James Hopkin

Winter Under Water

or, Conversation with the Elements

PICADOR

First published 2007 by Picador
an imprint of Pan Macmillan Ltd
Pan Macmillan, 20 New Wharf Road, London N1 9RR
Basingstoke and Oxford
Associated companies throughout the world
www.panmacmillan.com

ISBN 978-0-330-42679-4

1 3 5 7 9 8 6 4 2

A CIP catalogue record for this book is available from
the British Library.

Typeset by SetSytems Ltd, Saffron Walden, Essex
Printed and bound in Great Britain by
Mackays of Chatham plc, Chatham, Kent

for LAS, and for MMS

'Whoever had the choice would choose an eagle's
nest on the cliffs in place of a home.'

Juliusz Słowacki

'We have abandoned each other . . . and since we continue
to live we ought to meet again, for we were Life.'

Endre Ady

Chapters

1

A Woman in a Man's Voice or, Love, and We're All Asunder . . .

I will walk and walk until it is all familiar. That's what he tells himself. For he must reckon with the nights of fifteen below, the snow that pushes up his kneecaps, the cathedral's spire broken across the bend of the river, and the looming tower blocks – from here to their own horizon – only one of which houses a soul he can call a friend.

He is here voluntarily, self-ejected from everything he recognises, from the shape of the street to the pattern of his day. Though it's a mere ten hours since his departure, and a single hour forward in time, he has landed in darkness and unknowing, fifteen hundred kilometres from a notion of his own front door. And why? Why has he chosen to come to one of the coldest cities in Europe, and during December, when even the gaps between your teeth might freeze?

You might laugh if he told you it was for love, this journey to an unknown place, even less fathomable because trapped beneath a frost that fits as precisely as a press-stud. But what else pushes us out and away, our hearts set in courage and trepidation? If you ask him, he might put it another way. He might reply that he trusts only her to tell him what the back of his head is like.

The two of them are walking through the snow, disturbing the footprints of earlier block-escapees. Marta is late home. She had waited for the delayed train bearing her lover – such an ugly word, lover, it's soaked in sin and then kicked in the crotch. Better to say that Joseph Eadem is her love of six months, a short stretch of time, admittedly, but containing – so they insist to each other – more memories (yes, those) and more moments of elated living (not the only way of putting it) than some people experience in a lifetime. Their fear: they might not see many more such moments.

After three months of day-long communions, and nights of silence and skin, months during which they shared souls, clothes, words, bodies, some very watery soups, plus lasting looks and well-thumbed paperbacks – you might happily call this communicating bliss – they now face, after three subsequent months of dashed-out letters and pale-faced yearning, a reckoning, a coming-to-terms-with, a facing-of-the-music. And, yes, Marta is very late home.

You see, Joseph's train had broken down somewhere in the middle of the country, in provinces other than the night, where factory pumps and chimneys issue an industrial darkness. In his carriage, the already weary traveller had watched as golden motes of dust danced in the warm air from the heater beneath the seats, and it felt strange to be alone in this cabin that smelled of damp clothes and cold metal, strange to be stationary in a landscape of snow and smoke and silence, a silence not broken by the voices from the neighbouring compartment, but merely eased aside.

Yet he knew full well that he mustn't conjure up an unapproachable otherness just because of the endlessly white terrain at the window – emphasised by the greasy cotton covers of the headrests – or because of a sky as menacing as a highwayman's cloak, or because the train's notices are in four languages, not one of which is his own. No, he must make an effort. After all, he thought, perhaps it is the landscape that links us.

Earlier in the trip, a dignified old man had struggled into the carriage via the stiff sliding door that Joseph had also tussled with. The man introduced himself, in Joseph's language, as a professor of literature, and it turned out that he had once taught a student who later became one of the country's most famous writers, but the professor's proud voice grew timid, and his fingertips increasingly fond of his forehead, when he talked of the writer's emigration to America, and his subsequent divorce and suicide.

'Tragic,' said the professor, with a slight continental lilt giving the word a steeper precipice. Now he lowered his head still further as if to stare over this very same precipice. 'His parents perished. In a concentration camp. When he was only. A little boy.'

Outside, the darkness dripped into the snow. The occasional lights of a modest town passed, the isolated buildings retaining their bleak forms amid the melting contours. The faces of Joseph and the professor were reflected in the carriage window. Side by side in contemplation.

Impeccably dressed and polished – despite it being the middle of the slush season – and with a melancholy aspect that found expression in his tales, the professor seemed grateful for the ears of an attentive stranger. In succinct phrases, as if dictating a telegram, he told Joseph of the time when his father had taken him to London.

'By train. To Waterloo,' he said, looking up to the

luggage rack as if to locate the trunk he had taken that day. 'My father held my hand the whole way. We said goodbye. At the station. The sun through the roof. In my eyes. All that glass! My father went back to. The war. I never saw him. Again.'

Joseph leaned a little closer to the professor, until their shoulders were almost touching.

Peeled away a layer at a time, the darkness gave way to a lightening of snow followed by the yellow lamps of a station. Rising from his seat, the professor chuckled and said, 'A very fine writer of ours. Wrote that the difference between an East European intellectual. And a Western intellectual. Is that the latter has not had. A good. Kick up the arse! What do you make of that, mmm?'

The professor stood on the caps of his shoes to reach along the rack, his dark leather bag bearing the marks of years of knuckles and nails. At full stretch, he started chuckling again, as if someone was tickling his ribs.

'One final thing,' he said, 'for you to know. If there are two of my countrymen. In a room. How many opinions?'

Joseph shook his head until his grin was firmly in place.

'Three!' said the professor, stepping down with the case. 'Threeheehee.'

Then he shook Joseph's hand, urged him to keep warm, and, after another brief struggle with the door, he disappeared down the carriage.

As the train pulled away from the platform, Joseph tugged down the window's mosaic of ice and grime. He thrust his head into the darkness. His eyebrows stiffened. His pupils swallowed his irises for light. After a few lonely fields, the train passed a crossing. Joseph saw a nun standing in the snow.

Later, just as Joseph had reconciled himself to a solitary conclusion of his journey, two men in leather jackets and bleached jeans tried to enter the carriage, accompanied by a woman in a mini-skirt and high heels, and though these men were keen to get their friend inside as soon as possible so that one of them could begin to taste her lipstick while the other one held the beer, they first had to contend with the difficult door, so after pressing their moustaches against the panel, they tapped at hinges and grooves, while sticking their curses to the glass. Once inside, their bristles still burning, they tugged together the purple curtains to the corridor. Then they turned off the light.

In the sudden darkness, Joseph sniffed up the whispers and giggles and belches. Only in moments of illumination offered by track-side shrines – usually a figurine of the Virgin Mary surrounded by burning candles – did his senses resume their normal stations. A sound of zips and kisses and cans. The reek of an unfinished cigarette in someone's pocket. A man pacing up and down the corridor, his silhouette frequently pausing behind the curtain. '*Pee-voh! Pee-voh! Pee-voh!*' he sang, above the rhythm of the wheels.

When Joseph finally arrived, Marta was sitting underneath a white hat, behind pink cheeks, inside a green winter coat, on a platform bench. She might have been sitting under a spotlight, such was her glow. Joseph was over two hours late. Though the clock on the platform had stopped.

They held each other. Kissed, tentatively, unsure of the meanings their lips might bring. They studied each other's features to see how accurate their dreams had been. But quickly, it was cold.

'Your hair!' said Marta. 'It's longer. Really. It suits you!'

'And your coat,' she added, her tired gaze lying down the length of the lapels. 'A greatcoat!'

Joseph took it as a compliment.

So now, yes, they are walking through the snow as Marta takes the jaded traveller to a flat just round the corner from hers, a squat block of thick ledges and jutting stone, a block looking solid enough to withstand the harshest of winters and the most despairing of looks. You see, this block is in a difficult area of town, a zone of crumbling tenements and tin kiosks, where the shadows of dogs and vagrants collapse among the rubble, and petals of black plaster from the convent on the corner fall alongside snowflakes.

As Joseph makes his way over ice and stones, his walk full of false feet, he tries to recover his senses, but when he inhales it feels like there are tiny toothpicks jabbing the insides of his nose. His ears are full of cabin pressure and engine whine and whispers in the dark. He can taste only cold metal. His left hand is trying to hide in the lining of his pocket; his right is frozen to the handle of his holdall. (Cleverly, he had packed his gloves deep inside. Well, you never expect the transition to be so sudden, do you?) Only his eyes are free to report.

Joseph does not have to think he might disappear here, for it feels as though he has already, as if he, too, has slipped beneath the lining. Nearly every step across the cracked paving slabs is met with a slip or foot-flourish (like a slip, but usually with both feet) giving him the impression that he has not quite landed. Not properly. Not yet.

Again he tells himself not to make hasty judgements. In fact, any judgements. He knows his mind will deprive him of composure if he can't rely on his senses. Let alone his hands. His eyelids hang like the blank shutters on the departures board at the station. The cold whistles through his bones as though he is made of piccolos.

The two of them walk past a shivering bundle of strays whose gums are showing even in their sleep. Though Joseph is grateful for the coat he has borrowed from a friend, he is shivering, too.

They arrive at a huge wooden door that looks as though it has taken decades of heavily-booted abuse. Joseph imagines a portcullis. Marta fiddles with a wobbly lock. They step through an entrance within the bigger gate. To a cold and stony darkness. A courtyard? No, that's far too grand a term. It's really a pissing-hall, a lurking chamber, a place to stamp the snow from your shoes.

Joseph unpicks his fingers from the handle of his bag. He touches a wall. His skin takes on a similar texture. Goose-pimples in the blood.

A dog howls so long and dolefully it sounds like it is being tuned. There is a smell of stewed meat. They negotiate two other doors, before coming to the flat itself, where Marta tries a key, then another, peering into the lock as if for a way out of their predicament. Finally, with a shoulder-nudge, she enters. Joseph sees that the back of the door is padded, and he wonders in that moment if this is where he is to spend his time, in an isolation cell, or worse, an oubliette, deep in a country he knows nothing about. Again, he tries to convince himself that it will all look better by daylight.

They stand beneath the dim yellow kitchen bulb, in the black water melting from their shoes. They take off their coats. Back in the summer – oh, how the nostalgia grows! – they might have carried on taking things off, quicker and quicker, as if hoping to hurtle beyond nakedness itself. Now they are careful to put their shoes in order on the draining-grill.

Marta switches on the kettle. When it boils, the steam fills the kitchen, banishing the short-lived mist of their breaths. She makes toast. The small block of butter is the brightest thing in the room. She lights the brown-tiled stove that heats the bedroom. She closes the blue curtains that are as thin as a short-lived dusk.

'These cheese-plants on the sill,' she says with a smile. 'If they droop, get out!' She points to the taxi-rank beneath the window.

Shortly after, they are sitting on the edge of the bed, socks on the freezing tiles. Back then, it had been elbows, knees, necks – here we go again! – brown eyes in floating glances. Mischief in the sand dunes. The long dusk to perfect your loneliness. Or togetherness. Whichever their love had demanded each evening. But now these kisses are kisses of relief, and with trembling lips, like a conscience trying to find its voice.

Joseph notices that the light in Marta's eyes, usually so mischievous and tender, and above all else, open, is now trained in earnestness, even foreboding. The same can be said of the light that illuminates her from within. If Joseph still feels her heart beating against his ribs – how clearly he remembers their first embrace! – he believes this to be due as much to apprehension as to desire. Can everything have changed so quickly, he wonders. Has he been foolish to believe otherwise? But if you can't travel with love and faith in your heart then why travel at all?

He convinces himself it's all because of the lateness of the hour, plus Marta's long wait on the icy slats of a station bench. Not forgetting, of course, their three months apart. In summer, everything flowed. Now, everything is frozen. And therefore brittle. So what does he expect? Tread carefully or you will break everything, he tells himself. Even strong souls are affected by the seasons.

They sit on the bed, nibbling toast and drinking black tea. They say things like 'It's so good you're / I'm here!' and 'I can't believe you're / I'm here!' – phrases that reach for a conviction their voices cannot yet convey. A flashing look, a conspiratorial smile occasionally breaks through their diffidence.

'I'll be going,' says Marta, after finishing her tea and toast, the latter eaten quickly with still-chattering teeth. How Joseph likes this phrase of hers! As if the departure is only promised, and can therefore be postponed.

Marta disappears once again inside her winter wrapping. She looks very pretty, both young and naïve – that co-ordination of whites and greens! – and wise and mature – those ever-listening and questioning brown eyes! For this moment alone, Joseph knows his trip has been worthwhile. But he is also aware, painfully so, that there is more to be resolved.

'Reality,' Marta had said last summer. 'People eat, people work, and, if they're lucky, people sleep. That is reality. We must not expect to be excused.'

Well, maybe they did excuse themselves, for the summer at least, though they would much rather claim they had shaped their own reality. Found their own time. But everyone knows that conventional time, that relentlessly linear no-going-back time will catch up with you sooner or later. As for circumstances? They'll get you during one of those sleeps when, for a moment, you gurgle in a simple, trusting slumber.

Joseph offers to walk her home.

'Really,' she says, with the smile that sends his spirit soaring, the one that pushes up her cheeks and leaves them there, 'it is not necessary. We will meet tomorrow.'

A promised meeting returns Joseph to an approximation of joy.

Marta laughs, a gentle laugh that always drains any lingering clouds of bad weather. She has remembered something. 'Listen,' she says, as if Joseph's ears could ever ignore her. 'I should tell you this is a block for ex-convicts. Really! But don't worry! They are extremely old. Too old to be trouble. They smoke, drink, play cards. You only have to watch out for the toilets in the corridor. Yours is the first one on the left, OK? Be careful. Keep it locked.'

She hands him a key to go with the other three on a ring that could be a warden's. 'Yes,' she says, 'you must keep the door closed. Or your neighbour will maybe use yours.' Her familiar mischief now plays across her face, radically brightening her eyes. 'There are rumours he has syphilis!'

Joseph nearly chokes on the dregs of his tea. A block for ex-convicts and syphilitic poker-players? But by the time he swallows, the anxiety has gone. Besides, if you were told you had to live in a block of ex-convicts in your own country you'd certainly be worried, but in another country, it doesn't seem so bad. Everything is already spun from darkness and anonymity. How can such phantoms harm you?

Despite Marta's playful dismissal, Joseph accompanies her home. First, they renegotiate the doors and locks, with

Joseph imagining a series of decompression chambers through which you are returned, by degrees, to the plummeting temperatures outside. But when the outer door closes behind him, his breath is caught between his lungs.

Though they walk close, frequently brushing arms, they do not hold hands. The borrowed winter-coat and his tired limbs have put weight on Joseph's walk, and in all the wrong places, as if he has taken on the burden of someone else's past. And that hat! A last-minute purchase on the market, it looks more like a tea-cosy and doesn't quite cover his ears. To their right, the frozen river is a landing-strip for stars. Joseph might well be sniffing up these splinters of light, such is the crackling in his nose.

As he continues to pad across the ice without his usual rhythm or composure, each step hinged, not at the ankle, but at the knee, he wonders what on earth he is doing here, skating through a darkness that denies the existence of a sky, and surely leads only to sleep, but a quick glance at the woman beside him immediately repels the doubt. To paraphrase a great writer (who went east-west): her concavity fits his convexity exactly. Or, as your great-aunt (who went the way of all elderly relatives) might say: they're like two peas in a pod.

Now arm-in-arm, they follow their breaths across pavements as smooth as moleskin. They don't speak. The sound of winter walking is enough. They are both aware of what lies ahead.

Frosted bracken sparkles from the riverbanks, its knuckles and twists offsetting the solid arches of the iron bridge beyond. On the bridge's highest beam, luminous graffiti offers last rites to those who jump from one darkness to another, believing that gravity works best at night. Or doesn't work at all. It is 2.30 a.m, and, yes, Marta is very late home.

They reach her block, one of the newer ones, off-white as opposed to the otherwise ubiquitous grey. Marta points four floors up, to her kitchen window that faces the river and, on the far bank, the vast wingspan of the German-built university, an eagle seized forever on the edge of flight.

Marta does not have a key. She had planned to be home hours earlier. She presses the button of the intercom. She waits.

Moments later, she tries again, this time leaving her fingertip close, as if to order or accuse. Finally, she turns to Joseph. With a look from which her spirit has slipped, she whispers, 'He has locked me out'.

Standing a few metres behind her, Joseph leans back and looks up to the windows. The effort turns his head into a bucket of stars. Marta buzzes one more time. With the same outcome. She steps towards Joseph. She places a palm under each of his elbows, and draws herself close. Joseph holds her gaze, though the pressure on his eyes makes everything dazzle.

Silence. Save for the crackling of cold. A silence pressed in river-mist, and presented in a form too large for their ears. Their mingled breath hovers around them, a thin blanket to conceal their pulses. They continue to look at each other. Perhaps their eyelashes have frozen.

Still no voice from the intercom. No buzz to release the door. Then Joseph sees the decision in Marta's eyes: a change of light, a lowering of 'lids.

Marta shakes her head as if to disentangle her tears, which come now, to admonish her cheeks with warmth.

She takes a few steps back from the concrete path, sinking to her ankles in the deeper snow. She looks up to the bedroom window of her flat. A freight train worries the birds beneath the bridge. Dogs bark across the night. Stars shiver on their strings.

Marta cups her hands round her mouth and tilts back her head. From a distance she looks like she is praying. Or about to sing. She makes her voice as gruff as a drunkard's curse so that the neighbours won't be alarmed by a woman shouting in the street at such an ungodly hour.

She growls.

Then once more.

Her husband's name.

Joseph plots his sad retreat with cigarette stubs in the snow.

Letters

20 May [six months previously]

Here I am. At midnight. Waiting for Malena to demand my presence upstairs. I am writing this on lined paper as you can see. I like the idea of negotiating my thoughts. It disciplines my handwriting. We say, 'pisać maczkiem', to write in poppy seeds. Without lines, it is easy to stray.

Do you ever have the impression at this time of night that the borderline between the waking world and dream is blurred? It happens quite often to me. Especially when I'm reading. Images appear between the lines, images from dreams I once had. In these dreams, I always seem to be on a tour of some kind. I am running along corridors, tunnels, passageways. They are never relaxing dreams. I do not know whether I am pursuing or being pursued. I do not know what I am looking for. But they are not nightmares.

Except for the one about my great-aunt in her flat. That's pretty disturbing. It is an exaggerated re-run of when I had to look after her during her final days. I'm running around with buckets and tubs trying to contain her leaking away. She is in bed. Her lights flowing out of her like a liquid. Noises creep from beneath the blankets. A gurgle, a whimper, a struggle for breath. A smell of detergent stings my nostrils. I am scrubbing my fingers red-raw, trying to remove all signs of death approaching. Then she starts coughing up mucus. Each time I think it is her last breath. The sound is of a cough, a retch, a laugh, all mixed up. And her smell: of damp soil, or a forest after heavy rain. As though she's being slowly returned to the earth. Blood urine dribble faeces, all of her draining away. And there I am rushing scrubbing mopping weeping. For days. Until, finally, she dies. The relief is so intense I start feeling guilty.

After her death (in real life now, I mean), I cleaned the flat, a cobweb at a time. She must have had her hands full of spiders for the last few years. I moved in. During my very first week there, my great-aunt appeared to me in a dream. 'Aunt!' I said. 'Aren't you supposed to be dead?' 'Yes,' she replied,' but you still need to eat and drink. Shall I make you something?'

It was the only time she had ever been kind to me.

But more often than not, I dream of my grandmother. Usually warm dreams. She alone gave me the love I needed as a child. I used to love staying with her in the country. But I had to learn to say goodbye. 'Bòze mój!' My God! I'd hide in the stables for hours on the day of departure. Or in the less accessible parts of the orchard (painful, among the nettles). Disguising tears as a runny nose. When a student,

I went alone to stay with her. Those times, we cried freely on each last day.

What a subject for my first letter to you. Though I think you'll agree it's good to start where it's darkest.

Ps By the way, Marta is the patron saint of housewives. She is traditionally depicted as carrying a distaff or a bunch of keys, serving the Lord in the most humble capacities. I do have a busy key-ring. That part is true. House, office, university keys. I am not, however, under any circumstances, a normal housewife. Who is?!

21 May

It's a mild day. Not hot, but nicely scented, i.e. before the blossom gets boiled or blown away. I like English weather. It makes you feel so refined in your occasional melancholy. Or nostalgia.

I liked what you said the other day about people having to talk all the time for fear of discovering, in a moment of silence, that there is something inside them – like a soul. I think I have talked my life over so far, just endlessly raking the same old soil. I've hardly ever shut up to see what I really want or think or feel. Not that I fear emptiness, but I am afraid of confusion.

This little enclave where they put us 'foreign' researchers! Like asylum-seekers awaiting the verdict on their applications. Like them, everything about us is temporary. Especially in this provincial city in the bulging bit of England. Is this where the sinners and the sick come to feel reprieved? It feels like a long way from anywhere. Maybe it was a TB town a couple of centuries ago? Yesterday I saw a cat crawl under a camper van that looked like it would never leave this city again.

Nearly a month of my three has gone already!

Today I met a woman from Nigeria. She asked about my book. Whenever I talk about it, I remember an early conversation with my friend Patrycja back home. She's an academic, specialising in medieval women. She's all for nuns and mystics and inconsolable widows.

We were in a place where they do a café-au-lait in a large bowl which you hold in your palms and raise to your lips, like the coffee cup of communion. I told her the title of my book.

'Underground women?' said Patrycja, not so much stirring her coffee, as rowing in it. She was wearing one of her prim jackets, with padded shoulders. I think she has a thing about the 80s.

I told her my book is about European women. Women who had great ideas or energy. Women who, in some cases, have been forgotten. I showed her the list of names I had decided on at that early stage. Among them: Edith Stein, co-patroness of Europe, a philosopher and nun, born into a Jewish family, converted to Catholicism. She wrote about the spirit, and about 'Women's Significance in Contemporary Life'; Lya de Putti, a Hungarian silent-film actress, who left her husband and two young children to pursue her dream of stardom across Europe and America – her husband told the children she had died. Fatima Kapla who, having already served eleven years in Siberia for an assassination attempt, returned to fire six bullets into Lenin.

Behind dark glasses chosen especially for their gravity, Patrycja studied the list. Her eyebrows went down to mourning level. She took a sip of coffee, but quicker than a normal one, an affectation of hers to warm her lips before a weighty disclosure.

'As for underground women,' she said, 'I think it's a clear case of transference!'

I nearly told her that her shoulder-pads are a clear case of transference. From her mother's wardrobe! But for once I showed noble self-restraint.

I'll be finishing,

28 May

Funny how I write to you though I see you every day. But I enjoy our exchange of letters each time we meet, as if we are catching up with the hours apart. Also, because I am in another country, another language, perhaps I keep myself sane with these whispers across a white page. Your words, my words. A dialogue. Without dialogue, moving around can be dangerous. Isn't madness caused when all the borders come down?

I think that's something the women in my book have in common. Not madness! I mean, that they crossed borders. Or articulated new ways of seeing. Did I tell you about Edith Stein? She was born into a Jewish family in my home city on 12 October, 1891. The Day of Atonement. She saw this as a mark of election. Aged 13, she abandoned Jewish prayer, breaking her mother's heart. She converted to Catholicism. She studied philosophy at university under Husserl and became his assistant. It was very rare for a woman to study philosophy at that time. Together, they worked towards a rediscovery of the spirit. This study was known as Phenomenology. One of Stein's main philosophical concerns was empathy, an 'understanding so intimate that the feelings, thoughts, and motives of one person are readily comprehended by another'.

I think that is how I feel with you. Why I must write to you every day, even though my soul was not born to confess.

There is a guy back home in the flat below. He is always talking. Not quite confessing. His favourite conversation is with General Jaruzelski on the phone. Jaruzelski was our last Kremlin-appointed leader. He was known as 'the welder' because of his impossibly thick glasses. The guy beneath us begins his telephone call politely, but in a loud voice. He asks, 'Would the esteemed general like to come round for a meal? Because you should keep eating, general, sir, even though you are not on TV any more. We know it was you who kept the Russian tanks out of our country, so our cities didn't become like Prague, even though Martial Law could be a pain in the arse at times, sir – all that queuing!'

By now, the man's voice is a little louder. The odd word echoes in the stairwell. 'Come to think of it, I did see some tanks in our cities. Water cannon. Rubber bullets. Police. And soldiers, soldiers everywhere, sir! Sometimes squashing noses with their plastic shields. Or knocking heads hollow with their sticks. And those bloody queues! Really, general, they were worse than a bang on the head, because by the time I got to the counter, the last few crumbs had been licked from the shelves and any eggs that were left had hatched! So maybe it wasn't so good when you were in charge, general. Maybe it's just as well you're not on TV any more. Your head was far too shiny!'

Now the man is shouting.

'Yes, there were definitely tanks. Crushing heads and bones. Maybe it's not a good idea for you to come here, sir. You might not be very welcome, apart from old Kurczak on the ground floor who was one of your agents, wasn't he? His pockets were always full of bread and bottles.' At this point, he stamps his foot as if to alert the poor old man below. 'I am going to put the phone down now. I have found our conversation very disappointing. Please do not call me again. I never did like your glasses.'

By the way, this guy doesn't have any visitors. At least, I have never seen any. Nor does old man Kurczak. Even though the Institute of National Memory has been publishing the names of former Stasi members for a few months now, his name has not appeared.

When I was about twelve, I wrote political stories about bad General Jaruzelski and good Lech Wałęsa. Illustrated, of course. A friendly moustache always defeating those dark glasses. I knew I would be in trouble if anyone found these books. So I buried them in the communal garden by the fence, next to the vegetable allotment.

Boże mój! I have always had secrets.

I remember the police using tear-gas and water cannons to disperse the crowds. And my three-year-old sister shouting at them: 'Świnie! Świnie! Świnie!' ('Pigs! Pigs! Pigs!').

I also remember when I was staying at my grandmother's for the weekend. It was the middle of a ferocious winter. The river had frozen over. I was looking out of the window and across the icy lanes. When, all of a sudden, tanks appeared.

2

A Biography of Broken Bones, part 3

After a certain age, there is no going back. You can't go home again. At least, not again and again. Those who don't want to solidify into types have to keep moving, each day learning a little more how best to carry their bundles. How best to read the signs. When to hold on to something. Or someone. When to let go.

Educated by the small hours, by thoughtful opposition, by their own unhappiness or striving (which might be the same thing), these souls make their way, Joseph Eadem among them.

What more do you need to know about him?

He is 184 centimetres tall.

His family tree has an average ratio of burned to blossoming branches.

He swims four times a week to keep himself sane, which means: physically and mentally strong enough to resist currents not of his choosing.

His life to date?

Sometimes he went too far, other times not far enough. Either way, he would end up somewhere he had not expected. It's inevitable. Because you can't throw yourself into your latest project with passion and spirit and belief and expect to land safely, as the very same person, within recognisable limits. OK, so Joseph broke a few bones on the way (if you want to get physical about it. God knows the spirit needs a body to peep out of).

Aged eight, he broke his left leg. At thirteen, his right arm. At nineteen, his collar-bone. At twenty-seven, a wrist. Perhaps he frequently broke the wills of others; many times, too, his own resolve. Some wondered whether his neck would be next, it seemed a natural progression.

Yet Joseph was acutely aware of space, and the possible dangers of proximity. Like the time when, several summers ago, he had been on a train from Tower Hill across Canary Wharf, to stay with friends during one of his infrequent trips to the capital. There were endless glass buildings lit up on the outside and endless glass buildings lit up on the inside, and some of these lights were flashing, in red or yellow or white or blue, and some of the windows were mirrored so that their panels were flashing, too, as bodies lost for breath inhaled each other's concern, the train creeping along as if burdened by the weight, not of these bodies, but of the air trapped between them. With the passengers looking enviously at the water, Joseph felt it was all vast and beautiful and terrifying, these bodies in their sweat, like fish in brine, these buildings that steal the sky from the clouds, these lights that blind and bruise. And he realised, then, that amid all the talk, the grabbing hands, the desperate jumping-on and jumping-off, yes, somewhere inside it all, you have to find your way.

In that moment he decreed he would make his life small and clear and modest. Yes, he fully comprehended his task: how to fit his cosmology in a biscuit tin.

A month later, having packed up his latest temporary job

in the provinces, and with enough saved for a month or two of freedom, he drove to the coast, reversed his hatch-back up to a dune, and slept there, his legs a puzzle between the front seats. In the middle of the night, he woke, confused, in this box of metal and silver that smelled of cold plastic and the scent of a dream's tail-feather. He was sure there were stars bouncing on the bonnet. Or was it raining? Everything seemed set in silver. The moon was playing games. The sea whispered through an open window. He could feel the breeze upon his neck. He took a swig of warm water from a bottle reserved for the car radiator, a bottle filled way-back-when with God-knows-what. Not de-icer, he hoped. He rearranged his limbs in a semblance of comfort. As he struggled to get back to sleep, like someone trying to catch forty winks while rolling down a hill, he was sure he heard a woman's voice, an assertive voice, and this voice said to him: 'Startled, hybrid? I know you are hungry.'

In the morning, Joseph woke like a jack-in-the-box that has lost its spring. He clambered across a passenger seat littered with palm-size sketches, fag packets, apple cores. He opened the door and spilled out, his hands squeezing lumps of sand, and dune grass as harsh as wire. In a bid to restore his usual dimensions, he decided to strip off altogether, before ambling down to the water's edge, accompanied by sandpipers pumping out their reverse wolf-whistles. Splash-ing himself with palms of water so that the day's first words were exclamations, he watched a baby seal slither down to the sea. He thought about a swim, too, but settled for a waist-high wade. Such was the ache of his body, he didn't want to risk cramp, though it did cross his mind where the sea might take him: if not under, then elsewhere.

Soon after, his chest glistening with sunlight and salt, he

traipsed back to the car like a released captive who – for want of somewhere else to go – has decided to return to his cell. Not bothering to unpack his towel, he dried himself with his clothes and then, stretching them this way and that, he fitted them back to his frame. When he finally started the engine, water still dripping down his neck, the morning light a razorblade to his eyelashes, there was a screeching of gulls overhead. They might have been asking: 'Which way now, lodestar?' Or, perhaps: 'Whose furniture is your future in, traveller? Whose face?'

That morning, it might have been the rabbits, the gulls, or the outside air of things, but he recalled an image of a conservatory held together by rusting tin and damp wood, dead pheasants hanging from hooks all the way round, the smell of wet feathers and dirt. And he's seven years old and he's watching a cow being pushed into the slaughterhouse, spattering piss and shit along the concrete drains in a final gushing of fear. And then, the sound Joseph will never forget, the carcass slumping to the floor. Three years later, the business having been wound up, a garden with six apple trees replaced the slaughterhouse. These apples were bigger than cats' heads, and Joseph couldn't get his teeth into them. He often dreamed about them, these big fruit that he didn't know what to do with.

In the flowerbeds he loved to dig with his hands for the underneath of things. Finding bones, he would rush inside to show anyone who was interested, but nobody was, unless to get that filthy thing out of here, Joey, so he rushed back to tear some more at the wet soil. Later, he'd scrub the bones over a tin bucket, reducing his fingers to hard blue veins, fascinated, in particular, by the balls of joints that looked like the sheep's eyes on a tray in Grandpa's shop.

With this collection of odd bones, he then set about putting an animal back together.

At first he was thinking of a blue horse because a year earlier a horse had appeared in the meadow behind his grandparents' cottage, and he was told it was his, but no one could get anywhere near it, and a few weeks later, when he ran to the meadow, his horse was nowhere to be seen. For days, Joseph sobbed for his loss. So, at first, he tried to re-create this horse from the bones of pig and cow and sheep that he'd dug up under the apple trees, and he laid out his first attempt on the paving slabs between the coal bunker and the back of the conservatory. But it didn't look right, this skeleton he'd made. The neck veered off, and was too long. It was a dinosaur or a giraffe, but not a horse. So he shifted one or two bones with the toe of his shoe, the frustration growing, because now it looked like the mangy goat in the garden of the parish church. He kicked at the useless bones for the animal he could not bring back.

Yet he couldn't get rid of the tickles beneath his tongue, the excitement in his elbows, so he ran to the kitchen and, gagging at the smell of boiling ox cheek, he stuffed himself with cold cuts of ham, slices of bread soaked in dripping, and a bowl of custard made with brown sugar, but still he couldn't stop the tingling inside that drove him beyond himself, so he sprinted round the yard, past the now-empty pens that still ponged of crap and soggy fur, once, twice, several times he went round, until, finally, he collapsed by the coal shed where he found a piece of chalk and he started doodling on the broken concrete, sweat running down his arms, a tear in his eye for the unfairness of life, and he drew a shape that might just pass for a horse, its bones first, and then, with the smell of boiling ox cheek still in his nostrils, he added flesh and hide, and when he stood up to take a proper look, he was pleased with the shape but still it didn't move, so with a flourish of arms and chalk he made the horse look as though it was trotting along, galloping even, and soon he was galloping, too, this time elated by his discovery of how to bring things back to life.

Yet he didn't know what to do with this talent, so he kept it deep inside. No, he didn't want to expose it. In case that, too, was taken away. At school he studied ordinary subjects in an ordinary way, secretly drawing at night, fitting shapes on the page so they wouldn't become big fruit and block up his brain. But sometimes, when the street-lights were left to themselves, they did appear, these shapes too big for his senses, and they brought a bitter taste to his tongue and made his head go funny, so he'd turn on the light, but that didn't make them go away, so he'd turn off the light again, only to feel the fruit swelling in the dark above his head.

On one occasion, when everyone was sleeping, he grabbed his sketchpad to quell these strange feelings, and he drew his first portrait. 'Picture of Izzy Singer's Dad' – the father of a schoolfriend, who would come to sports days and stand on his own, a beard and a sad face, in a dark coat, wearing a little cloth dish on the back of his head, and though Joseph couldn't have said exactly what it was that made him want to draw this man, he felt he had to keep the light shining in Mr Singer's eyes.

Following the night on the beach in his car, Joseph spent weeks driving his hatchback up and down the country of his birth, perhaps trying to make sense of where he hailed from, or, more likely, looking for an exit. As he always did after leaving a period of work (he had been doing such jobs, usually in the building trade, for over a decade), he sketched furiously. Aggressively. On the back of petrol receipts, old maps, the inside covers of books, on postcards, in small notebooks, pieces no bigger than his hand. Yes, he knew he had to protect his vision, keep it alive until he had found its true form. He drew the rippling tarpaulins of juggernauts in the Midlands, he drew eleven horses standing in a field in East Anglia, he drew an abandoned mill in the Pennines. All the time, he travelled with the notion that there was a person or a place waiting for him somewhere, and that only then would he be able to unfold, fully, whatever he carried inside.

Measuring the miles in cigarettes and tins of popular fizz, he drove on, and when he had nowhere to stay and no one to stay there with, he'd spend the night in a lay-by, passing trucks rocking the chassis to sleep. Or he slept on the sofas of friends. Once, for three weeks, he stayed in the boxroom of a Victorian terrace, where the carpets crept round the house. He was woken each morning by the sobbing of the boy next door, the father of whom, Joseph later discovered, had died only weeks earlier. Each time he woke to these mournful sobs, Joseph would knock gently, just to let the boy know someone was there. The sobbing would stop while the boy wondered where the sound was coming from. When he finally resumed his crying, it was with far less vigour, until his mother came to open the curtains and return her son to the light.

Yes, that summer, in his solitary journeys, in the routes he plotted while not bumping into things, in the sketches he made in the palm of his hand, Joseph discovered gentleness inside himself.

If he lacked a cause, well, he didn't despair. The glove

Kochanie... tęi mały
wiosenny prezent.
Niech Ci przyniesie uśmiech
na buzi + radość w serce

JaJ Sebastian

ABU JANI
SANDEEP KHOSLA

MUMBAI

ABU JANI SANDEEP KHOSLA
Loving Mother, Arvind House
9, Darabsha Road
Off Nepeansea Road
Mumbai - 400 036
Tel. : 2367 3505 /2367 3401 Fax : 2367 3676
email : info@abusandeep.com
website : www.abusandeep.com

DELHI

ABU JANI SANDEEP KHOSLA
W/122, Ground Floor, Flat No.1
Greater Kailash, New Delhi - 110048
Tel. : 2921 4201 / 2921 3371 Fax : 2921 2609

BANGALORE

ABU JANI SANDEEP KHOSLA
A-13, The Leela Galleria
23, Airport Road
Bangalore - 560008

LONDON

55 Beauchamp Place, London SW 3 INY
Tel. : 207-584 7713 / 207-584 9490
Fax : 207-584 3327
email : abu.jani@virgin.net
website : www.abusandeep.com

compartment was filling with his work, the boot, too. He knew there was no mirror or measure for his long opposition.

So that when people asked, 'What have you been up to?'

Joseph would reply. 'Oh, you know, running and jumping.'

And another time, 'What have you been up to?'

'Oh, you know, fetching wood, carrying water.'

And another time, 'What have you been up to?'

'Oh, you know, spitting and catching.'

How best to tell those for whom cynicism and irony had become a way of life that he had been toiling away in the backyard of a person, living on the line between adventure and accounting, in attic rooms and basements, amid other people's furniture, on a diet of pasta and peas, trying to assemble his work, the structure of his life, while removing himself from the fatal flow of media and fashion and sales, where people talk about objects and not ideas, and where everything is snapped up instantly, like a digital picture, so that there is no room in the dark for development. No room for the growth of a soul.

Such solitary resistance is never easy. One night, on a camp-bed in the spare room of another friend, Joseph wondered if he would ever escape a life of debts and disappointments.

But just as you're beginning to believe that you have run out of time. Or space. Or desire. Something happens. The following summer, he met her.

Marta Balicka!

At last, an accomplice! Understanding with a look and a silence in which their complicity grew. Like a reconciliation with the world, a steady accretion of calmness and joy. He knew it from the very first time she said his name. She said it in a way that no one had ever said it before. As if she knew how he had come to be called by this name. As if she knew, also, the way in which he had carried this name through his life, sometimes like a candle-flame cupped in his palm, other times like a sack of wet firewood thrown across his never-quite-healed collarbone. He didn't have to tell her about his constant vigilance for a different order of things, because she was also looking. He didn't have to tell her about the past, because her memories became his own.

Immediately, he knew this was the person for whom his solitary journeys, his education in silence and stealth, had been preparing him. If he'd had a bucket of Baltic seawater thrown over him, he wouldn't have woken up to himself any quicker. Immediately, they sensed each other's light and dark places, and how best to approach them. They understood, too, that a person can't be fully explained, and that to attempt such a thing is to sharp-knife slices off the soul. Joseph was stunned by the subtleties of her thinking, so that every negative thought of his transformed itself in her presence, until he was ashamed to be associated with muddle or moan. And because they both had ideas and opinions, they argued. How they argued! But in a way that lifted them both, bringing laughter and clarity through occasional tears. Yes, sometimes they laughed until they were hungry. One moment, Marta would be singing into a hairbrush, the next she would be discoursing passionately on her favourite subjects: nations and stereotypes, and her underground women. Soon, there was another favourite: Joseph's drawings.

'Is that the artist in you coming out?' Marta once asked,

pointing to a heavy pencil-flourish in the corner of one of his sketches.

'No,' he laughed, 'it's the anguish!'

And another time:

'Funny. It doesn't apply to you. Nothing you create is ever stationary. But we have a strange phrase for a still life – *martwa natura*. Literally, dead nature.'

And another time:

'Your work is gentle, yet ruthless, too. Astonishing, really, this combination.'

During the hours before each rendezvous, Joseph lost himself in creative anticipation, a singing in the veins like a panic without the anxiety. He moved to different forms – collage, especially – and once or twice from pencil, ink and charcoal to watercolours and oils. He knew he was moving closer to the modes of expression he'd been seeking, closer, too, to the person he wanted to become. Yes, Marta had given him the gift of form.

Then, the simple things about her: the way she stamps her right foot when caught out or corrected, her determined yet graceful walk, the way she smiles, swings an arm, turns up her collar, the way she listens, really listens, sometimes turning her head to bring an ear closer, sometimes gently dropping a shoulder (as if her elbow has slipped, but on to something softer), and her sneeze! '*O babciu!*' she says, 'Oh Grandmother!' for she claims to have inherited her sneeze, thin and slightly croaky, as if all her vulnerability jumps out with that breath.

Yes, Marta was the second person singular Joseph had previously lost all sight of. And her look would always locate him. Her voice, too. Her playful intonation whenever she answered the phone: 'Is that you?' (Though she teased him by saying he exoticised her accent.) And the way she said 'Aha', an expression carried over from her own language, and Joseph liked that, too, because the gap between the 'a' and the 'ha' created a bridge between the speaker's comment and the listener's moment of comprehension.

Once, shortly after their third or fourth meeting, Marta phoned him in the middle of the night. Just to whisper his name. Afterwards, Joseph sang in his sleep. Another first. And it's right to say that – if for nothing else at all – we are here to start things anew. Yes, someone must have the courage to begin.

Letters
3 June
I am running out of paper. I have to write on the back of this form. Which is an application to buy my great-aunt's flat from the council back home. Because my husband and I already have a flat, they are reluctant to sell it to me, though I alone prevented it from falling to ruin (and being taken over by spiders).

I'm in the bedroom. I can't quite see what I'm writing. (I think it was Majakowski who wrote that to work on the word is to work in the dark.) But it is a midsummer darkness. Tomorrow is already pressing through. Like a new coin that can't keep its gleam to itself.

On TV last night, a brief report on peasant-life in my country! Did you see it? Shots of thatched roofs, simple farms, storks. We have the biggest population of storks in the world. People put out old tractor tyres for them to nest in. When someone goes overseas, we say s/he is like a stork abroad. Obviously, a stork is also where babies come from. The report was about American firms buying all the little farms. What can be done? It was a strange report, because these days you would really have to look hard to find a thatched roof.

Last night, I had one of my recurring dreams. About school. It's a maths lesson. I hated maths. In the dream I learn that I have failed the exam. I know it is because of the teacher. The way he has treated me. He makes me stand on the desk while the other pupils rejoice in my failure. I woke up in a panic. Then I remembered I am in England now. What a relief! Because here you can go and complain about someone like that!

My husband phoned earlier. He sounded absolutely exhausted. He spoke of the usual things – computers, invoices, tax matters. I began to feel a bit desperate. Sometimes I picture us travelling in opposite directions along those moving walkways you see in airports. We try to embrace. But we can only hang on for so long.

Later
You called. Your voice! It calmed me immediately. Everything that was up in the air settled. Everything gathered in range.

Now I am going to bed. My hands will serve as a distraction for a child who doesn't yet know how to put herself to sleep. So she plays with her mother's fingers to check that I have not melted into thin air, or to look for the magic one that will send her to sleep. Or she kicks me to test my solidity. To check I am not a dream. Or a memory. If these activities satisfy her, she murmurs like a cat, smacks her lips, and is soon asleep.

During the day she sometimes runs round the house calling for pan Joseph. I think I have told you already that 'pan' means Mr, and 'pani' means Mrs, the polite forms for addressing a man or woman. So don't go thinking you're a god. Or a goat!

Tonight, will I have more dreams of travelling? This constant pursuit of I never know what always makes me feel incredibly light. This reminds me of the actress, Lya de Putti, whom I'm researching at the moment. She travelled frequently across Europe, at a time when masses of people were in transit: after the First World War, the October Revolution, the fall of the Habsburg Empire. She often carried a pink cushion with her.

By the way, do you know the sensation of waking up with the birds and not at all liking the feeling? Like you've been born too soon. On the nights you don't stay with me, you are probably awake 'do białego rana' – until the white morning. You're moon-driven. I'm a child of the sun. Perhaps because I see so little of it. Especially in winter. So I collect the rays like twigs and store them in a dry place.

See you tomorrow, Joseph.

Ps Yesterday you told me that I keep you human. What a responsibility!

5 June, 1.38 a.m.
Here I am. I struggled out of bed, deceiving quite suspicious
Malena. I slept with her for an hour. I tried to leave a trace
of my body in her sleeping arms. I don't know how long I
can write until I am called back to my maternal captivity,
sweet but unpardonable.

Today, I spoke to my friend Ania on the phone. You will
meet her. She will come for a weekend. She has a strategy
of reassuring me by making problems sound normal, uni-
versal, inevitable, and all leading to happy endings. In other
words, a strengthening of marital bonds. But she doesn't
realise that the danger for me was not landing in bed with
you. Infidelity is not the most haunting. This is simply how
it happened. Now we can't stop fantasising about the
future, while thinking how painful it will be if it remains
just that, a fantasy. Whatever Ania tells me about sweet and
fleeting attractions, I know that what you and I have is
genuine. I am not able to stop it.

Later
Having read through my words, I think that what I am
trying to say is that I don't want this relationship of ours to
simply enrich my marriage. But it does force me to ask
myself what my marriage is about. Obviously. Painfully.
In dreams and slow afternoon thoughts. That is when I
go beneath the surface of things. At such times, I have
grave doubts. I have a home with my family, a real sense
of home for the first time in my life. There is affection,
devotion, cosiness. The things I missed out on as a child.
Yet I regularly feel a need to withdraw, to confront a feeling
of emptiness.

Despite my husband's sensitivity and love, I feel that

only you would make me truly satisfied. How can I say this when I have known you only a few weeks? But I feel it when I'm with you. I feel it when I think of you. Together, we would not need to seek other people. With my husband, and with most relationships I know, there is usually a need to look for company as if being by ourselves we would be threatened by boredom. Or forced to face a terrible truth.

So, as you asked the other day, with one of your wicked grins, 'What will become of us?'

Ps I was absolutely bewildered when Ania once told me that her parents' marriage grew from a loveless match (on her mother's side). And that they learned to love each other. Of course, a person has to learn how to love, but surely this is easier if that person feels love for another person from the start! The idea of the family is very strong in my country. Almost sacred. It is certainly taboo to fiddle with. A woman is expected to marry by the age of thirty. After that, it's a case of: 'Is she infertile? How many heads does she have? Even so, every monster makes its match!'

I remember reading a novel by a woman living in the DDR. She wondered where it is written that when compromises are necessary in the interests of the family, it is the woman who has to postpone her life.

I do not want to postpone my life. I do not want to live belatedly.

Whatever you pledge to your family, there must be love otherwise the act of imagining turns into an act of (self-) deception.

Joseph, I know one thing: you make me see how it is possible to mix the extraordinary with the everyday. I see, too, that this is only possible with you. And I want it only with you.

Maybe the problem is with me. Did I forget my status? My role? I will not destroy my husband's life by taking Malena away from him.

I can't help but sound sentimental. Like a 19th-century author of handbooks for good girls. I'm afraid perhaps I am just a good girl. In the end. Always doing what's required & proper. Maybe I did not have the strength to wait for you. Maybe I gave up believing that one day you would appear.

It is now 2 a.m. It must be insomnia urging me to write out my soul. There's rain at the window, falling lightly, as though trying not to wake anyone. The glow of the street-light competes with my reading lamp. Malena is asleep. The au pair is out. She goes out three or four evenings a week, in bleached jeans so tight she must wrap them on like bandages. Her hair is dyed black but with biscuit-coloured roots showing along the parting, like a muddy tributary. Occasionally she doesn't come back until morning, only minutes before I'm ready to leave for the library. Malena seems to like her. So it's OK for now.

Now it is definitely time for bed. Infidel wife again, I seek the arms of Morpheus.

Pps 'We have arrived,' wrote Anna Seghers, who lived and worked in East Berlin. 'Now, what happens will happen to us.'

3

The Ghost of Chuff-chuff

Joseph turns under the quilt, the blanket having long since slipped to the floor. He is wearing blue thermals and a sad, not exactly peaceful expression. He smells of whisky and a little bit of fright. Before going to bed, he'd taken a swig from a bottle he'd plucked from the dark, then he'd groped for light switches, the mattress, the tiny pillow, like a person blindfolded who fears he'll be able to see even less once the blindfold is removed.

How he'd longed for the warmth of her body.

Also, he slept in his socks.

At some stage during the night it is possible he encountered a ghost. Later the next day, he will certainly remember the voice of a very old woman announcing, in his own language, 'I am the ghost of chuff-chuff'. He will also vaguely recall having sat up in bed and scrutinised the darkness, such was the apparent proximity of the voice and Joseph's need to find a point of emanation, an image with moving lips. But all he could make out in the net-curtained night were the leaves of the cheese-plants on the window-sill – not unlike looming faces, admittedly, but mute all the same. He listened until he could feel a pulse in his ears, but there was no more chuff-chuff, possibly only a cough-cough from elsewhere in the block.

At another stage in the night – for the night here is nothing but stages, great blocks of darkness and ice pushed together – yes, at another stage in the night, Joseph woke again. The mattress had turned his skin to frosted glass. His bladder was full. He tiptoed across the floor in his socks, chasing the white beam of a passing headlight from one side of the flat to the other. When he slid open the bolt, the echo in the corridor sounded like a gunshot.

In the cubicle the bulb turned his eyelashes into matches about to be struck, and the walls to infected skin. He could feel the floor scratching at his feet through his socks. A picture calendar showed a mountain hut covered in snow, but he couldn't make out the year. A stench of dark water in the bowl. Plus a musty-smoky smell, an old man's smell, of cheap cigars, mustard, neglect. When Joseph pulled the string dangling from the plastic cistern high on the wall, the whole box leaned towards him. He let go. It did not flush. He heard a key turn in the neighbour's door. Or was it the lid of the spy-hole? Either way, Joseph suddenly realised he was in the wrong toilet. Not bothering to switch off the light, he rushed back to the flat, inadvertently leaping from one puddle of melt-water to the next.

Now, in an early-morning light issuing from exhaust pipes and egg-cups, beneath a sky that appears little more than the lining to another universe, Joseph's senses prise him from sleep. His nostrils twitch. His eyeballs move around excitedly as if polishing themselves on velvet-lined 'lids. Moments later, delivered on the cusp of a dream, he wakes. Not at all sure where he is. Not at all sure who he is. Or whether or not it's a good idea.

He focuses on the brown porcelain tiles of the stove in the corner. And then, before he even knows where it comes from, he experiences a terrible heart-sink.

Letters
6 June
Whatever I say and think I don't consider myself duplicitous. There may be a conflict of feelings and interests, but certainly there is no duplicity. A hug is the simplest gesture of affection, but how powerful this simplicity when we embrace.

Look, this is funny, but I really have the feeling that nothing else matters, that things are going to be easy anyway. The question remains: why don't I remember ever being held like this before?

I'm afraid that my short memory is not to blame.

Joseph, where does this tenderness come from, where?

I'm savouring the ripening summer. I am putting things in order. Like I always do after a period of strenuous work. Cleaning!

If I was home, I would be planning to make some vegetable preserves. And a fruit compote. To pickle summer's energies for the dead season. Which I know must always follow. After the brief and bronze respite that is autumn. These summer days here, though, I'm babbling to myself, singing, boring people to death with talk, and taking part in Malena's most weird fabulations.

Yes, my daughter and I splash around in the bath and sing at the tops of our voices. Is it really summer giving me this energy? Or is it you?

(And here I try not to inflate your ego. In case it blows up like a lilo.)

Today, in the library, I took some notes on the actress Lya de Putti. When Lya's father, a former Captain of Horse in the Austro-Hungarian army, passed away, her mother, a Countess, set about finding her youngest child a husband – surely confusing male role models in a way only the aristocracy can. Through her numerous contacts among the well-to-do families of northern Hungary, the Countess discovered Zoltan de Szepessy, a district judge with plenty of land and the beady eyes of a bachelor. The marriage took place in 1912. Lya was only sixteen. The book has a photograph of the wedding party: top-hatted men, tin-hatted hussars, ladies in big bonnets. Nearly as tall as her husband, Lya looks strong, even defiant, in her slender white dress, as if she is already planning to slip through his fingers. Zoltan is shrinking inside a fur coat and hat, looking very much like he has just come in from the cold. It is he who holds the bridal flowers. The Countess, meanwhile, sits at an angle to everyone else, like a monument dislodged from its pedestal. She looks quietly pleased with her work.

Today, for some reason, I thought of my great-uncle, perhaps because he ended up living in this country. As a young man in Nazi-occupied Poland, he refused to fight for the German army. So they put him in prison until he relented. Even so, at the first opportunity he surrendered to the Allies. He was held in a POW camp in the UK. When he was released, he found work in a factory in Birmingham where he stayed for the rest of his life. I'm not sure if he had many friends. I do know that he barely learned to speak English. And that he lived a very frugal life in the Polish community. He did not marry, nor did he return to his own country, where the communists would have branded him a deserter. Occasionally he would send us a tin of Bird's custard powder – I remember those tins with their coloured stripes, because custard was a luxury for us. Not too long ago, a few members of the family attended his funeral. His surname was Pudełko – which means, in English, 'box'.

4

An Easel in the Crypt

From the kitchen window, Joseph can see the frozen river – like a road paved with broken bottles – plus the barbed wire of twisted bracken, and a yellow tram going over the bridge. He wonders if this is where Marta's husband stood the other night, in the dark, ignoring the entry-buzzer or having switched it off so as not to wake the child, as he watched two silhouettes embracing below, one of whom looked very much like his wife returning home four hours later than she had promised.

Marta leads Joseph the few steps back to the living room. Her husband stays behind, stirring a pot on the hob, but slowly, as if winding a tightening coil.

In the next room, the walls are bare, except above Malena's playpen where several of her crayon doodles are fixed with tape. Joseph recognises one he'd helped her with over the summer. There is a faint smell of nappies and paints. It is far too cold outside to open any windows. Saddened by the absence of colour, Joseph directs his gaze to the shelves where he discovers the spines of books Marta bought during their time together. He knows these books once contained photographs of their outings, and perhaps his letters and sketches, too, but didn't she write that her husband had found them, and that she'd hidden them in a shoebox only for him to find them again?

There is a small dining table with three chairs, a plain white tablecloth, and three places laid out. Marta's husband carries in a tray with bowls of vegetable soup.

'We have a saying,' says Marta. 'To undress before the broth.'

Joseph stares at the skin on his soup.

That moment, Marta's husband raises his left arm as if pulling the hooter of a train or truck. It is a signal agreed between husband and wife if he doesn't understand. In fact, he can make out very little of Joseph's language. His eyes are heavily shadowed, especially beneath a bald head, so that he looks like he's peering from beneath a stone, and a stone that is as heavy as his thoughts. Marta explains to her husband. He tries to smile, but his lips betray him. Instead, he looks expectantly at the guest's face, convinced that the meaning will land there.

Joseph is still staring at his bowl. He can feel the husband's gaze warming his cheek. He begins to slurp the liquid from his spoon, perhaps believing this will set everyone's nerves at ease. But the soup is too hot. His mouth is caught in an 'ouch'. He releases a breath usually associated with cleaning the lens on a pair of glasses. The eyes of Marta and her husband turn to him.

'Well,' says Marta, 'here we are.'

Not long after the bowls have been removed (with one, in particular, inspected by the husband for traces of disrespect), the main course is served. Local sausages, red and fat and rolling in grease, with boiled potatoes, and dollops of raw cabbage to soak up the juices. There are also thickly-cut slices of white bread, and glasses of spring water.

'Will you be staying in our country?' asks Marta.

With the tip of his tongue, Joseph strips the grease from his front teeth. His words are hiding behind them, or behind each other. He has been in Marta's city for a period that, according to conventional notions of time, is ten days, but it feels more like a whole season pegged at either end by ice-clamps. Yes, here in the provinces, where the eyes are often deep-set, dark, suspicious, heads turned whenever he talked in his own language. Which wasn't often. So he tried to decipher the whispers across the ice, whispers that offered more words than you'd think a sentence could hold. He heard names like Ola and Jola and Anka. And other names that seemed, when spoken, to bestow grace upon the speaker as well as the listener: Magdalena, Agnieszka, Małgorzata. He wrote down words he overheard like 'bez sensu', 'rewelacja', 'jasne'. He observed old ladies in fur coats, some of these coats worn down to the wrinkled skin, others hung with the last tufts of black and brown fur, not unlike pheasant feathers, he noted, his nose twitching for a scent, and these old ladies stood chatting in the dark and cold, stroking the front of one another's furs as if to warm the place from where the words were coming.

Joseph was struck, too, by the number of 'Solarium' signs that shone down pot-holed backstreets. No wonder, he thought, that people go under the lamp during winters such as these.

Meanwhile, his greatcoat caught a suspicious eye, a whole street of suspicious eyes, like snowflakes falling on fur – *I am not from round here.* Yes, with its two columns of buttons marching down the breast, this cashmere coat offered more than a hint of a military aspect, and a Russian one at that. Neither of which, he knows, is a good idea round these parts. And those lapels! Each one the running-board of an old train carriage!

Yes, he was looked up and down so many times that he began to wonder which way round he should be. And to believe himself a dissident, an émigré, a refugee, as if all he has left is who he is and where he is. Even though, as he once told Marta, he is used to 'living on the fringes of the outskirts' in his own country, he felt he'd been delivered too quickly to the role of outcast.

Yes, he has been alone most of the time, in the snow and the slush of it, as if, ever since that first night, he has been slopping out his heart. Though he has been trying hard not to sink in the sentimental, Joseph soon discovered that a freezing industrial landscape, and his thus far luckless plight, might only be reprieved by a well-developed romantic outlook. Yes, he'd done his best to pilfer moments of beauty. Like the pastel façades of the townhouses crowding round the market square, their colours as cold as tiny pots of paint he imagined carrying close to his skin. Or, in the rare moments when the sun appeared, like a golden keep-sake in a pile of rags, he absorbed the reflection from car bonnets and shop windows, especially the *Cukiernia*, the sugar-shops, where yellow cream pastries are stacked on glass shelves alongside doughnuts squashed beneath layers of icing, and cheesecakes as thick as a brick. Despite these glimpses of light, he still couldn't quite shake the feeling that he was living at the bottom of a well, beneath routine and relations, awaiting the next bucket containing food or water or folded notes.

Each day, his first cigarette in the street stripped him of all resolve, and paraded his estrangement as a pair of weepy eyes in a cloud of smoke. In the freezing mist made of the sighs of hurrying shoppers, he felt, for the first time for years, the fractures in the bones he'd broken, not causing him pain as such, but an ache he often had to carry at an angle. Once, as if to put some grit in his resolve, he walked behind the man sprinkling the pavement with palmfuls of salt from a bucket.

Whenever Joseph had tried to sketch, he thought his fingers might snap. And it was criminal this light, or lack of it. The sky absorbed the dark patches from under people's eyes. He had to work in the dark for a gleam. And still he kept receiving strange looks. Perhaps it was his collar-length hair that emerged from the back of his hat like the tail-feather of an unusual bird, for most men seemed to have crew cuts or ponytails and not much in between. So he balanced these looks with looks of his own, until he touched something – a coin, a card, a wooden ledge – and then his hands would take over.

In a bid to keep himself busy, he went on excursions, hoping at least to invoke the weary enchantment of a tourist. But he stamped the ice from his boots to see a Hungary–Poland 1956–'89 Solidarność pamphlet that he found in a cardboard box in a basement bookshop, and his eyebrows went as high as his hopes when he visited an exhibition in the crypt of a church. A moment of white sunlight guided him down a wooden staircase, at the bottom of which he discovered black-and-white photographs: of small wooden crucifixes in Białystok, of a headless disciple in Rzeszów, of a plasterwork Christ carrying his heart in Przybysławice. (Yes, Joseph was careful to jot down the place-names, and to let them melt on his tongue.) He was intrigued, too, by a postcard reproduction of Malczewski's *Melancholia*, in which the artist shows three generations of his people struggling towards independence. But what really lit his blood was a student ceramics exhibition in which he found such a meeting of energy and form that afterwards he did not know where to go with this vision, or who to share it with, so he went on another walk, past kicked-in basement grills, lion-headed door-knockers, and a bearded queue for a soup-kitchen. Finally he sat at a tram stop, listening to the brakes. Yes, when in contact with a creativity that touched his spirit, he managed to reconcile himself with the fact that his plans for a future with Marta had thus far found only silence and a soft reception.

When the sky retreated from the roof-tops, and Joseph carried the cold in the front of his head, he recalled a line in the book of poetry that Marta had bought him: love is where cruelty and compassion meet. He is beginning to wonder whether this might be true. He hasn't even been granted much time alone with her. Only in public places, such as a crowded university canteen where, squeezed among pale faces and potted plants, they had touched fingers, all the time keeping the bowls and bread of everyday life between them, and usually under the scrutiny of strangers – and here, or so he felt as the lapels of his greatcoat flapped once more and the buttons marched down his chest, all strangers are scrutinised. Marta had even pointed out to him the church where she'd been married. Pretending not to hear her, Joseph had walked on, glimpsing only a green tin spire and a beggar on his knees in the snow.

One evening, Joseph had gone with Marta and her husband – in the latter's speeding car that at one point mounted the pavement like a derailed dodgem – to a jazz concert in the city's cathedral. The car park was packed with pilgrims and disputes. Marta's husband led them to the front of the queue where his hands dived like swallows among a hundred others and came out waving three white tickets. Inside, Joseph sat alone in the pews, like a lost soul who has only just heard that a church might be a good place to seek redemption. Marta and her husband chose to stand in a side aisle, closer to the stage. Outside, the temperature was minus twenty. Inside, among the silver crucifixes and icy acoustics, it felt even colder. Eight hundred pairs of eyes peeped over scarves. With ears of pink carnations, the people listened, devotedly, to the mournful wail of a trumpet as it rose to fill every vault and arch and enclave, its melancholy perhaps in response to its muting.

Joseph could feel the warmth pouring from his feet, as if his toes were unplugged rubber stoppers. He could smell the varnish of the pews, the breaths of the people either side, the puddle of black water at his feet. Marta looked over from time to time. She raised a palm. Joseph raised a palm in reply. Both gestures looked less a greeting than an attempt to stop something in the air. Then he quickly returned his hand to his pocket, perhaps thinking that it might otherwise freeze. Occasionally, Marta's husband looked over, too, his small dark eyes scanning the pews that for him became columns of numbers, until he found Joseph, this out-of-place integer, possibly in italics, certainly underlined, but in every way not adding up. Meanwhile, the melancholy trumpet played on, the breaths of the trembling congregation aiming for its snout.

After the concert, Marta's husband, chewing vigorously, drove the three of them to a bar, the short journey featuring skids, loud music with guitar solos, two wheels down the pavement, and a parking technique of accelerating, head on, into the smallest of spaces. Once they were seated around a single candle, Marta's husband ordered three Żubrówka vodkas with apple juice. Sticky on the lips, and fruity enough to protest an innocence of alcohol, the vodka encouraged Joseph to drink quickly, so that when he went to find the toilet, he had to chase his kneecaps down the spiral staircase, and even then he couldn't remember which toilet to use – one was marked with a triangle, the other with a circle – but just as he was about to take pot luck he remembered Marta's words that in her country 'men are three-sided, and women go all the way round'.

When he came back with three *Okocim* beers, Joseph found Marta's husband stroking his wife's hair as if he had just discovered a secret hand. Each touch made Joseph wince on the outside and howl on the inside until he wasn't sure if the inside and the outside had become confused. After putting down the glasses with the exaggerated care of someone yearning to smash them, he placed a hand in front of his mouth, perhaps thinking of that muted trumpet. Then he took a sip of the strong beer. It felt like sucking liquid through a carpet. He tried to swallow down his howl with his hops, while feeling that all his own attempts at tenderness during his time with Marta were now being sent back. Overwritten. Reversed. And in front of his very eyes.

Later, after a stiffening of shadows around the flame during which Marta's husband made sure of leaving his ring-finger on view, the couple offered Joseph a lift back to the flat. He declined, despite the shudder of cold as he spoke, his whole body cringing at his lunacy. Marta's husband smiled to see such pride. Though it is possible the sticky vodka had fixed his lips in such a curve.

Pushing his nose through air as stiff as frozen linen, and

his heart through untold despair, Joseph quickened his pace, trying to outwit the ice in his stride, yet his greatcoat and the treacherous paving slabs limited him to a one-man march, and a wobbly one at that, until his legs felt unrelated, merely lucky to be so close. Down the freezing underpass he went, thinking he could smell the luminous green graffiti that followed him along the wall, a cross between spray-paint and piss, '*Jezus cię kocha*' on one side, and '*Skinów!*' on the other, and he wondered if a city could be unlocked by its grafitti, then up slippery steps he went, inhaling darkness and salt, a gloved hand on a railing, the cobbles rising like swollen ankles presented for inspection. When he passed the bundle of strays, he heard a pulse in his ears, the howl inside, the steady moan of a trumpet.

When he finally crossed the wooden threshold to the sheltered darkness of his block (a squat block, the winter sky sitting on the roof, having pushed the first two floors into the basement), he startled a woman in a fur coat on her way out. Joseph touched her elbow to convince her he was human. But the look on her face! Eyeballs popping, head thrown back, as if all her fear had rushed that way.

Once in the flat, Joseph again found the bottle of whisky in the dark. He took a swig. Then another. Though he knew it wasn't such a good idea after beer and vodka. Raising the bottle aloft as if it were the burning torch that would soon lead him out of the woods, he carried it to the next room and planted it beside his bed. He heard coughing. A door slamming. Then, at last, the silence of thin blankets.

As Joseph sat on the mattress, covering his palms in muddy footprints as he grappled with his shoes, he thought of Marta undressing and slipping in beside him, and in another thought that also managed to separate itself from his drunken ones, and to find a voice above his internal howl, he wondered: what can you put in place of a person?

His head started to spin.

Your own shadow?

At that moment, he doubted there could be anything more important in life than the warm body of the human being beside you.

Now here he is with Marta and her husband. Again. This time, in their home. He is being asked if he will stay in their country. Despite the difficulties so far, he has already resolved not to give up too quickly. He knows that in the past, and on more than one occasion, his impatience led him to dismiss, albeit inadvertently, the very source of any future happiness. He tells himself to remember that there is always enough time. That resolution, and the stirrings of his spirit towards a new creativity, have convinced him he must stay.

'Well, that depends,' he says, pledged to an ambiguity he hopes Marta will relieve.

But Marta ignores the snags in Joseph's brief replies. 'Will you be visiting other cities here?' she asks, her words likewise carefully weighted to conceal their heavier load.

'Maybe,' he says. 'Where would you recommend?'

Marta's husband is chewing slowly, careful not to miss a word. Reading for false notes and fret-lines, he registers every change in tone. Sometimes he pauses, mouth open, his fork ready to scoop up any stray meanings. Other times, his knife takes command, scraping cabbage to the side of his plate, perhaps hoping that the porcelain might just transfer its clarity to the gestures round the table. Every now and then he smiles at his wife, with well-labelled affection, before touching her elbow to check she has not betrayed her form.

Marta tells Joseph the names of several cities. For all he knows they could be on the other side of the world. The other side of the well. Though they have similar shapes to the words he has heard in the street. Marta adds that perhaps they could visit one together.

Immediately, her husband's left arm rises to pull on the imaginary chain. Marta translates. Her husband replies, his voice like a whisper wrapped inside itself.

'My husband says he will be very happy to drive us to one of these places.'

Boże mój! thinks Joseph, nodding to Marta's husband, while biting the inside of his lip.

As if to emphasise his victory, Marta's husband stands up, stacks the plates, and carries them to the kitchen. Marta collects the glasses, gives Joseph a look he can't quite interpret – somewhere between love and contrition? – and follows her husband out of the room.

Alone at the table, Joseph listens to the dishes being done in a language of whispers and sighs. There are no tones of anger or irritation. Shortly afterwards, the three of them move beside the balcony windows, husband and wife on the sofa, Joseph on the armchair before them. Haven't I been here before? Joseph asks himself. Isn't this Einstein's definition of madness: to repeat the same act over and over again, each time expecting a different outcome? Or something like that. So here I am, four floors up from the frozen river, sitting opposite the woman I love who is sitting next to the man to whom she is married and I'm still anticipating that it's all going to work out in the end, and that, as Marta said to me last summer just before the three of us sat down together for the first time, 'We're all adults', as if that alone is enough to guarantee that we'll come to an amicable agreement, without violence, or unnecessary pain, an agreement that will take full account of the love in each of our hearts and the unquestioning love of the child sleeping in the wooden cot by her parents' bed in the room next door.

Marta's husband puts on some music.

'It's good,' says Joseph, in the local language.

'Yes,' says the husband, with a look that suggests he wants to change it immediately. He touches his wife's right ear, as if to check it's still correctly attached.

During the evening, minutes are not measured, they are felt – time as the ticking of pulses and tendencies. At one point during the silent cross-examining – the husband's looks going left to right as though he is trying to keep balance – yes, in a moment extracted from this fraught charade, Marta jumps up and goes to the bookshelves. She brings Joseph three books she has bought recently. 'Astonishing, *really*,' she says in that tone of voice he loves so much, the one that carries conviction and vitality, as if she is balancing, as well as can be hoped, a number of heavy and light things. They talk with increasing eye-contact. 'Lids going up. Lights going on. They fall into their familiar rhythm, re-establishing their complicity with ease, somehow managing, without even trying, to secrete all their emotions within words not designed to carry them.

Marta's husband stands and takes a step to the stereo. He changes the music and returns to his seat. He does not interrupt. He no longer reaches for the chain. He looks tired. Or bored. Or both. The strain of sifting every sound for a secret inclination has caused the darkness under his eyes to spread. As though reciting a prayer, he whispers to his wife, then leaves the room.

'He has gone to check on our child,' says Marta.

Joseph and Marta sit in silence, uncertain of their regained solitude, or togetherness, their heartbeats underneath the footsteps in the adjoining room. They look to each other for signs of how best to proceed.

Finally, Joseph gains the strength to whisper. Yes, it takes strength to whisper, to give out while holding yourself in. Especially as breaking a look with a word is also a perilous act.

'Marta,' he says,' it's me! Here I am. I'm still here.'

He opens his eyes wider to embrace the whole of her, or to encourage an equally emphatic response.

'I know!' she says, almost breathless.

Are the footsteps closer? Joseph can't tell. The floor throughout the flat is wooden parquet. There is a strange resonance to every step.

Joseph leans forward. His chair creaks. Or was it a floorboard? He looks round. No one in the door-frame. No shadow across the threshold.

'Marta!' he says again, hoping her name alone will be enough. Even though she has not spoken his all evening.

At that moment, Marta's husband strides back in the room, and with great purpose, as if he has already had a good night's sleep. His body carries a breeze in its wake, instantly dismissing any lingering looks or words or gestures. Sitting next to his wife, he puts his arm round her to guarantee her gravity. With his other arm, he reaches for the ripcord that will release his understanding.

Marta says a single word.

Her husband yawns, his newfound energy short-lived.

Belatedly, he remembers to bring down his arm. His stubble has now merged with the dark patches beneath his eyes.

Darkness and ice press at the windows. The full weight of winter. Withheld sighs on the inside maintain the air pressure.

Just as tiredness and silence threaten to take them all under, Joseph announces that he must be on his way. He must get a good night's sleep before setting off in the morning. Yes, there are other cities. He thanks them for the meal.

Joseph shakes the husband's hand, both trying to ignore what the other one knows. Marta leads the short way to the door. As she does so she hears a cry from the bedroom. So she says goodbye in the hallway, her husband in the room behind. Joseph kisses Marta on both cheeks, as lightly as he can, the familiar scent of her skin, and the tip of his nose against such softness (yes, skin as soft as froth!), adding to the night's many torments.

Having put on his shoes, Joseph pulls on his hat and coat and scarf, as though disguising himself so that the cold won't be able to find him. He makes for the door, Marta's husband close behind. Joseph turns and says goodnight. He is now in the stairwell. To his right is all darkness and glass. And metal banisters leading down. Joseph's right hand rests on the cold metal of the external door-handle. Marta's husband remains in the flat, his left hand on the inside handle. He looks as though he wants to speak. Joseph's eyebrows are as high as he can hold them, and his ears are wider than words. He hears a dog barking down by the river, the turning of a key, Marta whispering to her child. Again he feels the darkness pressing against the windows, like black water rising from the river, or a great surge of sleep. Still Marta's husband does not say anything. His mouth is open, his tongue perhaps already dozing. Once more, Joseph says goodnight in the language of his hosts. This time, though, he pulls the handle and closes the door behind him.

Letters
19 June, around midnight
Some people start and end the day with a prayer. Like Edith Stein. She prayed for hours in 'silent liturgy' as she called it. When she read, she read aloud, as if a book were a different kind of prayer. She would only be disturbed if she was called to the 'speak-room' by a visitor. Whereas I finished my day writing to you and so the next day started.

I know some of my friends would say, 'Marta, why all these letters? You see this man every day!' But I have always handwritten my most personal thoughts. There is something both calm and confessional about a clean white page. It reaches me deep within. I know that in this way, these thoughts will also find the most personal part of you.

Although a sinful daughter of God, I sometimes direct a few spontaneous thoughts upwards. It is a question of faith. You'll agree, I know, that it is possible to be an agnostic or a non-believer (and you tell me you swing from one to the other!), and still believe in the human spirit.

One thinker I have read believes that we all have a spirit, but that the soul descends upon a person, like a gift of grace. A gift that must be bestowed by another. In other words, we can't conjure up a soul if left to ourselves. So maybe those existentialists got it wrong when they argued that other people distract you from your authentic life, from your exhilarating fear and dread. Surely, hell is eternal solitude, wordless, without relations.

By the way, you know how little events can come together, squeezing us here, pinching us there, sometimes, without us noticing, changing the course of our lives? Take Edith Stein's conversion to Catholicism. One of the key moments occurred when she saw a woman praying in church. Stein wept for the peace and dignity of the woman. Her grace. The way she prayed as if 'talking to a friend'.

But you know what? I wasn't a good little girl at church. Was it excitement? Nerves? The first showings of my rebellious spirit? I don't know. But what I do know is that, aged six, something odd happened there. Maybe it was the incense swirling down the aisles. That smell always reduces me to solemnity. Gets in my lungs like a pious dust. Or the cold that played about my legs as I kneeled on the stone floor.

The first time it happened, it was snowing outside. I remember looking up to the stained-glass window to see if any flakes had landed in the prophet's beard. Rows of candles flickered as the midwinter greyness seeped in from the street. Like a beggar and all of his blankets.

In a Catholic service there is a lot of getting up and down. First standing then sitting then kneeling then standing again. And so it goes on. As if every bone and bend of you has to take part in the ritual. Let's say, you are encouraged to <u>feel</u> your mortality, to acknowledge how you are put together and therefore how easily you could fall apart! You should see the old ladies! How do they manage with their fragile bones, their trembling lips, their skin as delicate as the communion wafer?

Then, that day. The first time it happened. Just me and my mother in a pew. As always, she held her gloves as if they were the hands of the dearly departed. And when she prayed, she prayed intently. But what had this drone of voices to do with me? (I had no idea of the importance of the Church to those opposed to the State.) Besides, the muscles in my legs had been set in ice, like telephone lines in winter.

Then it happened.

The warmth of it. The relief. To feel human. To feel like a fully-thawed human being.

I peed on the floor!

Did I feel guilty? Not really. It became a little ritual of mine. Perhaps two or three times a year. In the winter. Then, one Sunday, the priest asked me to see him after the service.

I didn't pee during that service. But it was the only time I really needed to go. I trembled to think of my punishment. Would I be sent to a convent? Would my father be told?

I looked to my mother. Her eyes were closed. As usual. Oblivious to my terror. For the first time for a long time, I prayed. Really prayed.

Finally, everyone shuffled out, unsure whether to be blessed by the service, or blighted by the fact they must return, in humble human form, to the streets of dirty snow. And then, there he was. The priest. I remember the hairs from his nose were red, but flecked with silver. His hands were as white as his collar, apart from bursts of hair on his knuckles. (By the way, I remember his hands, especially, because at that age you live at the height of grown-ups' hands. I could often tell people by their hands, not needing to look at their faces.)

In one of his hands, a book. I thought at first it was the

Bible. But it wasn't big enough. The priest said that he wanted me to read this book. There was no sermon. No threat of being sent to a convent. I held the book as if it were a living thing. He repeated that I must read it, as God advises. I promised him I would. Of course. Look! I have opened it already. Look! I am reading the first page.

In a rare moment of maternal affection, my mother put her arm around me as we left.

And the book? It was about a girl, a little older than I was at the time. This girl was not sure of her faith. Every day she prayed to God for a sign. Until, one summer afternoon, she was swimming in the river near her home. She was a strong swimmer. On this occasion, however, there was a strange current and a dangerous outcrop of fresh weeds. She got caught up in them. She went under. She would have drowned if not for her brother's friend who happened to be jogging home along the river.

Though the girl was saved, she spent a long time in hospital. She thanked God for saving her. She took it as the sign she'd been asking for. She believed she would get better. As it turned out, her exhausted limbs would never be able to express her gratitude. Though the doctors did everything they could, the girl did not get better. Not physically.

She was paralysed from the neck down.

She cried and cried when they told her that the feeling in her body would never come back. She cried silently. Without whimpering. She could feel the tears running down her face, but she could not feel them when they dropped to her chest. Nurses and visitors alike wept at the girl's mute distress.

Not long afterwards, she was allowed to go home. She stopped praying. She was distraught for months. Until, one day, sitting in her specially adapted chair, looking out of the window, she realised she had received the sign from God, after all. Hadn't the accident released her spirit from the limitations of the body? Given her the lightness to aspire to higher things? Hadn't it assured her of her courage, her faith, her chastity?

Yes, she was more certain than ever that this was the sign she had asked for. 'She rejoiced in her soul' as it says in the book. She renewed her vows. And there, the book ended.

As I read her story, I felt something welling within me. I cried. I stamped my foot. I went hot and cold and shivery. My throat hardened. Until I could barely swallow.

When I reached the final pages, I could no longer contain the rising within me. I vomited. Several times. (My mother had to buy a replacement from the Episcopal bookshop on Długa Street.)

I continued going to church every festival and feast day. I no longer peed. I no longer prayed. I sometimes thought of God. After all, I decided, he did not write the book. But, then, why did he allow it to be written at all? Whenever I tried to wrestle with these questions, I felt the nausea rising within me.

So, you see, I remain an unorthodox occasional devotee.

Ps Why am I telling you all this when I haven't told anyone before? Really. I don't know. Other than I want to tell you everything! In return, Joseph, you must tell me more about yourself. For example, when you said the other day that you don't belong anywhere, did you mean that you don't want to belong anywhere, or that you haven't yet found the place? Which makes me wonder: does a person have to belong anywhere these days?

5

Pigeons in the Chandelier

The benches in the underground corridors are draped with bodies unlikely ever to return to their pre-street forms. They mumble among their bruises as if, even when dreaming, they can't escape their plight. There is a terrible stench of everything that can leak from a body. Joseph notices a man bleeding from a head-wound.

In the next corridor, where the concrete floor is dark with a stream of melt-water, elderly women in flowery headscarves and pale blue aprons are setting out stalls on upturned cardboard boxes. There are rolls of mountain cheese, piles of pretzels (like abandoned fairground hoops), hundreds of pairs of hiking socks, bras that look as though you could carry a head in each cup, furry slippers, purple plastic flowers, leather gloves, a stack of alarm clocks (their alarms going off, no doubt in a bid to convince everyone it's morning, despite the darkness, despite the cold), a wall of green bananas, and a dozen black umbrellas. Further along, there are stalls of tatty books, their covers flapping like wings held by a nail. Joseph notices a few art-books. One of them shows a shimmering portrait of a brown-eyed woman, and above this, in large letters, the name 'Witkacy'.

Joseph surfaces in the main concourse. Overhead, a

chandelier, once a proud welcome to an outpost of empire, now has feathers for fixtures and pigeon heads for bulbs. Again the smell of seediness and grime, of piss-soaked clothes and sweat that has frozen to become another layer of skin. The floor is scratchy with spilt tobacco and stones. Bench-sleepers are rising as the darkness thins. They rub at the places where a slat became a spine. They peer into empty cans like children with kaleidoscopes. They bundle up their belongings and shiver at their fate.

One day, you know, you might not make it home.

Once outside, Joseph looks back at the huge yellow station, an archetypal Galician design (so Marta told him) that he pictures as a hybrid of a castle and a post office and a giant wedding-cake. Ahead, he sees trams and trees and green tin kiosks, their outlines as if sketched in ink only moments ago. Over the pink neon sign on the roof of the Hotel Europejski, dawn emerges, a tone at a time, as if easing out its tongue.

Through senses numbed by tiredness and travel (that's an ear flattened against a greasy headrest, plus several hours of the train's muted thunder), Joseph hears rubber soles slapping across concrete and slush. When he turns, he sees a boy of about thirteen running from the station, with a pigeon flying low over his head, and at first glance this pigeon looks like a winged hair-piece, or a bat being shown the way home before dawn.

When this vision is followed by a noise of wheels across cobbles, Joseph wonders if the night train has deposited him in some mythical realm – a realm guarded by beggars and pigeons, at that – for hadn't Marta told him that this city is 'a magical city, a city of folklore and fables'? So perhaps he'd had this in mind as he stepped from the metal foot-plate, still carrying the images from the dreams he'd had en route and perhaps he can't disentangle himself from these dreams, though he doesn't remember one about a pigeon-boy, only fields of snow and blue horses.

As for wheels, well, he wishes he had some on his holdall. Why does it weigh so much? He has brought only woollen clothes, a couple of books, two small sketchpads with pencils and inks, and a bundle of Marta's letters. In fact, it was while re-reading these letters after the meal on the final night in Marta's city, that Joseph had decided to give the situation more time. How could he not? Her words still told him everything he needed to know.

Now, though, because of his tiredness and the coat that renders his gestures strange even to himself, his determination is beginning to ebb. Just as the neon of the Hotel Europejski is steadily draining its pink light, leaving in its wake fifteen lonely letters set in ice and metal and glass.

Again, Joseph hears wheels bobbling over the stones. When he turns, he sees two taxi drivers in caps and padded jackets, smoking beside their cream Mercedes. The silver radiators grimace at the day's first light. When Joseph looks back the other way, he sees steep tin roofs in red and green, like books that have fallen open. He sees men whose heads are lost among shovels of ice. He sees a blue tram pushing its muzzle through a mist made by early-morning kettles.

This time he locates the sound. It is a wooden board on wheels. The board is only inches off the ground. The man has no legs. His jeans are pinned up at the thigh. His arms bulge inside his coat. He wears leather gloves with metal plates at the knuckles that spark against stone as he propels himself forward. He wears a black woollen hat and a stubble of several days.

He wheels up to Joseph, coming to a gently rocking halt between two larger stones. Steadying himself with one arm, he reaches up with the other. He hands Joseph a small blue card.

The man speaks, stretching an accordion of consonants between Joseph's ears, and an accordion with little rips in the bellows, for there's too much air coming out, and not enough melody. Joseph shakes his head, for a moment sending into orbit the twelve rusting stars above the sign for the Hotel Europejski. The man points to the card. Joseph reads.

'Too old for youth hostels?' it says, in Joseph's language, on the back, 'Too young for park benches? Come to the Stranger Hotel!'

Letters
27 June
Joseph, you have a very strong impact on me. But that does not mean I am going to become your shadow. Quite the reverse. You make me stronger. I feel, at last, that I can begin to make the most of myself. This fuller self no longer floats around me, a secret darkness, tempting but not quite reachable.

I think there are too many people who, sensing their spirit all about them, are frightened of giving themselves to a cause. Instead, they choose the safe harbours of melancholy or abstraction, only sporadically entering life and even then to exploit it towards the protection of their souls. I never wanted to be this suppressed spirit. I always wanted to share. Though disclosure comes with its own difficulties.

By the way, have you heard of the letters of Bettine von Arnim to her lover? I thought of you, of us, as I read them today. Bettine wrote of their 'floating religion . . . a religion of joie de vivre, of sensory pleasure and humane attitudes' which would allow them to 'revolutionise the world while they laughed out loud'. This religion would be based on the principle 'that we do not allow any education – that is, no artificially taught behaviour. Everyone is to be curious about themselves and to unearth themselves the way one brings up ore out of the depths, or an underground spring. All education shall have the aim of letting the mind out into the light.'

Is this what we have, Joseph, a floating religion? Because aren't we bringing each other up from the depths? Isn't that what we recognised in each other, a certain solitude? Two people very much in the world yet at the same time somehow removed from it?

Later

Should I tell you more about my neighbours in our block back home? The old guy who complains that everyone keeps stealing his pots. He once showed me the axe he keeps by his bed in case he catches one of the intruders. Or how about the chimney-sweep? He called five times at my old flat when I was having a gas-heater installed because it required a clean chimney system. Each time he came round, he was riotously drunk, stumbling from elbow to ankle, unable to keep balance on the curb outside the door. His breath smelled like a fire-eater's just before the flame is taken. Of course, I wouldn't want to perpetuate the stereotype of drunkards in my country. 'Ivre comme un Polonais!'

O Matko! Now Edith Stein has popped into my head. So she studied the spirit and the soul. Faith. Empathy. Love. She sought to promote the status of women, too. As she studied, she felt herself moving closer to God. Inspired by the vision of the woman praying in church, Stein read the life of St Teresa of Avila. This story confirmed her faith. She took her vows as a Carmelite nun (known as the 'bare-footed' Carmelites), assuming the name Teresa. She believed that religion alone can keep a person human. She said that to seek truth is to seek God. And that all fugitive souls, whether they know it or not, are looking for Him.

Yet she once wrote that 'what I truly hoped for in my heart was a great love and a happy marriage'.

13 July

As you know, my friend Ania is staying for the weekend. As we chatted over soup last night, she suddenly said, 'Marta, are you not in love with Joseph?'

We both heard my teeth on the spoon. She said she could tell, not from my behaviour, but from the atmosphere around me! She claimed to have dreamed about it, too. We spent the evening in whispers. She is optimistic. She said it is a sign that I'm alive. She urged me to be strong. She was struck, she said, when she arrived the other day because I seemed tormented!

I don't quite think I am.

Ania is a good friend of mine, extremely sensitive and empathetic. Her life has not been easy. As a student, she delivered letters to a local Solidarność leader. Then, one day, two men turned up at her parents' flat. Her mother later said their moustaches looked like they were made from the bristles of a broom. These not very secret agents could have been models for the huge communist statues of workers you can still see in front of municipal buildings. They looked like oak trees in waistcoats. Ania's mother answered the door. They asked to see Ania. She was out.

'It is a shame,' said one of the men, the other no doubt mouthing the words in unison, 'that your daughter's education has today come to an end.'

But Ania is a not a person to give in. She continued her studies in secret. She worked in friends' flats late at night. She smuggled books in various bags, having collected them from designated pick-up points. A professor helped her take her exams, at great risk to his own career. Ania became like those women in the underground resistance during the war who 'lived on the 1 a.m.' – the time they could move around, find fresh dwellings, deliver plans, hold secret meetings, rendezvous with lovers, and disappear before dawn declared them. By the way, did you know that Solidarność was also known as 'panna S' (Miss S) – an underground woman indeed.

I would meet Ania with books in the cafés of seedy hotels, places frequented by businessmen and prostitutes, where the waiters ruled with smiles made from the rinds of rotten fruit. Because everything was rationed, you'd be lucky if you could buy a cup of watery tea and a stale cake. There was little or no sugar. The waiters would sneer at you if you asked, a sneer that would of course reveal their sweet tooth. Lipstick smirked from the rims of most cups. You had to be careful not to stick your elbows to the spillage on the plastic tablecloths. A cabbage plus hot water was served as soup. Only vinegar came in abundance.

Despite this, we tried to live as if Martial Law was not happening.

Boże mój! How we tried!

At home, there was often no shampoo. We used an egg mixed with a little beer. Not too fragrant, but a good shine! We had no toothpaste either, so we used salt and soda. Soap, like alcohol and cigarettes, was rationed. These coupons would swap hands quickly, the drinkers and smokers giving up their soap rations for more beer & cigarettes, the clean-living souls giving up their beer & cigarettes for more soap. You could tell who was doing what by their smell!

Then there were the frantic scenes outside shops whenever there was a delivery. People squeezing through the door ten at a time as soon as the shutters went up. They shouted, wrestled, fought. Shopkeepers ran out with brooms, garden hoes, pitchforks, and even cold-water hoses to keep the crowd at bay.

Nowadays there are whole shops selling soap.

Those years, they took something from all of us who lived through them. Apart from those with Party privileges, of course. (And even these sad souls will surely now be paying for their sins.)

I sometimes wonder: is it possible to be of our times, but not like our times? By which I mean, is it possible to live through a system, whatever system, and not be tarnished by it forever? Even if you were not involved in the enforcement of that system, can you be clear of it? Clean of it? I don't know. What do you think? Unless you become a hermit or a nun, I think it is very difficult to live in your period of history without smelling of it, soap or no soap. (Even Edith Stein could not escape.) Perhaps it is only love or some other delirium – drunken or otherwise – that can free us from our times and from all kinds of censors? Even then, only temporarily.

This reminds me of a writer living under communism who came up with 5400 anagrams of his name. Can you imagine? He said it helped preserve good mental health.

Now Ania is 'as nervous as a bird' as you said to me after meeting her. Her head turns every way. She walks lightly, still trying not to leave footprints. But she never lost her identity. She is brave. Even now, she takes risks, 'to lean out' as we say. She loves hitchhiking. As a university lecturer, she says institutions are never further away than when you're in the passenger seat of a stranger's car. OK, she has gained lines before her time where her face has folded in fret, or in disguise when she worked for panna 'S'. But she has gained wisdom and tolerance, too. She spends her life listening to other people.

How many people do you know like that?

I told her everything about us.

I will not keep you secret.

6

A Pebble in Each Pocket

Joseph did not have to accept the offer of accommodation from the man on the wobbly wheels, because Marta had already arranged a room for him in a private flat. 'Just say you're a visiting scholar,' she'd said, 'then you'll be well treated.' When Joseph claimed he didn't feel like a visiting scholar, Marta laughed.

'You look like a foreigner,' she said. 'So it's not a problem. Really. Besides, how are scholars supposed to look? You have a high forehead. For lofty thoughts. Big eyes. For reading and weeping. And you look like Rodin's Thinker – with a chin!'

'I'm not foreign!' replied Joseph, feeling the blood rush to his cheeks.

'You're far enough!' said Marta, who had only used the word to tease him. After all, hadn't she taught him that all nations are fictions, imaginary communities, who vilify others just to get a better sense of themselves?

When she felt his wince, she added, 'I know, I know, personality before nationality, as you like to say. I agree, by the way. As you know. In which case, I'll change it to fair enough. OK, fair enough?'

And she gave him a smile that he wanted to kiss from one end to the other.

Now as he heaves his bag towards a city that's rising above the snow with the help of roof-tops shaped like arrow-heads, he wonders how on earth he will cope without Marta's organisational skills. And her sense of humour! That wonderful sort of irony that unseats your pretensions without taking away your chair. Not that Western irony that's all clever-clever and intent on revealing your stupidity in the back of a spoon. What will he do without her laugh, her wit, her joy that leaps from the larynx? (If he is to be without her, that is, which he is far from accepting. Even in his tiredness.)

But he must not think of her now, he tells himself, with a gentle footstamp in the snow, a stamp that sets his print among those of hooves and paws, and of pigeons and ravens and crows. All these migrations marked in the ice! Is there room for him among them?

Through the early-morning mist, he can see buildings blowing out balconies. Bell towers and domes give up their sleeping-caps to reveal tender scalps of snow. The day's first clouds squeeze from chimney pots, as if pushed out by a foot-pump.

'ADAM' says a piece of paper held by a woman in a long dark coat standing a little way ahead. The grand building to Joseph's right, guarded by gargoyles, and disdainful of any snow that can't lay claim to softness, must be the theatre, for this is where they are supposed to meet. A bench alongside carries an ice sculpture of a summer sleeper.

Joseph's breath rushes ahead for a closer look. 'Pani Grażyna?' he says, approaching the woman, whose face only just emerges from the collar of her coat. Her hair, though, more than makes up for her diminutive frame. Having suffered a lifetime of bouffants and barnets, her raven-black strands spiral upwards in no particular style and at an imperious slant that the wind can only advise.

'Adam?' says the woman, tucking the paper in her pocket, before presenting a tiny hand.

'Eadem,' says Joseph, with a little bow to highlight his conscientious forehead. In his palm, pani Grażyna leaves a trace of cold fingers, like the ivory handles of butter-knives.

They make their way through the city gardens where the snow is soaking in shadows. Either side of the path, huge banks of ice stand like seawalls set, not against the ocean, but against the season. A group of trees looms like a seven-stemmed candelabra robbed of light. Beyond the gardens, a scrapyard comes to life as rusty trucks cough their engines to a start, leaving blue fumes in the air, and oil in the ice.

In black boots that peek under her long skirt like mice beneath a tablecloth, pani Grażyna bears the melancholy grace of a society lady without the society. Of course, she is far too refined to have met Joseph at the station, what with all those beggars and hawkers and half-wits, their fingers as yellow as their teeth.

'First, you sleep,' she tells him, in a voice that carries compassion alongside the command. 'Then my mother make you breakfast.'

Her mother? thinks Joseph. Out of the corner of a tired eye, he studies his host. Her hair! It must add 20 centimetres to her height! And it's been dyed black so many times that the roots have given up all competition and turned a mawkish ash. Yes, pani Grażyna's head belongs to another era. Likewise, she is stylishly dressed, but in the manner of a spinster of a certain age. She has pampered her solitude with velvet and wool. As for her small feet, they are surely indoor feet, made for soft carpets and pedicures.

Green gas-lamps, now fitted with electric bulbs, float above the path. Joseph can see their yellow lights ahead, popping with a flash in the snow. Crows peck at ice for their daily bread. Joseph slides his palms down the lining of his pockets. He feels a pebble in each one, his share of the binding stones as he and Marta called them.

Leading her new lodger from the path, pani Grażyna tilts her hair in the direction of the municipal library, a building half the length of a street lined by oak trees, their roots having long since pushed slabs and soil asunder, like the drifting anchors of a cruise liner. The library certainly possesses the might of an ocean-going vessel, even if it's stranded in an ice floe, and loaded with pigeons, not gulls. Though carrying his head towards sleep, Joseph remembers that as a scholar he must pay close attention.

Soon afterwards, they are outside a tenement block, its grey-green façade looking like it's been sand-papered by a century of leaves. When Joseph touches the plaster, a small piece crumbles in his fingers and so, for want of a better idea, he pops it in his pocket. Inside, the hall is dark wood and stone. Joseph is fast becoming used to the smell of cold and damp that clings to concrete as if winter lurks here all year round. They pass through wooden swing-doors that nearly give Joseph a double-palmed slap as he studies their art-nouveau motif: a chameleon? A salamander? A snake? It is difficult to tell for someone has scratched at the design with a knife. Of the coloured glass panels, only two remain, like a moribund Mondrian, and even these carry fractures. Further along, a wooden colonnade rises between the banisters, but it is painted a muddy orange to excuse its former grandeur.

As Joseph and pani Grażyna make their way up the wooden staircase, every step creaks under the weight of generations of feet. *'Dzien dobry!'* echoes in the bucket of an elderly lady on the landing – 'Good morning!' – as she mops the black tiles with spirals of wax. Joseph can only imagine the smell, for pani Grażyna's perfume has frozen in his nose.

They come to a chocolate-coloured double door. A brass plate is inscribed with a long name that Joseph can't make out, the arms and legs of the letters having been eroded over time by the proud breaths and polishing cloths of his host and her mother. Pani Grażyna takes two keys from her pocket and shows Joseph how to open the door for there are certain angles involved. Then she asks him to try. Another key in his hand, like an extra finger, though one drained of life, like the letters on the roof of the Hotel Europejski. In his exhaustion, Joseph struggles as though it's his wrist at fault, not the lock. He wonders if this is a country of awkward doors. He wonders if you can have stereotypes about a country's objects as well as its people. He opens the door. 'Good, good,' says pani Grażyna, with a quick clap of the hands from which no sound emanates.

Once she has taken off her coat, there is not much left of Joseph's host. Bright blue-grey eyes, like cracked tiles seen through water. A set of pearls tight to the throat. A slender frame that disappears in the gap between the white double-doors of her mother's room. And, of course, her aristocratic inclinations, no doubt championed by her mother, trampled over by her father (his longest-lasting bequest: the nicotine ceilings), and never lived up to by her suitors, most of whom have now trundled beyond an eloquent age. In the milky kitchen light that falls kindly upon her skin, pani Grażyna looks forty. In the damp green light of the bathroom, where the battered pipes spread like branches, and where a cat licks at the taps of the cracked enamel tub, she looks sixty.

The stillness of the apartment having been disturbed, it secretes an odour of camphor and sticky liqueurs, of boiled carrots and years of waiting in the dark. The air is heavy with geraniums and hidden latrines. Joseph suspects pani Grażyna has lived here all her life, serving her mother's shadow, while trying to ignore her own, for her perfume does not quite disguise her disappointment. Nor does her determined look of dignity prevent the lines of sadness growing round her mouth. Her hair must also be a remnant of former aspirations.

Pani Grażyna opens the door to Joseph's room. With a hurried hand, she beckons him beyond a threshold she no longer chooses to cross. Alongside one wall, beneath a picture of Pope John Paul II, there is an iron bed with a goose-feather quilt, and grey covers as coarse as horse blankets. In the corner there's a heating stove, its tiles the same blue-grey as pani Grażyna's eyes. There is a smell of warm dust and worry. Until her father's death, this must have been her room. Joseph pictures his host in her loneliness, like a Dresden figurine of a slender shepherdess, too delicate for her own despair, staring at the tiles until her tears absorbed their colour. There is also a brown wardrobe (yielding a single hanger with the name 'Chełmonski' inscribed in green ink), a chest of drawers with brass handles suggestive of the braiding on a hussar's tunic, and a desk

that does not look as though it could support a drawing
hand let alone a thoughtful elbow. The window, meanwhile, gives on to a great oak, its snow-strapped branches
filling quickly with crows. Pani Grażyna says, again, 'My
mother make you breakfast.' Then she vanishes through the
gap in the door.

Stepping from his greatcoat as though from the shackles
of a sleepless winter, and then from clothes that smell of
tarmac and smoke, Joseph finds the blank piece of paper
he's carried with him since he set out ten days ago. It's the
sheet that was attached to Marta's final letter at the end
of their summer together, the letter she'd tried to hide
in a book. Joseph considers the sheet talismanic, perhaps
believing it's the page on which their next chapter will be
written, or on which he'll sketch his finest work.

He slips beneath the rough blankets. The morning bells
of church and tram are distant behind crows reciting the
name of their city. A muddy light leaks from the sky, like
an emptying of pots – of tea, of paint, of plant. Despite
the boiled sheets, Joseph can't remove the scent of pani
Grażyna's perfume from his nose.

As he studies the bowl of the glass lampshade hanging
from the ceiling, Joseph can still feel the shudder of the
train from his night journey. Yes, you must be told if you
don't know already, that travelling does not let you forget
the skin and bones of it all, the skeleton standing inside
your skin. It's you and your mortality clattering down the
tracks, all right, your joints jostling, your vertebrae shivering
like a pile of coins small in any currency.

Joseph remembers stopping at stations in the dark, as he
dozed, disturbed, hearing announcements in a language that
sounded like water being poured from one tin to another.

Waking for a while, thinking it is the landscape that links us, he'd watched as the train passed through fields of snow and mist, and he'd never seen so many forests and fields, so many pine trees and silver birch, nor so much snow, and he wondered if Marta would be waiting at the station again, at every station, as the corridor of the carriage rushed by, the curtains blowing up like the manes of galloping horses, so that when Joseph next fell asleep he dreamed of these endless fields, and he dreamed of these galloping horses. Later, he woke to hear more station announcements as a woman's voice, as soft as a psalm, creased the cold air with consonants. The blue horses were still there, scratching their hooves on the platform, or cracking the ice with the sharp edge of a shoe, their snorts adding to the night mist that Joseph could sense behind the thin mauve curtain of his compartment.

Now, from his room at pani Grażyna's, he hears people passing two floors below, their footsteps in the snow (as if weighing themselves in ice), an untangling of keys, a door slamming against the cold, repeatedly, church bells, drills, whispers in the corridor, the rising and falling in tone as people say good day, the rattle of a tin bucket, then longer conversations, close to his door – perhaps pani Grażyna and her mother? – so that he is sealed softly inside by this gentle-sounding language, a language he cannot yet fathom but which does not at all alarm him, for it seems to be full of words promising sleep, and he's sealed in by smoke, too, for they are smoking either side of speaking, these people close by, and the smoke seeps under his door and into his room where it mingles with the yellow light of the walls.

Letters
20 July

I've had a nice weekend. Even though you were away. I went to the coast. I have never seen such a sky. It goes all the way from one side to the other. And the light! Surely artists come here to try to match their loneliness to the landscape. Or to plot their lives against the stars.

Tell me, Joseph, is this why you are here?

I went to this curving edge of England with my daughter and her au pair, who came home early this morning and left the door unlocked. When I asked her today if she liked this country, she replied, 'I like the economy.'

More and more people from my country are coming here now, in preparation for the changes next year. The other day I asked Ania who will stay behind to look after our country.

'The Ukrainians?' she said.

When you are not here, there is a hazy screen between me and the world. Warm summer smells are just so much nose stuffing. Or is that the English coast on a cloudy day? Now I have woken up with you, come to the surface, the last few years feel like a lethargy. Not a mistake, necessarily. But a waiting time. A quiet preparation for your arrival.

Maybe I have been wrong from the start to act as I did? To make such a dramatic declaration to you. But when you went away last time, and for a whole week, I couldn't eat. Really. Do you remember when you came back? You put your hand on my shoulder. You asked why I was so pale. Then you laughed and said I looked like a mushroom!

You made me a cup of tea to go with some nice little cakes you had brought, as well as a bundle of sketches from your journey north for a friend's wedding. You quickly stacked up magazines and books that I had left lying about the place, and a few of Malena's toys. But you simply smiled at the plates I'd dumped in the sink.

Malena was having her afternoon nap. So I couldn't refrain from telling you why I felt so terrible. We sat at the kitchen table. Your face was so receptive that it was easy for me to speak. Besides, my voice always feels confident when I am talking to you.

I told you I'd fallen in love with you. I tried to make it sound matter-of-fact. Inevitable. The last thing I wanted was to sound hysterical or romantic. I didn't want this great surge of emotion to sound like it was born of loneliness. Or boredom.

At first, you did not say anything. We stood and held each other. I had never felt my heart galloping like that before.

Is that already two months ago?

One thing I did not know then: there will now be more torture in being with my husband than being without you. Does that make sense? What I mean is, I won't be able to be more than friendly with him. I'll probably be cold and distanced. The thought of him suffering stirs me deeply. He has already started, I'm afraid. Our nightly phone calls crackle with suspicion and fear. I hear the hurt in his normally lively voice. I picture the dark skin under his eyes getting a little darker. He asks about Malena. He asks about me. Then, with trepidation in his voice, as if the line has suddenly gone thinner, he asks about you. Whether I have seen you that day. Of course, every day the answer is yes. He falls silent. Perhaps he is thinking of asking the exact nature of the relationship between us. So far I have only told him it is an intense friendship. In any case, he does not ask.

He steers his voice back to its normal pitch. He calls me the pet names he has for me, the names that used to make me happy. Now they make me feel childish. Not quite right. As if I have become separated from the image he has of me. Even worse, I almost pity him. I do not want to pity him. I do not want to think of the harm I could do him.

He tries not to give in to his feelings. He lets me know of any gossip from home. These stories may last five minutes. Then he tries another pet name. I try to respond. Really, I do. But my words are like stepping-stones that no longer reach all the way across. Painfully aware of my indifference, my husband trails off. By the end of the call he is distant in his despair. And I hate myself for it.

The complete trust of another person can be hard to bear. It is like guiding a boat across a lake at night with only your hand for a rudder.

Joseph, what can I do? When I picture you, I feel you close. But I don't want to have to keep you secret. Secrets can ravage a soul.

Later

I now know what happened when I first met my husband. He wooed me with his affection and charm. He acts quickly, too. In queues, he always seems to get to the front quicker than he should. The same when he's driving. Around the home he is always tidy, organised, affable and efficient. He is incapable of malice or deceit.

I could not have asked for more.

Now I am beginning to feel that it was my reason, my sober self, that was won over by him. My heart was only persuaded.

So we lived for the day-to-day duties, which we shared

with joy. We were young and hopeful and I translated this natural interest in life as being in love. Even if I was, it was simply more imagination than reality.

I see that now.

But I am making him suffer. So I suffer, too

I'll be finishing,

7

Light in the Eye

The tip of pani Grażyna's coal-black coiffure appears through a gap in the door. 'Pan Adam?' she whispers, now pushing her face through sideways like a moon tugged along by a mass of dark cloud. Then slightly louder, 'Sorry, problem.'

Joseph does not know which city he's in. If it is a city. His waking mind turns over the possibilities like the pages of a picture calendar. He rouses himself, but carefully, so that he might recover his whereabouts before he's fully conscious. He sits up. There is a layer of dust on his tongue. Or is it cat fur? He focuses on the small woman before him. She is wearing a dressing gown made of feathers and scrambled eggs.

'Sorry,' says pani Grażyna, again, like a person of frequent apologies who, in the first instance, cannot forgive themselves. 'My mother ill. No breakfast.'

And then the head and hair retreat.

Soon after, having pulled himself into his clothes, while hoping that his bearings will be just as easy to recover, Joseph is escorted to the bathroom under the raised wing of pani Grażyna's yellow housecoat. The route takes them along a corridor dark with wooden crucifixes and the discarded selves of erstwhile tenants. Joseph notices that pani Grażyna's gown has come open, revealing a small white breast. He is shocked to realise she is only about his age.

In the bathroom, Joseph struggles to find his face in the mildew-lined mirror. The cat is no longer in the tub. On the sink that is trying to detach itself from the wall, a tiny bar of mustard-coloured soap retains only a trace of its former utility.

After washing the sleep from his eyes, and the lack of sleep from the rest of his body – not easy using only a basin – Joseph emerges into a midday light of moth-balls and coffee-pots. In the kitchen, he finds pani Grażyna, still in her yellow housecoat, her hair a topiarist's tragedy. She is sitting at the white table, in a stately pose, her hands lost among the streets of a city plan. She is circling cafés and libraries, and with a certain relish, as if bringing these places into existence with a movement of her delicate hand.

Slipping the map in his pocket, and quickly drinking a cup of coffee – he was lured by a spoon of honey and a sprinkling of cinnamon – Joseph thanks his host with what he assumes to be the exaggerated courtesy of a scholar. After packing a day-bag – inks, pencils, pads, his special sheet, a couple of Marta's letters, and a huge apple proffered by pani Grażyna in the absence of breakfast – he heads for the city's main square.

Where every face, on every street, is featured in flakes. For this city is dazzled by snow, by already-seated snow, by settling snow, and by snow still enjoying its descent. Joseph wonders if he would have been better off wearing one of his host's heavily-fringed lampshades on his head and not his woolly tea-cosy, because his eyelashes can't deny the brightness. And the pavements are running with slush – purple slush, at that, for it was once a royal city, and Joseph is instantly up to his ankles in this slush – like a runny glue, or mashed potatoes with too much gravy – and he's up to his ears in the swish of this slush. And the whispers around him. And the midwinter breeze. Until he's not sure if it's words he can hear, or the syllables of a street under water.

On the roof-tops of buildings bearing designs from across Europe – ice-jagged Gothic, snow-turned Baroque, frozen-stiff Renaissance – he sees men tied to chimney pots by rope around their waists, and these men are running ridges to shovel off the snow, sending down solid clouds with a warning whistle or shout. As Joseph watches, he notices the blue sky, as tender as skin, stretching from a church spire on one side of town to a church spire on the other, and he feels, intensely (that's inside and out), his state of alone. Camphor and cold pinch at his nostrils. He sneezes. When he opens his eyes there is a young woman standing in front of him taking a picture of a building lit by red bulbs. Only, she is taking the picture through a flat glass bottle that she holds in front of the lens.

At the end of another street of trams – all those windows on wheels! – leather caps, cigarette butts, tin signs and gateways set with lilies, opposite a huge crucifix with a waxwork Jesus frozen in his suffering, Joseph finds the *bar mleczny*, the milk bar, as marked on pani Grażyna's map. Inside, there is a smell of anorak and steamed cabbage but this is soon overwhelmed by a stench somewhere between detergent and despair. The windows are held in place by condensation. A radio plays big-haired ballads from the eighties – reminding Joseph of his de-formative years – and the assistant boasts a style to match. He orders bacon and eggs by making a series of gestures in the direction of the menu – though he stops short of clucking – then he sits on a purple plastic chair, its sigh matching his own, nurturing the hard white roll he's been given, perhaps unsure whether it will take his teeth. His breakfast is served in the pan. He touches the sides. He loses his fingerprints on three digits of each hand. And it's strange this burning sensation, as he looks beyond the vinegar pots and carnations to a street where bright skies breed stalactites. Yes, he has noticed already that from the guttering of the Gothic cathedral, these stalactites hang in a row of descending length like organ pipes. From the drains of antique shops, they form the shimmering fringe of an art-nouveau lamp. From restaurant roofs, they hang like the teeth of the animals sacrificed for the menu. Above cafés, they hang like latté spoons. From the library, like bookmarks, or exclamations of silence. And from the yellow-walled church at the end of the street, they hang like the outstretched finger of the Virgin Mary, the Patron Saint of Wayfarers, because she is said to point the way to the child upon her arm.

Back on the streets, and loaded with brief inspirations, not to mention warm grease from the thick cuts of bacon, Joseph feels a growing sense of colour and light (and not just in his fingertips). Before meeting Marta, the intensity of his ideas often precluded their successful execution, or he didn't have time, or he didn't want to bring them to life only to have them obliterated by noise and light and commerce, but here he believes he'll be able to develop each idea steadily, quietly, along streets ending in white mist and sugar bowls and words that brush against him but do not leave a trace.

For example, in the evening, beneath the tin lamps

hanging high above the street, it is possible to study the constitution of a single flake of snow.

Led by his enchantment, he wonders if this city has more faces than feet. For there are eyes everywhere. No longer frightened eyes, like in the provinces, but inquisitive eyes, searching eyes, eyes that send out the light with which they survey, eyes that travel beneath the arches of the cloth hall or gather in cellars to listen, because listening may take place in the ears but it is measured in the eyes. (In other words, you can't see what's going on in an ear, but you can see what's going on in an eye.) And many of these eyes are set in heads that belong to the bodies of students, and many of these students are carrying large black folders, and this excites Joseph, too, to see so many people carrying their artwork along the icy streets.

He pushes open a wooden door, parts a curtain of dark velvet, and enters Café Prowincja. All the candles blink. Faces of hot wax look up to see a well-sugared hat and coat blown in by the wind. The outside walls are on the inside. The bricks are made of chocolate and cinnamon, the plaster of vanilla. A gingerbread staircase goes nowhere in particular. Or to a life of pictures, pencils, clocks, souls. Because – look! – people are reading! People are writing! People are drawing! And the clocks? Yes, there is a collection of Sława alarm clocks on every shelf, each one stopped, because time here is marked only by the banging of the coffee scoop. Joseph knows he must stay awake and watch. He is entranced by dark eyes over the rim of a white cup. By the yellow glow emanating from the pages of a book. And by the stillness of the body behind the book, for reading doubles the silence a body carries within.

The black water across the floor is a puddle of sleep. Or

the developing fluid in a darkroom. Just how are we going to come out? Women enter, unwrapping their slender forms from padded coats that cover them from ankle to Adam's apple and look more like sleeping-bags. Yes, Joseph is already struck by the grace of the women here. They are effortlessly upright, stylish, determined.

How can he not think of her?

And these eyes, in their curiosity, try to fathom the *fromwhereabouts* of this man who has just walked in. They look at his coat, the cut of his clothes. They look at his hair, the shape of his face. They listen closely when he orders. They watch as he opens his bag. Aha. Now they realise. For this tired-looking stranger asks for milk with his tea.

There is a kerosene heater in the corner. All the objects in the café float in its strange and flickering light, and in the fumes of smoke and coffee and conversation: a miniature rocking horse rises from its runners, the chocolate cake above its glass stand, the silver candlestick on top of the piano – all rise up in the gold-flecked darkness. And to Joseph's benefit. For he is sure that here in this city, free of everything that once bound him to a life without spirit, he has a chance of discovering the best form for his vision, a vision that Marta had been the first person in his life to share and understand.

Later, on the streets again, he follows eyes beneath the rim of a black hat, above a red scarf, between the upturned lapels of a winter coat. He charts the whites of eyes that put the snow to shame. He is drawn by the dark eyes of monks that speak of the silence inside. By eyes through the gloom. By eyes that lift you out of the gloom. Eyes that say if winter really is to be this cold, this dark, this deep, then so much the better! (Insert stalactite.) Let's test our endurance, our humility, to see this out, to guide ourselves with eyes and arms through all the darkness and slush.

Others have a different idea. Men in padded jackets elbow their way down the street with stares that don't let go.

Undeterred, and with a red nose for a rudder, Joseph steers a route over the slopping cobbles, and for the first time since he came to this country, he comes close to recovering his usual rhythm when everything flows together, just like it does when he's swimming, and he feels himself surging forward, on the verge of overtaking himself, his rushing blood full of images and ideas as if the source of these is his heart even his feet but in any case not his head, so that he can craft something from the street, from the senses, and not the intellect, and in these moments the weather doesn't bother him even though the sky is now snowing old women's bonnets (the furry ones, minus the ribbons), and the cold is putting a clothes-peg on the end of his nose – that doesn't bother him either, nor do the streets of crooked tiles and broken pavements where you can't tell the ice from the ash, because he is driven by his wonder and what's a slip when you have such momentum? what's a glimpse of ugliness when it's all going in? his eyeballs rolling from cracked pavement to cupola and back again, resting on a green set of scales in a shop window, a brown beer bottle in the snow, the purple-throated pigeons on the top ledge of the post office – and, besides, even a slip feels as though it is in her direction, and he'll take all this with him on the way: buildings with pastel-coloured fronts like paint poured on snow, former palaces stretching out a stone buttress, their angels and caryatids holding on (the tears of these grieving widows of Carya now frozen), crucibles and crenellated towers, and stucco like the iced saliva of smokers. Against a sky of coal-dust and snuff, each detail looks crisp enough to snap.

Yes, down streets made of paint and flake and feather, Joseph makes his way. He reads the signs hanging over the shops: *Kantor, Tania Odzież, Antyki*. And he lays these words across his tonsils. He listens, really listens, to passersby, to words like 'mówie' and 'dokładnie!' and 'tak!'. He collects the used springs of consonants that fall upon the ice.

Only occasionally, when his momentum is not so much lost as muddled – by a hissed word, an ugly elbow, a glare – does he feel dark tides tugging at the hem of his coat. As if he is only a spirit stuffed with senses. And a memory.

In such moments, he tries not to think of Marta. He inhales deeply. The cold crackles in his nose. He thinks of Marta: her brown eyes beneath a falling fringe when they shared their first moment, a moment that holds a glance or seizes a gesture, during which time itself holds its breath (as if time, too, had stepped from warm to perilously cold), while their eyes say, here we are, and for each other. Yes, your look says I am the only one who understands you, the only one who can teach you to be quiet inside, and I know my eyes say the same to you, and there is no need for anything that can be said in words because the way your shoulder inclines towards me suggests that you want to move closer and I know I do, too, because I am already beginning to think in terms of tenderness, of warming your skin with my breath, of showing you all I have learned until now of love. With my hair. My teeth. My tongue. What else is a body for if not to show another body love?

Joseph stamps his feet and moves on.

Letters
1 August

For the last ten days, in the rare moments when you and I were not together, I fretted about my husband and the harm I am doing him. It felt like the best part of me, the most real part of me, was the part conspiring against him. Today, I feel differently. Maybe my defence mechanisms have started to work. I feel calm. Maybe it is because I have returned to writing after ten days of blissful distraction with you. Reading about my women makes me stronger. How they fought to make the most of life. To be fully human: joyous, suffering spirits. How each one of them is so much more than the things that happened to them. I think that's where this notion of the human spirit comes in. A person's spirit exceeds the person, drives the person, pushes them through circumstances.

Take Lya de Putti, for example. She could never be contained! When she was in her early teens, and the Hussars rode their tight breeches into town, they would queue up to dance with this young beauty of the dark eyes and satin skin. As was the custom for men paying their respects, the Hussars drank champagne from her silk slippers. These slippers never lasted the night. And Lya rarely made it home on time.

As punishment, her father would lock her in the basement. But her spirit resisted. Aged eleven, she ran away to join a circus, only to change her mind after an unhappy meeting with the owner. Aged thirteen, in her parents' absence, she organised a night of singing and dancing at the family home, with a hired gypsy band. When the Countess found out, she sent Lya to a convent school. Even there, she found her way to mischief. One rainy evening, Lya was discovered beneath the ivy in the courtyard presenting a pair of knickers to a boy from a neighbouring school.

After six years of marriage, during which Lya appeared happy, but in the way that youthful energy can easily defeat the first signs of self-awareness, she met the poet Endre Ady. He was married to Lya's friend, Baruka Boncza. One critic called Ady 'a searchlight and a flame-thrower'. Ten years earlier, his second book had caused a revolution in the literature of his country: physical love as the highest expression of life. Attacks on the ruling class for their greed. A call for his country to rise from its backwardness. To embrace modernity. For its cities to emulate Paris, where he had lived with his first wife.

Having suffered a stroke, he was coming towards the end of his life. Even so, he relished the outing with his wife and her dark-eyed friend. He began by showing his new acquaintance his 'wizard marks' as he called them. Born with six fingers on each hand, the extra digits were removed, leaving thick stubs between his index and middle fingers. Apparently, he used to sleep clutching a recently extinguished candle in each hand, the fleshy part of his thumbs pressing down on the soft wax tops, ghostly replacements for his missing digits.

Lya was captivated by Ady, by the way he shuffled his bent but still towering frame, by his dark grace and sudden bursts of humour. Most of all, she was moved by the way he spoke to her, for he spoke of her most intimate thoughts.

His eyes confirmed that everything she carried within her was real.

'Don't be buried from the outside!' he urged her. 'Hope for forces you don't yet have!'

Years later, Lya told a friend that it was Ady who had given her the final push she'd needed to flee her family for the theatres of Budapest.

Later

Edith Stein once wrote that the soul is 'the absolute depth of a person, that which becomes perceptible only in moments of silent receptivity'.

Joseph, when we met, I think we met in those depths.

Funny how if you talk about the spirit now people think you mean the Holy Spirit. And if you talk about the soul, people think you must be a hippie. What happened to bring this about? Please put your list of reasons here:

You were right when you said I may be happy to see my husband. We do have things in common. Everyday things. This may imply boredom, difficulties, little but frequent irritations (this is me, especially), doubts, anxieties, even dullness, but it may also imply a simple, steady happiness, peppered with moments of joy. And shopping lists. And something else important: our shared delight in Malena, the reflection of us in her eyes. However far away my husband, he will always return in the eyes of my child. As parents, we will always be partners.

In other words, I won't be crushed. I can only develop. So can you. And you will. When I go back, we will be refined in our unhappiness. We'll be more aware of the world. And less alone. More aware of who we are and who we can become. Joseph, we can't afford to be sentimental. We would drown in the misery and mush.

9 August

Today is the anniversary of the murder of Edith Stein in Auschwitz, 1942. She was fifty-one. She was living with her sister, Rosa, in a Carmelite convent in Holland when the SS ordered the arrest of all Jewish Catholics. This was in retaliation to an open letter from the Dutch Catholic bishops denouncing the Nazis for the deportation of Jews. When the SS came for Edith, it is claimed she said, 'I am going to join my people.'

She was last seen on the transport to Auschwitz (in the Polish town of Oswięcim) when the train stopped in the city where Stein was born. My city. At that time a German city. It was a freight train with Dutch markings. It stopped before the Hauptbahnhof so people could not see inside. But a military postal worker remembers seeing the doors open to one of the wagons. He remembers the stench. He remembers the shock of seeing a nun standing in the doorway. She spoke to him.

'It's awful,' she said, gesturing to the floor of the cattle-wagon that was running with human waste, 'we have no containers.'

The postal worker handed her some water and two empty barrels.

'This is my home city,' said Stein. 'I will not see it again.'
The doors closed. The train went on to Auschwitz.

Now 9 August is her name day. Pope John Paul II beatified her as St Teresa of the Cross. He also ordained her as a co-patroness of Europe.

Remember, this woman was also a philosopher. She tried

to show us the spiritual structure of a person. What makes us human. What gives us faith. Yet she died in the most inhumane way possible.

She once wrote, 'We have no lasting dwelling-place'.

13 August

When I wrote the date at the top of this page, I wanted to find out if it hurts me. And it does. Joseph, we have only eight days after this one before my husband comes to collect me. Perhaps there is little point in scribbling these notes to you now.

That said, I do want to clear something up. Yesterday you asked me, in a slightly mocking tone of voice, if I 'identified' with the women I am writing about. 'Especially Lya de Putti,' you said, with that teasing look in your eye that also carries a hint of mischief, if not spite. I couldn't find the words for a quick reply. Not in your language, anyway. Also, I was a little bit disappointed by the way you seemed to enjoy my discomfort. Now I have thought about it, I can tell you that, no, I don't feel anything so crude as an identification with Lya. When I read and write about her, she is always supremely herself.

Joseph, our time is so short, we must spend it together. Urgently!

Words will only get in the way.

16 August

I am in the library waiting for you. You are already half an hour late. And not for the first time. I am not angry. I can keep working. But it makes me wonder: are you trying to tell me something? Are you punishing me because I have to go home in five days? Joseph, really, there is no need.

I am tormenting myself. I wake each morning turning over the situation in my mind. Desperately. Can I stay? Should I phone my husband and tell him not to come? To give me two more weeks? But what use is a postponement? The practicalities are stacked against me: my daughter, my teaching at the university back home. Above all, I owe it to my husband to discuss with him what has happened.

Underneath the hurt, Joseph, I know you understand.

8

'eltmeister Harmonies

This loneliness is lit with wonder.

Hanging across streets that lead to the main square like aorta to a single heart, there are blue bulbs and green tinsel, gold stars and red berries, bronze bells and transparent angels. Orange lights dangle from the snow-clipped branches of the linden trees like electrified Spanish moss, while the yellow cloth hall glimmers in the dark like a chunk of gold from a coalface.

Although the decorations point to Christmas, every date here is truffled by snow, or is lost among slate and stone and spire. You may as well study the drops falling from stalactites to calculate the passing of time. Or count footsteps in the ice. Or candles. Or crows. What else holds the day together, saves it from disappearing without trace into the depths of the dark season? A lost page? A shot of vodka? A chance encounter?

Pani Grażyna has not asked any questions. She has accepted her latest scholar. Every morning, she takes him under her yellow wing and escorts him past her mother's door. The bathroom smells of face-powder frozen in the compress of time. The water trembles in the bowl. Circular stains on the shelf mark the jars of cream and bottles of lotion from the days when pani Grażyna performed a toilet that left her only a brush-stroke from beauty. Alas, she could do little to enhance her height in a city of tall women. Leaving the tub to the cat, Joseph washes in the basin, covering himself with the sweet-smelling trail of a bar of apple soap, and though this might not leave him next to godliness – even taking the basin for a font – at least he scrubs away the heaviness of blankets and a yearning that came disguised as sleep.

Sometimes, though, he shivers to imagine mildew creeping under his skin, especially as his towel has taken on the odour of the flat, all boiled vegetables and furniture polish, so that he takes on that smell, too, at least until he visits the department store, as he does every morning, to spray himself with an aftershave sampler though he has to suffer looks of disgust from the beauticians who are beginning to get fed up with this Russian-looking tramp. Also, he has discovered that the washbasin lacks a plug. So, for want of another container, he has been shaving from a sugar-pot presented by his host.

When he emerges from the damp green bathroom – a room he pictured the previous day as the inside of a wet matchbox – Joseph usually finds pani Grażyna in the kitchen, amid the cut glass from Krosno and the Viennese-style 'Solitude' plates, a wedding gift for her maternal grandmother, the last of the family to be gently born among the lower echelons of the aristocracy. As always when seated, pani Grażyna lays a serviette upon her lips as a prelude to speech. Then she says, 'Sorry, pan Adam. No breakfast.' Nor has Joseph seen his host's mother. But he has imagined her, as a surviving piece of crockery from an otherwise decimated set. Yes, however much knocked about, dropped, mocked or banished – first by her husband, then by the times – she surely has a habit of resurfacing, her bluish blood animating her white skin in much the same way that porcelain is animated by the pattern it presents. Of course, just like the finest pieces, she appears only for very special guests.

What a world in which to wait! As if Joseph has found the place, the very apartment, where he can live as a soul in abeyance, among empty candelabras and other people's whispers, hoping that Marta will come to her senses and then come to him, just as pani Grażyna, both seeking and fearing her release, has waited all these years for the man to match her ambitions, the man who will give her back her future.

Later, when the crows have relinquished their wings to the night sky, and the trees are triumphant in their isolation, Joseph lies on his blankets beneath the picture of Pope John Paul II, grateful for the dusty warmth of the stove, or he empties his pockets of the leaflets he has picked up that day – his attempt to get to know a city from what is given hand-to-hand. One day, he collected matchboxes, a series showing pictures of old trucks: *Zuk, Nysa, Tatra, Star.* Another time, he brought back cards from an exhibition of abandoned churches in places with names like Jazłowcu, and he thought he would never get to sleep after visiting this room of ruins, where he studied painted ceilings with patches of sky showing through, altars overgrown with shrubbery, broken domes and pillars and porticoes, and saints who have stood still for four hundred years while the buildings behind them collapsed. As Joseph tried to sketch them back to their original forms he wondered if there could be anything more beautiful than a derelict church.

Other times, he reads Marta's letters. He is reading them chronologically, from the notes of last summer, which they exchanged every day, to the letters that linked them during their separation. He is thrilled to find her in the shape of her handwriting. He scours the pages for scribbled-outs and underlines, or he picks words out of the dark, like bad stitches. Sometimes he resolves his solitude with a sketch, marvelling at the ink, as vital as blood, under the green-shaded lamp on the desk. Like his drawing of the previous night's outing when a café owner, celebrating his own birthday, had built a pyramid of glasses on the bar and then filled them from a bottle of pink champagne. As the liquid splashed down the sides, the owner emptied his lungs to a rendition of the national anthem, *'Jeszcze Polska nie zginęła . . .'* Joseph drew the shimmering pyramid as a stack of open mouths on glass stems, consonants gushing along with the champagne, from the ears and nose and mouth of the owner whose half-red, half-white tongue ran with the colours of his country's flag.

When not drawing, or working on his scrapbook of the city, Joseph drops thoughts into his solitude, and waits for the echo. Among these thoughts (it is a room for thinkers, after all), there is one inspired by a German-Jewish writer Marta had told him about. This Jewish-German writer (Joseph never knows which way round it should be, and whether or not it matters) wrote that to live independent of community is 'the most European of all accomplishments'. Joseph isn't sure what to make of that. Yesterday, in the deserted Jewish district, he'd sat in a café as if on the border of waking and sleep, only a sheet of glass separating him from a bitter wind and snowflakes, and he'd become fascinated by the tattered lace curtain hanging at the window.

Looking long and hard at this curtain, he'd ended up drawing a ghost.

Whenever he leaves pani Grażyna's apartment, this museum of misfortune, this repository of undelivered souls, yes, as soon as he returns to the murmur of the streets, Joseph feels near-elation, an excitement at the elbows, like the blue sparking of the tram-wires reflected in the snow.

I will walk and walk until it is all familiar.

He sees a sign saying 'Alkohole' and he likes the idea that here it is possible to drink yourself into a pit. He finds one ceiling after another in the form of springing arches so that he stands there in reverence as if his head is being held. His lapels catch words as well as eyeballs and snowflakes, or if not words then sounds that are nearly words and seem to register joy or recognition – '*n-oh*', '*oh*', '*aha*', '*co?*' – as if the tonsils are merely flippers for keeping high notes in the air. He comes across names that Marta had introduced him to last summer: Białoszewski, Grehuta, Stanko, Kieślowski. And then there's the words ending in 'ka' sounds, and he knows these are diminutives, and in this way these words become no bigger than grains of sugar sprinkling the listener with affection. As Joseph pushes his shoes through the water lying across the ice, he wonders if he has found something he has only ever dreamed of: a language that might convey the spirit.

In the square there is a Christmas market. Green wooden huts display their wares, their asphalt roofs sticky with over-sugared snow. Open-air grills send out gusts of aromatic steam to taunt the cold and hungry: sizzling potatoes, frying onions, thick country sausages. There's a barrel-shaped hut selling beakers of mulled wine in which you warm your nose, the scent as welcome as wool, the breaths of drinkers turning the icy mist pink. Church bells put heavenly ripples in the air. Buskers mark time with boot soles in the slush. Everyone has their own way of not disappearing in the dark.

Yes, thinks Joseph, this loneliness is lit with wonder.

Until, one evening, a hand slaps hard on his shoulder, nearly forcing him to spit out his astonishment. He turns to discover a man whose dark woollen hat is either too tall or too tight, for his features have been sent to the bottom of his face.

'Eric,' says the man, with an English accent, and one lacking any regional provenance. A fingertip of facial hair sleeps in the centre of his chin, like a dribble of beard or a vertical moustache. 'In Berlin, I'm Erich. And here, here I'm Eryk,' he says, the last word clicking his teeth into a false smile. 'I'm related to all the nations of Europe!' And with that he removes a glove and thrusts his palm for a handshake. The grip is weak and swiftly released, like a man who has never had to hold on. Or a man who has long since let go. 'You enjoying a bout of *ost*-algia, too?'

Joseph is not surprised to be hailed by this Englishman whose sheepskin coat offers a threat, if not of menace, then certainly of middle age. He has noticed already that people from not round here stand out like luminous fish, and can recognise each other immediately by their troubled pallor or flap. Especially the Westerners. Even so, he's a little annoyed to be disturbed from his street reverie, because the clear night sky was helping him work out the lines of one or two architectural relations.

Nevertheless, he introduces himself. It's been days since he had a conversation, in person, in his own language. The shift in energies might do him good. They decide to go for a beer.

It turns out that Eric teaches English, and translates from two languages. 'Tell you what, matey,' he says, as they enter Café Galka, a bar favoured in the past by underground writers, but now by musicians and cardsharps and adventurous expats, 'English IS a foreign language the way I fookin' teach it!' Fluent in German – 'A beautiful language. Unfairly hated. Frederick the Great was wrong to compare its sound unfavourably to the neighing of his horse!' – Eric gets help with his Polish from his latest girlfriend, a former student of his. 'I call it the sleeping technique,' he says, running a palm up his face, over his receding hair, then all the way down to the back of his head. 'The best way to learn a language? To wake up in the morning with a local girl! That's the sleeping technique! *Andere Städtchen, andere Mädchen!*' Suddenly, his head jerks, his grin disappears, his face passes into shadow. His voice now a breeze across an open bottle, he says, 'We all suffer the same, but sleep in different languages.'

For a moment, they sit in a silence as thick as a frozen tongue, the silence of two people who have suddenly remembered they have only just met.

Until Eric beckons over the bartender. A person with frizzy black hair like candyfloss dipped in vinyl, and with a penchant for purple lips.

'Joseph,' says Eric, 'meet Bibi.'

Bibi makes a gesture between a curtsey and a bow. '*Enchanté*,' he says, offering his fingers but not his hand, before spinning away on soft heels.

'The first of his kind in this city!' whispers Eric, his

green-eyed stare always suggesting, if not delivering, concentration. 'No, really, he's wonderful. I've never seen pantaloons worn with such panache!'

Joseph looks to the bar. Bibi is arranging plastic flowers in a silver champagne bucket. Not so much dressed as veiled, he certainly has the seductive aura of those who dissemble their gender.

Eric leans in closer. 'And over there in the corner. See that bloke with the grey hair? That's Dmitri. Some say he's a lawyer from Lwov. Others say a former Stasi man. A gangster. An architect from Vitebsk. Or one of the local leaders of Solidarność. I have a friend who swears he runs Kalinka, the Russian restaurant. Always empty when it's open. Always a queue outside when it's closed! Dmitri's fond of saying "Pah!" in the continental fashion, if you know what I mean!'

Joseph sees a smartly-dressed man hunched over a book and a shot of blue vodka. At that moment, he looks up and nods.

'It's good here!' says Eric, his hand slipping from his neck to slap against the table. Yes, his hands are always landing. 'It's so easy to be yourself!'

'Or someone else!' says Joseph, his words overtaking his thoughts.

'Yes,' says Eric, then a moment later, 'yes', and then once more, as if unsure whether to savour these words or ignore their implications, 'yes'. Each time he drops his chin on his chest only to raise it again immediately, as if acknowledging charges in a court of law.

With a shuffle, a jerk, and a series of other scarcely related gestures, he gathers himself together. Like a man whose limbs have often been his only company.

'Where you from?' he asks, looking out of a face he has only just repossessed. 'Up north, judging by your accent. And I don't mean Siberia. Judging by your coat!' He fingers the lapels resting on the back of Joseph's chair. 'A leftover from your Gulag years?'

Joseph nods.

'I love the idea of the north!' says Eric, his eyebrows now heading in that direction.

'Ever been?' asks Joseph.

Eric slaps the table again. 'Of course not!' he says, only just removing his cigarette before his jaw snaps shut. 'That's why I like the idea of it!'

Joseph takes a swig of beer, already wondering how best to portray this character. Surely a sculpture of mixed materials for all the bits of him that don't add up. With screws for each of his joints, screws which wiggle out a little each time he jerks his body. So that he is forever rushing round trying to tighten himself up.

Shrinking in the silence, Eric returns to the subject that is the usual refuge of the garrulous: themselves. 'Did I tell you about my business venture?' he says, his eyes darting sideways, as if expecting someone to step from the shadows. 'We buy communist-issue radiators from former Soviet states. For next to nothing! As junk!' He looks to Dmitri. He drops his voice. 'We give them a good clean-up, export them to the UK, where middle-class boho types pay lots of money for examples of "Classic East European design"!'

Both his hands now rest on the edge of the table, fingers tapping. 'But I'm actually a classically-trained musician,' he adds, in a serious tone, or his best approximation of one, as if slightly bewildered to remember who he is. His chest grows bigger inside his green sweater, but bigger in the sense of a body preparing for a cough. 'I played piano in the student cabarets of Berlin. I also play violin, and . . .' He puffs out his cheeks. They are etched with little red veins. Joseph is reminded of a balloon stretched to its limits. Or the skin of an ageing paprika. Eric is playing three fingers close to his mouth, as if sniffing a trembling hand. 'The trumpet!' he just about shouts, with an involuntary twist of the neck, and an imitation of brass that sounds more like a bad case of wind. 'Jazz!'

As if not quite believing it himself, he laughs. His chuckle sounds like water going down a plug-hole. And soon turns into a cough.

Reaching into a pocket of his sheepskin, he tugs out an exercise book that appears to have spent most of its time being slept on. 'Look!' he says, flicking through pages littered with semi-quavers and lyrics and barely started sketches. 'I write music.' Again, he fans the book's yellow sheets under Joseph's chin. A smell of nicotine and leaf-mould. 'My dream?' he says, leaning closer. 'A book to better my dreams! A book of brilliant images! Lyrics! Melodies! The lot! A book that decomposes page-by-page, until you reach the end and your heart is sobbing and full of song, and the book has vanished completely, leaving only a brightly-coloured dust on your fingers, like the scales a butterfly sheds during mating.' He studies his knuckles to see if these scales have already appeared. Or perhaps he's checking for bruises. Or a ring. 'I have to leave something behind!' he says, puffing out his chest again, as though preparing to take his last breath. 'My birth certificate is slowly expiring!'

Someone is shouting in the darkness of an adjoining room. Joseph and Eric turn their heads beneath a solemn chandelier. They look over their two half litres of warm beer and cloves – a local speciality – that stand on their table like spirit lamps, a welcome relief from the darkness of velvet drapes and immovable walnut furniture.

At that moment, a sober man enters, followed by a semi-sober man, a drunk man, and a fat man carrying his belly. They order four beers, three cigars, two vodkas, and sit nearby, the fat man descending slowly as if he may never rise again. They pour a tin of coins onto the glass-covered table.

One of Eric's fluttering-down hands descends on Joseph's shoulder, but gently this time, a first gesture of friendship. Parted from another vision, this one of silver coins and bottle tops, of squeaky leather shoes and rust-red cigar smoke, Joseph senses his own sketch-book burning a hole in his pocket. His fingers twitch.

'Jazz?' he says, raising his eyes to the ceiling of bulging plaster. Joseph recalls the night in the cathedral in Marta's city, when he thought the organ pipes must be sculpted from his own insides. And that melancholy trumpet! He hadn't known whether to tap along or pray. Then, after-wards, in the car, behind the heads of Marta and her husband, he'd felt like he was eaves-dropping, though he couldn't understand a single word.

'Jazz?' he says again, the word dropping into his mouth like a coin returned to the bottom of a vending-machine. His throat tightens. He swallows back what might have been a howl.

Eric loves his dreamy new friend. He swoops to the floor and slaps Joseph's ankle.

'Do you like my goatee?' he says, on the way back up, scratching his droplet of beard. 'I designed it myself!' Then he polishes the tip of his nose, another stopping-point for his restless hands, and shaping the bone, over the years, into an arrowhead. 'This is a nation of goatees! You should get one if you want to fit in.' His head jerks. He changes direction. 'Anyway, what was I fookin' saying? *Also*, aha, jazz. Here, matey, jazz is for the people! Everyone was grooving under communism. People only felt free when jiving to jazz. It's religious!'

He takes a drag on his cigarette. His wrinkles gather round his mouth. However, as with all determined unaccountables, it is difficult to guess his age. 'Yes,' he says, with a nod that's more of a head-butt, 'I'll take you one night for some jazz.' He looks to the bar where Bibi is now perched on a stool, smoking. 'I think it's time for a Kawior.'

'Kawior?'

'God, you can tell you've only just got here,' says Eric, pausing to banish a sneeze with another pinch to the nose. 'The great European traditions? I'll tell you: Humanism, the Catholic church – and they're so Catholic round here, matey, that you have to visit a prostitute three times before she'll sleep with you! – the Enlightenment, the French Revolution, Socialism, Solidarity, Melancholia, and the melancholic's best friend . . . vodka! Kawior is a lifesaver, known only by connoisseurs! It's vodka with a squirt of lemon juice, a splash of ginger syrup, and a tooth or two of ice. Tonight, I shall avail the world of my astonishing capacity for alcohol!'

Once again, he swoops with the arm of an elaborate bow to slap Joseph on the ankle.

'On second thoughts,' he says, his features reappearing slowly from beneath the table, like the face on a jester's stick. 'I have to teach at eight in the morning. *Mehr Licht!*

Mehr nicht! I must remember to fix my miner's lamp on my hat. Without it there'd be no *Morgen früh!*'

Thinking that it's good to have some community from time to time, Joseph invites Eric for a reading later in the week to be given by two writers – one Transylvanian, the other Polish – that he'd seen on a bright red poster in the square. (Yes, he had been lured by the green poster towers, about two and a half metres tall, and wearing hats like a court-jester's, and sometimes containing a kiosk, a single window packed with cigarette boxes – *Męskie, Zawisze, Storm.* The posters are not geared to gloss and sales, no, they're expressive in the way Joseph loves, suggesting a hand at work across a page, and a secret energy that does not stop at the borders. Like the one for the Chopin festival that shows an angel with a single wing extended, and this wing is a keyboard with a feather for each key.) After the reading, they'll go to a jazz club – 'a famous quintet', promises Eric. On the steps of the building, as they leave, they pass two shivering Rumanian boys busy tuning the instruments of the buskers drinking upstairs.

Back on the streets, Joseph feels heavy with the dark enchantment of the day. Not forgetting the hopes that he balances between head and heart. Yes, without mentor or muse, wise person or patron, he travels from one hope to the next. A stranger to a city lives, initially, as if on an elastic leash – a variation of the rope around the waists of the men on the roof – and this elastic leash does not inhibit him so long as he remains in the centre, or close, where the snow is as white as a nun's coif, and there are cellars where he can fold himself in like a pigeon by an air vent, but as soon as he strays beyond the strip of frozen gardens that runs round the city, and beyond that, the ring-road, the elastic stretches like a caveat, a hand on the shoulder, a shake of a resident's head, and suddenly his back slumps with strain as if he is pulling a cart, his footsteps become measured as if it is fear he is now pacing out, not faith, as he enters provinces where shabby blocks of flats accuse each other for the lack of light, and where shaven-headed youths, as keen as terriers, gnaw at the footprints in his wake.

Yes, in the realm of chimneys and gated factories, scrap-yards and shacks, where cars whine of their fan-belt trouble and trees curse their roots, between buildings that have not quite been built and buildings that are about to fall down, the lease tightens further, approaches snapping-point, will give no more. Yet it is towards these areas that Joseph's creative sense draws him.

I am not from round here.

Working street by street, he is already familiar with the nearest pretzel-seller who stands behind the ice-struck land-yacht of her cart and wraps herself in its polythene sail, the skin on the back of her hand bearing the same leaflike veins as a page from one of the notebooks on the Christmas market, or perhaps these veins represent the rivers of her country, for her palm matches her country's shape, then there's the paper-vendor whose fingers have spent too long in ashtrays, the pale-faced girl with the black bob and big eyes in the twenty-four-hour shop who always glances at Joseph strangely, almost smiling, and once even brushed her shoulder against his, then there's the dark ink crucifixes that float in the air from the death notices, the white pages of which flutter on the wooden board outside the Church of Our Lady of Snow, sheets with names like Asnyk, Lenartowicz, Kasprowicz, and the blind beggar on his knees in the doorway of St Mary's, his eye-sockets full of milk.

Joseph's favourite? The accordionist who sits on his up-turned case beneath a green umbrella. Whenever the man extends his accordion – a Weltmeister with the 'W' missing – his smile widens, too, and he carries on playing in his fingerless gloves, hoping that by the end of the day his hands won't also be fingerless, and during quieter moments when the instrument barely needs to breathe, the man leaves his chin and brow snoozing atop his squeeze-box, as if he has left it up to his nose to sniff out any pending change in key.

Perhaps Joseph is trying to get to know every street, church, cellar, tree, as if, by doing so, he believes he could lure Marta back, even though it is not her city. He could say to her, 'Look, Marta, look how I have learned this city. I lit a candle for a compass and I showed myself around. From the painted freezes of the art-nouveau tenements to the worn wooden staircases of the Jewish district, from banisters smoothed by generations of palms to a begging-bowl held by only two, from the antique bookshop where I found a postcard of this city dated 1919 to a closed-down factory on the edge of town where I will sit and wait for you.'

Also, he has noted that the ring-road is not a magic circle like most roads that miraculously gather a city's girth in its belt. It is a holy circle, and not quite a circle at that. Viewed on a fold-out street map (available from any kiosk for the same price as a packet of crisps), the shape of the centre concurs almost exactly with the outline of the tilted head of the Virgin Mary, while the city gardens that border the ring-road match, to scale, of course, the shape and breadth of the golden braid of her headdress as shown on conventional portraits found on flea markets from Minsk to

Portobello. (For those of you who associate such markets with something your cat brings in, perhaps you should refer to the portraits of Our Lady of Sorrows by Leonardo, Raphael, Botticelli, and Dürer.)

Back in the seasonal market, where only orphaned shadows remain, Joseph has eaten a spicy sausage, and given a few cold coins to a busker. As he passes the illuminated Nativity scene down the side of the Gothic church, where the ice has been swept up to form pews, he may be thinking that, for now, he has had enough of families. However holy, however human.

Light flakes of snow begin to fall as if a flock of geese is being plucked in a neighbouring town. Even though it has been dark all day, he decides to call it a night.

Letters
22 August

Fortunately, my reunion with my husband has so far been Malena-centred. After five minutes of hiding behind a fat little palm, she repossessed her daddy. Completely. She even demanded that he come and hold her in bed. She fell asleep immediately. It is nice to find him as witty and sharp as I remember him. He will not play the victim. We laugh quite a lot. Yet at the moment I can't re-create our former intimacy. Our reunion hug was spontaneous, but only friendly. We didn't even need to kiss so far. Also, I struggle with a little taste of resentment. That it is him. Not you.

Yesterday, the last day alone for you and me. As we hid in the woods, by the lake, didn't we measure those disappearing hours in terms of sunlight and shade? I am sorry for all the tears. A film of the afternoon would be dependent on the music as to whether the scene was sorrowful or merely sentimental.

When you dropped me home, I fell asleep. Exhausted by those tears and all the day's torments. Both delicious and desperate. I try to season these feelings with a little irony. A little irony can help you survive. But only a little. Any more than that and you will never get to where you want to go.

I have had to hide all your letters and drawings.

23 August

I know my husband is a wonderful person. That's why I feel strange when I ask myself what I feel for him. That's why I felt as if the whole world was changing shape when I found myself attracted to you. Really. I have always been a good partner: caring, well-organised, putting forward our time together.

But deep down, all the way down where a person struggles to preserve an essence of themselves, I knew that my life was elsewhere.

The other night, I watched you walk up the street in a determined way, but lightly composed. Into the night where you belong. Where I'd like to belong with you. The two of us exploring each other and the world in which we find ourselves. How intensely I thought then, how desperately, that I want you to be happy. This is how I can now make use of my love for you. By sending you these stubborn implorings to be happy.

My husband is driving us home in two days. The waiting is

terrible. I fold clothes, then I do not want to put them in the case. Then I decide I just want to have it over and done with so I throw them in and shut the lid. Later, I take them out, brush away the creases, and start folding them all over again. The anticipation is always the worst. The time between the knowledge of the departure and the departure itself. I am living on the little bit of air left between the two. We will stay in London with friends for one night.

Funny, because the last notes I have taken here for my book are about Lya de Putti's first and only trip to London, in January 1929. To star in 'The Informer', a film adaptation of Liam O'Flaherty's novel. Lya stayed at the Ritz, went horse-riding in Hyde Park (she loved horses), and relished her role as Katie Fox. She is wonderful in this film, full of seductive energy and life! However, due to the onset of sound, it was decided that a talking-track should be added. As they did not like Lya's mixed Hungarian-German accent and her sing-song English (like mine, so exotic!), her part was dubbed by an Irish actress. The same was happening all over Hollywood. Actors and actresses from Eastern Europe could not find work despite the fact that until then they had been extremely popular with directors because of their wonderful expressiveness, and their 'romantic eyes' (so it says here).

'These eyes,' said Lya in an interview once, her pupils like ink-drops to infinity, 'these eyes, they do not lie.'

But now, catastrophe. There were suicides and wild nights as former stars tried to escape their plight. Still Lya's lover of the time would not marry her.

'The Informer' proved to be her last film.

Joseph, it is difficult at the moment to think in terms of the future. I am, somehow, always in connection with you. But I can't do it systematically. I know that you won't just disappear. But how will I cope without your huge, wise, always slightly sad eyes? Without your smile full of mischief and affection? Without, especially, our powerful embrace?

9

An Encounter at pani Stasia's

Chicken thigh? Pork knuckle? Cutlet *de volaille*? No, he went instead for the beef, thick slices of which now soak in a watery stock. Yellow chunks of potato glisten with butter and grease. Sour cabbage, sprinkled with tiny beads of cumin, sits packed in its own vapours. And Joseph is leaning over his plate as if it's a bowl of Friar's Balsam – like all convalescents, trying to get over a bout of too much of himself. As he gives the meat a good chew, he observes the kitchen between red curtains embroidered with violets. Huge shelves laden with pots sag in the middle like hammocks. In her apron and soft cap, the proprietress, pani Stasia – nearly eighty, according to local legend – is supervising other cooks with a long-armed spoon and a firm word.

Just as Joseph is negotiating another forkful, he is joined at his table by a man of about sixty, because that's the way at pani Stasia's, everyone sits together. After hanging up his coat (embroidered with snowflakes), the man takes a moment to run his large eyes over Joseph's face. He introduces himself as pan Oczek. Joseph introduces himself, too.

With a smile through which he could push most of his

remaining teeth, pan Oczek says, 'And you, Mr Eee-dam? Why are you here? Here, of all places? To pollute or to contribute?'

Joseph looks behind him as if trying to remember where he is and why, because this man is talking to him as if they are already half-way through a conversation. Also, it is not the first time he has been reduced to a cheese.

With a creak of wood or bone or both, pan Oczek sits. His features are not unlike those of the city's medieval gargoyles.

Having disentangled a gristly lump from his fork, Joseph realises he hasn't answered the question. He smiles and points to his plate.

'Aha,' says pan Oczek, his big eyes gleaming as if also soaking in grease. 'Of course, you are well aware that pani Stasia cooks the best meals in town. If you eat here now, in the winter, you won't get frostbite. And if you take enough salt, you won't slip in the streets! If you eat here in the summer, you won't get sunstroke. And if you come here with a hangover, it will be gone by the time you lick the last of the broth from your nose. A well-known fact.'

He scratches his chin as if to tickle out more words. Or to prevent his features from returning to stone.

'But no,' he continues, 'I don't mean here, at pani Stasia's. Forgive me. I am not making myself clear. I intended to ask, Mr Eee-dam, why are you here in this city? Aha, this city!' Inhaling deeply, pan Oczek's huge nostrils threaten to suck up the salt and pepper pots. 'Let me tell you, visiting this city is like visiting an old lady only to find her surrounded by mischievous children! Anyway, where was I? Aha, why are you here? You know why I ask? I ask,

Mr Eee-dam, because I can tell you are not from round here. I am good at such observations. For example, if you don't mind, I would say that you look like a chameleon who has forgotten how to change colour. I would say, also, that you are here for a woman. And I suggest it is not the Virgin Mary. Is that well said?'

Joseph's smile evens out, forming a ledge upon which his cheeks descend. He wonders if his heart is really so apparent. Perhaps it is slopping about on his plate.

'You are melancholy,' says pan Oczek, having now placed an order with a single gesture to the waitress. 'Melancholy because you came here with love in your heart only to find that the woman you came here for will not leave her family. Her country. Her home. You thought you were on the way to heaven but you find yourself *in purgatorio!*'

His eyes bulge as Joseph rescues another lump from the puddle on his plate. He continues. 'And however much you say you like it in this country, you are not sure. It is not home. You wake up in the middle of the night and feel something like fear. Or is it loneliness? You turn on a light and sit up in bed but there is no one else in the room. Only you and your dreams. Your longings. And strange furniture which does not make you feel comfortable. All that brown wood! The smells are not quite right either. And everywhere you put your fingers: dust! Medieval dust, then Tartar dust, not to mention the dust of the Ottoman Empire, and the dust disturbed by the double-headed eagle of the Habsburgs, followed by the dust left in the wake of our own disappearance, then Republican dust, Nazi dust, Communist dust, and finally – so some would have us believe – the dust of democracy!'

He flicks the air with the back of his hand as if some of that dust has gathered about his ears.

'Back to you in the night,' he says, his big eyes clearly believing they have seen Joseph there. 'The clouds scratch the roof as they pass. Even the sky looks wrong from the window. It would be different if she were beside you. But she is not. The bed carries no traces of where she slept. None of her warmth. None of her tenderness. You try not to think of her, but when you finally get back to sleep her eyes travel with you through your dreams. Her smooth skin. Her nose that you used to warm with your lips as she was drifting off to sleep.'

Pan Oczek's eyelids have become the heads of teaspoons. Whether his reverie is caused by personal reflection, the retelling of his own experience, or by savouring the meat and gravy fumes in anticipation of his meal, Joseph cannot tell. Though he thinks of another possibility: a language reverie. Perhaps the man's loquacity is that of someone who did not so much learn another language as move in, finding there as many alcoves and recesses as a Baroque cathedral and relishing the drama he can act out in each one.

'She has gone,' says pan Oczek. 'You are still here. The question is: why?'

The small windows of the courtyard restaurant have steamed up. The door bangs each time someone enters or leaves. A rush of freezing air strips all ankles of socks. At each table, heads meet over steaming bowls beneath another ceiling of springing arches.

Joseph looks more closely at his questioner. Pan Oczek has ears like cabbage leaves. They look as though they want to wrap themselves round his head. Starved of other people's words because of their owner's love of talking, perhaps they grew bigger to improve their chances. Joseph decides that he would have to render such a head in papier mâché. But there is to be no stopping pan Oczek.

'Are you still here because you think she will come running?' he says, his hand hovering over the one-sheet serviettes spouting from a glass on the table. 'In the dark. Across the snow. Just for you.'

After each phrase, he tugs out a serviette, flicks it up in the air, and watches it descend.

O Matko! thinks Joseph.

'First, her breath at the window. Next, her knuckles on the frosted glass. Then, the whites of her eyes. Listen, is that her plea from the street?'

As he watches the paper sheets settle to the sound of spoons scraping bowls, Joseph can't help but think of his very first week in this country. It's true, he had lain in bed each night, after his whisky nightcap, hoping that Marta would come running, and if not that very moment, then surely at first light.

'For this hope to survive,' declares pan Oczek, waving to an elderly woman in a mohair beret, 'you must still have faith in her. A great love for her. Allow me to say, an almost tragic love. And a desire that fills all your organs and limbs. Has it not yet seeped out of you, this desire? After all, the heart is a pump. It pumps outwards. Do you still believe you can stop this love pumping out of you?'

Joseph is sucking the meat in his mouth. Pan Oczek, meanwhile, is bubbling like one of pani Stasia's pots. 'Or here, here in this cold dark winter of this cold dark country, have you finally found the landscape to match the landscape of your heart? The landscape for your brooding spirit to

brood in? To lose yourself in the snow among the silhouettes of trees and all the other dark and stationary beings?
Here in our Galician valley of despair, beneath the cathedral
hill with its royal tombs, even your shadow will shiver when
you think of your loss. You have so many gardens where
you come from. Gardens well tended and seldom invaded!
But you have chosen here. Because of her!'

Pan Oczek's eyeballs rest either side of the last potato on
Joseph's plate. His nostrils are quivering. He almost sucks
his small chin into his mouth. He waves to elderly male
twins who have just entered, while whispering to Joseph,
'Actors! They were once seen as aristocracy. Note their
noble bearing! The way they carry their hands!'

Then pan Oczek returns to his point. 'Forgive me, please,
for my hypotheses. They are, after all, only hypotheses.
Only, don't think that we are more spiritual here just because
of all we have suffered. Don't make that mistake. Or you
will suffer too. We are just as spiritual or as superficial as
everyone else, be it east or west or in any other direction.'

He looks back to the kitchen, his eyes now running the
rims of all the pots.

'Though if it is God you are after,' he says, gathering up
the serviettes he has tossed, as if they were giant communion
wafers, 'we have an abundance of establishments in which
you can pray for your own salvation. If it comes to that. If
it hasn't already come to that.'

He waves a hand. 'Forgive me. Another hypothesis. The
Church, of course, being the oldest institution on earth!'

Joseph does not speak. He listens, as an agnostic might
listen, a little intrigued but largely despairing, to a priest.

'The final possibility?' says pan Oczek, knowing that his
food will shortly be in front of him. 'That since she led you

to this frozen landscape of ghosts and shadows, you have become trapped. Like a carp beneath the ice. Trapped by the traces of her you see everywhere. By which I mean: eyes, collar-bones, noses. Those cheekbones, you say, so Slavic! And just like hers! Delivering joy, then curving sorrowfully to the saddest expression you are likely to find anywhere on God's earth. How many emotions can a face be called upon to carry? Did I mention God again? Yes, I did. Forgive me. For here is God again in the grace of this country's women. See how they walk, you say! They almost float with their long legs, their upright posture, their elegant gait! And their eyes! I bet you have never seen eyes like these! But where will they lead you? Where did *she* lead you? To betrayal? Beneath the ice. Where your face is frozen in the expression you wore when you found out she would no longer come to you. And would never again come to you. Because that is the case, is it not?'

Joseph's eyes are watering. He tells himself he has never liked sour cabbage.

'Oh beauty!' says pan Oczek, plucking a final serviette from the jar. 'That's what beauty did for you! Your heart was full of love, and bursting with joy. Now it has burst. The joy has long since gone. However, do not weep while you still have laces in your shoes! For love has a way of holding on. That is because love lines the heart as well as filling it. So you stay in this city, keeping her in this heart of yours, trying not to let your love for her leak away. Trying, most of all, not to lose the lining.'

He wipes his wet lips with the serviette. 'Is that well said?'

Joseph's face carries the expression of someone who has just been slapped. His head is nodding despite himself. He recalls sitting in a café only two days ago. A café of green velvet and mahogany, with stained-glass windows. Waitresses floated in and out, only the hinge of the swing-doors betraying their presence. Old gentlemen sat in pairs, their whispers laying dust on the glass-framed grotesques sketched by the *Młoda Polska* artists who drank here between the wars. There were old clocks and cameras, faded murals and wine-red carpets, and chairs with spines like the handles of umbrellas. The tables were laid with lace doilies preserved beneath a sheet of glass. Everything loomed or faded in there, thought Joseph. He absorbed the light of skin beneath a waitress's cotton blouse. And her dark brown hair that every autumn should envy. Not to mention the pout of her lips! Surely formed over time through the sssh and cz and ps-sssh of her language. Just like Marta's lips. Yes, how could he not think of her? Cloaked memories steal from beneath the furniture in places such as these.

It's true, he admits to himself, back at pani Stasia's, while looking down at his plate as if into his cups, he does see Marta's face and form everywhere. As if, eye by eye, limb by limb, he is trying to put back together the body he has lost. Though a soul, he knows, is much more difficult to recoup.

Still pan Oczek hasn't finished, perhaps in fear that if he stops he will be overwhelmed by his hunger. 'Or possibly you did come here for the Virgin Mary,' he says, 'having heard the rumours that she bestowed an especial blessing upon our great country?'

Joseph recalls the city plan in the shape of the Virgin's head.

'No?' says pan Oczek, 'of course not. I can see your love is earthly, and because of that you don't have a prayer. In love, each kind word is a plaster that grows into the skin, so that when the time comes to remove it . . .' Here, a memory of hurt sends his features into an expression they can only fleetingly assume. 'And now there's nothing to stop all that love flowing out of you. Day by day. Night by night. And, if you'll allow me to say, probably in all the wrong directions. Unless, of course, yours is a creative misery. Aha!' he says, noticing a flicker in Joseph's eye. 'In which case, the art that reckons your groans may very well also deepen them. Forgive me. The beef, I see, was an excellent choice.'

On a plate carried by pani Stasia herself, pan Oczek's order emerges from the steam. He raises his mug of raspberry compote, first to the owner, then to Joseph. 'I drink to your health, Mr Eee-dam. To the end of suffering! To the end of all suffering! And, most of all, to the saving grace of pani Stasia's cooking!'

Letters
Saturday 29 August – on way back
I was trying to write to you today: on a bench, in a phone box, on the tube. Of course, it wasn't possible with Malena. She grabbed my notepad and was running all round Covent Garden waving it in the air. No secret thoughts when she's around. In London, as you know, everyone divulges.

The walk was wonderful. Though I had to carry Malena most of the way. My husband packed her buggy in the bottom of the boot. He did not join us for the walk. He is not in good shape.

I could roam this city for days. For weeks. And never be bored. But I would like to do it with you. All the strange trees and buildings and paths we would find! I again had the feeling that I will find life very difficult without you.

I cope. But I worry about my husband. He does not look well.

Joseph, Joseph, Joseph – never enough of that! I could keep writing your name. Always your name. Somehow I feel the warmth of you in these loops. Especially your smile.

I wanted to call you. But Malena would not give me a moment's peace.

Postcard from London

Passing through. Like emigrants whose time is tender, we carry these hours carefully. A sunny late-summer day when everything begins to soften. Crowds of people, but no danger you will disappear in them.

London seen through your eyes would be special. Without you, I feel the estrangement of a tourist being treated to the niceties of a place.

30 August

Do you like the green ink? Almost like the hills of Germany that we passed on the way back. I woke up in the car, my body aching, in the middle of beautiful landscapes. The country flattened only once when we were close to Hannover. We cut across from Eindhoven towards Berlin, then Dresden & Cottbus. The motorway took us between hills covered in forests, with villages distant on mountainsides.

At first, we talked. If we'd had a wicker grille between us and a change of clothes, I could have been back in confession. I told my husband all about you. I mean, about us. After each exchange, I could hear him thinking, even above the occasional tick of the indicator. He was humble. He said he could see why I liked you so much. We drove on in silence.

Close to Antwerp, in a rain that the windscreen-wipers could not cope with, my husband drove over a piece of metal. We got a puncture. We had to take everything out of the boot to reach the spare wheel. In the lay-by, in the rain, we must have looked like we were setting up a market stall. My husband was a little bit worried. It's a newish car and it was his first puncture.

Probably because he was anxious about the wheel, and my words, we missed the ring-road. We found ourselves on the way to the city centre. With its trams and cobbled streets, it looked like home. Desperate to get out of the city, my husband stopped to talk to a taxi driver. There was no point looking for signs. A mist had thickened to a dense fog. We passed Antwerp railway station: a huge, grim building rising out of the rain. Finally, we made it to the ring-road.

Malena slept most of the way. My legs were crossed over a bag, her head was on my right arm, her bottom on my left thigh. This packing and pressing of muscles and skin. I could feel in every part of my body how a person is put together. 'Od stóp do głów'. From head to toe.

My husband drove on in silence. I tried to sleep but my head registered every bump in the road.

At about 10 pm, we stopped near Berlin, somewhere flat and misty, for petrol, toilet and a pot of tea. They wouldn't accept my husband's new credit card, so we had to count out coins for the tea.

The area close to the German border is a wide belt of forest. We seemed to drive forever through the woods. A dark mist of fir trees and rain. Along the lit sections of the road, people ply their trades. A whole community of garden gnomes, characters from Grimm's tales, small white plaster Venus de Milos, one of which even had a flourish of pubic hair! The heads of wild boars stare from the verge – these are for country folk who like to drink their vodka in front of the fireplace, under eyes reflecting an imminent death. There are boxes of forest mushrooms with stems as thick as a farmer's thumb. They are now in season. Bulgarian prostitutes beckon from the side of the road. They are always in season. Black hair pinned on top of the head, dark eyes, good legs. Black leather jackets fitted at the waist to pump out the chest. Mini-skirts so short that you have a little of the buttocks exposed. Make-up thick enough to protect their skin from wet tongues and bad weather. Shiny tights to catch headlights and the moon if there is one. White high heels or sports shoes. A cross between school-girls and vamps. Every man's dream – right?

I read somewhere that these girls are sure to lose business after the changes next May. At the moment there are long queues of traffic because of all the searches by the border guards. So these women waggle along the line of vehicles, disappearing inside the cab of a truck, and then another. But what will happen when people can drive straight through? Will the girls sink in the mud with the gnomes?

Shortly after crossing the border into our country, my husband asked me if I had fallen in love with you. He did not turn to me as he asked. I sensed his grip tighten on the wheel. I did not turn to him as I answered. It is true, I told him, I have fallen in love with Joseph.

We did not speak again for the rest of the journey.

Later

The sun greeted us when we finally arrived home, along with fierce blasts of cold wind. We'd been on the road for twenty-two hours, with only three stops. My throat was sore. I could not speak. A smell of dashboard plastic and Malena's breath. I put a load in the washing-machine. It got stuck on pre-wash for several hours without anyone noticing.

Strange to hear the sound of church bells again. Every hour. Then a proper ring for first service at 5 a.m! There is no escape from bells here. To remind us of our sins. Where would the Catholic Church be without sin? No sin, no confession, no church. I'm glad I have not let them down.

Joseph, I am at a loss. I feel a wave of heat – love, longing, sadness – whenever I look at your photo.

What is faith in a person if we do not put that faith into action?

I feel fine here, though my husband is quiet with frowns. Yet what happened between you and me has turned out not to be a dream. Perhaps I should have had more consideration for you. I came back to my own place, where books inhabit bookshelves not boxes, and the furniture, though simple, is ours. Malena runs to and fro laughing. And my husband, despite his hurt, goes to great lengths to make it a home for us. But Joseph, where are you? Back in your car and roaming?

If not for Malena, I would have left my husband already. I would not have come back. I would still be with you. I keep wondering if I should have acted differently. But I didn't think it right just to slip away from a former life as if it had never happened.

10

Shadows

The time has come for the separation of their solitudes.

'Pan Adam, sorry, problem. Studentka from Warszawa come,' explains pani Grażyna, her words falling like petals from a flower too close to a flame. 'Warszawa,' she says, again, a one-word mantra to rouse all provincial souls and melt the snow on the roads into town.

Joseph knows he doesn't have a choice. He isn't from Warsaw. How can he compete with a capital? He's just a provincial soul, too. Can't you tell by his hair (more poetic than fashionable), the cut of his jib (more cut-price than dandy), the way he skirts around centres? Oh yes, he's more Pecs than Budapest, more Bela Palanka than Zagreb. It's not so much about East and West any more, he's realised. It's about capitals and provinces. Big cities and small towns. And the traffic between the two.

'Sorry,' says pani Grażyna, again, placing her small hands together, giving them the appearance of triangular sandwiches cut from white bread. As she bows her head in a gesture not unlike a Chinese greeting, her hair, more upright than usual, brushes against Joseph's chest. Joseph finds himself copying the prayer gesture, while thinking that it's funny how another culture will suffice when there's little you know of each other's. Pani Grażyna leads Joseph to the kitchen where the old wooden table looks made of dirty milk. The cat is in the sink. The only daylight to find its way inside licks at the 'Solitude' plates. With a hopeful look, pani Grażyna hands Joseph a card for an accommodation agency specialising in short-term lets.

When Joseph has packed his clothes, his sketchpads, Marta's letters, and his scrapbook, he finds pani Grażyna, as usual, on the other side of the door. This time there is no yellow wing, only a tiny white hand proffered as though to be kissed. Her hand fits inside Joseph's palm; her fingers are as cold as the silver on a Sunday morning. She attempts a smile, but the lines of disappointment re-draw the corners of her mouth. Meanwhile, her proud features seek anonymity in the shadow of her hair.

Though he is used to both sudden departures and difficult farewells, Joseph's face is also shaped from sadness. Here, in a flat reeking of church pews and long afternoons, he had found a half-way house, a warm room with a stove, a thick carpet, an en-suite aviary, where, each night, he had smuggled himself in from the streets of snow, after an evening spent with a beer and his inks, to settle beneath the horse blankets, almost completely detached from the faculty of suffering.

Pani Grażyna retrieves her hand. Joseph gives her the keys. 'Good, good, pan Adam,' she says, rubbing the metal between her fingers, grateful for the solidity of things. They part with the affection of two people unhindered by a common language.

Having arranged to look at a flat the next day, Joseph lugs his holdall along the streets in search of a cheap bed, and eventually, on the other side of the ring-road, he finds a *Noclegi* – 'Night-lodgings' in a building that smells of bookbinder's glue – or is it surgical spirit? – but in any case feels like a cross between a library and a hospital, and he is taken along a corridor by an elderly man who has something of a porter and a penguin about him (must be his walk and his waistcoat), and on the way they pass a woman arguing with someone in the dark, while waving her passport about as if in proof of her arrival. When Joseph is shown the green-tiled communal showers, he sees two cleaning women in red overalls smoking over their buckets. And his room? Another padded door. Glaringly white walls, so that occasional blood-streaks or other human deposits stand out, like the tails of shooting stars that have long since shot their bolt. A barred window. Two empty cans of beer crushed upon the sill. That night as he lay awake listening to shouts in the corridor while pining for the silence of pani Grażyna's carpets, Joseph wondered what sort of asylum he had found.

The next afternoon, he is outside a four-floor block on a street leading from the main square. High on the wall, by the entrance, a triangular lamp box of glass and tin carries the number '56'. A cold wind carries small cats and beer cans across the cobbles. The wind always blows in a poor person's face – a saying Marta once told him. He notes, with dismay, that there aren't any trees on this street. He turns his back to the icy breeze, for it is cruel enough to put doubt between his teeth: maybe he should have gone straight to the station? The previous night had been bad enough.

Now his gaze follows the flight of a long pink nail that is pointing to a window on the top floor. The woman beside him is very tall. She is dressed in black. Her mascara is so thick that she looks like she is peering out of a costume.

Studying the facade of peeling plaster, Joseph sees that the floor itself is tucked beneath the attic like an afterthought, and held up by drainpipes and green netting.

Inside the building, they climb the stone stairwell, its metal banisters laced by a creeper that eased its grip long ago. The glass roof sprinkles the steps with a dirty light. The woman's high heels echo like a hundred hammers. At the oval window to the courtyard, Joseph stops to look. Blue plastic bins stand tall in the snow. A scrawny black cat emerges, then another. Alert to his presence, they come together between the bins, several of them, the slightly bigger heads on either side, the smaller ones at the centre. With spines of wire to which clings an inconsistent fur, they have eyes like wild gooseberries, and crouch as if to attack.

In the flat, there is a smell of dried flowers and sleep, though Joseph wonders if he has carried this on his clothes from pani Grażyna's. Mosquitoes on the wall point their squashed limbs to the previous summer. There is an old parquet floor, each slat rising and falling in place, like walking over the notes of a xylophone, and one that could do with being tuned. Then the usual brown furniture, plus a cigarette stub in the toilet that has stained the bowl, tufts of purple dust, and yellow net curtains at the only window. A puppet theatre of pigeon silhouettes plays along the ledge.

Leaning on the cold storage heater, the damp wooden window-frame beneath his nose, Joseph looks across the roof-tops where snow as blue as sugar-paper covers a city in perpetual slumber. His gaze travels from spire to spire (on which you could snag almost any dream), between aerials (like the necks and beaks of storks), down to the tin tops of workers' huts, their tiny chimneys puffing out smoke like old men's pipes.

Next, he looks down at the busy street, on heads and hats and the bodies beneath them, on the dark pathways through the snow, on the long shadows that lead the way as the bodies follow metres behind, and he wonders for a moment if that's all we ever do: endlessly repeat our migrations, while trying not to bump into each other in the dark, none of us any clearer as to where we should be heading, and who we should be heading there with, as we plod along, at first nursing a vague idea of the soul, and how we should keep it close, but somehow losing track of it, because other, more pressing matters take over, more pressing because close at hand, and so we can't resist, we clutch all we can and press on in the dark, steadily losing touch with a sense of our selves, while hoping we will get to wherever it is we are supposed to be going before the light goes out completely.

Looking to the ground floor of the buildings opposite, Joseph sees a shoe shop, a *Gabinet Rehabilitacja*, a travel agent's, a Georgian restaurant, and what must be a convent because he can see women moving around in dark blue robes and white headdresses.

The rent is reasonable. Never before has he had his own place. He agrees to take the flat.

Rehabilitation? he whispers to himself.

Letters
2 September
Almost three days without you, the days which make me realise how bad it may be in the long run.

Since yesterday, I've had a strange feeling, a sensation

intruding from a dream I had over two years ago. This dream was about a fear of a terrible mistake. And a painful conviction that the mistake had already been made. Now, my waking world cannot evict this dream. I have a feeling that you're the truth I have found.

I often wake with a tongue too heavy to speak. As if I have returned to a reality with which I can no longer communicate. I can live. I can go on. I may even be happy in some ways, but always limited without you. How can I cope with this most basic truth? I am afraid it will be haunting me. Mocking me. It is possible to build a whole network of defences, even out of love, but dreams will always overwhelm them.

Later

Joseph, I know one thing: you are a real person, not a fantasy, so I will always yearn for you. In the end, isn't that how people bind themselves to one another, through yearning? The bond between us seems so strong. Even holding hands is a pulse of our unified strength. How can I be faithful to myself and live without you? Somehow, I have rarely been faithful to myself. The only moments when I have been were the saddest times, horrendous or nostalgic. Faith demands so much strength. Unbroken faith in your self, perhaps superhuman strength.

Now I am back, there are people everywhere. No space for mourning. Or even for silent liturgy. I have to keep a straight face and pretend. My husband is careful to please me. His hands are full of tentative touches. He is worried that his fingertips might not land on the woman he loves. He makes cups of tea. With honey for my throat. We take it in turns to prepare simple meals of chicken cutlets, broccoli, potatoes. On the way to work he often goes to the market to buy everything fresh. When Malena cries, and if I'm at my desk, he gets up and goes to the kitchen without speaking to prepare her some warm milk. He buys me little gifts. A bouquet of violets. A new CD. A toy or two for Malena.

When he is tired or, more rarely, relaxing, and I am reading, I see him looking at me, sadly.

3 September

It's getting a little colder every day. There's a damp mist made of vacated cobwebs. Yes, this is the season when the spiders come in.

In your last call, you told me you are back to driving round your country, thinking of ways to raise money to come here. Joseph, will you come? I can laugh at my current despair if I think you might soon be here. (At the same time, I suffer little pangs of guilt. Wouldn't it be wiser of you to save for a place of your own?)

Inside our block, the central heating is run by the city power plant, but they are digging up the pipes in the middle of our backyard, so all the flats are without hot water. Whenever I turn a tap, there's just a horrible choking noise.

By the way, I dream of floods, of rivers splashing over me, or of diving into water from high in the sky. Do I dream of extremes? Of course! I am melodramatic. I am East European! I adhere to the stereotype! At the same time, as you know, I cringe when people say that a certain behaviour is typical, as if it speaks for all of us, as if because we had to live for so long as a collective, it means we have only a single identity. (Though, of course, we do still love to queue. By which I mean, push in.)

Take a look at my family. For example, my uncle. Very individual. Once he was quite a well-known wrestler. Then he started to grow carrots in an allotment probably very similar in size to the wrestling-ring. But my uncle wasn't very good at growing carrots because he'd stand round talking to the neighbours all day instead of digging up a few carrots to give the others more room to grow. So he always ended up with very small carrots, not even as big as his fingers, which are like thick frankfurters with their ends bitten off. All the time he would make jokes about a whole nation of people, our nation, living in one giant block of flats, and how surprising it was that these people managed to outgrow the carrots – what with their similar lack of space, and the darkness from all the power cuts, it was like living underground!

And those power cuts! As if the regime was showing Solidarność that it didn't matter whether Wałęsa was an electrician or not, because he couldn't enlighten the people.

Joseph, our days in the summer – only ultimate feelings. Even tiredness was total. Now, even sadness seems to resonate with other voices. Sometimes I can be so calm, so quiet and undisturbed, and then, all of a sudden, like today, tears.

Edith Stein wrote, 'If only we didn't limit our vision to the little bit of life in front of us, and then, only to what's immediately visible on the surface.'

But to go deeper requires so much energy. So much faith. Some days it is just not possible. Though I feel I am there all the time with you.

Yesterday in the evening, we went to see my husband's friend and his family. The guy is my age, with a special talent for teasing. He even managed to annoy my husband. But he'll never outwit me.

His wife is an architect. By contrast, her main characteristic is a lack of humour. And a taste for bright lipstick. The husband runs a very successful business – an advertising company – and the wife with the shiny pink lips is trying to get some experience as a designer. I don't know whether she's bad at that. I only know she's been trying to get her diploma for three years.

In their flat they have all mod cons. Which they never fail to use, point out, or sit on. You know what? I'm already tired of all these toys for grown-ups. Not that this is my problem. I don't want these things.

'Uwaga!' Warning! This does not make me a technophobe. I just don't <u>need</u> these objects. I refuse them! This reminds me of one of your passionate rants a few weeks ago. Do you remember? When you railed against media and fashion and sales. 'I refuse,' you said. 'I stand still in the midst of this. I look around.'

But are you standing still, Joseph? Or are you rushing about in your car?

Perhaps it is a question of attachment. Most people have to attach themselves to something, whether it's a computer, a cigarette, the television, their phone, religion, drinking, even home improvements – maybe they think they can arrest time in this way? I have work and family, I don't need these extra things.

Perhaps this is genetic. At the end of the war my grandmother was relocated from the east of the country to the west. She chose Polish citizenship over Russian. She was allowed to take only so many kilograms of belongings: her essentials, plus one or two pieces of furniture, clothes, her pearls – 'moja perła!' as she says, after the actress in her favourite film, who clambers onto a horse-drawn carriage only for her string of pearls to burst. 'Moja perła!' screams the actress, rolling her 'l's in a way characteristic of the extreme east of this country, a region that has itself now been rolled under the auspices of an altogether different state. Anyway, as my grandmother lived on a farm she also took her cow down to the train, knowing that it would probably have to stay behind. But after one or two negotiations, they gave their consent! She travelled on a cattle wagon for six days with her cow.

How can materialism mean anything to me in the light of this?

There was a saying in Soviet Russia: 'What do you own?'

Answer: 'The sleeves on a waistcoat.'

Perhaps now that people are free to move around, they will take only the essentials. Maybe they will no longer want to accumulate great piles of unnecessary things.

Letters

4 September

On 30 August 1918, Fatima Kapla shot Lenin six times. Lenin carried the shrapnel for the rest of his life. Kapla was kept in an underground cell with other political activists. At 4 a.m. on 4 September she was taken to a garage. A tractor engine was started to cover up the noise. (Communist propaganda used to show farmers on tractors as paragons of good honest work.) Kapla was ordered to stand near the tractor. Then she was shot, with express orders that she should not be buried but destroyed so that not a trace of her remained.

More than a trace of her lives on in my book.

Joseph, I am struggling. I see you everywhere. Sometimes I get desperate. I flirt with the idea of death. Yes, as a fantasy, maybe. The ultimate fantasy, but in earnest. Sometimes I see no other way of resolving things.

But then the rebel in me returns. I am not a coward.

Joseph, I have never had such complete faith in anybody.

I won't write more about my husband. At least, not my feelings for him. Of course they are positive. We talk in terms of 'What time do we go to . . .?', 'How was work?', etc. We plot little trips with Malena, or go on our own to the cinema where we sit beside each other in a companionable silence. We never argue. Though we often try to outdo each other in being considerate. But I have such feelings for all my friends. In fact, I mean my female friends.

Joseph, don't you notice how frightened I am that these feelings can suffice?

Do you remember when we drove through the forest, on one of our day trips when you kidnapped me from the library? We were singing along to some nonsense on the radio. I rested my palm on your neck. We'd just been walking. Then running through the woods. A ridiculously childish game of hide-and-seek. You said I had an advantage because I could hide behind a pine. It was fun. Until, in looking for you, and not finding you, I felt the pangs of premonition. Of future feelings. Of the hurt that would have to happen.

In the car, I told you that I wanted to take care of you.

And that if I ever had another child it would be yours. These were not empty words, Joseph (though you insisted, with a delicious mix of mischief and indignation, that you don't need looking after!). These words may sound empty now, because I cannot look after you. Not immediately. Not in person.

So what can I offer? If it is only suffering and frustration – quit it.

11

Night Census, or, Until the White Morning

Joseph Eadem holds the newspaper before him, almost proudly, as if inspecting a sheet for a stain he knows he has already dealt with. Despite the events elsewhere, despite the events in his heart. (For doesn't a person always put their heart before history? Well, certainly before politics. Give me this government, give me that government, but don't give me unhappy love.)

When Eric arrives, late, he looks different to when they first met, as if he has brought the shadow but forgotten its source. 'Matey!' he says, jerking his body in the direction of Joseph's table, before striding over with a heavy step, dragging behind him a scent of nicotine and soap. Slipping out of his sheepskin, he reveals a white shirt with a big collar, long sleeves, and cuffs that hang like extra palms. 'Do I look a bit gay in this upholstery?' he says, twirling about like a dandy in search of an audience. Joseph shakes his head, though whether in disbelief or as a 'no' is not clear. Eric lowers himself on his seat, like someone aiming for a stool in the dark. His hands land on the newspaper, the pages of which he reads perilously close to the flame.

'As far as I see it,' he says, a few moments later, looking into the middle distance through slightly bloodshot eyes, 'the world is divided between people who are forced to migrate, and people who are free to migrate. Either way, it looks like half of Europe will soon be in transit.'

At the bar, the first of the ex-pat arty types to have gone east in search of their souls are exchanging lingering glances with their East European counterparts, most of whom look like they have tumbled out of attics in the fashionable Jewish district before rolling down the hill from the castle. The night's readers? A Transylvanian writer (once in prison; dark, grotesque prose) introduced by a Polish writer (once in prison; not so dark but still quite grotesque prose). Despite the freezing night, green leather jackets and distressed corduroy (boys and girls) are popular among the self-appointed cognoscenti, not to mention free-verse hair (mainly boys), bobbed black or red hair (mainly girls), scratch-me-again stubble (manly boys), and a look of intense distraction or distracted intensity (boys and girls marooned in their existentialist phase who follow the breeze beneath the arches of the old town).

In the Stary theatre – where the dust appears part of the design, like a layer of skin over velvet – the stage-set is the consultation room of a funeral parlour: soft yellow chairs, a plain round table, a dull-looking vase of dull-looking flowers (moribunds?) and a jug of water, so it's no surprise when the wraithlike MC appears, the boards creaking under his every step. Grave pauses haunt the professor's speech, and even longer ones when he repeats his introduction in the local language. Eric can't keep still in his seat.

The Transylvanian writer, grey-haired, with a thin beard like a partially discarded disguise, takes his seat, looking like someone who has always shown life his profile while holding his breath. He is joined on stage by his translator, a corduroy-clad midget. The writer lights a cigarette, his hands making strange shapes as if releasing a dove. Joseph can only imagine what this man has been through.

The Polish writer appears next, a man hewn from stone, you might say, though a great block of Polish oak might be closer. He certainly has a formidable trunk. His neck is as wide as his head. He'd also been in prison under communism, but not, like the other writer, accused of running an underground printing-press, no, he was in for refusing to do his national service. He sits down, immediately miniaturising his chair. Tugging out a cigarette, he tears off the filter. After lighting up, he takes a great puff as if trying to suck the whole thing down his throat.

'Someone fetch this man a cigar!' says Eric.

After both writers have read from their work, and been travestied in English by the translator and the ponderous professor, the Pole tells a story of hitching a ride on a truck in rural Hungary. Apparently, the driver of this truck pointed to an old communist monument, claiming it marked the centre of Europe. Ever since then, the Polish writer has been scouring maps to find exactly where the monument stands.

The writer from Transylvania percolates a little laughter in his throat. 'I, too, have hitched a ride on this truck,' he says, everything about him trembling. 'I, too, have been shown this monument. But what of it? Such monuments, such trucks, such drivers exist all over Europe!' His words struggle from his throat as if he is coughing up stones.

Soon after, and with gestures expanding his body from neck to knuckle, the Polish writer is again stressing the need for precise co-ordinates, while the Transylvanian maintains that sometimes a border can cross the river at night, while everyone sleeps in their beds.

A brief discussion of exile follows from the floor. An Irish writer (woman, dog-tooth skirt) announces that she considers herself an exile in her own country, a statement causing an incredulous Portuguese writer (man, green shirt) to jump to his feet and retort (in English, so the woman can understand), and with hand gestures that clearly spell exasperation, 'but you speak the number one world language!' Then a woman from the Czech Republic (pink polo-neck) pops up and says, 'In 1922, Karel Teige asked, who are the most popular men in Europe? The answer? Lenin and Charlie Chaplin – the former in Russia, the latter in Czechoslovakia!' At which point someone (indeterminate sex, neither shirted nor skirted, but from Belarus) shouts, 'We're all exiles' followed by 'Everyone is European by birthright! Viktor Shklovsky, Berlin, 1923!' Eric can't contain himself. Both hands slap hard on the wooden arms of his seat. He pushes himself up, waves frantically, his cuffs unravelling like bandages, and shouts, 'Europe will always be united with the help of vodka and beer!'

When the raucous cheers subside, the discussion is left behind, like a dog that has bitten one person too many.

The light in the foyer bar has turned the colour of an uncleaned aquarium. Faces float, collide, converge. Joseph and Eric are briefly split up in the drifting moss of the green-leather set who emerge from the readings ideologically recharged and surely in need of a drink and a smoke, and, no doubt, some politicised sex. Those from the West are probably feeling righteous and soulful now that they are in the East. Those from the East are probably feeling righteous and doleful now they've been encroached by the West.

As pink as coral, Eric reappears from the throng, his right hand hanging on to his left, perhaps aching from a number of handshakes. 'All this talk of the centre of Europe,' he says, 'when it might be this very city. It's here that 20th Meridian East meets 50th Parallel North. Or so I've just been told. Which makes me thirsty for a stein of beer and a high hat of jazz!'

On the streets, Joseph and Eric are surprised to find the stillness of snow. Their tongues lie flat in their mouths like ice along a ledge. Yes, Joseph has already noted that each return to the streets feels like it's for the first time, as if the whiteness can muffle everything, even familiarity.

Descending to a cellar where the dark spirits behind the bar look like bottled night, they sit at a low wooden table, kneecaps to the timber, the candle-flame threatening to ignite Eric's fingertip goatee which, in anticipation, has turned a pyrotechnical puce. But they're a little late for the quintet. In fact, very late. Eric grips his watch with the thumb and index finger of his right hand. He stares, and continues staring, as if trying to remember how the digits work. Joseph has never seen him so still.

'*Kurwa!*' says Eric, finally, displaying his knowledge of local obscenities. 'It was two days ago! Which means tonight it's Timo Brücke! A cabaret star *aus Berlin*! At the cellar Under the Sign of the Ram!' He sinks his bottle of beer, grabs his sheepskin, and heads towards the stairs.

Minutes later, trailing spurs of ice, they enter the former coal cellar. A tall woman is on stage in a dress of cigarette papers or moth wings or the skin of a hundred and twenty onions. The woman's hair is long and soft and blonde.

Joseph and Eric sit near a piano that sounds as if it is damp inside or, at the very least, tearful. Eric's hands refuse to land on his legs, his lap, his knees. He is staring at the keyboard, his fingers heating up like wax. Then he switches back to the singer, gives a violent nod as if trying to fling his head from his neck, whispers '*ach ja!*'s and '*also!*'s, slaps Joseph's knee, winks to the world, rocks in his seat, and presses down the air with knuckles like the small wooden hammers of the stand-up.

Joseph, meanwhile, is close enough to the stage to absorb the blue-black arches above the singer's eyes – arches that resemble those of the cellar's low ceiling – the powder in the fine hairs on her face, the false eyelashes and nails, the spittle that flies beyond the microphone like notes escaping the melody. And to see that the singer is, in fact, a man. For already this is Timo Brücke. With hands-on-hips, and a waggling rear, she (for that's the intention) plays a hundred expressions across her face, most of them flirtatious – though, like all flirtation, born of sadness as well as desire. Aha, *la grande coquette*!

> *Keep smiling, my dear*
> *Keep smiling!*

As she sings Pola Negri's '*Zeig der Welt nicht dein Herz*', red and white rose petals float down from the gods. Like one of the Fates abandoned, a thin woman with long raven-black hair plays the violin. Joseph tries to scoop the melting colours in his glass.

Timo's voice is both sinister and seductive, like the notes of a music-box found in a Weimar bordello. Her lips two segments of a ripe tangerine, she whispers, '*Leben ohne liebe kannst du nicht*. And when Timo growls the Alabama Song in a *Treib-mich-auf-die-Friedrichstrasse* Berlinese, Eric shouts the refrain, 'I tell you we must die!' like a man delighted to be on his way to the scaffold. As for Joseph, his favourite is a jaunty little number that sets his teeth on the rim of his glass:

> *Please,*
> *shoot your husband!*
> *Please,*
> *kill him dead!*
> *Go and do your stuff,*
> *He has had enough,*
> *Ma-rry me*
> *Instead!*

After the concert, Joseph and Eric sit under the domed ceiling of the bar, a ceiling adorned with a fading mural of goddesses and clowns, naked women on horseback, a devil with a clarinet.

'It's not easy being an ex-pat,' says Eric, a long way down another half-litre, his shirt like a sodden paper bag, his hands now obsessed with his head, as if looking for the best way to carry his memory towards a lasting hiding-place. 'Sometimes I don't know which language I'm in.'

Joseph agrees. Though he has been making an effort to learn the local language, it still feels like he is pushing at the hinge-side of the door. In addition to his jotted-down words and names, he has collected children's word-cards from bags of cereal: one week it was animals, another it was parts of the body, and he scatters these cards around the flat and pronounces them when he sees them. *Koni* and *kot* and *tygrys* (horse and cat and tiger) in the kitchen, *ręka* and *głowa* and *serce* (hand and head and heart) in the bathroom. Once, in Café Prowincja, he sat near a guy having a lesson with a female teacher, so Joseph took out his sketchpad and pencil and he wrote down the words as they sounded, sometimes even pronouncing them in a whisper over his steaming tea, and the meanings, too, when explained, as well as a few rules of grammar and, equally important, the day and time of their next meeting, so that he would turn up again, buy a drink, sit at the next table and have a lesson by proxy, and in this way he began, if not exactly to learn a language, then certainly to absorb one.

In terms of verbs, though, he is largely confined to infinitives. He must live, for now, an unconjugated soul. In the street, he is often lost to the slow paddle between the utterance and the understanding. He is learning different ways of disguising a face of incomprehension. Also, he is struggling not to get stuck in the phase he calls the phonetic-pathetic: this is when you hear a word in your new language that sounds very similar to a word in your own language so you assume it to have the same meaning. Like the time when Marta told him the word for 'excuse me' and it sounded very much like 'push past them' said very quickly, so now whenever Joseph is squeezing in and out of somewhere he says, very quickly, 'push past them' and, sure enough, the people move aside. Indeed, during this stage, you will try to press most of your new language into the gullies and grooves of your mother tongue.

Eric's head rises from his hands, but slowly, like a phoenix reluctant to leave the warmth of the ashes.

'Married! Did I tell you? I have a son, Jan!'

He takes a sip of Kawior, crashing the ice against his teeth. He disappears between his palms again, as if trying to climb into a prayer. The candle gives out a burst of entirely black smoke.

'Divorced! Did I tell you? They live in the UK!' This time he raises his eyes but not his head. The bald patch of his crown may be in the shape of a country, or his latest calamity, but it's a tonsure a monk would be proud of. 'I met her five years ago. Here! She's Polish!'

His long-worn incredulity raises his voice an octave.

With as much tact as he can muster from a heavy tongue, Joseph asks how often Eric sees his boy.

'Not often,' he replies, his whole body now in hiding like someone who has lost not only their home, but also any sense of shelter. 'Once or twice a year, if that. It's his birthday in a few days. I can't decide whether to go. I want to buy him a junior violin. I've seen a beautiful one in a shop window. A beautiful burgundy one. With proper strings. Just the right size. Don't know what his mother will say. She's not musical.' He sits up. His hands land on the table without a sound.

'Should I go?' he says, a few moments later, his eyes bloodshot and tearful, his voice as gentle as the breeze left behind when someone passes in the street. 'For little Jan's birthday?'

'Yes,' says Joseph, without hesitation. 'Take little Jan the burgundy violin.'

Suddenly Eric revives. He slaps Joseph's ankle, straightens his spine, and orders two Kawiors. 'And what about you, you fookin' northerner! What are you doing here?' he snaps, clearly fond of his cabaret regional accent. He slaps the table so hard the ash jumps out of the ashtray. 'Know the poet Julian Tuwim?'

Joseph shakes his head.

' "Even beautiful long legs have to end somewhere." '

They laugh, clink glasses, take a swig, then a drag.

'Well?' says Eric.

Even here. Underground. Beneath the snow. In a cellar famous for its political satire during communist times. And for its coal before that. With an almost-stranger. And a belly full of beer. Joseph must answer for himself.

So he says something about having grown tired of the life back there, of part-time building jobs where he slaved all hours for cash-in-hand, or decorated rooms for friends in exchange for board and lodgings. He does not mention his own work. Marta is the only person he can share that with.

'What was that?' says Eric, fiddling with his ears as if tweaking the walnut-shaped tuners on the neck of a violin. 'I didn't catch what you said. Got a problem. Had it for a while. Late at night. Sounds get confused. Call it *intercontinnitus*! Haha. Definitely a bloody ringing in the ears. On Sundays the whole of the old town is swinging like a bell! Or is it *delerium tremens*?'

Joseph senses his chance to slip off the hook. He says something about living on his own resources for a while.

'Of course,' says Eric. 'That's your wits plus your credit card, right?'

'Right.'

Another clink of glasses. But Eric is not about to let go. His palm travels from his chin to his brow, over his head and down to his neck, a gesture he often repeats while thinking. He flicks his cigarette, missing the ashtray by at least five centimetres.

'But you could be anywhere in the world, matey, living on your own resources!' He leans closer to Joseph, their heads nearly touching. 'And I'll tell you something else, you're the last one in before the back door closes. And the front gates swing open. It's gonna change here now. Quicker than you can say *na zdrowie*! Now it's being made safe for Europe's middle classes. Soon we'll be saying how quickly a city suffers! But you got here just in time, matey. Landing like a duck on the ice, just like the rest of us – safely, but utterly without grace! You and your big lapels! So tell me, what's her name?'

Like an arrested man given a sudden reprieve, he flings up both cuffs. Then he swoops down and slaps Joseph on the ankle again. When his head rises, like a face painted on a pillowcase, he snatches up his drink.

'I have the constitution of an ox!' he declares.

'You mean you're easily slaughtered?' says Joseph.

Eric loves that. He peels a grin from the top of his drink and thrusts for another toast. His glass shatters against Joseph's. His mouth drops open as though it is his teeth that have scattered across the table.

'Eryk!' shouts the manager with a voice already weary of that late-night appellation.

Eric is all palms in apology, his white shirt aiding him in his civilised plea. When he has helped the owner sweep up, he sits back down, and says, as if nothing has happened, 'Anyway, what was I saying?' He runs his hand over his face. Then he sprawls across his seat, as if he can't sustain the dimensions of a human being, let alone one of the adult variety. 'Aha, what's her name?'

What the hell, thinks Joseph, he's a few beers into camaraderie, and this guy, his only acquaintance here, has just broken a glass over his misery. Besides, isn't the most forgiving confessor a drunken one, whether drunk with

God or vodka or both? 'You're right,' he says, a tight grin nearly shredding the words as they leave his mouth, 'there is a woman.' A little ashamed to have reduced Marta to an impersonal noun, he drops his head.

'What's her name?' says Eric, sucking on his cigarette, which he leaves pointing towards Joseph, while turning his head sideways.

Joseph tells him. For the first time, Marta's name tastes strange in his mouth.

'Magda?' says Eric, a finger in one ear.

'Marta!' says Joseph, cursing himself for the double betrayal. He looks to the mural on the ceiling. It has started to rotate. There are golden horses in carousel, drunkards and monkeys, wobbly women in slow striptease, the devil raising his instrument.

Joseph is keen to change the subject. He doesn't want to go through the whole story. Not that he wants to keep Marta secret, oh no, perhaps it's his despair he wants to contain.

But he doesn't have to worry. Eric has gone again. He kicks over a chair then drops to the floor as if in search of a mousehole.

'This world would be a great place,' he mumbles, as Joseph pulls him up the dark stone steps, 'if only we could get out of it. And in one piece!'

Moments later they are once again in the keeping of the cobbles. They are the first to leave their prints in a fresh layer of snow. They sink into the softness as if stepping into sleep. Façades are now night-sketches shifting in the shadow-play between real and reproduced. Like a woodcut, thinks Joseph, though his art feels a long way away.

As dawn's emissary creeps across the roof-tops in filthy

slippers, Eric grabs, slaps, punches as if all his hurt is coming out of his hands. Finally, when he has spent all of his energy and most of his tears, he moves on, pulling Joseph shoulder to shoulder along streets deserted of tourist and trader, of beggar and busker, and, who knows, of God Himself, despite the churches on every corner enveloped by that special kind of darkness that sits about a sacred site. Yes, it is true, only history and the heartbroken stay up all night.

Letters
5 September

My city was a subversive city under communism, known for fostering rebels in Solidarność. As a result, the regime punished us by drastically reducing the municipal budget. You see this everywhere. Miserable cracking concrete. Derelict buildings. Potholes big enough to swallow shoes, wheels, horizons. Autumn will have trouble putting any colour here.

Between the balcony railings of their flats, people weave strips of plastic so that passers-by can't see their legs when they sit for the declining hours of sunshine. Oh for the Polish golden autumn! 'Złota Polska Jesień!' Now these plastic strips are cracked, dirty, devoid of colour. Inside, the residents are pleased with their brown units covering an entire wall. Ugly glass vases in the cupboards. The same cheap carpets. Or ageing floorboards. Obligatory net curtains. Or blinds, an innovation of the new wealth. (Did I say wealth? Of course, I mean credit.)

I know one thing: communism was about denying perspective. 'This is your flat, your job, your balcony, your little piece of sky. No horizon for you. This is all you need.'

It will take years to banish this legacy of ugliness.

A stupid thought, sentimental but true. I was an unplanned child, a disaster in terms of money, time, living conditions. A doctor told my mother the foetus had died. He told her it was necessary to terminate the pregnancy. But she didn't like this doctor. Never had. She said he looked at her strangely. She said she didn't like the way his eyebrows met in the middle, joined hands and went for a walk down his nose. And why did he act more like a priest than a doctor? Did he really believe he had been chosen by God to decide if there was to be life?

She waited. She pondered. She couldn't sleep. Finally, she went to another doctor, a younger doctor, in a different surgery.

Eventually, I was born.

And, later, love. I got involved with somebody, my first boyfriend, who I thought was absolutely in love with me. Or so he told me. He convinced me with his touches though I did not sleep with him. I wasn't ready. It turned out he didn't love me at all. It was sex he was after, so he grew frustrated and dumped me. Likewise, I thought that my work at the university was what I wanted in professional terms. An endless opportunity to develop. Quietly. By myself. Wrong again! They need conscientious teachers, good administrators, steady and predictable workers, not dreamy searching scholars. My book is not what they are expecting!

I thought I married for love. Now I am living the worst dream in my life.

Even worse, I find it manageable.

Tell me, Joseph, is this courage or cowardice?

6 September

My book has become a platform of stability. To return to work after all this uncertainty feels like a blessing, a silent joy.

By the way, did I tell you that when Lya reached Hollywood at the beginning of 1926, she spoke to her maid in German, her hairdresser in Hungarian, to several friends in French, and to the American directors in her awkward English? Yet the sad thing is she could not find the language in which to tell someone of her hurt.

Three months earlier, in Berlin, she was discovered by a broken first-floor window. She had been trying to smash her way out. She had fallen back on the carpet. She was found semi-conscious among the shards, babbling in her mother tongue.

It is a short walk from Babel to Bedlam.

A few days earlier, Lya had met her mother, the Countess, for the first time since she'd fled her husband and children, and for the last time in her life. They met in Dresden, on a blustery October afternoon. Despite the weather, they decided to walk the Brühlsche Terrasse, the southern embankment of the Elbe. Before the war, the revolutions, the counter-revolutions – how could she ever keep up with them? – the Countess would have scorned the idea of a bench in a public place – like sitting on society's lowest rung! Now, she didn't really mind. She'd had to put up with so much over the last few years, not least waking up one morning to be informed that half her village now appeared to be in Czechoslovakia.

Modern times! She didn't know which way to look for safety. Everything glowed or buzzed or rang. How much simpler the world had been when administered by candlelight! She was always relieved to get back to the country where time unfolded like her favourite lace tablecloth. There, she could sit for hours, undisturbed, among the shadows of her remaining antiques.

And these modern times included her daughter flouncing about on a screen in a smoky hall full of strangers, their faces flickering like candles on All Souls' Day. With a shudder, the Countess recalled the only time she had seen one of her daughter's films. What was it called? 'The Emperor's Soldiers'? Within minutes of Lya's appearance, the Countess had fainted, and the screening was brought to an abrupt end.

In the film, Lya played a semi-naked dancer.

If that hadn't been humiliating enough, the Countess had heard stories of Lya befriending 'erotic dancers', frequenting clubs, taking drugs and drinking all night, stories that made the excesses of her own youth seem like a slightly drunken garden party.

They must have looked a peculiar couple on that bench, the sturdy Countess, with her skirts puffed out against the years, alongside her daughter, the star face of the fleeting days, whose spirit was ruffled by every gust of wind. Only her large hands, an unwelcome genetic inheritance, seemed to give her ballast and thus secure her a place on this earth.

Why did the Countess finally agree to meet her? Had she come to admire Lya – or Mali, as she called her as a child – despite her reservations? Had she grown tired, a condition easily confused with tolerance? Or was she simply driven by a mother's imperative, that a daughter must never be abandoned?

She was a sturdy sort, a vessel of antiquity filled with the almost-synonyms of history and loss. In the end, she reasoned, you just have to get on with things because, if not, there is only suffering. And so, weeks earlier, the Countess had written her daughter a letter. When Lya broke the wax seal, it had marked the end of their silence. The letter brought Lya up to date with her girls, now aged ten and twelve. Photographs were enclosed. Lya cried tears like drops of milk.

By the river, Lya removed her hat. Her famously bobbed hair, her bubikopf, rose like a dark blossom from the enormous wreath-like collar of her coat. As the most famous film star in Germany at the time, Lya was quickly recognised. A young autograph-hunter bowed at the bench as if before royalty, surely prompting a regal nod from the Countess.

Lya took off her gloves, attempting to hide her hands beneath them. Then she signed with her usual inscription, 'Loving life and not fearing death'.

12

All Cities End in Sirens or Saints

Sometimes, in a new place, you have to sit up all night and listen. Joseph is finding this out for himself. Earlier, he'd enjoyed the sound of horse's hooves as he lay in bed wrapped in the darkness and dust, and he'd raced to the window to see, from above, a shadow of the horse's head and neck, and then the head and neck itself, gleaming in the lamplight and against the snow, the dark mane shivering like tassels, a red ribbon in its black hair, a white one, too, and Joseph felt the hairs on his own neck stand up to see the grace and form and movement of this horse, so dignified in its loneliness, its cold velvet shanks through the dark, a shoe coming away from a tired hoof, the carriage lined with white silk, the driver smoking beneath a peaked cap. Joseph pictured this horse's neck on his special sheet of paper but he decided against it because he needed new pencils, if not charcoal, and, in any case, he was very tired. Since the previous night's outing with Eric, his eyelids had been stinging, as if, during their dawn walk home, he had used them to scoop up beads of ice.

It was nearly midnight. Eight hours of darkness gone, he told himself, only another eight to go.

Returning to his bed quietly full of gratitude for the

existence of these creatures – one of God's better inventions, he concluded – Joseph dozed off, only to be thwarted by footsteps from above. Surely there isn't room for an attic? But there must be, because he heard anxious pacing, the dragging of furniture, then rapid steps from one side to the other, as if someone was measuring the length of a nerve.

With his senses raised against sleep, and thus condemned to an involuntary vigil, Joseph heard the false hooves of high heels. A chorus of giggles. He heard shouts in a language he had, until now, associated with Marta putting Malena to sleep, with whispers issuing from dark coats, or through a gap in the door, or with a woman reciting train times like a poem in the night. Not like this, with snarling 'r's and vowels like sharpening knives. He heard singing and laughing and slapping. The sound of a fist smacking flesh. He heard breaking glass, and so close that he tiptoed to the mini port-hole in the door to peer at the unlit stairwell.

Yes, it took this night for Joseph to learn by heart the nocturnal movements of this city. At one point, he imagined his flat as a compartment in a chest of drawers that was being wheeled across the cobbles. He heard metal beer barrels close by, as drunkards stole the empty ones, dreaming them to be full. And in the silence left in the wake of an emergency vehicle, he was sure he could hear the polishing of tram tracks in the dark beneath the snow.

All cities end in sirens or saints. And very seldom sleep. So he believed as he lay on the mattress and absorbed the sounds. With the footsteps above still manic, the building tossing and turning with several centuries of groans, the whole street now entered his block, came up the stairwell, and, without taking off its shoes, made its way inside his flat to gather round his bed.

Now, when finally sleeping, Joseph dreams, like all dreams, a mixed dream, about a shadow made of grimaces and gravel, about dark alleys he doesn't recognise, cities he doesn't know, blue horses cantering across familiar landscapes, but just beyond his beckoning, incomprehensible words, partial embraces, single shoes on every step of the stairwell, gargoyles dropping from the roof-tops, lips, eyes, uncertainties.

He wakes with a start, all head and torso above the duvet as if aware of a presence. Though he can't locate the anxiety, he doesn't feel safe. He is wide-eyed in the silence, the city now deserted save for the portrait of Jesus looking down on every street. The early-morning delivery vans will bring the dawn in bundles, but their drivers are only just beginning to reach for their alarm-clocks in the suburbs. Yet Joseph's night-head is relentless in its whirl of images. Their intensity suggests he ought to record them. Get them down before they get the better of him. But exhaustion denies him the privilege of control. Like a coin-operated automaton for whom the penny has dropped, Joseph's body suddenly slackens. He collapses back into the mattress. He is carried off to a deeper sleep.

Where he dreams the final dream of the night. He dreams of Marta's husband. He is holding hands with his daughter. They are standing on a mossy ledge over a rock pool. They both look tired and pale. Malena gives a little wave. They both jump in the water. There is not a splash. They both go under. There is not a sound. They both stay under. There are not even any bubbles. Their shadows remain on the surface, like funereal water lilies.

Letters
7 September

Strange to wave goodbye to my husband when he's going to work in his suit and a shirt which he humbly ironed himself. Though he hates ironing, he had to get used to it when I wasn't here. By the way, an iron with coal and steam was known as an iron with a soul.

My husband is quite happy this evening. He has been offered a very good job with a Swiss computer company. A better salary. He kisses me whenever our paths cross, which is often in such a small flat. He even offered to peel the potatoes, which I know he really dislikes. He's happiest with the training project, six weeks in Warsaw starting in October.

Joseph, you know what? I am OK. So long as I am busy or walking the streets of my city. Today, in the middle of Krakowska Street, I saw your image. Your huge brown eyes, warm and tender, your smile. I felt a tide of heat rise in my chest.

When Malena saw a picture of the seaside today, she reminded me that pan Joseph was driving us there. When I asked her if she likes you, she said yes and got all shy behind her palm. Her answer pleased me greatly.

Now I'm back, it feels strange to hear the radio in my own language. Sometimes annoying. As if I don't want to understand every single word. Don't want my head filled with voices all from the same country. Now I see what you meant when you told me you don't want to be 'infiltrated by media-speak'. One of our Romantic poets, Norwid, who lived much of his life in Paris, and died a pauper there, wanted to get to the true source and sound of a word, 'bez smazy' – without interference.

Perhaps when a person lives elsewhere, in a different language, you have more space to develop inside yourself because not every word touches you, troubles you.

As Stefan Zweig wrote: "Flee, take refuge in your innermost self, in your work, flee to where you are no more than your own being, not the citizen of a state, not a plaything of the infernal game, where alone your bit of intellect can still function rationally in a world gone mad."

I'll be finishing,

13

A Partial Thaw, or, Conversation with the Elements

A sheet of snow slides from the roof of the church, and folds in the street with a sigh. There are whispers across the ice. Dark eyes peer at the heavens and then down at their shoes before considering the relation.

It is Christmas Eve. Since dawn, the city has been all a-drip. The roof-tops are melting. At street-level, dragon-mouthed gutter-spouts have tongues of flowing water. Buildings lean forward to get a glimpse of themselves in the puddles below. Stalactites are melting in the sunlight. Perhaps aware of their limited time, they wink for all they are worth. It is possible they are aspiring to the light of the Christmas star.

Everyone is dashing between the drops, singing beneath their breaths, clinging to one another across paving slabs still perilous with ice. Some stalactites leak from the guttering. Other, more upmarket stalactites prefer a tympanum, and a flurry of drops, like a whole string of pearls in one go. A few of the caryatids have resumed their weeping for the husbands who will never return. And more than one committed churchgoer believes that Our Lady of Sorrows is weeping, too.

Each morning, having been not parted but torn from his

sleep, Joseph opens the curtains and dreads another strip of sky as bleak as the tongue of a shoe. The darkening of one day seems to be quickly followed by the darkening of the next. There is barely room for words or shapes. At least since his night out with Eric. Or beyond ordering a meat cutlet in a milk bar, where he pronounces a phrase on the menu, each word a coin he balances on his tongue, and accompanied by a look of fearful curiosity as though he is trying to understand the gestures his own hands are making. He gauges the efficacy of these words according to the movement of the assistant's eyebrows. If he's got it right, these sculpted brows go up and the woman whispers into a microphone – as big as an onion – that's connected to the kitchen. If he's not even close, these brows congregate at the bridge of her nose; she shakes her head, her dyed raspberry-ripple hair remaining perfectly still, and she waits, with increasing impatience, for him to try again.

And then, other words, his phone calls to Marta, as he stands under one of the plastic hoods in the square, like a penitent-in-waiting, watching a whole city turned upside-down in ponds of melting snow, or being mapped in footprints, the receiver nibbling his ear, but sometimes warm from a previous caller, or smelling of perfume or else it's sticky with a trace of foundation. Each time, he wonders just what he's doing, for surely what he and Marta have to impart to each other cannot be poured into a single heart let alone a frozen ear.

Besides, in his own language, hasn't he always pictured words as knives and forks trying to get to the meat of the matter, but usually ending up in the string and gristle? Even if his new language feels different, based more on intonation than explanation – or so he imagines, as if it's about keeping the meaning in the air between listener and receiver, and for as long as possible – it's not as if they can sit in silence at either end of the line, in the light of each other's eyes. Sometimes, though, when he listens very closely, he is sure he can hear her smile.

And what of his plans for Christmas? Well, he has a carp in the fridge. A bony old fish. His solitude is edged with sadness, like a silhouette set in silver. But it's that soft melancholy that he knows is good for work. So long as he does not succumb to the tides of darkness and difference. Yes, he tells himself again, he must stay awake and watch. He must not be deterred by a city turning to mud as entire streets head for the drains, or by the man in a black leather jacket and obligatory moustache who is frequently standing opposite Joseph's block looking up at the window, or by the ravens in the city gardens that look like mini-vultures, or by his own arms that are already weary of gestures – the weight of that coat! – or, and most menacingly of all, by the doubt playing on his nerves that if something bad happens would he be able to rush out to the street and find someone who could help?

He must stand firm inside his sense of self, and keep these tides at bay. Yes, he knows from experience that it is easy to become indoctrinated by your own darkness, especially along strange streets in the middle of an unlit winter.

The previous day, he'd walked the city open-mouthed, his eyelashes wet with flakes, as he pictured image after image in the ice. He was trying to figure out how to combine a city's seediness, the dirt carried in nostrils and nails and pockets, in bad consciences and deeds, in filthy words and grimaces, along streets of sodden cardboard and slush, where the beggars carry plastic bags full of smoke, before freezing beneath their beards, yes, he was trying to figure out how to combine all this with the beauty of the sloping buildings and all their inset figurines, the light (when it comes), the women, the wonder. And so he ventured down side streets of two-seat *Fryzjer* (hairdressers) where the combs are pickled in a jar of detergent, past hat and shoe shops no bigger than confession-booths, watch-menders, key-copiers (with a sideline in shoe-laces), twenty-four hour shops smelling of mud and warm bread and tended by middle-aged women offering well-stacked hair, a teetering fringe, a spiky finale, altogether redolent of a Knickerbocker Glory, and in similar colours, and then there are the little tea houses where you stand at raised wooden counters, a nose in a cloud of vapour, and there's an old man in the corner playing a xylophone and the notes may well be his own bones or those of his dearly departed, and Joseph now holds more tea than a samovar, perhaps thinking he'll be able to burn his way through the ice or at least move about under his own steam, but he sat and sketched, having first walked his ideas into circulation, the cold making his whole system sing, and to the plinkety-plonk of the old man's bones he came up with a sense of something vulnerable yet indestructible. Recalling Marta's letters, he wondered if this is what she meant by the spirit. Also, he'd had to fix his belt round his greatcoat because the last black button had jumped off the lapel.

Back at his block, he'd dashed to a stack of wooden vegetable crates by the bins. He grabbed three and leapt up the stairwell. Driven by the smell of cat piss and putrescence, he smashed them up, scrubbing away the dirty ice and frozen cabbage leaves as if scraping all traces of winter from the city's roof-tops, until the thin slats, bristling with splinters, were ready to take his paint. With a few cheap pots of colour, he'd set about work, with fervid strokes and rapid adjustments, sometimes with his head tilted as if expecting to hear Marta speak.

His aim? To catch the city as he sees it now, before it disappears under the predatory wing of the West. Or trickles away in the thaw. For in this city, nothing appears complete. Flying buttresses, green copper towers and beams preclude a view of the whole, just as heavy roof-tops, their eaves serrated like pastry-cutters, dismiss the sky as scraps.

For example, he has taken to sketching the bin-searchers and pigeon-punchers as they lurk for God in bars no bigger than an armpit. They scratch away at the veins on the outside of their skin that hang like the creeping-vine stucco of the art-nouveau façades. But Joseph gets agitated because he can't render the stench as they wrap themselves in beer fumes and newsprint, their skin as tough as bark, so he rips the label from a *Tyskie* beer mat and he draws on that, or he smudges pages from his sketchpad with beer and ash and spit, sometimes stamping them with muddy boot-prints or encouraging one of the men to doodle across the page. When he's done, he hands out a palmful of silver coins with eagles on the back, or he shares a beer and a bagful of curses. In his guts, he believes them to be the true residents, for they curl alongside the foundations of the city walls, under all the shelter a single sky can provide.

He is also sketching buildings. Like the former coach-house, the name of this city dropping off a crumbling wall, one huge Gothic letter at a time. And the disused train station on the edge of town, where, beneath its moss-eaten brickwork, he found the words '*Rauchen Verboten!*' With his knuckles inviting blue blisters of frost, Joseph stopped in the street to sketch a pile of coal in the snow. (On first glimpse, he saw a stack of cats' skulls.) Pushing charcoal round the page with numb fingers – the flesh now just insentient padding about a bone – he stopped, too, for a rapid portrait of the busker with the harmonica who plays the same Christmas carol over and over again, his lips frozen on the metal of his Hohner as if sucking on a spoon for an elixir long since spilled.

Now, Joseph can hear singing from a nearby church, its great door open as latecomers cross themselves in the dark and press up to one another in the porch. When he bangs open the rotting window to lean out and look, he sees a gold crucifix floating in a sky of black water.

Yes, Joseph will sit out his solitude. He has candles from the Christmas market. With candles it is easy to sanctify a room.

Letters
9 September
We had a bit of a fight yesterday. Malena fell headfirst into a bathtub of water. She had been standing on the toilet seat beside my husband. I hadn't realised he had turned away. But he has quick reflexes. He caught her by the legs. Her head was only under for an instant. She got a mouthful of water which she spat out right away. She was so shocked that she cried, but in a puzzled way, and with much sorrow. She looked at us suspiciously for the rest of the day, often breaking into little snivels and sobs.

My husband took it the worst. He knew how easily she could have drowned. He developed a terrible backache. Early evening he went to bed for a couple of hours. I was astonished how composed I felt. Terrified, obviously, and feeling guilty, but the guilt that comes when you don't feel the whole burden of responsibility.

When my husband appeared after his lengthy siesta, he looked even worse. As if his face had taken on the creases from the pillow. He moped about the room. Until, at last, he confessed he had again been pondering the situation between us. He whispered, as if he did not really want to hear the words he was saying, or to touch them with his tongue. He said he'd been imagining I was about to leave. He said he could see it happening. He said I should tell him if that was what I wanted, because he wouldn't stop me.

Eventually I couldn't stand his gentle pleadings. I cried. Not out of misery, but as a release. My husband knows I am missing you. But when I tried to explain that it feels strange anyway coming back after such time away in a different country, he was not satisfied by my answer. Or he found it inarticulate. Which it surely was through my sobs. He went back to his desk. To a pile of tax forms he has been working through. For several evenings.

I went and sat on the edge of the bath, and finished off crying. As quietly as possible.

Next day

Today, we started brighter, if still bruised. We have been excessively polite to each other. In the evening when we went to my parents for dinner, I realised again that I cannot tolerate my father. I see my mother lower her head each time he speaks. These days she can't give much more than a scared look. Like an animal that has been hunted but, at the decisive moment, reprieved. She has been worn down by years of illness and worry. Thanks to him. Under her eyes, my mother has pouches the same colour as the ash of burning incense. In these pouches, she packs all her sleeplessness and fret. And it is never fun to see how time settles in a person, especially someone you love.

When I was twelve, I saw my mother fainting, vomiting blood from her ulcers, from all the stress my father placed her under. Where were the aunts and uncles? Sometimes a family is just a coincidental sharing of genes, and genealogy only good for a gravestone. Relatives would rather avoid my father than confront him. I can't stand his foolish laugh that gets louder when he sees no one is joining in. His whole body erupts. I can't stand his conviction that he knows everything. Or the way he rolls his eyes if you challenge him. He molests his visitors with stupid questions. Sometimes he uses his belly to run people out of the room. Really! Without using his hands! I told my husband that we do not have to succumb to the convention of visiting him any more. The fact that he's my father does not mean much to me.

My husband looked at me warily, perhaps suspecting me of dismantling the entire family, a person at a time.

14

Swimming in Europe's Only Uphill Pool

After two lengths, it feels like his face is coated in wax, a thin layer of *I'm not from round here.* The water is sticky and warm. Small diving-blocks retain only traces of their lane numbers. Over the pool hangs a pink life-ring that appears to be made of Terylene and toilet paper. I could drown looking like a drag queen, thinks Joseph.

In the narrow pool, in a lane divided by chains of plastic blossom, he is trying in vain to complete an unimpeded length. There are skinheads sharpening their shoulder blades by doing the butterfly, heaving aside great swathes of water and corrugating the surface. Like eagles held by the ankles, these swimmers repeatedly rise. One head reappears each time with a tumult of teeth as if he's been shouting under water.

Continuing his breast-stroke, Joseph soon realises that it is much harder to swim towards the windows at the far end, windows stuck with iron bars and the wings of dead pigeons. The more lengths he does, the chemicals combing the hairs in his nose, the more Joseph is convinced of the increased difficulty when going that way. At first he attributes this to a post-Christmas lethargy, until he remembers that he'd had the quietest festive period he had ever known.

On Christmas Eve, or *Wigilia* as it is known, the city had been stripped down to its divinity. Drawn by the voices of a choir rising among the roof-tops, Joseph, trading ice for incense, went to midnight mass in St Mark's across the road, where he'd sat among the bonnets and furs to give thanks for his lot, not feeling at all out of place, instead rather grateful for the elbows at his side, and for the elderly lady who tapped him on the arm and pointed to his hat which he immediately removed, and he mouthed along to hymns, or whispered the words he has learned of this language thus far in response to the prayer, and even though they were not the right words, they seemed to fit inside the massed recital, and Joseph was taken by the singing, a choir of nuns, so that he wondered if he had ever heard such clear voices, unless in the waters of the thaw, and then came the words that seemed to bring relief, so many words in an exhalation more gentle than a sigh, granting everyone a moment's rest from the lives left at the door, and he crossed himself as everyone else did before the golden altar, its beauty completed by those who descend upon its cushions. With something like holy reverence and a tear in his eye, he may even have prayed when everyone went down on their knees.

That was after his meal when it had taken him nearly a whole candle to pick the bones from that fish. (He was very happy to waive the other eleven courses.)

The next day, as he'd sat among his candles, each one a star on a stick, in 44 cubic metres of silence (the size of the flat), he'd consoled himself with the idea that you don't survive this much solitude without deepening your resolve.

So he ran that silence through all five senses, and possibly a sixth, while wondering if he was reaching the level of equanimity he had always been seeking, and of which he knew he was capable, given the right conditions. Who knows, perhaps even goodness was not beyond him.

Christmas rolled away like the slow procession of trucks that carry the snow out of town. On New Year's Eve, Joseph visited a few cellars and he'd smiled in the dark to see the pupils of eyes dancing on the tips of candle-flames, and to hear the whispers that wrapped themselves round the wick. When he'd popped into Café Galka, he saw Bibi veiled in lilac and pink, with silver streaks sprayed in his hair. Bunches of mistletoe protruded from the champagne bucket. Joseph nodded to Dmitri who was sitting with two friends, one in dark spectacles, the other with a bald head at the front, but from the back, he was all Rapunzel. Joseph drank three half-litres of beer, before consoling himself with a glass of *Krupnik*, honey vodka with warm water plus lemon slices studded with cloves.

Later that night, he'd been taken up by the crowd flowing to the square for the fireworks and chimes of midnight – that's if you could make out the bells among the popping corks and the rainbows shattering against an ice black sky. The cold air made Joseph feel more drunk than he'd thought, and he giggled to see medieval buildings flapping like sheets behind a mist smelling of spicy meat and gunpowder. They're not buildings, he sang to himself, they're paintings. He'd watched like a child as giant shadows peeled themselves from stone and curled up with a resonant flap. An arm with a hand on the end handed him a bottle of champagne. A firework went off from a nearby lump of ice, leaving a sad stick in its wake.

Objects are enticing when you're drunk, because they retain a composure you have already lost, so Joseph plucked up the stick with one hand, while raising the green bottle to his lips with the other. He gulped down an exploding ball of sugar and ice. Then he looked at the city through the dark green glass. Yes, it's a painting, not a building, he giggled, not a frillding, a fainting, as he pointed his new stick at the cloth hall hanging above its arches in the dark.

Soon after, he became embroiled with a group of students from around Europe – medical students? Mythical students? – and he went with them toe-poking corks along streets of crushed cans, spent streamers, abandoned bottles – as if a whole year had been consumed in one night. Still mumbling about frilldings and faintings, he tried to get his tongue, now a peach slice in syrup, to push out Happy New Year in Spanish, Ukrainian, Polish, German, Latvian (such was the many-flagged assembly, o, Europa!), or to join in with their folk songs – in spirit and tone if not the words – because he didn't know any folk songs, either from their country or his own, but his stick became a conductor's baton nevertheless.

'Where you from?' asked one of the students.

'From here!' said Joseph, putting his arm around the questioner.

'No,' said the student. 'I mean, originally.'

'Oh,' said Joseph, his tongue now a rollmop herring.

Off they went, kissing strangers and statues, to a flat not far away, via an iron-gated courtyard already littered with the fingernail foil of silver wrapping, and in this courtyard the stars made their way down from the sky, bouncing from one wooden window ledge to another, sometimes catching a balcony railing or tympanum or a white eagle painted on a red tin sign, and so Joseph leaned back, clutching his head as if it were a bowl into which these stars might drop, but he couldn't focus beyond an orange lamp in the top window, and so these stars crashed past his ears and eyes and ankles, before turning into the silver bottle-wrappers at his feet. Next thing he knew, he was going up a wooden staircase in the dark, following the outline of the shoulders in front.

Back in the pool, Joseph decides it is not the after-effects of Christmas slowing him down. No, there must be a slight slope. Especially as he has noted that when swimming back the other way he almost can't keep up with himself. Either way, he can't find his normal rhythm, the strokes that usually swim his thoughts to clarity. He wonders if he has been going to pani Stasia's too much – all those forgotten chickens and pigs! Or perhaps he is heavy with longing, for unspent tenderness can also slow you down.

For a while he floats on his back, in a momentary peace, and in that moment he realises that both his life and his work aspire to this state of suspension, this supporting of the weight of a head. He thinks of Marta. He thinks of his work. He wonders why there is no longer any call for a vision that can't be shown on a screen.

His meditation is broken by a stampede of footsteps. It seems that in this country there is always someone up above.

Starting each stroke with his hands in the shape of a prayer, Joseph swims through a serious of mini-baptisms (he counts fifteen submersions per length). In the shallow end, two of the shaven-headed youths stick out their elbows as he approaches, their glares falling in the water with a fizz.

Joseph swims on, regardless.

Letters

12 September

I want so much for you to come here. I am sorry if I didn't sound too enthusiastic when you suggested it again on the phone today. Of all the things I am afraid of there is one I am afraid of the most. I know that I am capable of plotting and lying. My 'tender' years at home, my de-formative years, as you call them, trained me in this. I know how one lie is usually followed by another, how one scheme demands a shadow scheme, and so on. This blunts sensitivity, and makes you truly wicked. I don't at all have to be a saint and you know the best that I am hardly a puritan. I just know that this secret plotting would be the surest way to lose you. I wouldn't be able to make you an accomplice in my rather sly projects. When I meet you, I don't want to feel like a fugitive. Or you, a refugee.

Today I saw a young man in the street. He bore only one resemblance to you: the dark curls at the collar. It was enough to make my heart leap.

I scribble down my dreams to record your appearance. As a slightly restrained and out-of-the-limelight figure, a shadow passing behind a lamp-post or down a dark corridor. Carrying your smile with you through the night like a well-cupped candle.

How I want to go with you!

We came back unwell. My cold was rather violent. My husband took the spare duvet out of the cupboard, evacuated to another room and so far stays there. Without complaint. Which does not mean – forgive my candour –

that my husband and I live in celibacy. We don't. Though our intimate moments are rather brief and rare. He treats me like glass. No, I don't mean he thinks I'm fragile. I don't know. I shouldn't be saying. Maybe as if he is treating me to something rather than sharing it with me. It's not unsatisfying, but on my part, narcissistic.

Whenever I kissed you, whenever our bodies flowed together, I knew why I felt so happy. I wanted to give as much as I was taking. Or even more. My body had never felt so sensitive. So, I am at a loss. I need you. To speak to you, to hold you, to be close, the closest.

Come closer!

Can I be radical in the circumstances? I don't even mean the pragmatic aspects like me being 'bez grosza przy dusza' – without a penny next to my soul. Perhaps I lack the courage of the women I am writing about. Perhaps I lack their spirit. I am deep in reading and writing. A silent liturgy, indeed.

I am looking at one of my favourite photographs of Lya. How forlorn she is! Her bobbed haircut looks as though it was slid on when she was not paying attention. Like a black rubber swimming-cap. She poses with the frown of a scolded child. Her eyes are moist, as if they have recalled all the day's tears. (I have a doctor friend who says this film across the eyes can be caused by taking cocaine.) Her expression asks how her life has brought her to this point, while also pleading: 'Don't tell me! Don't answer! I know!' She is all too aware of the details of her fugitive life. An unattached soul who, having torn up her roots, often feels unfamiliar to herself. She wears her loneliness all about her. And the guilt she will never come to terms with. Under the eyes, too. Where the skin is darker, like the bruising on porcelain where a tap has run for years.

This is an early picture. She abandoned her husband and two children only a year or so before. To what end, this huge act of bravery? This huge act of betrayal? Where is the spirit of her driving her?

She wears a velvet turtle-neck which gives a vaguely Gothic impression. She has the dark fire of a melancholic, the fire that flashes from time to time and ignites the spirits of all who see it. But when not supervised by others, this fire ravishes its source. She already looks like a woman who is frequently in peril, and capable of endangering those who do not look beyond her. That is why those big sad eyes seek guidance. Really. She has made all the difficult decisions. She has escaped her bourgeois background, the more or less fixed marriage, the joys and duties of motherhood. Now she is free to fulfil a dream born in adolescence: to dance, to act, to travel! The world is bursting into modernity, and she is bursting with it. Yet she does not look happy. She already knows the cost.

Later

Today, when the world was quiet for a moment, I remembered the day of my wedding. It was after the evening reception. I was sitting in the bath of our hotel room. Not a luxurious hotel, but one of the better ones. The brass taps, the fluffy white towels! I had a glass of champagne on my knee. Bubbles up to my ears. It should have been the happiest feeling: my husband in the next room, humming a pop song, waiting for his bride to appear naked and fragrant, full of love and passion and laughter. But you know what? I was crying. Desperately.

Joseph, I will <u>not</u> let you turn into my memory of you.

Ps Would it be wrong of me to whisper: hurry, hurry, my heart is here!

15

Bratysława 333

'Come on! What you don't know can't kill you!' says Eric, pulling Joseph by the lapels as he ducks in the front. 'Unless, of course, it's dark and sharp and heading your way!'

In the passenger seat of the Fiat, Joseph bounces and jerks, his bones borne low to the ground, as the car wheel-spins between buildings squaring up in the snow. Having been persuaded to join Eric and his friend, Jurek, on an afternoon trip to By-m, he feels like he is careering down the street in a three-man toboggan. His muscles tighten like a tuning of strings. His fingers are clenched from a memory of steering, his feet reach for the brakes.

Jurek takes the next bend like a chicane, no doubt thinking that two wheels are all you need for turning. As the tyres skid across the icy tarmac, Joseph can't help remembering Marta's husband, the way he drove that night as if the road was only a suggested route, and traffic lights merely advice.

In the rear-view mirror, Joseph sees Eric's head bobbing up and down as he slides along the back seat, and he's pointing and clapping, this boy in the back, before lurching between the front seats to say: 'You know, I appear to

be in the right mind, but the wrong country!' He jerks
his head from Joseph to Jurek. 'Or is it the other way
round?' He gazes down the road ahead. 'You know what?'
he adds, his spirits lifting. 'If we keep going this way,
we'll end up in Berlin. All those big windows and brilliant
heads!'

This city has collapsed in the dark. For here the darkness
does not fall, it flourishes. There is a stench of chemicals.
'Welcome to Prussian industrialist hell!' says Jurek, with his
best Satanic chuckle. They pass a mineshaft with a lift
tower, the wheel of which, having reeled in the sky, will
never turn again.

'Jurek! Enough of your Slav pessimism!' says Eric, still
bouncing in the back. 'This place is being rebuilt!' He
points over the driver's shoulder to a confusion of scaffold-
ing and cranes.

'Yes,' replies Jurek, blowing smoke against the glass. 'On
quicksand!' Again his laughter rumbles from the depths.
Then he handbrake-turns round a corner, nearly sending
the chassis into a spin.

Joseph hangs on to his head.

The Fiat shudders back into a dusk that's abseiling down
facades as if it can't escape quickly enough. The few
remaining clouds are punched away by broken chimney
pots. They come to another derelict site, completely dark as
if lying in a puddle of oil, save for a brick outhouse with a
bare yellow bulb. They park alongside. '*Biznes!*' says Jurek
as he and Eric get out, leaving Joseph alone in the diving-
bell.

Later, back on roads that glimmer like tin trays carrying
water, Joseph takes in the circles and scoops, the bowl-
lamps and balconies of three art-nouveau buildings, and

suddenly he feels he could be in Budapest, or back in the city in which he now lives, and not in a forgotten mining town in Silesia, in a tiny car full of smoke, swigging from Jurek's bottle of Wiśniówka, a cherry vodka, a sweet and sticky antidote to the dark, and lining your veins with fur – at least for an hour or two – but just as Joseph is beginning to rescue notions of beauty from the icy muck and granite, to see similarities in all districts – it *is* the landscape that links us – the car slows down at a junction, alongside a sign saying 'Bratysława 333', and trees appear, and these trees splash their limbs against the windows, their toxic branches having died many winters ago.

Letters
16 September
Since I came back from our days together, everything has been rolling too fast. My mother works. My mother-in-law has many mysterious visits to the doctor. So in the last two weeks I have been trying to combine child and house care with preparing materials for my book and my teaching. There is no longer enough of me for myself.

Yesterday, my husband offered to erect a mirror on the balcony. To reflect more sunlight for my pots of herbs that were neglected in my absence. Especially as the sun is sinking further every day. I laughed. I thought it was a joke. He looked very sad standing there holding the mirror. When he turned, his shoulders sloping with disappointment, I saw my expression in the glass. I shuddered to see the face I had presented to him.

He thinks of everything that could comfort us.

16

ħistory at ħand

The woman walks with a rocking motion, a swaying back on her heels, to rescue her momentum before each step. Her right arm swings beside her like a pendulum that's escaped from the case, but not yet from the clock. She is upright for her age, which Joseph estimates as late sixties. She wears a dark green winter-coat, a thick black band in her grey hair, and large, tinted glasses, similar to the welder's.

Joseph knows she is swearing. Thanks to the late-night drunks beneath his window, he is familiar with fuck in a foreign language. With shit. With whore. With worse. With the growling curl of consonants, the rolled and snarling 'r', the catching of the curse in the roof of the mouth.

People step out of the woman's way. Some laugh. All stare. No one listens. No one really listens.

It is possible to go mad looking for someone to talk to. The woman's voice startles pigeons, scratches shop windows, tests the hinges on the flip-top bins.

When she reaches the shoe shop opposite Joseph's block, the owner comes out and takes her by the swinging arm. After a brief resistance, the arm stops. With little circular movements, the owner rubs the old woman's hand as if to maintain her circulation, or to erase the memories stored between knuckle and wrist. But gently, because the old woman's hand is like the grilled skin of a *Lawasz* pancake from the Georgian restaurant next door, thin and blotched and browning. Still talking, the old woman nods at the end of each sentence, her voice now only slightly louder than for a normal conversation. Joseph bangs open the window and leans out to hear a few phrases. He jots them down. Phonetically. With a hand curled against the cold. He will ask Marta what these words mean. Maybe the woman is ill and she has no one to look after her? He hears her every day.

With a final pat the shop-owner lets go of the woman's hand, having first returned her arm to her side. But cautiously, as if laying down a pearl necklace in its case. The old woman rocks on her heels, her swinging arm begins to swing again, finally pitching her forward. Joseph watches as she walks away, palms open, fingers extended, as if she is wading out to sea.

At first, she is silent. Joseph is pleased the encounter has done her good. But before she reaches the end of the street, the woman resumes the shouting and swearing that orchestrates her plea.

Letters
17 September
I'm at the station. It always reminds me of when I was leaving to go to my grandmother's. When the train came in, the rush of the crowd, the doors immediately blocked, people balancing with one foot on the metal step, the other foot kicking off those behind. The men rushing down the narrow corridors, claiming spare seats. I tried not to see my father pushing people aside with his belly. I see my mother,

following meekly. Then her relief. Not so much from having a seat but from having avoided her husband's rage.

Now we're going north through the city. Over furtive bridges that feel as though they don't know whose side to be on. This is a city of 117 bridges! You see the back of the theatre, the side of the town hall, then later the factories, the warehouses, the derelict sites. Funny, but I feel like I am seeing the city from the inside out: gas pipes, building sites, roadworks never ending. Like one of your sketches. This is the way to leave a city. Via its intestines!

But where are you? Still racing round your country in the car? You once told me that you seek 'a life lived close to the blood'. I was certainly overwhelmed by your passion. But must you always take off like a dog that's found a fresh scent? Isn't there a danger of forgetting what it's like to be still? Even to fear it. Stillness, that is, and the self-appraisal that goes with it.

In other words, Joseph, I get the impression that your wheels are always just above the ground.

'Doesn't this give me an angelic aspect?' you once said.

'No,' I replied, a little annoyed that you hadn't taken me seriously. 'Probably just tragic.'

What I am trying to say is this: when will you land, Joseph, and where? And the question that hurts me the most: who with? You said when we're together I cure you of your restlessness. But sometimes I wonder: for how long?

You are a hyphenated being. Always between two places. Just make sure you don't reduce your life to the dash between two dates!

We're passing through countryside. The sun is bright, the horse-ploughed fields a dusty shade of brown, the topsoil frequently disturbed by the wings of bathing birds. There are apple trees in the gardens. Huge apples, red as a peasant woman's cheeks, and taking half an afternoon to eat. Boggy meadows glisten between forests of birch and pine. In this light, the barks are more white than silver. Trees and trees and more trees! Long shins in the sunlight. Bless you, o forests! Then come run-down farms with old peasant women in their cardigans and skirts and ankle boots. They are bent double from a lifetime of pressing their faces to the soil. They collect vegetables and leaves in their wicker baskets. Sometimes it is possible to see a whole community sitting along the station platform with these baskets, waiting for the train to the market. There's a pile of rotten window-frames waiting for a fire. Entire villages made of wood and tin. Rusting bits of farm machinery leaning against a barn. A dozen or so deer in a meadow staring at the passing train. And there's a horse and carriage going down a lane, the driver in a red jumper sitting high on a bright green seat.

I love the simplicity of life out here. I would like to share it with you. Here, it is still possible to be a quiet human being. To gather yourself about you. Here, Joseph, I would cure us both of restlessness.

My paper! I should be writing those last two paragraphs. I return to the seven other people in the carriage. A smell of sweat and sandwich fillings, especially salami.

Again, Lya forces her way into my imagination. All the trains she took! Each time leaving behind a discredited life. As if she was trying to keep ahead of her fate. When she fled her family to go to Budapest in early 1918. Or escaping to Bucharest in November 1919, in a first-class sleeper, with her lover, the leader of the Rumanian army, General Marderescu. Then, less than a year later, another night train in haste, this time via Czechoslovakia to Berlin, where she finally achieved European fame. It seems a train carriage became her home. Or at least a resting-place for her transient soul, the rhythm of the wheels, the gentle rocking of the carriage helping to console her as she parted from yet another aspect of her life.

This morning, my husband tried to get me to buy a first-class ticket. I was ideologically opposed. With his long legs, he ran up and down the platform, leaping inside carriages, trying to find the best seat for me. He looked happier when I was comfortably installed, though he is worried about me going away again so soon. When the train left the station, I could still see his anxious smile pressed against the window by my seat.

Joseph, I wonder where you are. And if you're coming. I can't die of remorse.

17

Towards the End of A Season in Sepia

There has been a farewell flurry of snow, as if the white eagle has laid down its wings, or maybe all the sugar-shops have got together to produce a cloudburst of coconut, or else the residents have thrown down their woolly hats and scarves in protest against winter's tenacity. Tympanums shrug their shoulders and carry a final load. Bell towers and trees are close to recalling their true forms after a season as black felt, pressed between heel and horizon. And the lumps of swept-up snow that have survived all winter long? Well, the first explorers of these archipelagos of ice have long since marked their discoveries with cigarette butts in the sludge.

Joseph is sitting in a patch of sunlight, the only light to smuggle itself into his flat past the greedy eaves of the tall buildings opposite. It is the first sunshine for days. On such a well-lit afternoon, he can do decent work, no longer rubbing his eyes to dispel another sack-cloth sky. He lets this light spread across the table, until his paper looks like parchment, or the skin of the woman with the swinging arm. He sketches feverishly, the light putting rings on all of his fingers. He selects a thinner charcoal or licks the tip of a water-colour pencil. He lights a cigarette to quicken his system. Or he munches on a bone-dry pretzel, its poppy seeds scattering to form goose-pimples on the page. And he likes this for he wants to capture the texture of streets still awash with salt and sand and slush. Or is it sugar and chocolate and cinnamon? And the texture of peeling posters, of feathers, of skin – for the walls look like skin in this sunlight, while other blocks of masonry look, from a distance, like charred wood, or the cardboard inlay of an egg-box, or they're creased by the light like a fan made of paper, and then there's the pastel façades of burned orange, mustard mixed with ash, a rose-petal that's been bruised between the thumbs, all softly incongruous against the filthy snow, and held in place by giant coping stones occasionally sculpted with feathers and leaves, a lions's head, a gargoyle or an eagle.

Yes, sometimes Joseph wants to all but destroy the medium under the weight of his work; other times he wants to touch the page as lightly as possible. Just as he has to lick the short-lived sunset from the window-panes opposite, like crème-caramel from a plate. Or he thrusts a brush in a pot and rushes it up and down a wooden slat as if he is ringing a bell.

Though his work is gathering in intensity, he has not fully broken through. The delicate light and its brevity reduce him to short bursts, as the day yields to another darkness of wet mohair. Nor can he quite fathom the paradox of Marta's absence and proximity. Or the feeling of being elsewhere that he wears like a wrapping of tiredness or someone else's skin, so that he first has to break through to himself each day before he can even approach his work.

Sometimes, when he looks over to the nuns living opposite, he wonders if he should devote himself to the

Church and transfigure his longing into liturgy – after all, wasn't that what Edith Stein had done? Yes, why not let God sort the whole mess out? But then again, he thinks, perhaps God is responsible for the mess in the first place. I mean, if she hadn't been a Catholic, surely things would have worked out differently? But no, he's not going to blame religion. To be absolved of all responsibility for one's own actions! For isn't this the anxious pulse that beats in the heart of all fugitives? To be emphatically unattached to the outcome?

On darker days, when the city is tired of its history, and the buildings in need of a good scrub, he patrols the streets under the surveillance of crows and the stupidity of pigeons, refreshing his gaze with a pair of red boots – as welcome as a smiling face – or the lime-green of a passing tram (like a giant caterpillar in the snow), or, like a swallow in search of an eave, he dives into a sugar-shop, where the pastries are all fluffy and yellow and he tries to absorb their brightness so he can take it back to the streets and hang it like golden pears in place of the heavy green lamps. Yes, he is moved by simplicities now. His day is made of them: a tram ride, a stranger's smile, the red collar of a Daschund.

On these days, the sun gives out scarcely more light than the yellow cloth hall reflected in the back of a shovel. A cigarette outside tears strips off his lungs and pickles him in nicotine. In a rapid sketch, he makes a strike for clarity only to succumb to abstraction, his fingers so cold that his left hand has to carry his right hand home.

He has been phoning Marta less frequently. Perhaps because it is still too cold to lean your bones against metal, and speak like a supplicant who has used up his humility, or maybe it's because they now communicate as if they're talking across continents, afraid of being disconnected at any moment. Joseph knows his voice sounds strange after days of solitude in a language not his own, days when he feels like a bell with no tongue ringing in the dark, because there is frequently an echo and he hears words as if spoken during sleep, his tone faltering between resentment and exhaustion, and he is disconcerted by this, unsure whether to go on, each word a coin down a well that's running out of wishes. Also, when he is called to the speak-room, he's not sure which language will work best: his own already feels like the memory of a language, as if he is walking among ruins, while his new language has him fumbling through the phrases he has learned so far as if he's turning out a drawer.

Are you still there? Can you hear me? How do you mean?

Sometimes he hears Marta aiming her voice into a cupped palm and pouring away its warmth, or, because she has so much on her mind, her voice points in a direction other than his and he looks through the hood of the phone box, and he sees the horses in the square blowing out their noble indifference through both nostrils, and he wonders if he would have been better off if fate had found him on four legs – I drink from a bucket, I sleep in the hay, the horses sense a brother.

On other occasions, his frustration gets the better of him, he tries to hold back but he can't, it's too much, so he accuses her of falsehoods, of cowardice, of fear. Only to wonder if, in his own language, bitterness is all he has left.

And did she really imply that he didn't appreciate the practicalities of her situation, especially regarding her child, when she surely knows already that he loves this child like his own and will never forget the day of blue skies and seed-pods when they drove to the coast (without the au pair who was busy vomiting in the bathroom). Once by the sea, they were reading the papers, playing in the sand dunes, sketching with Malena, taking fresh peaches from a brown paper bag then blowing in the bag and popping it to make this little girl laugh, and later down on the beach with the sea going out, collecting pebbles, rinsing them in the froth of a wave, hoping they would keep their colour, and after that in the car in the harbour, eating fish-and-chips, the sun going down over wooden boats held together only by scales of paint and seaweed and the shaded eyes of onlookers. With Joseph and Marta in the front, Malena in the back, vinegar breath floating out the windows, and at one point Joseph turned and, squinting for the setting sun, he looked straight into Malena's brown eyes and he felt happy to be looking into the eyes of this peaceful child, a child whom he already loved, and Malena must have felt happy, too, because she gave him such a smile, a knowing smile, and she reached out a plump little arm with a plump little hand on the end and Joseph leaned over to hold her tiny fingers, each one a centipede he gathered in his palm.

On the 'phone, when Joseph and Marta are able to speak for longer, it is different.

'It's good to hear your voice,' she says.

'It's good to hear yours,' he replies.

Now feeling her breath in his blood, his joy heats up slowly, like a tin-kettle on a camp-fire, until, a little later, he is whistling, too.

Until 'I'll be finishing'.

A silence into which Joseph drops his jaw.

If love heightens the senses, then longing finds strange ways to feed them. He must get back to work before he

comes undone. Yes, the phone is against them. Perhaps the
line that links them is made of their own unravelling.

Even Marta's letters are beginning to trouble him. They
often pick the bones from their latest misunderstanding,
and put them back together in different shapes. Sometimes
he recognises these shapes. Other times he rips the paper to
shreds. Or he splashes her words with spirals of paint.

Even so, he dares to kindle a hope: perhaps the relief
Marta felt when she returned home was not, after all, about
re-discovering her love for her husband, but about re-
discovering her language.

He knows he must not give up the habit of hope.

Each day he fills pages with verbs and words and phrases.
He ignores the fact that learning a language without a
definite article is bound to be fraught with uncertainty. Or
that the word for reality is feminine. He kicks up the purple
dust in his flat, pronouncing his kiddie word-cards with
theatrical pomp to the approval of the pigeons on the sill.
One day it's 'ch' words – *schemat, wschód* (sunset), *schron-
isko* (youth-hostel), the next day it's 'rz' – *rowerzysta*
(cyclist), *rycerz* (knight), *orzeł* (eagle). And he's fascinated
that the word for midnight – *północ* – is also the word for
north. And that east and west are the same as the words for
sunrise and sunset. Or he listens to the huge Communist-
issue radio that's birthed in his flat, like a child's wooden
replica of an ocean-going ship.

Though these words don't yet have the potential to hurt
him like words in his own language, and their shapes are
much more interesting, sometimes their value eludes him,
so he flicks through the paper in search of images for his
scrapbook, or he retunes the radio to a classical channel
where he is becoming familiar with Lutosławski, Pender-

ecki, Karłowicz. He returns to his own work. There, back down the well, he scratches at the darkness, trying to find the hieroglyphs that might lift him to the light.

The sun is slipping behind the ridge of a roof. The dusk will be short-lived. Like a giant sheet, it will be unfolded from the top floor of the building opposite and then dropped to extinction in the dark.

Looking down at the street, Joseph sees a nun slipping in the ice. She does a dance of flashing feet as if trying to stay on top of a rolling barrel. The crucifix round her neck swings from side to side. Another sister grabs her under the arm to prevent her from falling. Clutching their rosaries, they laugh in gratitude for the kindness of their Holy Father's will.

Immediately, one of them slips again, this time pulling the other to the floor, where they sit on their bottoms looking stunned.

Letters
17 Sept – 2 p.m.
I'm in a café near the town hall: gothic, but serene. There are many colourful townhouses, Renaissance, I think. On each street, they squeeze together like a dozen faces trying to fit in a photograph.

The coffee is not too good.

It's the home city of Copernicus, so forgive me if I get philosophical. Or astronomical. Funny how the metaphor of the sunrise and sunset has endured despite his discoveries. Of course, the monks of the time were horrified. They committed suicide in great numbers. They couldn't believe that the earth was not the centre of everything.

This city was seized by Teutonic knights. Copernicus helped design the fortifications because he started as an engineer. Those Teutons were clever and barbaric. Under the guise of spreading Christianity, they murdered the entire Baltic people living here, just wiped out the poor pagans within a century, leaving a few immense and beautiful, mainly red-brick castles.

How does a city escape the memory of so many deaths?

Joseph, I am missing you. (No matter how inadequate these words, I must use them.) Maybe the excitement about the conference took over from my despair. Maybe I am slowly coming to terms with the crooked ways of life. What I want to say is that I am no longer gushing tears, but I think of you, I talk to you, I picture you. I think, endlessly, frantically, of what we can do.

The world without you is narrow. The people around me are very nice, but there's a lack of depth in my encounters with them. And an inevitable inhibition in my contacts with my husband. Sometimes I am bewildered by my indifference. Other times I feel a kind of tenderness for him that I cannot decipher. Not a wave of passion, but a need to confirm my friendship. Warm like a memory of love.

19 September, 10 a.m.
Joseph, were you teasing me when you said you tried to get a coach-seat to come here, to the conference, and it was fully booked? And did you mean it when you said you will come to my home city before the end of the year? I shall hold you to it!

13.50 p.m.
I'm desperate. I came early, not knowing the exact time of departure. There are policemen leading football fans along the platform. A stamping of boots on wet concrete. The air is very close. I have had a feeling of heaviness in my chest for two weeks. Sometimes I feel I'm suffocating.

Last night, my husband told me on the phone that he will never believe me again.

18

Rationalist without a Nation

This city does not know which season it's in. Down side streets, winter raps its bony knuckles on every door, like a tinker on his last legs, one final lump of ice in his beard, perhaps making night-time sojourns to lie across the cobbles, or to whisper up flakes that will not have the heart to land.

In the city gardens, meanwhile, the trees are slowly removing their winter sleeping-suits. Branch by branch, they perform a strange striptease, a morbid striptease, because it's not flesh being revealed, it's bone. A stocking of snow falls away from a pine to reveal a glistening shin. The branches of oaks appear like giant fingers crippled from knuckle to nail. And having given up the white silk that perfected its whalebone dress, the willow now stands in the skeleton of its original shape.

Not wishing to surmise a city from behind the froth on his latté, or, in fact, to surmise a city at all, Joseph is heading away from the centre on one of his walks. If this decision has led him over the ring-road and down the unsanctified streets beyond, the elastic straining at his back like a stiffening muscle, then so be it. He has already left his footsteps in all but the remotest parts of the city, and even here he has left his gaze.

Now he's down an alleyway, a gloomy rivulet between immense tower blocks, where the eagles are worn on the skin. A woman walks ahead of him, each strand of her yellow hair shining all the way to her waist. The colour floods Joseph's retina and stings the tip of his nose. Already he is working out how to suggest the silky texture. His fingertips twitch. He'll have to mix egg and beer with his paint.

The buildings brew a filthy dusk. The clouds are threadbare. There is a change in the air, like a gradual lifting of a lid, though it is the lid you can smell, not what's beneath.

Joseph approaches another decision. Left or right? Left is a blind corner, a tight turn under a brow of stone that's more a turret than a tenement. Right stretches past a playground, adjacent to a wire fence, before dwindling to darkness. With a grace in her walk that defies the gloom around her ankles – yes, her spirit gives her dignity and a lightness of gait – the woman goes right. Joseph watches the colour drain from her hair.

Then he turns left. To find himself among a gang of blocks. No season can recommend them. Cobbles peer through the last of the ice like punched-out eyes.

He speeds up. Perhaps a shape or a line will set everything in relief. Though the sky is not an ally.

Suddenly, he detects a movement. A silhouette with a lit tip for a tooth. His stubble chattering in the shadows, a man flicks his roll-up in the gutter. He turns his shaved head in the direction of the passer-by. He raises his nose as if to sniff.

Joseph cannot walk any quicker. His greatcoat feels like a carapace. His shoes may as well be buckets.

I'm not from round here.

Like a suspect in an identity parade, the man takes a step

forward. Joseph feels that step as a change in heartbeat. He hears the suck of trainers across the wet road.

Joseph looks to the semi-stripped trees ahead, their green barks proffered like throats. Pavement slabs rear at him, showing teeth of broken glass.

The blue tongues of the man's trainers are now at his side.

'*Spokój!*' says the man, in the local language, 'calm!' a word Joseph has already learned, a word that hisses and spits and promises anything but. The man raises his hands, palms down, to just above waist-height, like someone about to climb over a wall.

Buildings either side of the street stretch their necks for a better look.

'Please,' says the man. 'Excuse,' says the man.

His hands are still raised as if not knowing who will go off first. He has more nervous tics than the clock on a detonator.

What Joseph sees then makes him catch his breath. And struggle to release it. On the man's pockmarked face, running from just below the right eye to just above the chin, lies a curving scar.

'*Zehn Geld! Ich muss es haben!*' shouts the man, with a mouth that could bite its way out of a muzzle.

The shift in language has given Joseph the alibi of ignorance. The scar has levered him off his haunches. He shakes his head. He shrugs his shoulders. He shows his palms face-up by his sides.

The man switches back to the local language. He rattles like a tram. Words spark off him.

Stride for stride they walk on. They pass three anoraks drinking from dark bottles.

The man is shedding words. In Russian, in Polish, in

English, in German. As agitated as a nationalist who can't recall his nation. He mixes these words with melting ice, with lumps of gravel, with growls.

He is as formidable as a dockworker from Odessa, his head is serious cargo.

Like rats flushed from a drain, the two men emerge, scampering, past a tiny shop with a window display of empty bottles and toilet-rolls. Joseph crosses the road, heading for bus stops, kiosks, the first of the flower-sellers, navigating a route he hopes will take him back towards the ring-road.

But there is no nearby.

The man introduces his body for ballast. He bumps heavily against Joseph's shoulder. He thrusts his stony knuckles against Joseph's ribs.

'Shake hands!' he orders, his smile a scratch on a bone.

Joseph knows that to do so will leave him off-balance. But his assailant pulls him in. Joseph's fingers are squeezed from the palm, like a rubber-glove being filled with water.

Now their skulls are side by side. From a distance, they look like two drunks leaning on each other. Joseph feels eyes and lips and cheeks all aquiver beside him. For a moment, they breathe in each other's intentions. He smells of cemetery flowers, thinks Joseph, and roll-up cigarettes.

The sky is scraping itself in from the horizon. Shadows are made of dried blood.

Joseph slides his hand from the man's grip. Rehearsing the steps to safety, he strides on, looking ahead for brooding balconies, entrances unpeeled by daylight, odd corners and ice clots, the places where he could be sacked by his own shadow.

The man is even more insistent now. In Joseph's own language. 'You have ten money! Give!'

His face is a mess of expressions. His scar threatens to remember the gash.

'Shake hands!'

This time, Joseph merely taps the man's palm with his fingertips. The sky is swollen with unreleased rain, like blood trapped in a bruise. He feels as if he's carrying these clouds on his back. In the distance he can see the trees of the city gardens, all bandage and bone.

The man is sick of words that don't work. 'This country, *scheisse*! Your country, *scheisse*!' He pretends to be firing a machine gun. His skin is boiling on the bone. 'Iran!' he shouts, 'Iraq!' His laughter is the same as his fire.

Still the blue tongues match Joseph stride for stride. In his battered German the man insists they go to a banko-mat. When he says this word his face lights up as if he is suddenly carrying a block of gold.

Joseph pats his pockets, shakes his head. He crosses the street. The man follows. They are like two previously shackled convicts, one of whom refuses to accept they are no longer bound.

The ring-road is just ahead. Before that, there is a cash machine. Joseph sees it first. He steals a glance at the man. The man is looking at him. He has not yet seen the bankomat.

Dropping his right shoulder, Joseph dashes left. Two angry hands grab at his elbow. There is a scuffle. A slap. A push. Joseph slips on an icy step. He falls back and bangs his head against a wall. He manages to spin on his haunches and jump to his feet. Next moment, he's dodging car bumpers, horse shins, tram snouts.

'*Bis bald!*' shouts the man from the other side of the ring-road, a giant palm raised, his scarred face hoisted as if on the end of a bayonet. 'See you soon!'

Letters
23 September

My husband was waiting for me at the station when I came back from the conference. I saw him before he saw me. His eyes, intense and fearful, were looking up and down the platform trying to spot me in the flood of passengers. Did he really think I might not return?

He was wearing the clothes he knows I like best. His first words: 'How beautiful you are!'

We embraced. For the first time in a long time, for me, sincerely.

After a take-away pizza with cokes and traditional raw salad of cold carrot and cabbage, we talked. I was washing up, my husband drying. I told him that I couldn't prevent myself from falling in love with you. I told him that such a feeling had never happened to me before. Not in that way. I told him that the fear for me was coming back to a person I no longer loved. I told him it had been the greatest relief to find the feelings still there. My husband rubbed the tea-towel against knife and fork and plate as if trying to make them disappear.

He did not ask me the crucial question: what I feel for you now.

Later, during one of his brisk tidying sessions, he discovered a letter of yours. The one with the first batch of sketches you sent me. He paced the room. He read the letter. He paced the room again. (Not easy in such a small flat.) He looked for a pen. He couldn't find one. He took a crayon and a piece of scrap paper from Malena's drawing box. I had to restrain a laugh, because, at first, I thought he was going to try to outdraw you. He was very careful not to betray too much emotion. He sat at the table, smoothing out the paper. I heard him scratching a note. Then he stood up and handed me the page. I glimpsed only a sentence or two before he snatched it back, saying he was ashamed of himself because it was written in jealousy. I saw only the words: 'Now the end of any contact whatsoever with . . .' and 'You won't be the most important person in our relationship any more.'

Now I have told him everything, exactly as it happened, I feel less like a criminal. Even calm, with the interior silence you gain from a confession. Though I wonder if I confessed all I had to, or just what I wanted to. Either way, it is true what I told him. I do contain two loves in my heart. They do not exclude each other. They are of a different order. But when I am silent, and by myself, it is your eyes I see, Joseph.

11.30 p.m.
Another letter from you today. My husband carried it from the mail-box downstairs. He handed me the envelope with a wince, as if he had thought so hard about burning it that he had begun to feel the heat in his fingertips. But he is an honest man. He wouldn't do it. He did ask me, though, to keep your appearance in the flat to a minimum. He said he cannot ask me to stop the correspondence. He just does not want any letters under his nose.

Later, we talked again, after my husband had spent a few

minutes crushing the empty plastic spring-water bottles – something he often does when he needs to put his thoughts in order. This flat has never been so tidy.

When he had stacked up the flattened bottles and carefully slid them into plastic bags, he said he still couldn't understand why I had spent so much time with you. If I had known something might develop, why hadn't I stayed out of your way? I said if I had stopped seeing you, the feeling might have grown even stronger.

Then, the worst thing. He asked me what he should tell his mother. Can you imagine? I laughed, maliciously. 'Do you need to tell her anything?'

'But, Marta, she has already asked,' he said, his eyes now feeling the weight of maternal scrutiny. 'She has asked, "Is there somebody from England coming to see your wife?"'

25 September

It always seems to be midnight or dawn when I am talking to you. Is this the only place where we can meet? If so, does this make me bohemian? Or just busy? Definitely not bourgeois!

I've been listening to the CD given to me by my friends, Gary and Joanna (English husband, Polish wife). Joanna is funny. An intelligent academic but obsessed with fashion, whether clothes or music or film. Sometimes she talks loudly in English even when she is with Polish friends and her husband isn't there. Other times, she talks about American film directors, telling us that we're missing the point ('the references!') if we say we don't like their films. She keeps saying how exciting postmodernism is. When I offer the opinion that surely it's not all good, she tells me

I don't understand. Her flat is furnished in glass and pine. There are magazines stacked against every wall.

Yet she saves some disdain for her husband, too. We always speak English when Gary is present, because his Polish is not yet up to scratch. When they came round, Gary, at one point, very tactfully corrected Joanna's English.

'Gary,' she replied, nearly cutting her tongue with her sharp tone, 'I wouldn't consider you my language expert.'

Later on, she addressed him as 'my little husband'. OK, we Poles are big on diminutives, but this was cruel. I had to lose myself behind the CD case. I have never understood couples who humiliate each other in front of friends.

Later

Joseph, your last letter. You now send more pictures than words! Among the few you write, you ask, 'Why wait for what is certain?' This makes me sad. Are you trying to make me feel like a coward? I have already written to you of the complexity of my situation. Are you listening, or merely rushing round your country in search of the reasons for my delay?

I have learned to shape my waiting. This is an action in itself. Tell me, are you still planning to come before Christmas?

I do have a different life, Joseph. Not necessarily secret. Not necessarily underground. But it is another life. I remember it sometimes as if it has already happened. That's the strangest thing about it. It comes as a recollection.

You see, not only artists have retrospectives.

Recently, I was watching a film in English with Polish subtitles – an odd thing in itself, because there is usually a 'lektor', a man who reads all the parts in Polish. 'Okropna!' Dreadful! This dubbing-out of difference! Anyway, at one point in the film, a character said she was a feminist. This was translated in the Polish subtitle as 'man-hater'! Can you believe it? That's what the majority here thinks of feminists! (By the way, I am not a feminist. I don't need a label. But of course I demand equal rights and opportunities for women.)

Maybe the translator's backward ideas are not surprising when you consider that under Stalin and after, women were encouraged (just about ordered) to have babies 'for the nation'. 'O Matko Polką!' They were deemed 'Heroic Mothers' if they had more than ten children. More than ten? That's not heroic, that's super-human! They received a medal for their, ahem, labours. As did the mothers who pushed out seven to nine. They were awarded the 'Order of Maternal Glory', shortly after being stitched up and told to go and make another one. Women who didn't see their lives in terms of having babies were labelled 'unreliable' workers or 'bad' mothers or 'inattentive' wives.

Of course, I would have qualified as all three.

I know one thing, though: the world is made by mothers!

And my mother was heroic for putting up with my father. Now she often sleeps during the day. Just to have her own space. To be out of his way. But her skin never gets lighter beneath the eyes. Her smile is rarer and losing its sides. I only see it when she is with Malena now. Or occasionally when my husband makes one of his jokes. She has always liked my husband. Such an ordinary man compared to the tyrant she's bound to. I wonder where her secret life takes her. Where does she go to be herself apart from the sanatorium, the hospital, her bed? Where can a person go? Of course, for those like my mother who believe, it is still church. But for those who don't. Or who aren't sure. Where do they go?

This is what Edith Stein considered in her essay, 'Woman's Significance in Contemporary Life'. She believed women should go beyond house and cloister. Beyond husband and hearth. To find 'breathing spaces', the time and space to return to themselves.

But where?

Under communism most people had a job, though this might have been counting leaves or passing cars, as my mother tells me. Women, too. The ones not racking up medals for maternity, that is. Now, as the money comes in from the West, the majority of entrepreneurs are men. Many women are back to menial jobs, extended motherhoods, or low-paid jobs like teaching. Sexism is rampant. Television adverts show naked women in the shower, or mothers waiting for the return of their husbands while cooking and cleaning and looking after the children. Welcome to the 1950s! No wonder so many women are planning to go and work in America or the UK.

Monika's husband grins like a pawnbroker when he sets his briefcase on the kitchen table. After unclipping the catch, he flings open the lid and grabs a pile of notes in his stubby fingers. Then he counts out the housekeeping in front of her nose. He hands her the dirty notes as if she was some kind of navvy. I saw it once. He did it in front of my nose, too. In front of a guest! I remember the inky smell of those notes. Plus his aftershave. A proper little businessman. And with the kind of bright blue eyes that always make me suspicious. Like polished metal, they record something only if it moves.

This country has survived fascism then communism. I'll be damned if we're going to put up with male chauvinism. I won't let it happen!

After all, haven't we had enough of brotherhoods? The Nazis claimed a brotherhood:

'If you don't want my brotherhood
I'll smash your skull and smash it good'

– an SS chant in the death camps. Then, of course, communism tortured and killed in pursuit of a 'brotherhood of man'. Elsewhere, in other times, a cry of 'fraternité ou la mort!' Funny, too, how a language secretes an ideology. For example, we have the phrase 'język ojciec' – translated as 'mother tongue' but literally, in our language, it is father tongue. Whereas for soulmate, we have 'bratniej duszy' – literally, 'brotherly spirit'.

Boże mój! We have had enough of brotherhoods!

(Besides, please remember Europa was a woman, a Phoenician princess, abducted and raped by the Cretan, Minos. Perhaps things haven't changed that much, after all.)

Earlier, I was looking at your latest words and pictures. I knew it would not be wise to leave them on my desk. So I put them out of sight. When I went to the balcony to hang out the washing, I heard the key in the door. It was my husband. He had gone to the bank but forgotten his ID. (You need to provide ID here wherever you go.)

He went to the chest of drawers and rummaged. With increasing agitation. Until he pulled one drawer clean out. (He caught it across his arm.) I saw his shoulders hunch. He fiddled with the collar of his rain-jacket, in the process folding only half of it down. Beads of sweat ran down his

forehead. For once, he didn't care about his muddy footprints.

When I asked him what was wrong, he answered that he
was just anxious about losing his ID. But no, he hadn't lost
it, there it was.

When he left, I saw the photo of me and you and Malena
on the beach that you sent with your last letter. It was on
top of the chest of drawers in which he'd been looking.
I'd forgotten to hide it away, after all.

Later

My life is all tangled up. I have a feeling my husband has
also seen the notebook in which I am writing this letter to
you.

Yesterday he was telling me about his plans for the flat.
All of a sudden he said, with a little bit of anger, 'But you
don't care at all, do you?'

And this morning, Malena wanted to get to the bathroom. She doesn't usually respect anyone's privacy. My
husband was in the bath. Instead of walking straight in,
I mechanically pressed the light-switch (which is on the
outside), wanting to switch the light on, but instead switched
it off.

'I played a little game,' said my husband. 'I thought that
if the light goes off, it will tell me for sure that you came
back only to finish your book.'

19

A Minor Apocalypse

There is no arguing with concussion. Even if Joseph doesn't believe he needs his head examining at the military hospital in Nowa Huta, it still feels like someone has given his bell a bloody good ring, or whacked him on the bonce with one of pani Stasia's copper-plated pots. And right at the point where the skull curves towards the neck, where a caressing hand would suspend the world in loving contemplation.

Strangely, though, he carries with him a sense of calm and sleepwalk: street-lights as night-lights, buildings as scenery, blue horses for riding in a well-designed dream. The whole of life is singing softly round his skull. The blood swimming in the bruise makes his eyeballs vibrate at a different intensity, allowing him to glimpse his limits, his own extent, the space he takes up in the world. Yes, he feels he's closer than ever to figuring the relations between this city of cellars and his own subterranean self, and to trembling with the tension between the two, the tension that will prevent his vision from bursting like a watermelon beneath a horse's hoof.

When it comes to work, he will not rest. He must make the most of this movement towards clarity – if that's what it is. Lately, he's been scavenging from the skips that are appearing in the streets as landlords renovate their flats for the hordes soon to swoop from the West. Rummaging for a rough surface, he brushes off lumps of bird shit and ice to inspect shelves, cabinets, drawers, window-frames, doors, the thin backing of dressers, the panels of chunky sideboards and sofas, the slats from old parquet floors – all those forgotten feet! – lacquered wood, brown wood, dead wood – a history of communist furniture in a single skip. Wondering if Eric has already snatched the radiators, he grabs a hubcap for a mixing-dish, but leaves the fixtures and statuettes – a miner, a ballerina, a Lenin bust – to the old man who ties his clanking assortment to the rusty wheels of a pram.

Then he gets to work, manic with charcoal, as if rubbing for relief, his latest idea now growing beyond his head, while he tries to figure out if this city is losing its identity or coming-into-being, and he has to fight to get the image to his fingertips, so he leaves his preparatory sketches in the body of a work to keep the piece tentative, and flourishing, so it doesn't dry into conformity, or leave itself vulnerable to a single interpretation. He throws paint, then the brush, sometimes strangling the picture into a new perspective, so the wood or cardboard or canvas is no longer flat but warped, even corrugated. (He refers to his clutter of surfaces as his 'boards', relishing the suggestion of movement, performance, fight.)

Living on a diet of chocolate and fish, he eats while working to the rhythm of hooves and heels and chatter from the street, and to the bells from the church tower, or to pigeons at dusk that sound like they are calling to each other from inside a watering-can, or he listens to the gentle hammering from the kitchen of the flat next door as the wife prepares another cutlet for her husband's evening meal, or else it's Górecki or Preisner or Szymanowski oozing from the radio like oil in the dark. He often tilts his head as if expecting Marta to enter and speak, as if still working to the pulse of her breathing by his side, for hasn't he always believed in working with someone, in collaboration, in dialogue, as Marta herself would call it, and if not with someone, then with a place for he believes that such grand notions as truth and beauty and goodness can only be glimpsed when many heads come together and find a form in which these visions can be held.

As he works, he gulps from mugs of black coffee, his nerves vibrating like the strings of a cabaret violin. In the evening, he might have a bottle of beer, or hack open a tin, cold-spooning peach slices between his teeth, or a jar of corn and pea salad, and he'll work through the cries of the last drunk in the street to the first pigeon to bring the morning to his sill, and only then will he collapse on his pillowless mattress and sleep the dreamless sleep of the drained. Some evenings he races down to the Georgian restaurant opposite, where he orders a *Lawasz* pancake stuffed with vegetables and a creamy garlic sauce, which he then hurries back across the freezing street, like a hot brick wrapped in a blanket, his muddy footprints chasing him up the stairwell, the skylight spattered with pigeon shit and stars. Afterwards, he lights a cigarette to stop the trembling, or to increase it, often forgetting to smoke, or he presses the stub on the canvas, with the help of molten wax.

He knows it is going well. His muscles have tightened round his vision: yes, of something vulnerable yet indestructible that might suggest the spirit. He took some rubbish down to the bins just to snarl at the courtyard cats.

When he stops working, everything changes. The first hour is the most dangerous. He is still lucid, but defenceless. He tries to withdraw his heightened senses. Or pacify them. Instead, they turn inwards. Unfinished works taunt him. Unstarted works hail him. Loneliness creeps up his limbs. Plus a yearning for green landscapes and bigger skies. A key in the ignition. A voice he understands. He has pangs of wanting to drink himself into a ditch. He lights a cigarette to soften the solitude. But then immediately puts it out. He can't get still. He is teased by different forms. Like all the shapes made by the candle-wax congealing round the room. In need of voices, he retunes the radio. He finds a station called Radio Maryja. There are hymns and carols and patriotic songs, and sermons he doesn't like the sound of.

He lies down. He tries to sleep. He sees a vision of himself, alone in bed, trembling for her touch.

So he springs up, disturbing rough sketches and Marta's letters strewn across the duvet. He grabs his greatcoat and boots and keys and once again disappears down the darkness of the stairwell. Back on the streets, he can re-engage his senses. Point them outwards. Empty his head of big fruit.

It's not quite so cold. Just as well. He has forgotten his gloves. His fingers carry spots of yellow paint and the sneer of a squashed tomato. A gentle throbbing remains in the back of his head, as if his heart and brain have merged.

That evening, he sees a figure hunched on a bench in the city gardens, opposite the conservatory of an upmarket café. He is surprised to discover that Eric also exists by daylight – though it is very nearly dusk. His friend sits beneath the reaching boughs of a tree. From a distance, these boughs look more like trailing roots, as if the tree is upside down.

'You waiting for someone?' says Joseph, grateful to see a human form other than his own.

'*Jestem allein*,' says Eric. 'Sorry. *Ich bin samy*. Sorry, sorry,' he says, a palm running over his head. 'I'm alone!'

Joseph offers him a cigarette. Both of Eric's hands descend upon the packet.

The sky is a patchwork of puddle-stained feathers. Joseph asks after Eric's girlfriend. But Eric does not seem to hear. His palms flutter down as if they have fallen from the tree. After taking three big drags, pushing out cheeks as worn as leather patches, he knocks the glowing ash from his cigarette, then he puts the unsmoked half in his pocket.

'I met my wife there,' he says pointing to the yellow glass of the café, behind which the silhouettes are cut from velvet. He jerks his head. His boots kick up black water. 'Sorry!' he says. 'Ex-wife!'

Night is now gathering quickly in the upper branches. It will soon be too cold to remain. Joseph asks Eric if he took little Jan the burgundy violin. With tiny, rapid movements, Eric's body answers the question using all of its parts, except the mouth.

Joseph knows better than to press him.

Suddenly Eric springs from the bench as if he's taken a pin to the arse. '*Kurwa!*' he shouts, rolling the 'r' to such an extent that the word turns round in his mouth. Both hands dive into the right-hand pocket of his coat. He plucks out his smouldering exercise book. He hadn't extinguished his cigarette properly. Pages float away, mocking his panic of palms. He tugs off his hat and wafts it about furiously, though nowhere near the book.

'It's not just winter you have to live through,' he says, when seated again, a minor apocalypse averted. 'It's your life!' Shortly afterwards, with a smile that simply lies across the dried skin of his face, he announces he has to be on his way. He has a lesson to give. They agree to meet later in the week. Joseph watches the sheepskin fade between the trees, a thin ribbon of smoke still trailing from the pocket.

Letters
27 September

Distractions? Integrity? Gap between life and dream? (A gap surely wide enough for most of us to fall through.) My life is now a memory of something absolutely essential but evasive. I wake from my afternoon siesta with a taste on my tongue. Before I can even structure this sensation, I know it is about being with you.

Now bubbling in the kitchen, a soup of onions and potatoes and carrots. A good autumn soup that packs everything in. 'Too watery!' you would complain, before spooning it down like a man unsure whether he is hungry or thirsty.

By the way, did I tell you Edith Stein was, for a time, Husserl's secretary? He was her mentor in the study of the spirit. On his death-bed, Husserl shouted out his last words, 'Oh! I have seen something so wonderful. Quick, write it down!'

Joseph! I'm bursting! I know a space will clear for me soon. For my book. And for my words to you. My beloved daughter fills my life to the brim, but soon she will start with a childminder. As the proverb goes, 'The wolf will be satisfied, and the sheep alive.'

Yesterday, even my husband conceded that he is expecting

you to visit. We were looking at furniture to replace the old communist-issue tables and chairs that we have put up with for so long. We were looking at a modern armchair (and bed), quite painfully – for me – expensive. My husband said, 'If pan Joseph comes, he should have a nice bed to sleep on.' I said that you would like to come and that perhaps you'd stay at my great-aunt's old place – which the council finally let us buy; we rent to a student. My husband did not protest.

I'll be working at home today. Later, I will drink some Arabic coffee in a new café where they give you a little pot on a small blue flame. These blue flames at each table provide the only light.

Joseph, no one has taken anything away.

Your smile! I always liked its complexity. It was usually affection mixed with a little bit of naughtiness. Sincerity underpinned with cynicism.

Perhaps I find meaning now that I didn't find then. But isn't that how meaning arrives? Belatedly, but hopefully not too late!

Faith keeps this meaning resonating.

1 October

Joseph, I wasn't at all angry with you on the phone today. Just unhappy. I have made a few resolutions. I can't be unfair to my husband in my letters to you. I see clearly that I have been scapegoating him. Otherwise it was too difficult for me to understand what happened. This is my explanation. The way I see it now.

The time of my research trip to your country coincided

with Malena reaching the age when I stopped being absolutely indispensable to her, in physical terms at least. It felt
like my body was my own again. My breasts no longer
cried for. My nipples no longer sore. I started to relax after
the hectic, tiresome but, yes, wonderful time of early
motherhood. This is when I came to the city where you
were staying. Before then, I had planned everything with
my husband, now I had to organise everything on my own.
I felt free. I began to ask myself, 'Shouldn't I be missing
him a little more?' For the first few weeks, my phone calls
to him were happy, affectionate, if slightly matter-of-fact.
I did not think of writing.

Then I met you. I looked into you, deeply, as you did
into me. We first met in a car, on a trip organised by a
mutual friend. You in the front, in the passenger seat. Me
in the back with my daughter. We talked as if picking up
an old conversation. We couldn't hide our smiles. Nor did
we want to. You kept turning round and the light in your
eyes lifted me. Even from that very first meeting, I was
thinking of stroking your arms, of holding your hand, of
somehow linking our smiles.

After four months of us being together, including four
weeks of being apart, I wonder how guilty I am of being
indulgent. Our times were heady, and of the heart. 'Love is
energy' as Tolstoy wrote in 'Anna Karenina'. But it is not
always energy going in the right direction. (As that book
proves.) Or energy that is employed for the benefit of
others. Where there is love, someone gets hurt. Whether
a person within the relationship, or someone alongside it.
A simple truth.

Now I have realised that in my letters I have occasionally

diminished my husband. His sensitivity is immense, his will to understand great. Yet the things he and I enjoyed together before my trip, the little everyday excursions and chores, now seem distant to me.

In the end, we bought a bed for Malena. A fold-out settee. Very simple and nice. My husband said he was sorry for enjoying such unimportant things. He said this without bitterness or irony. These things mean a family to him, whereas I saw only a piece of furniture.

You know what the most painful realisation is for me now? I lost my happiness, my home life, of my own volition. You are my discovery, but I can't have you, nor my husband. Not as I used to. Not as it was. At least, not yet. That's why I'd like to go away by myself for a while. (My husband was appalled when I told him this.) I might go to the mountains, where the air is fresh and the sky so wide that it is difficult not to feel the wonder of life, even in autumn. Especially in autumn.

What is it you say sometimes? 'Life is simple, people are not.' Of course, I agree. In the mountains, alone, I could open up like a fir-cone after a storm. Learn from what has happened. Grow the strength to face the day-to-day of life all over again. And rediscover simplicity.

Later

My moods swing from elation to inconsolable sadness. From patience and understanding to irritation and confusion. I am healthy because of my daughter. She tries to ask questions, and with impossibly exaggerated expressions – she thinks that if she finds the right face then the right word will follow. Her favourite expression is earnestness, plus sticky lips.

You once said that in such a volatile world we should act according to our joy. Be together. Overcome circumstances. And as soon as possible. But I wonder, Joseph, if in such a volatile world it is best to nurture what you have already chosen, for in acting differently, in breaking away, aren't we just adding to all the uncertainty?

I'll be finishing,

20

A Person from the Back

When Joseph arrives at the large municipal building that doubles as a cinema, he makes his way along corridors of black tiles and full ashtrays – all those forgotten fingers! He wonders if the dust of democracy has really found its way through such a heavy portal.

The previous day his nerves had flared like sparklers when he saw a poster for a silent-film festival, including – could it be true? – a Lya de Putti film. His heart scattered in all directions, like the bucket of chicken hearts he saw in a local butcher's and which he imagined flinging across the ice.

That night, he couldn't get still. He felt he was trying to get to sleep on an opening and closing door. In the small hours that often yawn to belie their slenderness, he got up and lit two gas-rings, their blue flames the lashes he looked through. He warmed some milk, wrapping his fingers round the ceramic mug he'd bought at the student show in Marta's city. He heard every single shoe in the street. Every whisper in the stairwell. Every breathing in-and-out of the building. Every water pipe, door key, clock. Plus, the usual footsteps in the attic pacing out their plight. Even the moon he could hear, moving across the sky like a ball through wet grass.

Now, on the second floor of a building that has all but disappeared in the dark, he finds a large room with wooden benches arranged in front of a pull-down screen. Six people are huddled in their coats as if sitting at a tram stop. There is no heating in the building in the evening.

Joseph takes a seat at the back, alongside a red-haired woman at a small table with a lamp and an old-fashioned microphone, like one of those used for early radio broadcasts. The woman has just started to read, in Polish, a translation of the word-boards between the scenes originally in Czech. The production itself is German.

O Europa! sings Joseph to himself.

In the film, Lya de Putti plays Bertha, a lovelorn circus acrobat who, despite the vitality demanded by her vocation, is often being put to bed. In one scene, she stands on a table looking like an overweight child in a white outfit comparable to body thermals. Or bandages. She is round-shouldered and full of sulk. In another episode, she dances in enormous heels and a glittering gown, rising and falling in a rapid dance as if trying to fill the length of her dress. She moves like an image from a flick-book.

And how she smokes! From an ivory cigarette-holder, she smokes. Exhaling through her nostrils, she smokes. Seductively, she smokes. With the light of devil-may-care in her eyes, she smokes.

Joseph is surprised by how many shots there are of Lya from behind. Yes, he decides, a back is more expressive than you may think: why are you turned away from me like that? What are you concealing from me? Or from yourself? And do you know you have a bump on the back of your head?

Lya's bobbed hair curls inwards just above the nape.

Joseph knows the nape will always set him dreaming. Isn't this the most tender part of a person? Not only because of its delicacy – its tantalisng blend of tough skin and sensitivity – but because another's touch is needed to bring your nape to life. Despite himself, Joseph thinks of Marta. She has such a long and graceful neck, as if it's always rising from water. A nape upon which he liked to play his lips, as if composing a lullaby on a harmonica.

He stamps a foot for his sentimentality. Then he takes a quick look round to see if anyone noticed.

In silent films, it is all in the eyes. One moment Lya sticks up her lashes with childlike incredulity, the next she is doleful to the depths, her tears as thick as drops of honey. Her eyes are so dark, notes Joseph, that you'd have to take a walk in the woods during a particularly heavy rainfall to find a corresponding colour.

In another scene, Lya jumps on the back of a departing lover, her big hands in a desperate clutch, her head flung back. (Because despair, while pleading one way, often flies the other.) As her dapper ex-suitor strides away, Lya slides from his shoulders to his waist, her bared teeth registering a click on each of his vertebrae. She continues to slide, scratching at his hamstrings with her nails, perhaps accompanied by someone doing the same to a double bass or cello. Her departing paramour drags her along the carpet. He tries to flick her off. Down by his ankles, Lya finally lets go. She beats the carpet with her fists. Soon after, she opens her mouth for a scream made more terrifying by the absence of sound and the close-up of a larynx as big as a punch-bag. Then she throws herself down the stairs, but fails to fling herself free of despair so she cries giant tears, smashes glasses, and, in a later wine-drinking scene, sucks the goblet dry in a single gulp, looking very much like a woman who knows how to put away the booze.

'Nobody marries women like that,' says one board, according to Joseph's rough interpretation of the woman's whispered Polish. He is saddened by a sense that the Lya on screen was all too close to the Lya in life.

Towards the end of the film, without warning, the on-screen word-boards, until then in Czech, transform themselves into Dutch. There are a few giggles from the women on the benches in front. That's to say, Joseph thinks they are giggling. Perhaps they are sobbing quietly, for the film has started to unravel its bleak denouement. It is difficult to tell from behind, he concedes, looking at the backs of the women, their shoulders twitching gently in the dark.

Letters
5 October

I must remember to rip the page from the calendar. I'm still on September. I don't have time to keep up with time! A very nice calendar of Witkacy's portraits of women. Underground women? 'Pewne jak amen w pacierzu' – that's as certain as amen at the end of a prayer. These women are muses, hostesses, lovers, models, aristocrats dedicated to their own dissolution. And to patronising painters with gold coins and sneers. Watch out! All smoke and bandanas, they are seductive. And morose. Those big, unblinking eyes!

Witkacy was one of our leading avant-garde artists: he wrote plays and novels, painted, directed. He often marked his canvases to indicate the influences he was under at the time of composition: alcohol, cigarettes, cocaine. But never family, history, country! I should say avant-guerre not avant-garde. For having fought in the First World War, he could not cope with the outbreak of the second. When the Germans invaded, he fled east. Days later, the Russians invaded. Witkacy and his lover were in a field beneath the stars when he took his fatal overdose.

October shows Nena Stachurska. Big blue eyes, thin red lips, a pout that is not far off a bite. She is like a squirrel, all eyes and almost no body.

Joseph, listen, I have moments during the day when I am desperately sad. I know it is easy to say 'come!' But I am frightened. Not of seeing you, but of facing life which is so changed now. I am living in hope, but I don't see any solution. Only fantasies of an illness, of some miracle or cataclysm.

But I am not resigned. I'm waiting for the right moment to act. In what way, I don't yet know. Yesterday I tried to convince myself that I should be afraid of you. It did not work. I am afraid only of myself. Of doubts, guilt, longings.

19 October

There's still no central heating or hot water here. I think this is a tribute to a past era (only a few years ago) when everything broke down every couple of days. And there were frequent strikes. Half my childhood was lived by candlelight. Which did not make it in any way romantic. Funny, though, because a lighted candle in the window was a way of showing your support for Solidarność. Yet the secret police couldn't arrest you because you could blame it on the power cuts!

So here I am sitting in the cold and damp, warming myself up with these words to you. It was a quiet weekend.

Colourless. Malena fell asleep for more than three hours after her friend had been round.

Joseph, I'm not playing nostalgia by missing you. I want you here. I want to show you to the world. Also, as I once said, having discovered you, I want to discover something for you. And with you. A city, a book of pictures, a secret place. I don't want to be looking round in the street to check no one sees us together. I don't quite like this underground existence. And I am underground. There I have my freedom. And you.

1 November

The day to honour our dead. The tram to the cemetery was packed. Every face hovered over a bundle of blooms, mainly chrysanthemums – and they're always gloomy, aren't they? Like today, All Souls' is usually dark and damp. Between the headstones and trees, thousands of candles burn in coloured pots. A smell of leaf-mould and wax. And flowers too sweet for darkness.

At the entrance to the cemetery, there are stalls selling candles, pots, flowers, chocolates, bags of nut toffee, as well as trinkets to adorn the graves. Beggars, often amputees from the East, sit at the gates.

From the chapel in the cemetery, amplified by hidden speakers, a priest recites the names of the dead. Shadows move solemnly along the narrow paths, a sound of brushing anoraks. Occasionally a hidden congregation repeats a verse, or sings another 'Amen'.

I went with my husband. We visited the graves of his family. And then mine. Each one was already consoled by about twenty candles in pots of orange or red and green – like a flame in an inkwell. I kept looking up to see a whole landscape flickering in these colours. And to hear the ongoing list of the dead.

The candles send out many strange shadows. Flowers become giant trembling stalks with almost human heads. Families become three generations of wobbly caricatures, warming themselves with the smell of burning oil. Stone angels open their wings and take flight. Some graves are monumental, a mini-chapel, others have a simple cross. Some are well tended and loaded with light, others are visited by a single candle that has already gone out.

In the dark and cold, all these trees and people and candles. The smell of lives and flames extinguished. A mist of damp and smoke. The mournful poem of the list of the dead. It is difficult not to feel your own mortality.

My husband took my hand.

It was on 1 November 1925 that Lya was found on the pavement beneath her first-floor flat in Berlin. This time she didn't try to jump through a window, she 'fell' from the balcony. It happened soon after the meeting with her mother, the Countess, in Dresden. All Souls' Day must have been a painful reminder of the family she'd left behind. Apparently, Lya escaped with only bruises due to a thick covering of snow, though this sounds a little fanciful to me. Neighbours said she'd been shouting at her lover from the balcony, begging him not to leave. Each departure must have reminded her of her own. Must have brought back all the guilt and pain. She demanded that her lovers stand between her and her past.

Yet 1925 was Lya's most successful year as an actress, the height of her fame.

Ps Also living on Lya's street at the time, a scientist by the name of Albert Einstein.

Pps People are afraid of being left alone, whereas hiding in solitude usually brings about apathy. Or anger. Most of us are capable of all kinds of feelings, from good intentions to wicked motives, but you can't survive left only to yourself. Don't take on the whole world, Joseph. There's too much of it. And too many people looking for a fight.

21

A Coatstand Away from
A Floating Dream

He must have pulled up gravestones to get here, for a smell of moss and soil and stone hovers about his fingers. Inside, the rooms are the yellow of ageing ivory. The walls slope and curve as if rendered by a lunatic. The floors rear like the deck of a troubled ship. The candles on each table stand at an odd angle as if stuck on by someone about to fall over.

Despite his recent knock to the head, Joseph does not lose balance. He is more concerned with a series of small wooden doors. He presses a cold spoon-latch with his thumb, but it does not give. Instead, his fingers find velvet curtains, like a hanging tapestry with tassels. Drawing one aside, he steps through, to see the giant shadow of a smoking hand. He has never seen such an intricate shadow, the little spirals of smoke faithfully reproduced like curlicues in lace. There's an unoccupied table in the corner, though, of course, it's not a proper corner, it's a collusion of walls, a casual meeting of angles (like the meeting of two raised beer glasses), giving him the chance to recede into a soft patch of shadows. He unbuckles the belt round his great-coat. A wisp of purple dust lights up his lapel, like the first flower of spring. In the corner, he can wait for Eric.

Nearby sit two identical women with ash-grey hair. Such

is their pallor, they look like they've been rescued from the same plot. Their gentle chatter strokes the heavy walls with feathers. Joseph is grateful for this, his sleepless ears having been battered like bin lids each night by street oaths and sirens and screams.

In the room – a competition of nicotine and mauve that both are too worn out to win – Joseph notices a mirror with a gilt frame. He wonders why smoke reflected in glass always assumes a face. His hands are fidgeting. His fingers are brush hairs and nerve ends, both still trembling for the refuge of paint. It's his first trip to a bar since he became immersed in his work again. He feels about as real as one of these shadows, only not so well attached.

On the way here, trained by a season of snow, he'd lifted his feet like a horse in dressage. Apprehensive of the faces he passed, for the words they might say, for the looks they might give, he'd tucked his face deep between lapels that flapped like elephant's ears. The clouds were patched up. The roads could not drain themselves of dirt. Every sound made him flinch in a different part of his body, until he wondered if it was the city or his work that had stripped him of his self-assurance.

Looking round the underground room, he sees more shadows: of heads, of noses, of bouffants, plus a huge pair of eyelashes that, when closing, look like giant cymbals (though mercifully silent). It's as if people hand in their corporeal selves at the cloakroom, leaving their souls and shadows free to drink and smoke and natter, and they seem to be having quite a good time trembling in and out of focus, depending on the feverishness of the conversation taking place around the flame.

But no, thinks Joseph, let's not be hasty to enter the

spirit world, for the candle also does a good job picking out gold crowns and rotten teeth, as well as the sachet of liquid in which an eyeball sits. Smoke hovers about the group, braceleting wrists and necks, and stretching across the table, a safety net for their spittle. Just to make sure, Joseph checks hair and nails for signs of post-mortem growth, but again he is reassured. Yes, these people are smart, if somewhat dowdy, in clothes preserved from previous decades, fifties and eighties especially, he notes, perhaps the clothes of their parents, a sartorial incest, an outward fashioning of unfortunate genes. That goes for the hair-dos, too: those beehives and barnets! He smiles to imagine the shadow of pani Grażyna's hair.

However, such is the chill air down in these chambers (enough to make your teeth scratch but not chatter), that when he lights a cigarette, Joseph cups his hands as if he were standing at a bus stop on a windy October morning by the sea. He orders a beer. It arrives quickly – though, thankfully, not of its own accord.

Still no sign of Eric.

While admiring the shadow of the curving prongs of the coatstand – six bass clefs gone berserk – Joseph tries to listen to the conversation, all whispers and wool to the ears. In addition to this country's curses, which he can now conjugate in order of severity – *kurcze, kurde, kurwa* (chicken, shit, whore) – he has picked up words from beggars' quips, from counter-girls and waitresses, from the woman in the street with the swinging arm, from the busker with a 5-string guitar singing Solidarność songs, from poems and papers, his word-cards, his lessons by proxy in Café Prowincja, and a dictionary he daily torments with his thumb. He is no longer living in infinitives. He can conjugate 'to be' and the first- and second-person forms of several other verbs, and he wonders if this is what makes a person European: to be able to say '*Jestem*' – 'I am' – in a language of the continent other than your own. And to go further. To love someone in a language other than your own. Like the young couple he'd met in a Ukrainian restaurant (a nice trout with a pout served by waitresses in traditional folk costumes): he was Finnish (not the trout, the man he met), his girlfriend was German, and they communicated with each other in Russian, and with Joseph in English.

Also, his next lesson by proxy will start on the past tense.

Despite his steady progress, however, words overheard in his own language still reach him like a rush of ice through the blood. However much he'd like to resist. Today, for example, he heard a young woman say in English, and with a lovely lilt to her vowels as if they were all facing skywards, 'There are words in Łodz that don't exist in any other city'. And, despite himself, Joseph wondered what those words might be. Later, he heard a middle-aged man say, 'Everyone's outside, let's go inside,' and Joseph, though trying to send these sounds back out through his ears, couldn't help but consider this a philosophical insight worthy of future attention.

Now, in the bar that's more like a house that's been buried alive – yes, the walls are boarded-up soil – there is a rush of copper rings along the curtain rail. It must be Eric, at last. But no, there is no sign of a sheepskin or a tumbling hand. Instead the velvet drapes divulge a young couple. Their eyes scour the room for a corner in which to conceal themselves. The only remaining seats are the two wooden chairs at Joseph's table. Having asked after their availability – while looking at each other – the couple sit down.

With his eyelids now moths batting about the flame, Joseph observes them. She is in her early twenties, pale as a November sky, with an expression that suggests life is tense and if it had been up to her in the first place then she probably wouldn't have bothered. Yes, he thinks, her face is impatient for change, tight round the lips, as if she is trying to hide her teeth, while also straining for a resolution she does not yet possess. She has cheekbones to deal with the easterly winds, cheekbones he would render using melting wax. There are smoker's gulps beneath her eyes. Smoker's gulps? Yes, those dark pockets made of caffeine and nicotine and night, in which a body gathers up its deficit.

In silence, her face unbroken by speech, she is pretty, but as soon as she opens her mouth, her teeth stretch from cheek to cheek, forming a row of turrets. It's a funny face, as if put together in jest, only for her features to have made a last-ditch dash for beauty. Her hair, meanwhile, is a calamity of curls in dark brown, as if she has only just extricated herself, lock by lock, from her latest passionate engagement. Yes, she has the melancholic's air of absence and intensity.

At that age where you associate cigarettes with sensitivity and the decent prospect of a premature death – if only because nothingness seems much more desireable than middle-age – she smokes Virginia Slims, long and white and smooth to the fingers, like a phantom digit for beckoning lovers in the dark. She smokes almost continuously, confirming the link between her and the insecurity she carries inside, like an undiagnosed illness she wants to keep to herself. She holds these cigarettes in such a way that it looks as though it's her ear that's smoking. When she takes off her stylish winter-coat (gathered at the waist, narrow lapels), she steps as if from a fold in the night sky. Often, she looks sideways at Joseph.

The guy with her has a face like over-rolled pastry, a long ponytail in an elastic band, light brown corduroys with radiator-ribs, a leather jacket beneath his not-so-stylish winter-coat (big at shoulders, flared at hem). Totally in thrall to this enigmatic beauty, he frequently leans over to kiss her, despite the smoke being blown in his face.

When the man-with-the-mane goes to the toilet, the girl looks directly at Joseph.

'*Deutsch?*' she says. '*Italiano?*'

Joseph shakes his head.

'From whereabouts?' she says.

In a room both curving and crepuscular, Joseph is not sure if it's the place for geographical certainties. He pictures the maps he'd studied in the antiquarian bookshop, a dot marking a specific city – how many lives that dot conceals! He looks to the wall behind the questioner. The shadows are shifting continents. Or the wings of fledgling nations.

He says the name of his street.

She shakes her head. A watery smile.

He says the name of this city.

She shakes her head. Sucks in her teeth.

So he tells her where he is from. No, not where he's from. How do you say where you're from? Especially when he's lived in so many places. And for such short periods of time. He simply tells her where he was born.

'But my birth certificate is slowly expiring!' he adds.

The girl puffs out a cloud of smoke, this one darkened by her disdain.

'I pity you,' she says, 'for coming from Imperialist country.'

Letters
3 November
Today you told me again that you will come here before Christmas. That you might sell your car. Is it true? Time is running out. Or running away. Are you not exhausted from racing round like a man in search of a homeland? Really. You had better not be teasing me. My heartbeat quickens when I think of you here.

On 3 November 1919, the Rumanian army, led by General Marderescu, stormed across the River Tisza into Budapest. And where was Lya? Wasn't she in that city? Yes, she was performing a dance called 'Migrating Swallows' at the Royal Orpheum, a theatre well known for naughty operettas, featuring fresh-faced soubrettes from the provinces. Apparently, the dark pink interior was perfect for secret liaisons between concubines and counts, society ladies and acrobats, chorus girls and government officials. You could say that at the Orpheum, plenty of groping took place beneath the gilt.

Of course, that week there was a tension that the crumbling yellow stucco could barely absorb. Coughs rattled ribs in the private boxes, opera glasses were dropped in the stalls, prompting a flurry of hands among sweet-wrappers, cherry stones, melon rinds, and the butts of fake Egyptian cigarettes. Especially when Mr Somosy, the owner, let it be known that General Marderescu was in attendance. Whispers circulated as quickly as a bag of fresh plums.

Lya – or Amalia as she was then known – was accompanied by Red Elek, the gypsy bandleader. With her hands pointing to midnight, and clasped together as if in prayer, she swooped to grab her skirts, her spine doubling up like the Danube bend, her bright red fingernails disappearing in the dark tresses of her costume. Then she'd stamp her foot and throw out her layers with a swallow's shrill cry, before flinging herself into dizzying spirals, her small wooden beads in orbit about her head. Kicking out her legs, she leapt and leapt again, her naked heels landing with a thump against the boards. When she threw off her bright red headscarf, her black hair shone like vinyl in the stage-lights, offering more curls than a sky of crescent moons. Her body glistened with greasepaint and sweat. Her powdered breasts and thighs flashed as her garments gaped. Then, with a final cry, and a tragic leap, she threw herself to the floor.

A week earlier, in new silver slippers, Amalia had walked the plush carpet of the Soviet House. As she stood beneath the mirrored chandelier, she was approached by a pageboy in a midnight-blue uniform.

'Malika! Malika!' he said, using the friendly diminutive.

'Laszlo, how handsome you look in your new uniform!'

Laszlo felt like a boy in his buttons. Nevertheless, he told her about the Rumanians.

Lya turned her eyes to her childhood acquaintance. He was three years younger than her and besotted ever since he'd once seen her on the way to school. On the fringe of their discussion stood a hussar, time slowly smoothing his breeches towards the lustreless sheen of an anachronism.

The room darkened as a storm cloud came down from the sky and squeezed itself between the walls, like a bundle of soft elbows.

Amalia looked grave. She asked if they could get back to their homes in the north.

Those eyes, thought Laszlo. Like the Danube at night on the banks of St Margaret's Island.

'Laci, we can get back, yes?'

'There is no way,' said the page boy, returning reluctantly from dream to detail. 'The railway links to the north have been cut. The Rumanians control all the roads.'

Amalia's face looked so delicate with worry that Laszlo had to look beyond her. How every part of him strained for a more intimate conference!

But Amalia would not give up her thoughts so quickly. She asked if they could travel on the back roads, at night, dressed as peasants. In bare feet!

Anything for these eyes, thought Laszlo, his heart close to taking on history.

'Malika,' he said, finally, with the tenderness he always found inside himself whenever he pronounced her name. 'There is no way back.'

22

Europe as an Eyrie

They drink. More beer, more vodka, the translucent potato potion that, when not thrown down the throat, is taken like little sips of sin. Joseph points at bottles glowing behind their labels. Passover Slivovitch. Yes, a shot of that, *prosze*. Passport Scotch? That's sure to take us over the border!

Suddenly, the sloping walls make sense. And the shadows are swift accomplices.

When the ponytailed man had been ready to go, his friend, Ewa, said she would stay. Though he tried to take her by the hand, she insisted, even threatening to stub her cigarette in his palm if he didn't leave her in peace, so he kissed her once more, his arm clamped round her neck, presumably hoping that the memory of his grip would keep her chaste, then, with his face as long as a waterlogged sock, he'd done his best to give Joseph a look that said (in any language), 'Don't you dare, because something bad will happen to you if you do,' then his ponytail followed him out of the building.

Now, much later, in the near-dark because the candle has gone out, and the night-light collector has gone home – the man who replenishes the flame on each table from the mobile shrine across his arm, a silver tray aglow with a dozen slim white candles, a hand-held chandelier – and because Joseph is drunk and his tongue will outwit him and because words can't scare him as they're no longer attached to anything, least of all to meanings or emotions, especially as he has been speaking in his new language, a word here, two words there, and so he says, after another shot, and a cool sip of beer that has, cumulatively, put a lisp in his loquacity, and so he says, for absolutely no reason whatsoever other than it's that time of night when all is dark and kept up by desire, and Eric didn't show, and because he can see for himself – it must be her delicate ratios: of eyebrow shape to forehead space, of pupils to eye-whites, of curving cheeks to full lips, of chin-glow to the shadow that falls beneath her jaw, and, perhaps most telling of all, the distance between her eyes (a distance to hold all three of them: him, her, the night) – so there's no need to ask, but in any case he asks, out of mischief, out of loneliness, or desire (which might be the same thing), out of the stickiness threatening to seal his lips, he asks: 'Are you beautiful?'

'Of course,' replies Ewa. 'I am Russian.' She blows out a thin ribbon of smoke, her cheekbones a match for her collar-bone. 'No, not Russian. I'm joking, for sure. Beautiful? Of course, yes. Can't you see? Another drink? A cigarette?'

As he fumbles for a smoke, Joseph giggles, his fingers tickled by the tips. It turns out Ewa is an architecture student from Silesia. 'For sure, almost *Deutsch*!' she laughs. Unlike some of her friends, she does not want to leave the country. She wants to stay and help rebuild the former mining regions, such as K-wce and By-m. She works in an *Antyki*, an antiques shop, one day a week. Last weekend she helped renovate a church by polishing the altar.

'About as close I get to God,' she says, her cheeks now puffs of smoke. 'No more church! No more confession!'

When Joseph tells Ewa that one of his favourite buildings in this city is the Church of the Transfiguration with its epaulettes of stone, iron-lattice bell-tower and gold detail, Ewa tells him it is built on the site of an old brewery. 'It is where drunkards go smell God!'

Then more shots in glasses so small you have to be careful not to swallow them, too. And more beer, this glass a pleasure for a palm. Maybe Joseph is trying to drink down all the darkness of the season departing. Plus a gulp for each of the eighty-nine steps of the stairwell that separate him from the city. And a shot for the spy-hole in the door. Then there's the darkness of her eyes. The darkness of his predicament – of being left in the dark? The darkness of this city, where the nights are lit only by the end of your nose or by the yellow teeth of beggars or by the golden 'taxi' signs that float down the street as if on their own accord. Then there's the darkness between one end of the phone and the other. Not forgetting the darkness of memory, and of memory's shadow (which might be even darker). Yes, Joseph is a radiant void, ever ready for a refill, having found his drinking rhythm, the rhythm of removal, that takes you out of yourself, one glowing glass at a time, with the promise of an elsewhere where all your senses are sated, all your hopes of love fulfilled.

In the toilet, he smells the cold night crouching in the bowl. He sees big muddy bootprints facing the other way. He reads the graffiti: '† Pamietaj! Katyn, 1940'.

As he splashes his face with cold water, he suffers the memory flash of a dream. He was walking streets of snow carrying a candle on a butter dish. And what was he wearing? Something heavy and hanging and tied at the waist. It might have been his greatcoat; it might have had a hood. He was trying door handles, rapping on iron knockers, ringing buzzers. He was met by shaking heads, shrugged shoulders, raised palms. He woke in the dark, the sadness trapped under his tongue.

Back on the other side, they are soon dancing to mad accordions and plucked violins – give me *dumki*! Give me *chastuski*! – Joseph grabs the coatstand, grateful for its straight-up spine in the midst of all this sloping, and he kisses the cold wood where it curves at the top, where it's all forefingers and thumbs, and he whispers, 'Life is short, but you, Madam, are tall,' and when he swivels on his heels, not quite dizzy, but almost deranged, he finds Ewa immediately behind him, so he kisses her cheeks, and how warm and soft they feel after varnished wood, and with a slight scent of body-milk, like cream and cloves, and he knows at this point that he is steadily pouring himself into this young woman's eyes, just as he is steadily pouring pools of colour and light down his throat. Yes, he is simply pouring now, not drinking, pouring from neck of bottle to neck of Joseph, as if trying to fill up the well, so that he might float to the surface and escape, but not now, not yet, because didn't Ewa just put a hand on his filament to see if it is glowing?

And they smoke. Almost continuously. Perhaps proving that smoking is the yearner's comfort and curse. Lung-hungry, they suck for dear life, one drag after another, like an endless series of sighs, plus a privilege of smoke. Entranced by Ewa's teeth in the candlelight, Joseph wonders how she doesn't grate the filter each time she pops a Slim between her lips.

'When people want to smoke,' says Ewa, sliding open a matchbox, 'they go to Paris, or they come here!'

She laughs, but not her usual laugh, like a small brass bell in the dark. No, this time her laugh comes out like the yap of a lapdog: short and harsh and strangely aristocratic.

They order blue Bols vodka, four small glasses on a tray, each one looking, for Joseph, like a distillation of a summer dusk, or a dental rinse in an egg-cup. He wonders, with a cruel grin, if that's why Ewa chose it.

'I find your view of this city very . . . I try to think,' says Ewa, referring to Joseph's recollection of his stay thus far, 'impressionist!'

Her voice is full of music. She finds all the bright notes in Joseph's language. Joseph touches Ewa's long fingers. They are cold. He leaves his palm across them, and wonders if the bar is still open because you're still beautiful and if we drink enough, smoke enough, talk enough, then this night might not end, not if we don't want it to, especially down here among the foundations, beneath the roots of grass and tree and everything else that rots and crumbles before trying to grow back.

But Ewa's features have absorbed a shadow. She slides her hand from beneath his. Her teeth retreat behind a frown. 'Why you here?' she asks, this time snapping off the words from her second (or third?) language as if she shouldn't really be touching them.

Joseph's eyebrows don't know whether to go down with dismay or up with incredulity. Staring at a bead of candle-light on the edge of a frame, he envisages a future when we're not called to answer for the actions of a government we didn't vote for, or to answer for the excesses of a nation with which we have no deep affinity. Let alone the Treaty of Yalta! He tells her he was being buried alive back there. He couldn't find a place. He tells her, too, about his building work, and then, reluctantly, about his other, more personal work, the pain of disclosure numbed by the beer, otherwise he would never have dreamed of revealing his creative self to a stranger.

Hoping his sincerity will make it through the night's syrup, he says, 'I'm just a person, trying to create good . . .' He can't find the last word. In his old language or his new one. Besides, he can't explain what he does. He's never been able to explain what he does. In that moment, he feels like a well-upholstered ghost.

Ewa gives him a long sideways look. 'I don't know if to believe,' she says.

Joseph's eyes sink the length of his beer.

'Please believe,' he says.

As quickly as the serious moment had descended, it now departs. Ewa's face is renovated by a smile. She tilts back her head, as if about to laugh, but she is silent. Joseph loves this image of teeth and silent laughter. The way Ewa balances her contentment on the end of her chin.

So he returns to his impressions, telling Ewa of a time when he'd gone swimming and there was a nun at the side of the pool in a black robe and headdress, with blue plastic bags on her feet, and this nun was giving a lesson and Joseph had hoped for a benediction but didn't get one, only more clumsy strokes, as if swimming for ever against those tides of incomprehension and greasy cutlets and nights when his blood turned to cherry vodka.

'You know nun?' says Ewa, her eyes, for once, inadequate for her astonishment.

'Not in the biblical sense!'

Ewa does not laugh.

By the light of the candle, Joseph studies the dusty fingerprints on their glasses. He pictures all the things he has held in his hands since he last held Marta.

'Funny,' says Ewa, always accompanying this word with her most serious expression, her eyebrows exuding the same aura as recently erected, but as yet bookless shelves. 'All eagles of Europe. We have crowned white eagle. Germany has black eagle. Hungary has eagle. Russia has two-head eagle. And France? I think eagle mean once royal family, no?'

As Joseph pictures the eyrie of Europe, a man with wild grey hair approaches their table. He is wearing a dress-suit with a tail as stiff as a board. Looking like he has not slept for generations – as if he alone has witnessed the many histories of this city – he suddenly straightens up as if about to follow his father's coffin through the village of his birth. Barging into every leg (whether human or furniture or phantom), the dress-suit begs men for money, and women for a dance. Ewa declines. The man speaks as though he has a pipe-cleaner's brush in his throat, his syllables eroded over the years so that only portions of words fall out.

The man finishes. He is staring at Joseph. Ewa is staring at Joseph, too. For Joseph's left arm has shot up in the air in search of the chain of translation.

In any case, Ewa translates, 'He ask why I drink with foreigner.'

Shaking his head enough times to give himself the spins, Joseph exclaims, 'Not foreign!' He stretches his arms in despair. Like an eagle unsure of its colours.

Ewa relays Joseph's reply. The man laughs. He speaks again, also waving his arms. But as though he's imitating a chicken. He nearly loses balance. He leans back on his coat-tail until it becomes a perching-stick, or a ramp down which he might lay an egg.

'He say he not sure,' says Ewa. 'He say maybe until you get to German border. Then you can talk to border-guards about that. *Ausländer*!'

Joseph has found instant despair in his hitherto blissful drunkenness. How quickly all those glasses can turn against you!

Mumbling something about being related to all the countries of Europe, he suddenly remembers the letters on the roof of the hotel by the station.

'*Europejski!*' he yells, with a fervour not dissimilar to the better-known exclamations of Orpheus or Archimedes.

Ewa and the old man laugh. They throw their shots down their throats. Joseph's spirits rush back in the right direction. Such is his grin it may have been lit by the stars on the roof of the same hotel.

Like a ghost deprived of his luminosity, the old man gathers up his groans. He retreats, but only after a bow from which he threatened never to return, tucking one of Ewa's Slims into his top pocket while still bent double.

Later, his senses softened if not altogether saturated, Joseph observes Ewa's stuttering grace. She is tall and slender. Her body leans and curves like his favourite streets and buildings and trees. He likes, too, the way her curls bounce on her shoulders, while barely touching them. She shows him a folk dance. A polonaise? 'More walk than waltz,' she says.

Pausing for a moment, perhaps unsure of the space her body takes up, she totters on her toes, before absenting herself with a quick dash. As if she had never been there. She is full of indecisive life, notes Joseph, and therefore highly flirtatious.

'Yes,' Joseph tells her, not once but twice during their waltz into the small hours, 'you are beautiful.'

A waitress is putting out the candle on a nearby table, for the quarry twins have just left. She pinches the wick with a quick thumb and forefinger. Some of the walls have straightened up and turned the colour of cold coffee. Tables have traded their silhouettes for stability. Empty glasses are ribbed by marooned froth that catches the last of the light like slug-trails lit by the moon.

Is Joseph drinking himself pint-valiant? Or all the way to lunacy in half-litres? More fist than palm, he reaches for his beer, only to punch away the glass. He laughs, but like someone who has instantly forgotten the source of his mirth.

'I've lost the use of my faculties,' he says.

'What are the faculties?' asks Ewa.

'They're like senses,' says Joseph. 'Only, there's more of them.'

The bottles behind the bar are filling with ink and ash. Joseph and Ewa dance again, their bloated shadows wrestling on the wall, because they have commandeered a fresh candle and stuck it, in its own wax, at an angle that may well be pointing to the time, but which, of course, they don't notice.

As they dance, Ewa whispers, 'By the way, *Europejski* is for European object. Not person!' Joseph doesn't hear all the words. He is lost to her 'by the way'. It opened a trapdoor to his soul.

When they finally return to their ribbed wooden chairs,

they are grateful for the extra spines. What with all the whirling and twirling, it is easy to lose track of your upright. Joseph is saved from further reflection by Ewa's lips, her teeth gently grazing his cheek. After all, he has carried his features, uncomforted, all the way through winter.

When he wakes late morning, she has gone. A scattering of creases across the sheets. Joseph places a palm where she slept. He goes to the bathroom and discovers she took a shower before leaving. The tiles are sweating, the mirror has sucked in a mist. Though he knows he shouldn't drink from the tap, he gulps down as much cold water as he can, imagining his oesophagus to be the pipeline to the source. Then he cups his hands and splashes his face. After drying with a damp towel, he wipes the mirror. Palms on the slippery tiles, he stares through a headache that is pulsing from forehead to bruise. He stares out of bloodshot eyes, trying to rescue the image of her body, how she looked as she stood there, naked, only minutes ago. A glimmer of limbs, a memory of curves, at least her light and dark places.

He peers more closely, trying to find where she rises and falls, where the skin is stretched and tender just inside the hip, and where she had arched beneath him, because he can remember that, but not as a tenderness, nor a sensual comfort, just a memory of release, like a thrust in the dark for a thrill, both of them writhing as much from tiredness as from pleasure, as though merely stumbling over each other's bodies on the way to somewhere else. And whatever else they glimpsed in the dark, in their tangle of limbs and pulses, through the smell of skin and sweat, of body-milk and smoke, yes, whatever it was they glimpsed soon gave way to an intoxicated sleep, side by side, but not embracing, not pressing skin to skin, as he always had with Marta, no, he can't even remember Ewa's fingertips, and so here he is now, alone, when he wants to give and receive tenderness, with his head sore and his heart heavy and his tongue set in aspic (a sticky residue of all his mispronounced words, whether drunken or in his new language) all he wants is Marta despite the fact that on the phone yesterday his frustration had got the better of him again, and he accused her of lacking courage, of living for books and not people, or something like that, something bad, something he didn't mean, and now, when his limbs are all for stroking and touching and giving love, she isn't here and Ewa isn't her and she's gone anyway and he's left trying to glimpse her contours through the condensation, to rescue her form from the steam, to unveil a legacy of hair and teeth, exactly where she stood only minutes ago, as naked as a human being made of faith and warm water, while he was still sleeping off the booze in bed, but all he can see in the mirror is his own pale face and dark eyes, his slack features pinned out as if on a corkboard, his attempted smile an over-used elastic band, his developing beard giving him the look of a man peering through a thicket to see which way his spirit went, while his body, left behind in boxer shorts, bears a goose-pimple for each of the lost moments of love.

He touches himself to see if he remembers her there. He looks again at the mirror and sees a face painted on a puddle. His attention is drawn by one of the word-cards he'd placed on the glass shelf. '*Usta*,' it says, 'lips'. And even though he can feel a pulse somewhere, he is not sure if it's a heart or a haemorrhage.

He continues to stare, still hoping to conjure her form,

or to banish his own. Of course, he isn't stupid. Thick-witted, yes, but not stupid. He knows it is Marta he is looking for. He knows it is her tender dimensions he is trying to evince.

Shortly afterwards, the effort becomes too much. His tears fall as hard as cherry stones.

Letters
11 November

Today is Independence Day. When we hang red-and-white flags from our balconies. A whole block can ripple in the wind like a giant sail. This day commemorates our emergence as an independent Republic at the end of the First World War, after 123 years of the partitions, when the country was divided between Prussia and Russia and Austria.

Do you know that we have a crowned white eagle on a red background to denote our royal heritage? (I think you need to know these things for when you come here. Tell me you are still coming!) Anyway, the communists went round painting out these crowns – as well as annulling Independence Day, which was reinstated in '89. But people secretly painted the crowns back on, or made little paper replicas and stuck those on instead.

Remember what I told you about a nation being an imaginary community, always needing to have scapegoats to sustain its own identity? Of course, the anti-EU parties are now preying on everyone's fears about fat businessmen from foreign lands coming to buy this country block by block. Especially Germans. We'll end up an Imperium Germanicum, they say, especially round here, not all that far from the border. They don't say anything about the thousands of people who have already gone in the other direction. I have a dentist friend who has gone to work in the UK. I know a couple of academics, too. And students and builders have been working there illegally for years!

I paraphrase the words of a writer I once told you about – What is most important to you: where you're from, or that you are a human being in the world?

27 November

They found her squatting in the corridor. Her gown had come undone, trailing is long cotton ties in the pool of urine by her side. It was the middle of the night. The previous afternoon, she'd had an operation to remove a chicken-bone from her throat. The anaesthetic had all but worn off by the time she'd taken to wandering the hospital in the small hours. She looked desperately pale, as if all her life-blood had leaked away.

The next day, she developed pleurisy. She felt like she was coming apart at the seams. As if the past was being torn from her in strips. To expose the emptiness she could no longer conceal. Even the guilt had gone, a guilt she carried for so long and which no one could appease, though she claimed to make daily confessions at the Catholic Church. Perhaps she was free at last. That is, released from memory.

The following day, she contracted pneumonia. She fell into a coma. She was put on extra oxygen. Her condition deteriorated. She received the last rites of the Roman Catholic Church at 5 p.m. on 26 November 1931. At 1.05 a.m. on Thursday, 27 November, Lya de Putti passed away. Official cause of death: double lobar pneumonia. She was thirty-five.

Months earlier, in what proved to be her final letter to her mother, she had written, 'Stay well, don't forget me.'

3 December

It is now that heart-breaking hour of a winter afternoon, around three o'clock, when the light is made for loneliness. The sky is trailing bright pink and orange stripes over the factory chimneys. Like ribbons left behind after a party.

But there is always something more powerful than the human soul to take this beauty away.

My work on Lya is advancing quickly. Funny how things fall into your lap when you are focused on a subject. The other day, I found a salacious little book about the glamour days of the German movies in the 1920s. Lya is described as 'an erotic whirlwind' who courted many 'tragic affairs' in sustaining her 'first-class reputation as a femme fatale'. The author claims Lya was infamous for carrying her film roles into real life, even auditioning her screen lovers at home. She often turned up for shooting looking like she had just got out of bed, or hospital, after one of her all-night parties. During production for her best film, *Varieté*, she is said to have demanded a break, exclaiming, 'Time for a man!'

A critic in *Der Tag* wondered,'how could this woman become a film star?' Another wrote that Lya de Putti is 'beautiful, stupid, snake-like, lascivious'.

The book says she pressurised men to become lovers by staging public suicide attempts. Just as in her films, when she swoons in front of suitors. Of course, they cite her jumping from her balcony in Berlin.

A nasty little book, but it does not put me off Lya. This great and troubled spirit. This dark star. Can you imagine?

During that burst into modernity when souls were trampled by speeding machines, to have such a spirit was to have a talent.

An opening caption for one of her films reads, 'Desire! Desire! What is there to life but desire?'

I'll be finishing,

Ps Desire, in German, 'sehnsucht' – a beautiful word!

Pps Tell me again and again, Joseph, is it true? Are you really coming next week?

23

An Ordinary Day is a Gift

Joseph feels as though he might vomit from a standing-start. His skin is paper carrying too much paint. His eyeballs hide in inkwells. And what's that pressing against the inside of his forehead? A strip of wood like a sawn-off chair-leg? Though last night's beer was enough to put hairs on his throat, he has also discovered that in this city the potency of a hangover is directly related to the heaviness of the furniture in the places where you drink.

He is no longer teased by visions of light and colour; he is tormented by them. Because he can't reach them. Can't feel them in his blood. Or taste them on his tongue. His fingers are a clutch of fibres gone stiff. He can't even bring himself to look at his work. He jumps on empty plastic bottles round the flat, cursing himself in his new language for the momentum he has lost – that coming together of discipline and desire without which he's all suffering.

In the street, Joseph puts his faith in people but everyone looks duplicitous as if he has found only the faces of burglars' look-outs (with an eye for a keyhole), fraudsters (with an eye for a coin of suspect currency) and adulterers (who can't keep their eyes to themselves). And it dawns on him how much his life has changed: from travelling about in his own country, in his car, on his own, to living in the centre of a city in a strange country, entirely dependent on his own two hands and feet, his tongue, his talents, and where you have to have faith in people – even in Marta's absence – if only because of their number and proximity and because you understand only one in five of the words that they don't so much speak as rush out of their mouths.

Belching up a sour reminder of the previous night, and deciding that he can't do people today, after all – his new language having evaporated from his system along with the water and minerals – he puts his faith in objects. Upright buildings reprimand his soul. He takes hold of sign-posts while turning a corner, though the pavements are no longer icy. He sinks his fingers in his pockets to conceal the fact they're not at work. He is relieved to find the binding-stones. But no, there is only one. He checks his other pockets, flinging out receipts, painkillers, buttons, the doodled-on silver tongues of cigarette boxes. He stamps his foot, says '*Kurwa!*' under his breath. He goes to the shop to see the kind eyes of the girl who sometimes smiles at him. She is not there. In a phone box, receiver held not against his ear but somewhere between head and heart, he dials Marta's number, only to hang up after a few rings – an act he repeats three times.

His teeth are cigarette butts from the previous night. His legs are stilts, his spine made of candlesticks, his head a pail of sawdust and sleep. At one point, in his despair, he posts his sacred sheet in a flip-top bin in the street, only to change his mind instantly, thrusting an arm all the way down until his fingertips retrieve the page. Two women cross to the other side of the road, carrying their contempt to safety.

Noises don't disturb him, not even a magpie's shrivelled-up scream. He wonders if he has a case of *intercontinnitus*, that illness of the inner ear. Ever since he has been away, he has carried his head at a slight tilt, like a nervous animal, or a very curious human being, but over the dread curse of time the muscles in his neck have stiffened, and he has become trapped at this angle, in this hyper-sensitive state, a keen mind in quarantine, super-responsive to every word and intonation, to every footstep on the stairwell, to every change in weather on the sill outside his window. Today, though, he is numb. Paranoia sits on him like a pigeon on a crust, but it is a lazy paranoia, a steady withering of nerves. He jumps aside as a matter of course when three skinheads come hollering down the street, leaving in their wake a spray-painted swastika, an up-ended pretzel cart, a fright of pigeons, and a beggar on all fours in the gutter, looking for a tooth or a coin.

Just as the sky is turning the colour of a coated tongue, Joseph's senses start to return, along with the first of the swallows. He has to squint to keep back the darkness, as if someone is trying to pinch out his wick. The buildings will not keep still. They shuffle in their shadows and threaten to spit out their coping-stones. Or they shimmer like dark sheets in a breeze, but sheets with rips in them, allowing painful flashes of light.

On his usual route past the Church of Our Lady of Snow, his eyes are again drawn to the flapping white notices of death. Placing a palm against stone, he reads: Chmielewski, Rej, Ryba, Jelinek, Oracewicz, Czapski. He is not sure if he can take his hand from the wall. With a smile that's merely a prelude to a wince, he wonders if he should stick to streets named after saints.

Forcing himself back in the direction of work, he enters *Tania Odzież*, a second-hand clothes shop. In a white plastic crate stuffed with textures that scratch his fingertips and issue a shiver of static down his spine, he finds an oversized shirt, in light blue cotton. When he has torn off the cuffs, this will be just what he needs, though it is too late to save the clothes already derided by paint and wax and turpentine.

Has the whole street really become his tail? He keeps turning round to see who or what he has in tow. The thin strip of sky is a bandage trailing from his head. Every muscle in his body bears the burden. The few words he utters in the baker's are too big for his mouth, the loaf he buys a mild form of punishment. Yes, in whatever language, he tries to stick to nouns.

'Mr Eee-dam!'

Joseph freezes on the spot, like a cat on its claws that knows only stillness will ensure its survival.

'Mr Eee-dam, how do you do? You are still here, I see,' says a shortish man stepping from the doorway of an antiquarian bookshop. Or did he slip from the roof?

With the relief of recognition, Joseph yelps, 'pan Oczek!'

They shake hands. Pan Oczek puts away a set of keys in his leather bag. 'Good to see you have not lost your memory as well as your . . . your . . .' He turns back to his bag and fiddles with the buckles. 'Forgive me,' he says, talking to his fingers. 'I meant only to say that you look in some way differently.'

Joseph notes that pan Oczek looks in all ways the same, like one of the gargoyles on the guttering of the Słowacki theatre. He is only surprised to find a body attached to such a head.

'How do you mean, differently?' says Joseph, who might have been standing there with his heart in his hands such is the way he proffers his loaf. In anticipation of the answer, hot blood rushes to his ears.

With his bag at last correctly buckled, pan Oczek rolls his formidable eyes back to Joseph, and says, 'Forgive me in advance, Mr Eee-dam, but may I suggest you have spent the night in the city gardens. And not, perhaps, just one night.' He steps closer, places a hand on Joseph's shoulder, and in a whisper smelling of fish and hours of contemplation, says, 'You are now very close to losing the lining. Is that well said?'

As much as he'd like to, Joseph cannot deny it.

'Aha,' says pan Oczek, looking up to the sky. 'In this world there is too much waste!'

A short walk later, they are sitting in a café of dark tables, varnished until you can see your face in the wood, each with a single white candle – a chimney made of moonlight – and a rectangular lace doily that looks like a sheet of music for a fairground organ. An unlit chandelier hides overhead. As does, for some reason, or for no reason whatsoever, an empty birdcage. The light blue, rough-plastered walls emanate a chill. On two sides they are covered with sepia photographs of families from the Habsburg days.

'Ahh, Mr Eee-dam,' says pan Oczek, staring at his coffee, his great gaze possibly keeping it warm. 'Have I told you the story of pigeon-boy?' Picking little drops of molten wax from the candle as if lifting the scabs of memory, he continues, 'Every two years, an elected pigeon of this city – and there are tens of thousands as you have surely seen –

is sent out to find and accompany a boy of about thirteen. The boy is said by locals to have something monumental about him, by which I mean, some hidden greatness, that will one day be immortalised in stone. You see, Mr Eee-dam, only pigeons can foresee this, such is their unrivalled knowledge of monuments the world over. If you see the latest pigeon-boy, it should bring you luck. If you are chosen as a pigeon-boy, you are destined for greatness! But, of course, for you, for me, too late!'

Joseph places a trembling finger on top of the tea-pot as if it's his composure he is trying not to pour away.

'What about pigeon-girls?' he asks, his voice dampened by the previous night's nicotine still trickling down his throat.

'We are hoping for the first!' says pan Oczek. 'Of course, the pigeons of this country are slow to catch up with the equalities of the West!'

Joseph worries up a wheeze that sounds like the accordion played by the man under the green umbrella. On the accordion Joseph pictures, however, the white buttons are made from the filter-ends of cigarettes, the instrument having been stuffed with smokes.

'Anyway, Mr Eee-dam,' says pan Oczek, his features turning grave on receipt of Joseph's discomfort. 'Let me tell you, if I may, that perhaps a heart has to freeze before it can break. In which case, you certainly came to the right place! However, a broken heart will not kill you. It may only affect your circulation. That is why you are as pale as *petit pain*. Well said?'

Sore with the prospect of a dozen dancing flames, Joseph's eyes can't focus. Two small windows throw in coins of light that bounce upon the tables and spin across the floor. Pan Oczek's features have absconded from the portraits behind. Joseph sits with his loaf between his knees.

'But it is for you to decide,' continues the mouth beneath the eyes, between the ears, above the chin. 'Which will it be? The nose-bag or the noose?'

Unsettled by a dozen melancholy moustaches now floating from their frames, Joseph shakes his head. But gently; he is worried it might come off.

Pan Oczek points to the empty cage above. 'Your bird has flown,' he says, 'leaving you to face an immediate choice. The nose-bag? Aah, the nose-bag!' and here he rolls the nub of wax on his thumb, in remembrance of sensual delights.

'The nose-bag?' says Joseph, perhaps picturing a sick-bag. Or the horses in the square. His intestines feel hollow and lined with silk. He looks inside his pot of tea. And sees, not a tea-bag, but a drowned mouse. Oh, where in the world is shelter to be found? As he shifts in his seat, his ribcage creaks like an old cabinet that has survived a flood, only to betray all the marks of its time under water. His skin flushes pink, but not the pink of rude health after you've been for a walk or a swim, no, it's the irritated pink of dehydration. He tells himself he mustn't drink again. What was it someone once told him? A drunken soldier sobers up on his horse, but a lonely man is drunk beyond repair.

After dipping the word-wafer of his tongue in his coffee, pan Oczek explains, 'In the nose-bag, Mr Eee-dam, you will find other oats! Let it be said, plenty of oats! Have a wash, have a shave, find a shirt, find a woman! Ask her nicely, very nicely, and in her own language, and she might just put your circulation back where it belongs! Tell me, how are you doing with the language?'

Joseph recites a few phrases.

'Splendid!' says pan Oczek. 'You speak like a nineteenth-century aristocrat with a mouthful of Lithuanian meatballs!'

Joseph thinks of returning the compliment, but doesn't. Nor does he tell pan Oczek about the previous night with Ewa.

'The noose?' says pan Oczek, startling Joseph's eyes from the sugar-bowl. 'Do you choose to wear your lost love like that? Each time you think of her, you will search for an oak tree or a beam. But then you'll hesitate: is there not a chance she might still come? So you carry on wearing this noose and before long everyone in town thinks you're an escaped convict or a man given a last-minute reprieve. Is this what you choose, Mr Eee-dam? Because, at the moment, if I may say so, you have the complexion of a slowly-hanging man.'

Joseph does not know whether to laugh or cry. Pan Oczek has the bulging eyes of a slowly-hanging man. Is he talking from experience? Joseph takes a sip of tea, but his throat remains the neck from a bottle of vodka.

'As I said during our first delightful encounter,' pan Oczek continues, 'there is always Our Lady of Perpetual Succour. She will give you eternal sustenance, in exchange, like most women of course, for your perpetual devotion!'

Pan Oczek swills the last of his espresso. Joseph stares at the bottom of the tiny cup until it becomes an extra chin. When pan Oczek's lips reappear from behind the white porcelain, they are already moving. 'Haven't you had enough of the gentle whispering of these women? Their laughter, you say, like water from a celestial fountain! But

I warn you – do not collapse into beauty! It is a long way back. Besides, this city is just a city in a tea-pot,' he says, now tapping his finger on the lid. 'A nest! And one in which the royals and nobles once laid their eggs!' He breaks a final piece from the candle as if plucking the last feather from Joseph's solitude. 'But do not be afraid Mr Eee-dam, there are brighter days ahead! I have been reliably informed that spring will arrive this Thursday, on the 12.42 from Żywiec!'

Rising with a squeak of the chair, pan Oczek stands over the candle, his ears and eyes in grotesque relief as if preparing to return to stone. 'Please forgive me. I am known for saying it as I see it. If it makes sense to the senses then it makes sense to me! I hope to see you again, Mr Eee-dam,' he says, shaking Joseph's hand. 'May God bless your beard. Though I would recommend a trim. The Messianic aspect is less fashionable than it used to be. I see, also, the benefits of a pot of tea. Please enjoy your extra cup!'

And with that, pan Oczek disappears into the evening's unpainted gloom.

Later, when Joseph opens the door to his flat, his smile drops to the floor and slithers beneath the wardrobe in search of other silverfish. He writes his name in the dust. Though suffering a bad case of the deadbeat chills – the shit'n'shivers born of dirty beer pipes, lack of sleep and chronic dehydration – he tries to rescue one or two hours from the day, like ice-cubes from a bath of warm water. He tosses out jagged cans, sodden cardboard, ruined works. He scrapes up purple dust, the seedless pulps of fruit, odd socks, lost brushes, puddles of ink and wax. He empties the ashtrays and washes the dishes in the sink. He collects the loose pages of Marta's letters scattered around the room.

He puts on a load of washing, but forgets to add the powder. He makes calculations as to how much money he has left. He wonders if he could sell some of his work, gain a commission to design a poster, or join the doodlers doing portraits in the street. But no, he's not much good at likenesses; it is the spirit he is after.

That night, in need of a pure-veined sleep, Joseph lies down early on his bed. When he finally gets warm under the blankets, he can see through his eyelids. Like a moon wrapped in skin. His beard feels like the legs of nesting spiders. He can sense big fruit in the dark above his head.

He tries not to think of Marta. Nor of Ewa. Though he longs for a body bearing kindness. Already, false hooves clatter-stagger down the street as if the alcohol ended up in the hollow of those heels. Then real hooves, a tired clippety-clop across the cobbles. A woman shouts a man's name. A siren gathers itself in its cups. The stairwell echoes last things.

In the middle of the night, that interminable middle whose unnumbered hours are said to hold unspeakable events, Joseph is flung from another dream of futile searching. He turns on the lamp. He takes a gulp of water from the glass beside his bed.

Footsteps pound across the attic. And is that a bird in the air-vent? It must have fallen from the roof. Perhaps it has broken its wing and is singing of its distress. Or is it merely the humming of the fridge?

In any case, Joseph leaves the light on, for a light can sometimes banish what a life perhaps can not.

Letters

14 December

Tomorrow, you are leaving my city. I just wanted to say that I am sorry for all the things that made your stay not as we'd have liked. It was all my fault. Things seem to be not too good for me. Or there is something wrong with me. I wanted you to feel like a very special guest. But I was distracted and full of fret. I can't remember any stretches of time we had to be relaxed and happy.

I am not jealous of people, I am jealous of time. I am jealous of the time that people will have for you. I have to focus now on treating this city as a stopping-place. Nothing more.

You left without a hug. Where is the embrace you once wrote to me about, the embrace that is 'above circumstance, warm and strong'? All you gave me was a sulky goodnight kiss, when once you had arms for me. The whole world.

Also, I seemed to be the one making all the effort at the dining table. I felt like I was entertaining two gentlemen. While not being much entertained by them. You were as quiet as a mouse under a broom. My husband's English was melting in your presence. Then it disappeared altogether. He'd hidden away the music you once gave me. You will never have to see how much I struggle with despair.

Your leaving so abruptly! My husband told me you shut the door in his face! That was rude, especially as he held it to shut after you. In our country, you see the guest to the door and then wait until they go down the stairwell. He didn't deserve this at all.

I know you have gone to another city in my country. But for how long? Did you do it just to tease me? You seem to enjoy such teasing now. Is this the price I must pay? Really. Have you forged a bond with my country? In such a short time? Joseph, will you become a stork abroad?

I'll be finishing,

17 December

Now you have gone, the world has sunk into slumber. And slush.

I am everywhere beneath.

Yesterday, I fell asleep after having a bath with my daughter. At 9 p.m! As usual, she named all my bodily parts, but I dozed off before she got to the brain. I didn't wake up until eleven hours later. I wanted to write this morning, but a splitting headache rushed me out of the house. Now I'm back after a cup of strong coffee in the Arabian café. Those blue flames! Like tiny wagging fingers, chastising me for not working.

Today, I looked for you along every street. At times I really believed you were still here. My search became desperate. I found only grey buildings glaring from behind broken glass. Sometimes, it feels like you haven't been here at all, and I am still waiting.

Later

So little is allowed. So much denied. This room has a memory of your presence, though my husband has made every effort to roll up your shadow and take it away. He has sprayed air-freshener. He has moved one or two items of furniture (including the chair you sat on). And carefully dusted to eradicate your fingerprints, one by one. He does not realise that my senses have memories, too. The light through the window is of a different intensity compared to when you were here.

You see, Joseph, I'm truly underground now. Where you are always with me. At the same time, I don't quite like this underground aspect.

Bettine von Arnim wrote, 'I will not give you up . . . You cannot be merely a figment of my imagination: you really are alive, aren't you? . . . How strange, if you, too, should prove to be an illusion.'

24

Endless Examples of Beauty

This is a city where the spring comes in. Half a moon previously, chandeliers of ice and light had crashed from every rooftop as if a glittering empire was coming to an end. (And most empires, like most winters, feel like they will never come to an end.) Caryatids wept the last of their tears until the long nights return to restore their mourning. And the dregs of winter dripped down the drain in a mixture of vodka and slush.

When time raced forward an hour, all those whizzing clock-hands must have whipped up the weather for the very next day brought the first rain of the season – a whole city over the font! Joseph is happy to be out, the cool drops running down his neck to remind him of his spine.

Round the back of the Gothic cathedral, he walks, the the clear pavements helping him to recover a more familiar gait even if he still looks like a *clochard*, what with the beard in which his face has nested, the boots made of mud and blisters, and the greatcoat that has certainly seen better days but not too many as warm as this one, but on he goes, singing to himself beneath the well-rinsed pillars and the porticoes, as if all his uncertainties have been transfigured into song, and he realises that he hasn't really been singing since he came here, and, in part, he blames his coat for this, too, its weight closing up his lungs like a strapped-up accordion, plus, of course, the weather that froze the song inside him and the looks that deprived him of a tune, so isn't it about time he gave his lungs a good stretch? After all, the air has been cleansed by the more sonorous bells and lightened by the withdrawal of mohair bonnets and furs, and Joseph has come to believe there are no solutions, only varying degrees of acceptance and understanding on one side, and bitterness and ignorance on the other, and he wants to move beyond resentment, yes, he wants to move on, for surely in this city where even the fire hydrants have an aspect of a crucifix, he has learned forgiveness, and so he sings, and keeps singing, perhaps aspiring to the clarity of the *Wigilia* choir, while hoping the melody itself might show him the way.

One afternoon, smoking for a shift of heartbeat, and perhaps catching sight of the tail of his painting shirt, he had a sudden vision of a self-portrait, his first since coming here – in fact, he had only ever attempted one other in his life, and even that he'd destroyed – but in the meantime, he'd executed a couple of landscapes inspired by a trip to the countryside, past wooden churches that threatened to collapse in the wake of winter, in a rackety blue-and-white bus that sputtered along as if choking on its own fumes, and through a forest thick enough to help you forget about the existence of the world on either side. And he'd noticed that one of these pictures evolved into a landscape familiar from his childhood. It is the landscape that links us, he thought, before cursing his nostalgia for his nation, this nation, any nation, if such a notion still exists.

On his walk, he passes through sunken arches hoping to resume their street-level status, and then alongside benches nailed together out of driftwood, and on which old couples were now sitting, in silence, as if not quite thawed from the winter, or shocked into wordlessness by the arrival of another spring. For yes, there is grass and greenery! After a season when window-panes rattled in the sash, doors banged, noses were blocked, and lights were always just about to go out, yes, when it felt like the city resided in an ash-tray that had been half-filled with water, this greenery is a blessing, and it's no wonder, thinks Joseph, that people still believe in God here, for after so much ice and dirt and darkness, how can you not give thanks to a higher power for leaves and rain and sunshine?

When Joseph hears the first of the songbirds, the ear-wax of the dark season melts fast away. All those nights of dust in the blood! Of yearning and Wiśniówka! All those mornings when he woke with grass between his teeth and a blue sky across his brow, only to go to the window and find dirty water, distressed clouds, concrete!

Now the black winter sky has been undone like a screw-top cupola or lifted like the lid of a *bierstein* from Bavaria, Joseph is satisfied by the sight of a swallow, and he is content, too, to think that creatures who fly away might one day return, though he does not extrapolate this to include human beings, who, he has come to believe, are not nearly so determined.

Meanwhile, the great stone buildings are not to be overlooked. The domes of the Słowacki theatre rise silvery-blue, almost transparent, like the heads of newborn babies. Tiny balconies emerge as delicate as nests, one for each of your beliefs, or for each of the beggars sleeping in the basement, flecks of plaster under their tongues. On external church walls, frescoes of Mary and child reappear like celestial stamps.

And Joseph sings, and keeps singing, just like the people of this city who are emerging from a season in the cellars, their clothes no longer coated in cobwebs and ash, their skin no longer pasted with tea-leaves and smoke. Yes, this whole city has come out of hiding! Cafés move their wicker furniture into the square. On every corner, there are green buckets full of blooms tended by old women. And younger women are carrying daffodils or tiny bouquets of purple petals wrapped in a thick green leaf, and Joseph feels as if he has been pressed from a wax mould so that it might at last be possible to recover his rhythm, his bearings, his purpose, yes, to return after love, as everyone must, to see what's left of himself.

For example, has he become a resident of this city? Well, he is always somewhere between what he is learning about this country and what he knows all too well of his own. Here, he knows the man with a face like a boiled hog who points and shouts, 'These people made money under communism and they won't give me 50 grosze!' He knows, too, the woman with a face like a used tea-bag who sits in the city gardens, playing 'If I Were a Rich Man' on a child's plastic keyboard, and the carriage driver who, whenever he adjusts the harness, says to his horses, 'Really! Do I have to think of everything?' Yes, Joseph knows the peal of individual bells, the intimacies of every street, the zones where padded jackets and hoods await an eye-to-eye.

It is a sunlight for gathering dust. Joseph feels the warmth on his back like a blessing from behind. But it is rare for a

body to be blessed all over; his feet hurt because the baked-
apple crusts still claiming to be his shoes are chafing against
his heels. He needs some lighter clothes. Even though he
presses his jeans under the mattress each night, they are as
creased as cake-wrappers.

Once more, he visits the *Tania Odzież* shop. Among the
winkle-pickers and sports jackets, the funeral-suits and
underpants, he senses the generations of souls who once
walked these streets, surprised, like him, that it's this life
and not another. After a brief search among the dry-cleaned
shadows, he picks up a flowery tie (made in France), a pair
of black linen trousers (Italy), a black leather jacket (*echtes
Leder* says the label), three T-shirts (made in Germany,
Rumania, Poland), and a close-fitting dark blue shirt (Hungary). Yes, all Europe has a say in the re-fashioning of
Eadem.

He changes behind a sheet hanging from a rail, stuffing
his old clothes into plastic bags. On his way out he brushes
a sheepskin coat by the door.

Once again, he passes the Church of Our Lady of Snow.
He recites the names: Cyrankiewicz, Prylinksi, Staff, Kor-
zenowski, Wiosna, Badylak. He gives himself full marks for
pronunciation. He hears pianos from the music school
opposite, all the tympanums having turned into keyboards.
He realises he does not know Eric's surname.

That moment, a breeze fresh from the mountains rushes
at Joseph's new linen trousers, turning him starboard in the
street. To come face-to-face with a woman, her shoulders
glowing through a white linen blouse, her shadow cut from
blue silk.

Tall women will inherit the earth! sings Joseph, into the
scented breeze, for this woman is so tall she must already

be on her way to heaven, and so upright, she must be impervious to sin. Then he curses himself. His plastic bags have become buckets of lust. Hasn't he learned that lust begins and ends in the body, tenderness in the soul? Yes, on the lust side, it's been a full six months since he saw a stranger's nipple; on the longing side, he has forgotten how it feels to hold a human being. His winter-long yearning for Marta has filled him with a tenderness he has yet to bestow. Sometimes, like now, he can feel the blood in his fingertips, and sometimes the singing in his blood. Like the other day when a Ukrainian waitress – who also speaks the local language with difficulty, but in a different direction to Joseph – twice touched him on the arm, and Joseph had trembled in relief to find himself still human.

This thought makes him melancholy. He tells himself he doesn't yet want it to be spring. Doesn't want to be deprived of the darkness of his longing.

But the moment lifts. The sun overhead is busy shortening shadows. How good to be in contact with a blue sky again! Perhaps it is spring, not winter, that encourages submergence and forgetting. Yes, as usual, he is saved from himself by the external world. The smells! Admittedly only dog shit and fumes, but smells nevertheless. Plus, the bodies are back! Other people's bodies! Buried for a season under layers of anxiety and wool, the form of a person returns. Elbows first, then collar-bones, legs, knees, stomachs, napes, thighs. He sings these words in the local language, as if putting himself back together, and he wonders as he does so if it is possible for a person to be uprooted from a landscape, set down in another, and still prosper.

Looking around, he is surprised to have forgotten so

quickly the beauty of a body. Perhaps because a body can so quickly disappear. He can recall Marta's intimate form, a pulse close by, a breathing light. He can recall little of Ewa. Only her teeth against his skin, and the moment when, on the way back to his flat, she took his arm in the dark.

But it's true, the women of this city are returning to the surface, raising their faces to the sun after a winter when their spirits, like dynamos, kept their eyes alive, their hearts warm, despite the darkness made of ravens' wings and ice, but now these very same spirits light up the flesh of their arms and legs and throats, which is not to suggest they were miserable in the dark season, oh no, but surely then their laughter was muffled in their hoods or smothered by their scarves, or when they clapped with glee their gloves made it sound like a pat on the back.

Later, it is dusk, and a dusk no longer afraid of the dark. The horses are living sculptures, the trees, too. Though the man who cycles behind the horses with a bucket – he doesn't think they're sculptures. '*Ciepłe!*' he shouts, 'warm!' as he shovels up the steaming dung, before pedalling *szybko!* to the convent flowerbeds.

Carried along by a prospect of tenderness, people come from all directions, negotiating their safe passage over the cracked slabs of the main square, taking side-steps and excuse-mes, most of them unaware that their careful migrations are mirrored overhead – if much more inventively – by the starlings swooping round the towers of the Mariacki Church.

Joseph would have to walk a long way to tire of twilight. Even when poorly shoed, like a neglected horse. Great medieval facades, licked by the tongues of lilacs, have fallen to a startled hush. Yes, even the stone has turned sentimental. A dilapidated gable recalls its royal chambers. A rusty fire-escape that doesn't reach the ground becomes a staircase to other realms.

Joseph sits on a bench and listens to the blood in his heels. 'I could go mad for all this beauty,' he whispers, before urging himself back to his boards.

Letters

28 December

We had a Christmas Eve supper, the mandatory family occasion. There should be 12 dishes on the table – poppy seeds, honey, almonds, sour cabbage, prunes, mushrooms, dried peas, dried fruit, marinated herrings or salted fish, especially carp in grey sauce. Those who know prepare the soup with 'the soul' – the special souring ingredient, fermented beetroot juice. You ferment it by adding brown rye bread. Delicious! It is traditional to put some hay under the tablecloth, a candle, an additional setting for an unexpected guest. I wondered where you were. I wondered if you might turn up.

The meal is followed by a special mass at midnight, Shepherd's Vigil. The churches are packed. The priests deliver sermons full of pathos. The congregation sings carols, sending thick alcohol vapours straight to heaven.

Long before Christmas, Malena was stripping her dolls, wrapping them in toilet paper, announcing the coming of her little Jesus. After her bath, she insisted I wrap her naked in a duvet and sing carols in which little Jesus features. A child's love is vast. And about the body. But it is not a desire to be satisfied. It is all tenderness and touch.

I won't write much about the grandparents gathering for

Christmas. My husband, fed up with my father's manic tirades, announced that in this house there is to be no bad talking about Jews. I also argued with my father. Not too seriously. But enough to feel annoyed.

Unable to relax, my husband reinstalled the programs on my computer. By doing so, he deleted all my recent files. All the edited chapters of my book thus far.

The row was earth-shaking. I shall have to go back to the drafts.

Later

In between festive food and drink i.e. when everyone was sleeping, I did go back to the drafts. I remembered that Lya had planned to spend Christmas 1927 with her mother back in Hungary. But Zoltan refused his ex-wife access to the children. So she decided not to go. She would never see her daughters again.

Perhaps she recalled a poem by her friend, Endre Ady:

'I do not know why and for how long
I am going to remain with you
but I hold your hand
and guard your eyes'

New Year – first Monday

It makes me both happy and sad to think how many more years can appear in the right-hand corner of our letters.

Last night I saw some handwriting imprinted beside of one of your drawings. I struggled in vain to read this secret script, hoping it was a message from you. It felt like reading words in a dream.

I have been thinking about my grandfather. I think you inspired me to unearth my past. A sensitive man, he had rows with his wife that used to blow out all the candles in the house, and make next door's Alsatian bark. 'That dog,' he used to tell me, 'it barks with its ears, its eyes, its legs, the whole of its being!' At the end of each row, or sometimes in the middle, my grandfather would lower himself out of the first-floor window, landing his limbs in the soft grass below. He would then run, sobbing, across the fields, his bent silhouette trailing a length of rope. Each time he rowed with my grandmother he was sure he would do it. He just couldn't stand the heartache of arguing with the woman he loved. By the time he reached the oak, he was breathless, his face sticky with tears and sweat. He had used up all his misery, too.

Half an hour later, he would trudge back to the house, the rope behind him like an unwanted tail. At the back door, my grandmother would be waiting for him with a warm hug and a forgiving silence.

It's a ritual they repeated for every major row. They have been together for over sixty years.

Joseph, I have the perfect right to miss you.

3 January

Joseph, I want to write your name a few times. A name is magical. Your name. As if you are present in these loops and flourishes. It gives me a feeling of being in touch. I say your name to myself sometimes, when I am alone in the room.

Edith Stein wrote that at a higher level of prayer, 'The

soul is no longer in the position to reflect intellectually or to make definite decisions.' Perhaps this is true of all elevated states. Perhaps it helps explain my own indecision.

I have also had a few sleeping sessions. There are always two or three days a month when I never wake up. Not properly. Especially in winter. It's as if all this darkness demands more respect, i.e. more sleep! I doze off in the afternoon with my daughter, then again when I put her to bed in the evening. As I'm sure you're finding out for yourself, the temperatures can drop quickly. The icy cold seeps in through air-vents and drains. The walls in this flat are white. Like a nun's cloister. As you have seen. Otherwise there would be no light at all. In the end, my husband chose not to erect the mirror on the balcony.

Today we went with Joanna and Gary to an exhibition of work by Kathe Köllwitz (1867–1945). Bleak charcoal sketches of the underside of the Weimar Republic. Köllwitz wanted to show the poverty suffered by the working classes in Berlin, a city that was otherwise alive with film (Lya) and theatre and all kinds of decadence. She drew hollow-faced workers. Exhausted mothers. She drew a darkness that cleanses the forehead but buries the soul. A stony-faced determination. Her pictures look as though she sketched them with lumps of earth, her characters as though they are sheltering in mines. Mothers and babies. People who struggle. She refracts feelings through gestures and facial expressions. Like in 'The Weavers', her depiction of a scene from Hauptmann's play of the same name: Silesian weavers in dispute as the industrial revolution sweeps across Europe. She was especially concerned by the plight of women. One piece, 'Waiting', shows a troubled mother in prayer. Köll-witz lost a son in the First World War. She was the first woman to be elected to the German Academy of Art.

Maybe my perception of time is not linear. I refuse to acknowledge the loss of you.

25

A History of Rot

They sound like the old man's xylophone in the teashop, these wooden frames knocking in the wind. They're either spiritless imitations of masters or the sort of mournful picture that can be found in cheap hotels across Europe: a gypsy girl in ribbons, a horse with clean teeth, a landscape suggestive of the route to the cemetery. Joseph prefers the work done by the lice on the frames.

On his haunches, leaning against a corrugated iron fence, Joseph is up to his ears in Soviet cameras, shoes, prosthetic limbs made of wood for wartime amputees, electrical fittings that no longer fit, pig-skin valises, hearing-aids, books without covers (a few titles in Cyrillic), Kama watches that failed to out-tick their time, a handleless hurdy-gurdy, porn magazines in five languages, small busts of Stalin and Lenin, the insides of a television, bicycles, spectacles, Erika type-writers, a blue-eyed Jesus painted on soft, wet wood, Art-Deco dressers and mirrors, porcelain pots marked 'Zucker' and 'Salz' and 'Pfeffer', Solidarność badges, Grünewald medals, gold coins in cellophane, flick-knives, cleavers, a tin of film of the 1936 Olympics. It's as if the last century was given a bloody good shake and this is what fell out.

All cities have their gutters. All cities have their charms.

At the flea market, the two come together. Especially here, where people lay out their wares on blankets and rags across the muddy concrete.

Joseph sits with a thick wad of his sketches held between his boots: a detail of the castle, a Baroque turret, a view down the street from the back of a tram, two Jewish cemeteries, his series on the homeless, several studies of buildings now demolished, snow-sweepers with shovels for heads, a field of chicken hearts, a cupola like the stopper on a crystal decanter.

The market is plundered by the wind. Clouds are in a hurry to find a sky they can stick to. The ornate anchors of chandeliers rattle their fixtures and glass. How forlorn they look when brought down to earth! A design of black chrysanthemums clings to an art-nouveau vase. There's a scattering of disciples and saints. A slim figurine of Our Lady of Sorrows topples over, prompting a collective making of the sign of the cross, and then a collective intake of breath when her head is seen rolling away. An old man walks about with a brown toilet seat (faintly embossed wood) around his neck – a harness against the elements? Or a sad reminder that, in the end, time will flush us all away?

Near Joseph there is a stall of war memorabilia, fronted by a trader with a burning stub for a diamond ring. He grunts behind yellow smoke as he rootles for change in oily pockets or licks at filthy notes. Joseph sees the dark burgundy cover of an Arbeitsbuch. He wants to touch it, just to see if his fingertips will spark. Even through the plastic cover. And then he doesn't want to touch it, because he's sick to the stomach that such objects endure. An SS medallion stings a box of blue velvet, plus knives, swords, scimitars, some of these also embossed with a swastika. He clenches his fists still tighter when he sees that many are reproductions, the Nazi insignia clipped on to secure an easy sale.

Young skinheads surround the stall. In one palm they study medals and blades alike, while with the other they sandpaper their scalps.

From late morning to late afternoon Joseph sits, without success, beneath the racing clouds. There's an occasional visitor, a flick through his sketches, including one elderly man, a tinker by trade from an adjacent plot, who, after studying half of the pictures, avows, '*To nie jest moje miasto*' ('This is not my city'). Later, just as Joseph is preparing to leave, a man picks up *Cabaret Nights*, a piece Joseph painted on a shelf from the skip. The man raises it horizontally against the wall, the paintwork face-down, using his moustache as a spirit-level, his nose as the first ornament. When he asks the price, Joseph says three; the man offers one. Enough for two rolls of bread at a push. But Joseph is not sad to see it go. The sale is in keeping with the spirit of the piece.

As he leaves with his vision of this city in a tin box he bought earlier in the day – a cross between a tea tin and a hat box – he has a look at a final stall, a stall selling postcards in long thin boxes, like homeless drawers. The first block is tourist pictures: Warszawa, Budapesz, Lvov, dated 1922–1931. Then local wedding pictures. With bride and groom looking very young. And severe.

Joseph decides to switch to the pile under the rusting paperweight. This stack of cards is of single portraits, with the name of the sitter printed beneath: Gaidarow, Nielsen, Bow, Moore, Nazimova, Esterhazy. The women in gowns and furs, the men in top-hats and tails.

And then, tucked for all anonymity a good two-thirds of the way down – yes, a hundred layers of companions to help her sleep through history – there she is: Lya de Putti. A Ross, "Verlag" card, Berlin, 1925.

Reproduktion verboten.

Letters

7 January

Yesterday I thought by what means anger can be conveyed across the continent without losing its charge. Then I remembered you are still in my country. The phone line can be so bad that I automatically think you are a long way away. Sometimes I have to be angry in order to bear sadness. And there are always things which, the more they are clarified by one side, the more misunderstood they are by the other.

When I told you that I missed you over Christmas to the point of being dizzy, I did not do anything wrong. I know you experienced a lonely Christmas. So sometimes, wait a fraction of a second before you feel resentful. I have never argued with anybody I consider close as much as I have with you. I can be stubborn. You can be stubborn. There is nothing wrong with that. But I don't want our correspondence to become a case of how many reproaches we can fit inside a single call. Or envelope.

Tell me, Joseph, am I bad because I hurt you? Bad because I hurt my husband? And myself. But we transformed each other, didn't we? Isn't that as much as anyone can offer another human being? Some understanding, some tenderness, some encouragement. Whether they are together every day or not?

Later

During a dusk walk home from work, I felt my city again. It is a city of newcomers. It is a place where the past has been forgotten. It was completely destroyed by the Germans. I have never had a sense of roots here. I like the city. I like its youthfulness and its fin-de-siècle villas in the green areas. But I do not belong here. It makes me want to move on. And I will.

By the way, the woman in the street you told me about. With the swinging arm. I have tried to translate the phonetic rendering you gave me. Not an easy task! Anyway, I think this woman is talking of her daughter. Something about exams. Of her daughter not being allowed to take her exams.

I will keep sending these letters poste restante. I don't believe in women writing letters and then being too timid to send them. If I write you a letter, then you are going to get it. Wherever you are.

I'll be finishing,

Ps How is your flat, by the way? Four floors up from the hooves sounds nice. Though I'm not sure about the purple dust – we call such big tufts, 'koty z kurzu', dust cats. Whereas cobbles are known as 'kocie łby' – cats' heads! Have you found some comfort among these hooves and heads? Among the stars and stalactites? Tell me, Joseph, have you found a place to be? Or is home just the body you are in?

10 January

On 10 January 1896, Amalia de Putti was born in Vesce, Hungary, to Countess Maria von Hoyos and Julius de Putti, reputedly a baron of Italian descent. Amalia was the youngest of four: brothers Geza and Alexander, and a sister, Mitzi.

Today, in my writing about her, I decided to stick to the details of her films. Titles such as The Scarlet Lady, The Heart-thief, Manon Lescaut, the latter including a fight scene with a young actress called Marlene Dietrich.

Lya played peasant girls, maids, a Russian princess in exile, a spy, usually the 'other woman', a mixture of virgin and succubus. On the cover of the February 1928 issue of 'Picture Show' magazine, Lya looks very young and unsure of herself. She hugs a bunch of roses. She is thirty-two years old. Her career is about to go into steep decline. The headline reads, 'She is NOT a vamp'.

Later

I think about it sometimes. Desperately. About coming to you, I mean. I have to cope with the thought that you are only a few hours away by train. Sometimes, Joseph, I don't know in which direction my strength is going. Am I strong to stay or strong to leave?

Despite these days that are dark at either end, I refuse to forget your charms. The first time we arranged to meet. Was it the end of May? You in jeans and a well-fitted T-shirt. Your strong arms and chest. Your face already lightly tanned. Your smile and sensitive eyes: green in the sunlight, brown in the evenings. And your slender hands with their long fingers, and good strong palms. I thought straight away you must be a poet or a thief!

As our pleasures progressed, so did their intensity. And desire, if it goes on long enough, is love.

I like the sound of the scrapbook you are putting together – at street level. You're surely already finding out that the city contains plenty of histories, many of them brutal. Plus a raised-nose conservatism – lots of people claiming links with the aristocracy of old. The genuine ones probably own palaces in the centre, the others merely add a few letters to lift their surname above common currency. Such snobbery! It's all in the family. 'Korzenie' – roots. 'Rodzina' – family. Families of lawyers, families of professors, and if you're not in one of these families, or close, it's very difficult to get in. Such is the weight of tradition in that city. Aristocracy on one side (plush fur coats), peasants on the other (plucked fur coats), everyone else squabbling in the middle. Patrycja always laughs when I mention the place, she calls it a stagnant pond, before quoting statistics about the steady erosion of the medieval buildings due to pollution from the steelworks at Nowa Huta. She says even the gargoyles there are toothless.

Ps In 1896, Hungary was celebrating its 1000th anniversary. The city's underground system opened the same year.

Pps re: Lya. How desperately she needed confirmation from others that she was real. Perhaps the more people who understood her the more real she became.

26

Parting, for the first time

Joseph is working on his self-portrait, drawing from memories that, at the same time, he is trying to escape. And in a forward direction. Today, he remembers the end of the previous summer when it was time to part, which means at least one of them was free to leave. Marta had decided to give him a book of poetry, a bilingual edition, annotated with exclamation marks in blue pen (on the English side of the page). On the night before her husband was to drive her back to the other side of Europe, Marta stood in the kitchen, clutching the book to her chest as if warming herself with its wisdom. Her husband, meanwhile, hovered behind the intended recipient. Like a reluctant shadow.

'Be very careful with this book,' said Marta. 'Very careful. They are precious poems. By a precious poet.'

With ceremonial gravity, and a smile Joseph couldn't quite decipher, she carried the book towards him.

But Joseph missed the wink in her voice. He missed the stress on the first syllable of 'very'. He even missed, or paid no attention to, the repetition of that word. Such was his concentration in the presence of Marta's husband – as if trying to look at two people at once, while attempting to think of neither of them – he saw only a book, and not the site of a secret. Besides, they were covered in secrecy, Joseph and Marta, and this secrecy gave their skin a sheen that was far from invisible. Every look, every gesture, every word betrayed them. A rhythm and complicity united them. Even when simply standing in the room, their bodies tensed the same way, and spoke to each other of their distress. Earlier, when the three of them had sat down at the kitchen table, Joseph's bare arm brushed against Marta's, and he wondered if her husband could hear the singing in his heart.

Joseph reached for the book.

And dropped it.

The hardback fell open, face down, standing on the edges of its cover. A piece of paper had spilled out. For a moment, all three of them stood in silence, staring at the paper as if expecting it to ignite under their scrutiny. Finally, Joseph swooped to a single knee, ushering the letter within the book as if it were merely a badly-behaved page.

With the clumsiness of bodies in doubt, the three of them retreated to the lounge. Just a few steps, but the atmosphere changed. A partial release amid books, newspapers, Malena's toys. As if these objects might absorb the tension or at least make a mockery of it.

As there were only two chairs in the room, Marta's husband sat, having first offered the seat to his wife. Joseph took the other, opposite, while Marta, mischievous Marta, her cheeks pink from the wine, settled on the floor between them. Then she stretched out her arms and legs. Joseph knew she had not yet told her husband. His tired eyes seldom left the body of his wife as though trying to discern if Joseph's lips or fingertips had ever landed there.

A sleepy cry from upstairs. Marta sat up, preparing to go to her daughter. Her husband, too, leaned forward. Linked by the act of listening, husband and wife looked to each other. Malena did not make a further sound.

When enough time had passed for a polite departure, Joseph thanked them for the soup. Everyone stood. Joseph shook hands with Marta's husband. The eyes that had observed him all evening had receded to small dark points that were more powerful for their lack of light. More suspicious.

'I'll see you out,' said Marta, doing her best to make Joseph's exit sound like the routine departure of a friend.

Her husband took two steps. He paused in no-man's-land, a short carpeted space between his chair and the front door.

Their shoes on the gravel in the late-summer evening. A starless night. A faint smell of cooked blossom and brick. Joseph felt he was crunching across a fallen constellation. Such was the feeling in his stomach, he might have already swallowed his sadness.

They embraced. But differently from the first time, from all the other times, as if they were simply pressing their ribcages together. Yes, he could feel Marta's bones. And most of his own. He could not believe this woman was being taken from him.

'I'll be going,' said Marta, pushing up her wet cheeks with a smile. 'See you soon.'

They shared a kiss that only hinted at the blood in their lips.

Over Marta's shoulder, Joseph detected a twitching. Though standing inside the house, her husband cast a shadow across the doorstep. Occasionally, this shadow moved over the stones.

Letters

30 January

Each time I pass the metal pigeonholes (painted tomato-red, but tinned tomatoes not fresh ones) in the foyer of my block, I peer through the grid with my number on it. If it is empty, then I carry this emptiness upstairs.

Edith Stein: 'Things that withdraw from the glance are accessible to the touch.' I like this. It makes me think of Lya, forever in the public eye as a star. Yet when it came to her private life she could not be touched in the way she desperately needed. As if her skin, having soaked up all those flash-bulbs, gave her a luminosity that repelled finger-tips, however much she craved tenderness.

I think Lya wore her loneliness as armour. Perhaps also her guilt. In the end, she could not detach herself from either. She tired herself out with a despair that could be lightly worn and enchanting, an energy like a mad steam. Yet she was often desperate, even violent. I don't think anyone could get through.

Stein's idea is important. That it is possible to withdraw from the gaze, to grow, silently, to become more receptive, more human.

Joseph, isn't this how we encouraged each other to grow?

But I wonder what it means for us now. Have we withdrawn from each other's eyes? Have we returned each other to the world, albeit with our spirits revived and touching?

This morning at breakfast, as my husband made coffee, he asked me what I had dreamed about during the night. It is the first time he has asked me such a question. I sensed the muscles tighten in his arm as he finished pouring from the pot.

'How do you mean?' I said. 'I don't remember what I dreamed about.'

He sat at the table, careful not to scrape a chair leg. He took a piece of toast and spread the butter so that not a glimpse of bread remained. He asked if I could at least say whether it had been a good dream or a bad dream.

I told him I would have remembered a nightmare. I asked him the point of his question. He took a bite from his toast, while trying not to make a sound. He swallowed awkwardly, eyes bulging. He said, 'Why were you speaking in English in your dream?'

I had to stop myself from laughing. I told him that surely it's because I'd been living there for four months. I told him that, as he knows already, I often write sections of my book in English (especially the Lya sections), before translating them, because I like the language so much, and feel less constrained after a lifetime in my own language. I told him that I often see and read words in my dreams. Especially after a period of writing. And that this is what must have happened.

'What were you saying, then, in your dream?' he asked, his eyes soft with apprehension, like someone who has received one slap and is not sure if there's another one on the way. He swept a crust of bread across his plate. 'Were you dreaming about . . .?'

He could not bring himself to say your name. He picked up the piece of crust and chewed loudly, as though it were full of nourishment.

Joseph, where are you? Really. I mean, I know which city. But, I'm wondering, sometimes desperately, which space? Have you found a place to be? Away from my prying gaze?

I remember you saying that you don't really have a sense of home. Not as a physical location. I know you see yourself as European. Is this, then, what it means to be European: to have a second home, but not a first?

27

Street of Crooked Tiles

The darkness no longer drops as quickly as a coin in the tin of a back-street beggar. The air is soft and warm to the skin, and Joseph is beginning to feel dizzy with the full extent of the evening's promise even though he has learned already that a meeting of loneliness and lust is as volatile a mix as vodka and tabasco sauce, a shot known as 'Mad Dog' and favoured by the dawn drinkers who knock back one after another until, leaving their grins in the ashtray, they slide from their stools like slugs.

As the sun melts down the back of former palaces, for a moment reinstating their grandeur with a gilt made only of light, Joseph hears a horse's neigh, a violin, the laughter of women, the clinking of glasses, the rolling of barrels across cobbles, and the opening of wooden trapdoors as these same barrels are lowered into outstretched arms.

Having come to an *impasse* in his self-portrait, he's decided to brave the streets again, at night, and possibly for the last time. As usual after a period of intense work, he feels about as real as a daguerreotype, save for the cold tea and smoke clinging to the enamel of his teeth, but he needs a shift of energies, another dose of difference, an encounter with a soul other than his own. He just hasn't been able to find the form that might contain him.

This dusk does not need persuading. It seeps from cellars, wraps hanging-baskets, and beards roof-top figurines who give up their poses and sing themselves to sleep. In the city gardens, purple blossom buzzes like neon, and, for Joseph, the long flowers of the chestnut are the glowing fixtures of a chandelier. Leaves shiver in greens and greys forming a mosaic dark enough to drink. Feeling the bliss of release after a near-holy confinement, he walks with an eager rhythm to his step.

In Café Galka, after nodding to Dmitri, Joseph sits at his own table, respectful of their individual pools of loneliness and light. Purple stars of Loosestrife protrude from the champagne bucket, but there is no sign of Bibi. As usual, Joseph sketches on napkins and beer-mats, and with a speed suggesting he wants to resolve the issue before his street-inspired elation turns to dread.

As he looks to the bright congregation of faces around each table, a pile of sketches between him and their joy, he realises – what? – that he has never been happy? Unless with Marta? His wrist stiffens until every movement is a false one, and his images float face-down in a pool of blue vodka and beer.

When the bubbles of his vision no longer reach the surface, he's back on the streets, cracking his ankles across the cobbles, trying not to think of a colony of cats rising from below, as he sways from window to doorway, resting an elbow here, his head there, as if laying down his thoughts, or imprinting them on a wooden ledge with the ink-stamp of his forehead. His thoughts? Yes, blurry images of a departure, of an end to his waiting.

He tugs at his linen trousers, now shadows desperate to leave him. He wonders what happened to the night and all of its promise. Is it hiding behind one of these big wooden doors? Is it still singing beneath the streets? Or did it pack itself in the boot of the last taxi to leave the rank?

Resting the darkness on his shoulders as if carrying the sky on a hod, he scuffs his shoes and the last of his hopes against empty bottles of *Krakus* vodka or *eau de cologne*, the favoured tipples of penniless drunks, and he sidefoots one of these bottles, sending it spinning like a fat star across the stones, while giggling down his chest to think of breath so sweet, or he kicks an old iron grill for cleaning the mud from your boots, as he tries a latch, a handle, a padlock. Yes, he could get drunk on doors that lock him out, if he wasn't drunk already.

On he goes, carried by the tide of intoxication that pitches your body forward while at the same time pulling it back, and by the sleeplessness that has washed against his soul ever since he came here, like waves of darkness and salt, plus memories of brittle light, indecipherable syllables, a whole city set in ice and paint, so that he can't believe these dry and dusty streets are the same streets he had struggled along, full of frosty despair in the winter.

Kissing his laces one moment, the moon the next, he carries his ragbag of bones over disused tram lines, before cutting down a side street where the tiles are made of brown porcelain – or so it seems – and he looks to the frescoes of Mary and child, only to wonder if the stars around the Virgin's head have anything to do with the stars of the European Union, or at least with those rusting on the roof of the Hotel Europejski.

As if a current has passed through him, he stumbles

again, picking up chalk on the shoulders of his *echtes Leder* jacket, cold-slapping plaster like a canvas to be primed, until his nose comes to rest against the bars of a basement window, where he catches a whiff of flat beer and distress, and he hears moans and grunts and curses, and he knows straight away that it's one of the city's sobering-up tanks, underground rooms in which the *policja* throw the *spierdalaj!* drunks (f-off in local speak), strapping them to a bed beneath an old army blanket, as they shit and piss and puke, defenceless against everything a body can throw back.

When he pulls himself up, Joseph sees that the ground-floor window is taken up by the display of another new real-estate agency. He gives a groan to match those coming up from below, and then he's off again, carrying his hope like a wingless bird in his palms, as he passes the crucifix outside the Church of the Transfiguration, the suffering Jesus beneath which the can-crushers sit, two old drunks who lurk in the double-darkness of night and beard so that you know of their existence only by the stamping of boots on tin.

Visited by a sudden memory of *Wigilia*, Joseph crosses himself as he falls headfirst into another half-tumble, only for the townhouses on either side to rear like neglected headstones. He squints for the one bearing 'Eadem', thinking, if he finds it, at least he'll get a bloody good night's sleep. He stops in a doorway to read the names alongside buttons as shiny as those of a bell boy's tunic: Twardowski, Rajska, Szostak, Parandowski, Skrzynecki, Ptak.

He sings for the absence of Balicka! For the absence of Eadem! For the absence of Eadem-Balicka! He wonders if Marta has changed her surname.

Unable to bale out the weariness flooding his limbs, he

dozes across a car bonnet, like a cat content with a still-warm engine, until he lurches forward, chin to the heavens, as if someone has pulled him up by the tie. (Though he had smartened himself up with his new French neckwear, he now looks like he has been lassoed, half-hung, a head in a sling.)

He stumbles on, before resting across another chassis, and he giggles to himself to think that they're not much bigger than pillows, these little red cars, so, if you don't mind – and here he has a quick look round, but like someone wearing a blindfold about to cross the road – I'll put my head on the bonnet, here, just like this, his ear flush against cold metal, the windscreen reflecting a face creased by all the strange expressions he has worn when not being himself, or being himself, or being too much of one and not enough of the other.

Suddenly, he is aware of a breath that isn't his own. He sees, immediately before him, a giant in padded clothing, an overstuffed silhouette.

'*Dowód!*' orders the giant in a thunderous voice that flies up drain-pipes and echoes among the gables. Though Joseph knows this means 'ID', he has no ID, so he says, '*Nie mam dowód*' ('I don't have ID'), and he pats his pockets for proof. Apart from his keys, a few coins, the last binding-stone, and his pens, Joseph carries only his blank sheet and he isn't about to hand that over, so he promises the guard he is on his way home, while thinking that he really does not want to go to the tobering-up sank, sorry, the sobering-up tank, and so he sets his features in earnest-ness, and the guard, after a pause that seems to pain him, says, 'OK'. Billowing out in his stance like a well-tethered tempest, the guard then points down the street. Even though he is pointing in the opposite direction to Joseph's flat, Joseph follows the finger, scuttling down the lane like a spider in fear of the slipper's killer blow.

Once round the corner, Joseph stops for a moment, dropping his palms on his kneecaps, perhaps thinking that's where his heart has slipped for safe-keeping, or maybe he wants to unscrew these caps and let out all the beer, but, no, he doesn't unscrew the caps, he merely giggles to himself and sets off again, moving with the same eerie presence as a car with no lights being driven down the road at night.

Among the dark shapes of the city gardens, where the benches are now strewn with drunkards and lovers and lunatics, plus tourists who have underestimated the strength of the local beer, Joseph makes his way, saddened by the silence of the trees, a whole town with their backs turned.

Suddenly, a man jumps in front of him, palms in the air, and shouts, 'Is it good or bad to live in this country?'

'*Dobrze!*' shouts Joseph, automatically. 'Good!'

With a belch that disturbs something in the bushes, the man steps back into the darkness.

Away from the gardens, Joseph comes to a halt in a puddle of pink neon outside a '24h go-go bar'. He wonders if this is where the night's promise has gone. He rings the entry-buzzer. A clank of iron from the inside. A sixty-year-old woman with a fifty-a-day habit (always a fag or a mascara pencil between her fingers), orange hair, and turkey wattles dredges up a welcome from lungs like the spent bags of a vacuum-cleaner. She leads him to a tatty sofa, where he sits beneath his knees, trembling. From the darkness of a door-frame, with a television flickering behind, three bodies appear in fluffy slippers, their limbs silvery-blue in the light of the screen. In transparent nighties, they shiver in their pockmarked skin, thumbs of fat poking through garters and lace. They look as if shaken from a state far deeper than sleep. A sagging of jowls and breasts from gravity's lasting grope. A smell of burned toast and trepidation. Sour breath and wet carpets. Joseph mumbles his excuses. He knows that whatever he is looking for, he will not find it here. When the iron barrier comes down hard behind him, he feels like he's been locked up.

He is relieved to find himself back on the streets. He inhales, deeply, and moves on, the moon now bouncing against his forehead like a puffball fresh from the lake. After buying a bread roll from a twenty-four-hour shop where the open hatch divulged a cloud of sugar and flour, plus the assistant's nettle-sweet perfume, Joseph went on another wander, past advertising hordings that stretched from attic to pavement, obscuring the medieval façade beneath, and before long he ended up back in the city gardens and this time with a woman whom he'd found while trawling the maze of old-town streets one last time, and this woman had a plastic bag of beer cans, and a wooden high-chair – a bouncer's seat – that she'd pinched from the doorway of a club.

They sit on a bench, sniffing the key-holes of their cans. In silence, they smoke one cigarette after another, the gap shortening between each one as if they, too, measure the steady leaking away of night. They change benches, carrying the high-chair between them, one at either end, because it might be all that links them. Joseph scratches the pavement with a coin, looking for the first sign of dawn.

All at once, there's a whistle and a scrape. The arm of the woman's tatty anorak reaches round Joseph's shoulders. She pulls him close, and then closer. And there they sit, on the bench, waiting for the world to end, until Joseph's off for a piss behind the bins. If Marta could see me now, he shudders, before tripping over a shin-high section of the city wall. Thrown into dizzying spirals, he carries himself beyond the huge aluminium barrels, where he finally stands upright, only to arch like a cat for the rising within, and now he's bent double and dripping cold sweat, his palm on the handle of an old water-pump. He lets out a long and terrible howl. The blackbirds fly out of the trees.

Next thing, the woman leaps at him, just as he'd unzipped himself and she grabs him and begins to tug away, perhaps focusing on that water-pump, until Joseph feels as if his whole being is going backwards and forwards, backwards and forwards, and he has to take little steps forward and back, forward and back, just to keep balance and to make sure she doesn't yank the thing off completely, so they keep moving forward and back, forward and back, with Joseph looking to the palm-sized leaves of the nearest oak, perhaps for a helping-hand before remembering that a helping-hand is the last thing he needs, so he looks to the copper-beech shimmering in the coming light and he pictures a bobbed haircut, just like Marta's, just like Lya's, and as he is wondering if everything goes round and round, or at least, backwards and forwards, they emerge slowly from behind the bins in a strange dance of limited steps but abundant facial expressions. Yes, more of a walk than a waltz.

Shortly after, they are back on the bench. Dawn comes in under a pigeon's wing. Joseph looks to the spires deposited by the lifting mist. They stitch themselves into the morning sky. The whole street is a mural freshly painted on the monastery wall.

They light two more cigarettes and drink beer that now tastes like water full of coins. The woman puts her arm round him. They are secure in their embrace amid the brightness gathering around them, the hurrying clouds above them, and everything in between that is beginning to whisper or move.

But then Joseph breaks the silence. He jumps up and begins to babble. He does not know why. He is beyond self-analysis, save for the patting of a pocket for a lost cigarette. He babbles. Not in any one language. But in an idiot litany, a melting of consonants, a pouring away of sounds.

After a while, the woman's eyebrows shape an apology. Joseph drops his cow-haunches back on the slats of the bench. He remains untranslated like a bridge that disappears before it ends. He takes out one of his inks. He starts drawing on his palm.

The city emerges, drained of all darkness, a chimera made of stone and spire and sticky pastries, or of history and sour cabbage and loneliness.

When he's finished with his palm, Joseph removes his shoes and socks. He rushes across the flowerbeds, hurdling budding tulips who whistle at his antics. Leaping from the soil, he pads down one of the streets that leads from the square like a strap from a saddle. He buys a bunch of white violets from a peasant woman. He holds the woman's blistered fingers in his own. He rubs his cheek against hers. 'What's your name?' he asks in the local language.

'Iga,' she says with an amused smile. 'Jadwiga.'

'Where you from, pani Iga?' asks Joseph.

'From here!' she laughs, pointing to her bucket of blooms. 'And you, sir?'

'Here, too!' says Joseph, pointing to the unearthed roots of his toes.

He shows pani Iga his palm.

'*Orzeł?*' she asks, leaning across her buckets for a better look.

'*Tak!*' he says, though it may have been a bigger bird of prey he'd been after. '*Orzeł!*' Taking out his pen, he adds a crown to the eagle's head. Pani Iga claps her hands.

After exchanging greetings with passing bin-collectors, shop-workers, and a couple from Athens who have just had their camera stolen on the night train from Bratislava, Joseph returns to the bench, like a sleepwalker retracing the route to bed.

As well as the high-chair and his shoes, only the white stubs of the woman's roll-ups remain.

Workmen appear in blue dungarees and orange T-shirts. They are carrying pots and thick brushes. Joseph is mesmerised by these busy moustaches on sticks. He recalls, with a wince, his barely started self-portrait. He wonders if they have come to finish the job. The men work in threes: one paints, one smokes, one watches.

'You been here all night?' asks one of the men, dipping his brush in a pot.

'No,' says Joseph, shaking his head, until he sees stars in the morning sky. Like diamonds in a glass of milk.

The man looks at the chair, then at Joseph's filthy toes. He pretends to give them both a lick of paint.

And with that, Joseph moves on, carrying the husks of his shoes in his left hand, and the chair over his right shoulder. The city continues to emerge sober and bright. Too bright! And to a deadly chorus of drills.

A little further along, Joseph takes a side path, following

trees and benches and bins, the latter like upside-down bells with a cymbal for a hat. After kissing a monument to the poet, Boy-Żeliński – yes, we're all clever and penniless here! – he discovers next to a children's sandpit, in the morning-denying shade of oak trees, a wooden platform. He puts down his shoes. He puts down the chair. Taking the two steps up to the platform, he sees, stretching out beneath him, a map of the world.

Measuring out distances in fairy steps, he giggles for the sand and the sycamore leaves, for the little stones scratching his feet, for the tiny changes in texture when crossing forests and mountains and seas. He maps the route he has taken across Europe. In a wobbly stride and a half. Before swooping low, spinning round, skipping East to West. For a moment, he is overcome by the futility of his travels. Of all travels. Perhaps he should have listened to someone, and not just to his fugitive heart. But to whom should he have listened? He thought he had found the only person in his life whom he could trust.

From a nearby bench a mother and child smile to see this funny man with a beard dancing in his flappy trousers.

Joseph pictures all the time and space reduced. The memory of the bruise on the back of his head begins to thump. The city revolves around him, a mad carousel of horses and inhabitants, of the loved and the dejected, of those who are annoyed with themselves because they don't understand and those who suffer because they do, of those who want to leave and those who want to stay, of those who believe in love and faith and goodness and those who laugh at these ideas while reaching for the sugar.

Again Joseph dashes East to West, not a single border guard grabbing at his toes. From some part of his brain, he recalls the words of an eighteenth-century traveller, 'Pooh, the world is an orange!'

Still, he surmises, as he pulls up his spirits by the laces, the exercise having delivered him not far short of sobriety, it's not every day you get to walk on water.

Letters
6 February

Joseph, if you don't start seeing the world as less hostile to you, you'll be in trouble. Where has your soul gone, where? You must be trailing bile across the cobbles, like hot wax.

Your little witticisms and nastinesses. Perhaps you should take heed of Russian poet Alexander Blok in 1908: 'The most vital, the most sensitive children of our century are afflicted by a disease unknown to physicians of body or mind. This disease, akin to psychological ailments, may be called "irony".'

And stop asking if I'm wearing white socks! Do you want me to send you a pair? I remember the fuss you made about socks when you were in my city. We were walking to the train station. You with that big green holdall over your shoulder. I had so many feelings. A mixture of hopes and premonitions. I thought we had to time to grab a quick coffee before you left. I wanted to show you the little blue flames in the Arabian place. To have the time to say a few important words. But, no, you needed a pair of fucking socks! And you wouldn't stop talking about them until I took you to a store and you bought yourself several pairs. You looked happier than I'd seen you all week.

Also, as much as you'd like it, my life is neither motion-less nor sedate. I am not, and never will be, the adverb to your verb! If you carry on suggesting this, I'll hammer tent pegs through your feet, then we'll see how far you travel!

So drain off this resentment, Joseph. Before it poisons you.

In other words, put a sock in it!

Later

You're lucky, I'm calmer now. Your last phone call, your teasings and provocations, simply pushed me over the edge. Hence the rant above. Next time you ring, eat something first, you'll be kinder!

I forgive you, Joseph, but please stop complaining about things because I know you don't really mean it. I am sorry if people sting your back with curses when you change at the swimming pool. It's just young men being young men. Personality before nationality, remember? As for being locked in the changing-rooms until your 45-minute session began, I am sorry to say that in a way that's a legacy of communism. You get your time and you swim that time with everyone else. That's why people give you strange looks when you get out early. Not necessarily because you look different, but because most people will stay in the water until the whistle blows.

I suspect, Joseph, that you are secretly in paradise. All these staring eyes must force you to examine yourself every day. Haven't you always fancied the role of pariah?

I've been thinking: some people don't have much luck, do they? Can you be born blighted, and then spend the rest of your life trying to outwit your fate? Is this what gives extraordinary people their spirit? And do people with this spirit feel compelled to keep going, as if they can find nothing on earth with which to oppose their destiny?

In other words, how much hurt grants a star its light?

Early in 1923, Lya's second husband died. Louis Jahnke had been ill with tuberculosis for some time. Though Lya reguarly went to visit him in a sanatorium in Davos, Switzerland, she blamed herself for being a negligent wife. On one occasion, when they were still living together in Berlin, Lya had returned home at lunchtime after a drinking session that had begun the previous evening. When Louis demanded to know where she'd been, Lya picked up his soup and poured it in his lap. Then she locked herself in her room and sobbed herself to sleep.

In the sanatorium, because of his increasingly frail condition, Louis carried a pink ring-cushion from chair to chair. When he died, Lya kept the cushion, and took it with her on her travels.

28

Laughter from Above

He has begun to imagine the sound of his own falling down. The collapse of his carcass upon a concrete floor. Striking his limbs into odd angles, his body is keen to defy him, as if it was only by accident that his spirit came to inhabit the form of a human being. One heel catches his chair as he sits, so he stretches a leg under the table to form a supporting hypotenuse. An elbow slides across the surface, so he grabs himself by the arm. And his head, in gentle wobble, requires a steady hand.

To make matters worse, the table rocks. Joseph folds up his sacred sheet to use as a wedge under the short leg. As he leans forward, a thousand stars rush from the back of his brain, a rain-stick turned upside down. Oh God, he thinks, whatever your size, your shape, your existential status – yes, whether or not you even exist! – you must be having some fun!

That morning, following his long night of drinking, he'd got straight back to work, having emptied his pockets of bright red tomatoes from a trip to the market where he'd also bought a tub of yellow buttermilk, a legendary local hangover cure as well as a strong lining for the soul. Throwing on his cuffless old shirt already encrusted with oils and juice, he might have been hoping to paint himself an exit from this city for his thoughts had been travelling that way for some time. He wanted coffee to appease the sour milk that was setting about his system, but he poured from the kettle, thinking it had already boiled. The sound of cold water in a mug always sinks his heart. Then he pulled up his newfound high chair to his boards, sitting and dabbling while biting back the yawns, or jousting as he stretched from a rung. Once he even stood on the seat to look down on the versions he had thus far assembled of his impermanent self.

All the time there was a hammering against stone from the builders below. They have been there for days already, constructing two shops in the entrance foyer. It sounded like they were trying to knock down the block with spanners. And then the drills began.

Early in the afternoon he paused from hunger and the shivery demands of a body deprived of sleep. Flopping on his mattress like a star uncertain of its original form, he disturbed pages of Marta's letters, which he now likes to roll upon but no longer reads. But he awoke after a dream in which faceless workers in blue overalls, each one carrying a brush or a hammer, a ladder or a drill, lined the entire circumference of the ring-road, before crossing over and marching towards the old town, yes, he woke with the belief that he was running out of time, and, besides, he had to make use of the light. The roof-tiles opposite shone like leather patches in the sun.

As he clambered up his high-chair, he wondered if love is a hanging in reverse. You start with the ecstasy, eyes bulging for the beauty. Slowly, you start to regain your own rhythm of breathing. Everything clicks back into place. Finally, you untie the knot, step down, and with an enormous sense of relief, walk away.

Yes, he told himself, surely it is time to walk away.

He stepped down. He was no closer. A shot at himself but not aimed at the target. The piece didn't tremble. He despaired that even in his work he could not bring her back.

Again he collapsed on his bed, this time sleeping until dark.

Now, back within the wood-panelled walls of Café Galka, he is leaking loneliness like a bad scent. He recalls the harsh light pouring from the glass roof in the stairwell when he'd come back that morning, mixed with the smell of his neighbour's aftershave, a businessman who always leaves by seven.

Dmitri is here, sitting alone, grumbling behind his pipe smoke and 'Pah!', looking like someone who has carried around a bucketful of bitterness for twenty years, only to end up washing his face in it. Bibi is filling the cigarette slots, sliding down the red and blue and white packets one at a time like bars of soap. No one has seen Eric for a while, but they accept his disappearance as a matter of course, though there are rumours of unpaid alimony, court cases, an attempted escape to Berlin. Others say he has gone back to the UK to work as a translator for those going West who have learned their new language only from pop-songs and films, though someone said he was really going back to set up an agency of long-legged lap-dancers and escorts supplied through his contacts in the East. *Biznes!*

Joseph lights a candle for company. And winces. Living in a candlelit city, he has come to accept that on a good day you're a sculpture, a beautiful head, on a bad day you're hollow, a convict's skull.

Today he has heard, not the ringing of church bells, but the creaking of the rope; he looks like he has been pulled out of a reverie by the eyelids. Yes, a lack of sleep pushes out the eyeballs in search of other darknesses. Perhaps his retinas are emblazoned with everything he has seen since coming here: Gothic towers, crows, other people's eyes, the bruises of beggars, Corinthian columns, stalactites like piccolos playing, not music, but light, the insides of mouths, snow-crested cupolas full of lonely echoes, a bowl of broth from which he scooped a boiled egg, the courtyard cats, a back-street bordello, the breathing of forests at night.

It is a quiet evening. Bibi has run out of chores. He fusses with the purple blossom in the champagne bucket. He adjusts his veils of lilac and black. He hovers by Joseph's table, his painted lips sucked in. Then he retreats to a candleless corner, knowing that to take this man's drink would be to leave him more than alone.

The air is stiff after a day in the sun. Buildings are baking-stones, warm as if fresh from the kiln. The dusk will not give way to darkness. In a first-floor window across the road there is a blur of violet light, and a box of geraniums. On the second floor, Joseph can see, with a squint, a woman's yellow hair, as stark as a bunch of daffodils in a coal-shed. He feels for the lump on the back of his head.

Perhaps that's where he keeps his vision of this city.

Just at that moment, he notices other people sitting only three candles away. He looks over and a sudden breath brings all his selves together for the first time for a long time, perhaps even since he came to this city, for there is a beautiful woman facing him, talking to her friend, yes, those eyes are large and brown and full of Joseph, and she keeps looking in his direction and when she gets up to fetch a candle from the bar Joseph sees that she is tall and slender with long, chestnut hair and her shape speaks to him and the way she moves speaks to him and by now he feels a tingling from his spirit to his socks, a calm music that fills him like warm blood, for the woman keeps up the steady appeal of her glance, a kindness in her eyes, but more friendly than mischievous, empathy – is that what it is? – a sudden affinity, an instant acceptance, and when her friend briefly leaves the room they simply carry on looking at each other, Joseph and this woman, without need of gestures or even smiles, as if in sweet relief that a hope at last has been granted, that now there will be an end to the lonely journeys that have taken you from dusk until the white morning and all the way through life, and so they look and keep looking, as softly, as peacefully, as a first falling of snow.

Letters
10 February
I became ill soon after meeting you. Looking like a mushroom, as you told me. Because I knew my homelife would never be the same again. I knew I would always want you. Desperately. Even violently.

Do I like the word 'violence'? I certainly know it. As an adolescent, I was beaten until I decided to threaten with legal action. I always felt strong at such moments. I knew I'd get over everything. But I would get sick whenever I saw how it really worked. And I did not get over those images of me and my sisters suffering. We experienced things that made me think an afterlife is necessary, otherwise people like my father will never have a chance to pay his dues.

I used to think that nothing good could come of me, as if this hatred would trickle down the family tree like poisonous sap. Now I've realised that by telling you these stories over the summer, stories I was once too ashamed to whisper, even in confession, their demonic aspect has been removed, leaving my father not a powerful Satan but simply a failure in all areas of his life.

The lingering trauma is only the longing I had for my mother. Her inability to protect us. I remember visiting her in hospital. She looked so calm. I couldn't tell her how wild my father becomes when she is not at home. How he forces us to drink stale milk. To praise him for a meal that is inedible. To bring him beer from the fridge, even help him to bed. Which I hated most of all – the horrible heat emanating from his body.

Today, I discovered a photograph of Lya aged six. She is wearing a white smock. Her eyes are dark. A gypsy child with her long black curly hair. She looks mature, not of mind, not of body, but of the heart. Because, for whatever reason, she knows already what it is to feel unhappy.

The Countess stands alongside her. Looking the other way, of course. She has her hand on the head of her youngest son.

I have also seen a picture of Lya aged twenty, with her two young daughters. The photograph was taken only weeks before she met Endre Ady. Her hair in distress, Lya's skin has an underground glow. A sullen vitality. Like the moon the night after it's been full. Her eyes are two olives dropped in a bowl of porridge. Her youngest daughter is crying and looking the other way, just like her grandmother. The other daughter, sporting a bubikopf bob, is tucked under her mother's arm. She is staring quizzically at the camera.

Lya looks buttoned up by the eyelids. Lost beneath herself.

Is this what happens to us if we do not live for love?

13 February

I like very much the two pictures you sent me from your series, 'The Homeless People'. I feel you trying to see them as they see each other, a desperate camaraderie.

In return, please forgive my indulgence about Lya. On this day in 1928, she left for Hollywood. It was her second attempt at success in the States. In Berlin, she organised an auction of unwanted belongings. She owed $25,000 to dressmakers alone.

I have seen a photograph of Lya on the boat from Bremerhaven to New York. Pale, with soft black locks in the sea breeze, she is wearing a plain white blouse, a knee-length black skirt, and a beret. She looks like a school-mistress and a star. Perhaps this is how beauty works, when young <u>and</u> old, vulnerability and charm come together?

Lya's chin is raised in a defiant smile towards the camera. Defiant, because she is battling her fears. Of the failure she sensed was coming. Of the aspects of her life she had been trying, without success, to leave behind. Could it be that she recovered her true self only in her suffering? Perhaps with no one to whom she could truly confess, her guilt became boundless, uncontainable. Her isolation, too. This is the saddest picture I have seen of Lya. She looks so lovely, her spirit all about her, so deserving of love. Yet utterly alone.

Her films in America were only moderately successful, 'The Sorrows of Satan' perhaps her most accomplished. She lived the same life she'd led in Europe: mysterious illnesses, accidents, lovers. She befriended young people about the age of her daughters. In Hollywood, she employed a young male chauffeur. He lived in a room above the garage. She just could not find consistency. Or, more importantly, the person whose love might keep her consistent.

There were sessions with the famous photographer, E O Hoppé. He believed that 'to confirm the spirit behind the eyes is the test'. And he certainly confirmed the infectious, mischievous, frightened spirit that propelled Lya though life. In 1927, her photograph was used to promote Chester-field cigarettes.

Later, when sound displaced all the East European actors, Lya turned to theatre. In November 1930, she played a French maid in a lightweight piece called 'Made in France'. A production assistant, meeting Lya for the first time, later described her as 'a small, slight person, unaffected, appealing and vulnerable. Her skin was delicate and without lines. I thought her very young'. Lya was thirty-four, and would live for just one more year.

The critics were derisive of Lya's performance. 'More dash than skill', they said, while mocking her 'rather genial Berlin accent'. The play closed after only five nights. Citing illness, Lya pulled out after three. She would never act again.

Later

I fell prey to flu while roaming this city of snow and smog. Maybe I got it from Malena or my students. My husband has been very kind. He made endless cups of tea, or milk with honey. Dried toast with a careful covering of butter. His kind eyes, still with their thin film of disbelief, or confusion, as to what happened when I was away. Or, rather, why it happened. His gentle kisses on my forehead to convince me of my fragility.

Later, he retreats beyond my sneezing range, from where he observes me tenderly while getting on with some work. He takes good care of me. His hugs are more relaxed since those first days of our return. Back then I felt he was trying to squeeze the life out of me. Or a confession. While not actually touching me with his hands, as if that's where he kept his anxiety. Though there is still hurt, he is beginning to accept what happened. He is a good man. His pride will not destroy him.

Now I shall squeeze half a lemon into a cup of hot water. I shall place the cup by my bed, and then smell it in the dark.

28 February

By the way, last time we spoke, you told me I'm aggressive. Why? Because I asked you if you'd just got out of bed? I would never scold you for staying in bed late. I would never say 'Pobudka wstać, koniom wody dać!' Wake up and water the horses! I know how late you go to bed. And that you're not a good go-to-sleeper.

I feel guilty when I sleep late but that's because I secretly read or write. I love the stillness, the night breeze through a slightly open window. Sometimes I open the balcony door during severe frosts, just to feel the ping of air. On nights like these, I feel as if I hold all the keys to the city.

Later

Do you remember the pebbles you gave me on the beach that day during the summer? 'Binding stones' you called them. The tide was out. The sun had no intention of unwrapping itself from clouds like used tissues. And you English, you determined or stubborn English, were sitting on the beach in your swimming costumes and jumpers!

You and I were not in our costumes. Though you were wearing your tight blue T-shirt. The hairs on your arms were standing up in the chill. We tried to read the papers in the mischievous breeze. (Yes, you didn't seem bothered by 'media-speak' that day.) We had to pin down the corners with stones. Then we read the pages on all fours. Like dogs sniffing for a scent. Malena played around us, clapping with joy at the sea going out, as if it was she and she alone who had ordered it to leave.

These binding stones you gave me are the only talisman I have ever had in my life. Maybe it's wrong of me, I don't know, but I was never bound to objects. I never cared for them. Even if they had a special meaning, this meaning always passed. I don't know where the piles of books are that I read in my adolescence. I loaned some books, I never asked for them back. Boxes of jewellery were taken by my sisters. My elder sister even took all my soft toys. I didn't care. My material past has been divided among many people. I gave away Malena's baby clothes as soon as she grew out of them. And all the 'good parenting' magazines. Of course, I didn't need those anyway! But now I keep letters. I keep my books. My own scribblings.

Words endure. However precious or trite they are, they always find their way back. Like the imperishable stones of jasper and sapphire, emerald and topaz, beryl and amethyst. Even their names suggest they're of a different order. And then, these two little stones you gave me, the binding stones, fading slightly on the shelf above my desk.

29

The Weight of a Head

Joseph is stretched out like someone who has very nearly concluded his business here on earth. And certainly in this city. The sound of melting stalactites emanates from hidden speakers. Over skin glistening with oil, a firmament of moles, the shooting stars of scratches from holdall straps and benches and rough mattresses – yes, Joseph's back! – the woman proceeds with the falling fingertips of her touch. When she traces crystal nodes of tension (those residual dot-to-dots of the lives we lead), she gives them a good rub before pursuing their disintegration. Yes, she squeezes and probes, pinches and soft-slaps, as if wishing to leave finger-prints on his skin.

Joseph feels a sadness growing within him. A tenderness, but a tenderness that is not attached to love. He thinks of the brown-eyed woman he had seen the other night. By the end of the evening they had worn each other out with their glances. Barely able to keep his eyes open, Joseph had stood up to leave, landing a final look upon her face, and as softly as he could, but she was not looking back. She was looking at his table for signs of a possible return.

Now the woman vibrates Joseph's thigh with a rigid hand, her thumbs more dexterous as if released from the burden of digital complicity. She works her way down to his feet. Heel in hand, she attends to each toe as if contemplating which one to pull out, like the rod on a mechanical giant, to animate or lay to rest forever the cadaver before her. Joseph feels the callused skin, the pulsing blood in his feet – all those icy pavements! Perilous cobbles! Anxious kilometres! – and he wonders if toes, in the evolutionary scheme of things, were really such a good idea.

Palms slippery with grape-seed oil, the woman moves to his shins. She strokes these sharp edges to a soul as if wiping down a window-frame. When her hands move near once-broken bones, she senses them, her fingertips barely landing. Yes, she is aware that although a person is more than the sum of their experiences, a body, alas, is not.

It has been a long time since Joseph has felt so keenly the way a body is put together. It seems that not only horses are measured in hands. These palms are pressing his shadow from within another shadow, and possibly his spirit from this city, but carefully, so as not to leave a trace of departure.

Gradually proceeding upwards, the woman folds the yellow towel over Joseph's left leg to expose his thigh. He feels a deathly coldness, as if his hip-bone is poking through his skin. And breathing on the edge of intimacy.

His body has gone soft with sadness, as if in contemplation of all that is being removed: every touch left by every body that sought to show him love.

Slowly releasing the leg as if laying it down in its casket, the woman adjusts the towel to permit the fleshy parts of her palms to work the lower abdomen. With these thumbs at his stomach, Joseph can tell exactly where time and space have gathered within him. Not to mention bread rolls shaped like the hair-buns of the women who sell them, the meal in pani Stasia's known as 'a piece of meat' and proving so stringy it had tied up his teeth, barrels of beer, sour cucumbers to bring tears to your tastebuds, thick cuts of rubbery cheese, candle flames that turn your eyelids to butter, a loneliness given extra layers by unfamiliar skies, a harsh light, winter trees like municipal furniture, not forgetting desserts that compensate with sugar what they lack in taste, yes, this is a *ciasto-miasto*, all right, a cake city, and Joseph's extra layer of skin is surely a pastry case, or else it's marzipan and misery that have set about his form. It's been weeks since he swam a decent length. In this city, he has learned, you not only indulge in your vices, you develop them.

The woman takes the weight of Joseph's head in her hands, the remnants of his bruise sleeping in her palms. With the backs of her fingers, she begins to brush his forehead. Thoughts fall from his mind like the letters on an idiot-board suddenly deprived of its magnetism. She smooths his cheeks as if removing the cold-wax mask reinforced daily by inquisitive looks. She lightly traces his closed eyelids, rendering them as blind as the walled-up windows of Renaissance townhouses, thus freeing Joseph from the burden of constant watching.

Does his spirit now occupy the space between the human and the holy? For Joseph has only ever felt such calm, such religious wonder, when his head is being held.

Next, the woman takes Joseph's hands. Without lingering over the scales of coloured paint, she strokes his knuckles. Then she smooths his palms, like a fortune-teller who has decided to have another go.

Inadvertently, Joseph squeezes her fingers.

Letters

3 March

I lay down for a few minutes to gather my thoughts for the next round of writing. I fell asleep. I saw tower blocks. A fragment of a hill. You could see the layers of sand and soil overgrown with grass. There was a pine tree on top of this hill. Through the branches, a watery light of silver and gold. The tower blocks were dim, the hill and tree translucent. I felt I'd seen everything before. Then I realised. The hill and pine were exactly like the ones at my grandmother's towards the end of her life. I felt very light. It gripped me by the heels, this lightness.

I woke up, crying.

What should I do? It is always a terrible time, those hours of mid-afternoon. I can't beat the light. The emptiness. The feeling that the world is away doing what it does best. Bombs murder terrorism. We can write or draw as much as we want. The suffering will not cease.

Joseph, did you colonise me with your underground ways? In a dream the night before last I was waiting for you in my grandmother's village, at a bus stop overgrown with shrubs. A smell of rain and honeysuckle. There were people I knew as a child, now grown-up, often in pairs, often with children. One after another, the buses kept coming.

Without you.

I waited.

And kept waiting.

Ps Do you know something, Joseph? When I came to collect you that night at the station, I got the impression you had arrived from all the cities on the board. Not just one.

6 March

I often think of how to meet you again. Properly. Just us. Will we have to settle for friends not lovers? You are frowning at the word, I'm sure. At both words. At all words!

Joseph, have you ever promised to share your life with someone? I'm perhaps living the 'for worse' part of the vows. I can't promise you that I won't be unhappy. I am afraid of complacency and mediocrity more than death. Does this make me a proper little bourgeois?

But you must never forget that ordinary lives can also brim with dangerous feelings. So you don't have to keep giving me your boho manifesto! Boho men are often balding types in tatty leather jackets who drink too much and chat up young women by candlelight – the only light by which they can get away with their age! Look at your friend Eric! They claim to be poets or musicians, and not the desperate human beings they are. They cling to the underside of the night like spiders on a crumbling ceiling, spinning out a web as thin as their hair. Is this your bohemia, Joseph? Is this what has kept you there? It sounds more like a refuge for the dejected! I'm not saying there are no genuine characters among them. Of course there are. At the time of night you meet these people, though, do they talk of work which – like them – never sees the light of day?

But tell me, Joseph, just to hurt me, how do you like your boho women? Brown-eyed, obviously, and stepping from the canvas of a Klimt, a Schlemmer, a Schiele, or Witkacy? Eyes by Gustave Moreau? Will they retain their mystery as they slip from their sequins? I would go for a black feather hat. Chiffon ruffles anyone? Haha. If they still exist. Does boho still exist? It is an attitude, above all, isn't it? (And I'm talking of serious bohos now.) Ideas, plus assertiveness. A spiritual trajectory. To develop quietly, creatively, not in a direction dictated by convention. To elude 'taught behaviour'. I respect that. I only disagree with the amount of drinking that seems to be involved!

Probably, this is easier for women to do, to go underground, that is, to withdraw from the gaze, as Edith Stein put it, to evolve as a person, quietly and without fuss. It requires a certain selflessness, to resist the vanity that insists on being seen. Whereas men, as well as being the principal gazers, cannot bear to be out of sight! They are stricken to the surface, condemned to float.

OK, the women's clothes can be quite interesting. Antagonistic (or tangential) to fashion, in a way timeless and elegant. A look that says, 'I know how to take care of myself. I have lived and loved and travelled.' Here, at the moment, it's berets (I have one!). Le bonnet rouge. Black patterned tights. Leather boots, but not with too high a heel. Little green leather jackets (if it's not too cold). Or big-collared woollen coats, with silk headscarves. Yesterday I saw a woman wearing a 1920s pilot's cap, leather with earflaps. I wondered where she'd flown in from. Though I'd prefer a hat designed by Maria Likarz, you know her? Of the Wiener Werkstätte?

Joseph, I know you appreciate how thin the dividing line between comfort and despair. However 'ordinary' my life may look from the outside – and I may be taking a step back for safety – I still feel the vertigo behind my kneecaps. And in my stomach. My life does change. Continuously. I am changing it. I want you to remain a part of the process. I lead a simple life. But it places demands on me that are often contradictory. This is what I mean by complexity. I know that to feel alive, wildly alive, is to be dancing along death's borders, sticking up two fingers to nothingness and fate, yet a steady life must have its pleasures, too. Good things come from quiet application.

Are you still underground? Collars up to the cellar dust and the plaster that plops in your 'piwo'? Candles picking out your eyelashes, the wings of a ladybird preparing for flight?

Uwaga! Watch out! The place you sit in might be a catacomb.

Yours!

Ps Ladybird in my language, 'boże krowki' – literally, God's little cow!

Pps I nearly forgot. You asked again about the woman in the street. The one with the swinging arm. I translated your latest phonetic renderings. You are definitely improving!

But this woman is talking of torture. Of the Red Army, perhaps even the SS, the Kapos. As you noted, she is reciting addresses close to your flat. She claims these are the flats of the people who spied on her. One of these addresses, she says, is where the tortures took place.

Boże mój! Is anybody listening to this woman?

30

A Biography of Broken Bones, part JJ

All love is lost in time, because isn't that what time is for, in its crass linearity, to prise us from what we hold dear? Joseph is learning this. If painfully. Perhaps Marta did give his restlessness a reason, a tender validation, but you could also put this restlessness down to the same impulses that send us out to the streets late evening when the curtain trembles, or when, sitting alone, we hear rain on the roof, or footsteps on the fire-escape.

In the months between Marta leaving and Joseph going to see her, he'd returned to mapping out his own country, across moors and dales, hills and flatlands, past lonely fields and forests and farms where thousands of sparrows descended for a scattering of seed. Not knowing if he wanted to sketch or sing, but either way to strike through the uncertainty with a clear line, a bold form, he drove along A roads and B roads, in variations of north and south and east and west, past snack caravans with tatty flags of St George flapping from their roofs, and fat bottles of ketchup glowing in the sun, like jugs of blood. Racing round as if impatient for eternity – or at least a glimpse of it! – he drove country lanes, at night, past out-houses lit by a single bulb, and cottages with smoking chimneys.

Believing each kilometre to be in her direction, he journeyed up and down the motorways – all those eyes! The green eyes of the slip road, the red eyes of the inner lane, the orange, the yellow. His hatchback squeezed between a convoy of trucks and cars, a darkness of brake-lights and the backs of people's heads, and every now and then a honk, for he'd lost himself in a reverie as the tarmac disappeared beneath the bonnet, so he'd change the cassette on the stereo (only one speaker working), open another can of popular fizz, light a cigarette on the orange mini-grill, and sing along.

During his trips, he tried to invoke Marta's spirit, and the way they'd encouraged each other towards the people they could become, while mindful of the space each needed for that growth. One way to do this was to write to her. Perhaps for the first time in his life, Joseph did not find words as difficult as pulling on wet clothes. He scribbled away, each sentence collapsing the distance between them, the page already taking on the light of Marta's eyes, for he had to keep in motion whatever it was they were sharing.

We will travel so far together, Joseph had thought at the time, no doubt believing that the situation with Marta's husband and child could be easily resolved. Because, of course, love would triumph, and the singing would con-tinue.

'Now I have found you,' Marta had told him earlier in the summer, 'I want to find something for you.' And she'd read to him from the work of a writer from her country (who had spent much of his adult life in exile) and he'd written that anyone who wants to feel truly European, and free, spiritually, must view their own country as an obstacle rather than an advantage. 'Do you agree?' asked Marta.

Joseph wasn't sure. Though he certainly didn't view his country as an advantage, he saw it more as an encumbrance than an obstacle. You can climb over an obstacle, whereas you have to drag an encumbrance. And he dragged his country along in his holdall, didn't he? Or was it a stone in his shoe?

And there was that evening when Marta had insisted, with her usual blend of gravity and light-heartedness, that he show her, exactly, the bones he had broken. As if she wanted to run a finger along his seams. Find out where he was held together. And so there were fingertips and kisses for his left leg ('in two places'), his right arm ('just here'), his collar-bone ('don't press too hard!'), his wrist ('you'll never be a classical pianist now!') and his toe ('aha, just who were you dancing with at the time?').

And they talked more, argued more, kissed more, sometimes even waking with their lips still touching. Other times, they found deep silences that neither of them needed to break. Yes, she gave him what he had always been seeking: an identity he could go to sleep with.

Now, back in the car, in the small hours, plotting out his trip to see her, he'd run two wheels along the rumble-strip, just because he liked to feel the ripples through his blood. In a dawn light of muddy fields and brake fluid, he overtook post-office vans and the strange vehicles that journey round with only one headlight, trying to outmanoeuvre their fate.

Yes, on he went, in his rusty crate on wheels, with his two holdalls of clothes, and his boot full of belongings, including the volume of poetry Marta had given him (which he'd wrapped in newspaper for safe keeping), with the special blank sheet inside.

In a ten-day period, as if trying to keep up with the

clouds, he drove 1200 miles, through thirteen counties, sleeping in seven different rooms, and a couple of lay-bys. On one side of the room, there were boxes and bags: he was moving in. On the other side of the room, there were boxes and bags: he was moving out. As the rain pressed tiny palms of leaves against the windscreen, Joseph tried to keep singing, despite the silence from the passenger seat. Though he kept his hopes slim and well-behaved, he couldn't stop the tingling in his blood for the time when he and Marta would be together again. The breeze through the driver's window was not unlike her fingers through his hair.

As October introduced a gathering gloom, the night air smelling of water in which flowers have died, Joseph tried to learn how to hold on to hope. He had taken another temporary job to raise money for his trip. Plus he was thinking of selling his car.

Occasionally, in weaker moments, he remembered their less positive exchanges. Once he had been late to pick up Marta and Malena from town. He'd left them standing in the street.

'What's a few minutes?' he said to her, after she'd quizzed his disregard. 'You're so English!'

One night on his travels, a night spent behind the peeling window frames of a provincial town, he had a terrible dream. A dream of a swan with two necks. He could see this two-necked swan coming down the river with its characteristic surge. When closer, he saw that one of the necks was, as usual, erect and serene, but the other one was different, the other neck was broken, bloody, trailing in the water. Though he fought hard not to interpret the image, he wondered if a person is only whole when they're devoted.

He knew he could not let her go.

When the winter sun rested on the parcel shelf of his car, trying in vain to warm the nape of his neck, he vowed not to let himself go either. Not to get into drink or drugs or that equally disruptive narcotic, despondency. Even if winter always does demand so many adjustments, he had to keep his resolve. For hadn't he glimpsed a kind of freedom, a vision of the person he wanted to become, and the person with whom this was possible?

But one night, after a particularly bad week of work during which he felt like a horse that knows it wasn't born in harness, he took to drinking with friends. So long as they were around, everything was fine. Not one of them knew what he carried inside. Around 2 a.m. when his friends took a taxi home, Joseph insisted on staying out. 'Yeah? Like where?' they said. 'Here,' he said, with a vague gesture down the street. They laughed and swore at his idiocy. It was raining, and you're asking for trouble.

Joseph made his way down to the canal that runs through the city, old brickwork and licorice under a single streetlamp. He knew the prostitutes and the homeless would be down there. He walked in the mud of the bridlepath, handing out the last of his cigarettes. He couldn't tell if he was crying or whether his face was wet with rain. When he looked to the water, he saw the whole night stagnant. A whole life. Either side of being with her.

Now it is twelve moons since he first met Marta. He is living in her country. He has found space there, an atmosphere in which he can breathe. And possibly create. Perhaps he is truly European now, and spiritually free. He is keeping faith, against the circumstances, learning patience and humility, and other languages, while ignoring the advice of the friends of his still eager for his co-ordinates, who view his extended stay not in terms of the growth of a soul, but in terms of the growth of stupidity, or, as one of them put it, a death wish. As if he was still down by that canal. Waiting for his luck to change. Or to run out for good.

One day, you know, you might not make it home.

Will he leave soon? Perhaps he is walking these streets as if he's already left. Unsheathed of history, unembellished by his gaze of curiosity, his favourite buildings flap like death-notices, their foundations merely dust and water in the drains.

Yes, there are other cities. Cities full of people on their way up, people on their way down, and people who open things with their teeth. Besides, he has learned that it is not the city that's important, it is the space you make within it, the routes you radiate when quietly seeking.

If he does leave, he will take with him everything he can carry in his palms, everything that isn't another person's hand (though hadn't that been the purpose of his trip?). Not to mention a leaked-out heart, lungs scarred by cheap cigarettes, creases on his face from the lack of a pillow, a season of boiled sheets and bad stomachs – confirming, or so he laughed to himself, his European constitution – plus nail-dirt, ear-wax, a stone in his shoe. Yes, though you can leave a city quickly, it takes much longer for that city to leave you.

What else will he take? An understanding that he has found more than he has lost? Plus his favourite trees (the alder opposite the concert hall)? The springing of the arches? The metre-long tin Jesus high on the wall of Kanoniczna Street? Lace doilies and latticework, spiral stair-cases and gutter-spouts? The very old woman who goes round the cafés selling knuckles of garlic? Or the city itself, painted on a sheet that he forces through the zip of his hold-all? *Niemozliwe!* Impossible! The train station is sticking out.

Well, he has his tin from the flea market: his sketches, his scrapbook, Marta's letters.

Joseph will certainly not stay here thinking he is less lost for doing so. If he has learned one thing it is that we are all moving round in the dark, trying not to bump into one another, while remaining vigilant for whoever might show us a different way. You just have to keep account of your position between suffice and sacrifice. Besides, he knows that wherever you are, people will always come up to you and ask, 'What've you been up to?'

To which he'd reply, 'Oh, you know, running and jumping.'

And another time, 'What've you been up to?'

'Oh, you know, spitting and catching.'

And another time, 'What've you been up to?

'Oh, you know, fetching wood and carrying water.'

Wearing each new horizon as a halo (only because it sits nicely on his head), he goes in search of goodness. Yes, he has learned that all things end in time. Our hearts beat through the narrative, we travel from beginning to end. What else is there to fear but ourselves lost in time?

But occasionally, it is true, on a dark evening, standing in a doorway waiting for the rain to stop (yes, as in a train-station novella), Joseph Eadem might be thinking:

People slip through your fingers.

People slip through.

People slip.

Don't they?

Letters
8 March

Women's Day, another left-over from communism. Women are given flowers by husbands, friends, colleagues. Was this day inaugurated in the hope that if women get their day, they will accept that men get the other 364? O Matko!

A student bought me a plastic rose.

My husband, I know, will drive home 200 km from Warsaw with a dozen real ones.

Here, as you have seen, we have lots of days. Feast days. Name days. Teachers' day. Children's day. Workers' day. Every day is a day!

But not a good day for Lya's first husband. On 8 March 1932, Judge Zoltan de Szepessey booked himself into a single room at the Ritz Hotel in Budapest. A few hours later, he shot himself. He had not been able to come to terms with the death, four months earlier, of his former wife. Once again, the children had been abandoned.

Eleven years earlier to the day, Lya had featured in the Berlin papers for only the second time. Billed as 'the beautiful gypsy', she was dancing in the 'expressionist, cubist, futurist Kostumfest', with five orchestras, at the Scala.

Later, when she was famous, she would tour the city most evenings with her friend, the erotic dancer Anita Berber. They would call at the Bristol for cups of tea and Viennese cigarettes. At the Eden, it would be schnapps with beer. At Kempinski's, while dancing the czardas, a knocked-back Scotch and soda. At the Adlon, where her school-friend, Laszlo, was now working, having made it to Berlin among the masses of people going West for work, it would be 'Rotwein'. In the small hours, on the dance-floor of the Eldorado, cognac straight from the bottle.

Lya would lead the way with the confidence of a star, as if supported by every one of the glances directed towards her. Berber followed. White face, black rings painted round the eyes, crimson lips. A permanent Persephone. The step into darkness that Lya often craved.

At their favourite haunts, the young 'Schauspielerin' would take out their cigarette-holders and smoke at that classic angle of indolence, as if testing for rain behind their backs. (In a 1928 interview, Lya described smoking as 'my only remaining passion'.)

Though everyone was moving at great speed around the city, as if trying in vain to keep up with the rate of inflation, the two friends would take a horse-drawn white carriage. There were child prostitutes at Weidenbrucke, people sleeping among the barges at Humboldt Haven – perhaps subjects for Kathe Köllwitz. Lya and Anita would break into a rendition of 'Black-eyed Natasha' and brave the streets of unillustrated darkness.

A well-known phrase of the time proclaimed, 'Heute nacht tanzen sechzigtausend Menschen in Berlin!'

20 March

I had a dream you called and my husband answered. You didn't hear his voice. You assumed it was me. You said you loved me. My husband slammed down the phone. Yesterday someone called three times and did hang up each time my husband answered. I knew this would not be you. Probably just someone dialling the wrong number and not caring to apologise.

I think I am learning from my women. I am learning that when you've suffered before, you adjust your sights. Not necessarily lowering your expectations, but refining them. By accepting that if you're ever going to get there, it's not going to be all in one go, in one precise and magical leap. Rather, in little steps and rushes, hard won and well deserved, and – if you're lucky and open-minded – with sufficient glimpses of mystery and promise to keep you on course.

I'm thinking more and more that I don't want to stay in this city. Maybe not in this country. I would like to work at a university abroad. Their facilities are better. The pay is good. I have talked with my husband about this. Understandably, he is not keen. Not yet. If it ever happens, though, he says he will certainly come with me. Even if it means giving up his job.

You told me a while ago about a writer saying that an old communist monument in Hungary marks the centre of Europe. I disagree. I think the new centre of Europe is the toilet in the tail-fin of a budget flight between one side of the continent and the other!

31

These Words He Has Collected

How difficult it is to live in the world without taking up
time or space! He slips the folded sheet from his pocket.
With his right hand, he smooths the paper across the
peeling slats of the bench. For a moment, his palm becomes
a part of the page. The paper is stained in many places.
With the dye of his jeans, with butter, with grease, with
coffee splashes, tea, ash, with the green-brown rubbing of
bark, a circle stamp from a table leg, with beer, wax, thumb
smudges, with grass, soil, a tear or two, with blood, where
he once pressed the page to his mouth, perhaps hoping to
transfer a spoken word, and when he very gently peeled it
away he took the top layer of skin from his lip and he
wondered if this is how two people leave each other; there
are also sleep creases when he woke to find the sheet in his
bed, but he can no longer see the little black stars that were
cast across this same page the last time he took it from his
pocket, as he lay on the grass, on his elbows, in the sun,
listening to himself living, and he liked these stars on the
page, these shadows of daisies, that he pictured as Stars of
David.

What hope a single heart in the face of history? He has a
brief flash of Laszlo in his buttons, reaching out for the trail

of a star with his hands still wet from the dishes. The page flaps in the breeze and turns blue in the twilight. Joseph has been in this city long enough to come to an understanding. He has rounded up words like a bundle of strays. For these words have had to fight for their existence, words emerging in his new language, words receding from his own. They rub each other up the wrong way and merely scratch at meaning. Though these words are for Marta, he knows his spirit will depart from them as soon as the ink hits the page.

He grips one of his pens. He has a feeling of big fruit. He doesn't know if he'll be able to melt the shapes through the nib. He strokes his bare arms. Is it good to be in the world? He looks up. The sky is a sheet of newspaper from which all the print has run. He looks down. His boots are bookends with nothing in between. He looks ahead. He takes a deep breath. It is good to be in the world. And so, on his sacred foolscap, even though he'd much rather sketch his feelings on a horse's hoof, a raven's wing or, in chalk, on the back of a wild boar, he prepares to write.

But he must write around the stains, or the meanings will melt in the wax and butter and grease, and he likes this spacing-out because if he is to limit himself to language, then he doesn't want the straitjacket of a sentence, no, these words must come crashing down like a chandelier dropped from a height. And so he writes, pressing so hard that he leaves an imprint on the wood of the bench beneath. Yes, in letters as small as a scattering of poppy seeds, he writes, and keeps writing, until the page can hold no more.

Letters
3 April

I've just re-read an early letter of yours. From the days when you were still writing to me. Wonderful and vexing on many levels. But is the world necessarily twofold? The 'wicked' and 'the rest', 'night' and 'day', 'magic' and 'reality'? Maybe it's twofold because language works through plus-and-minus logic. But are the above terms mutually exclusive? For instance, does there have to be security at one end and insanity at the other?

I think this also applies to your view of the city you're in. You swing from the fanciful to the fearful. The boys are geeks or brutes, the girls are geeks or beauties. One day you are enchanted by church interiors and by old women smoking under their bonnets, and the next you are angry because men in padded jackets try to walk through you, and everyone can tell you're not local, and it's all so parochial, and people, in general, are not friendly 'i tak dalej', etc. But it's just life Joseph, isn't it? Magnified, because it's a city. In other words, not a place to escape your fate! This reminds me of a Jewish friend of mine who visited there. He had just arrived at the station and was waiting on the steps to be collected by a colleague when a man came up to him and said, 'Auschwitz? You wanna go to Auschwitz?' Even though it turned out this man was only selling day trips, you can imagine how my friend felt.

Joseph, I once said that your work presents paradoxes – perhaps, then, you are a seeker of contradictions? Perhaps you feel contained by them, between the yes and the no of our times? Like one of your abandoned mills or churches.

Edith Stein wrote: 'For now, the world consists of

opposites . . . But in the end, none of these contrasts will remain. There will only be the fullness of love.'

In death, perhaps, yes.

Joseph, when you came to my city, you let your warm hand slide from mine. Was that heroism or lack of love?

You use the word 'betrayal'. I don't want to make it sound like a justification when I say they are a part of an adult's perception of the world. Betrayals of dreams, visions, plans, of people, of oneself. But please try to understand I never made my choice against you. So there's no need to block the light when you used to bring it.

Maybe I have come to an understanding, a painful understanding, that love is not the only destiny.

Later

I have been putting the finishing touches to my Lya story. Of course, you must be wondering: how did she come to have a chicken bone stuck in her throat in the first place? (Remember? The operation.) The answer is as fairy-tale tragic as the rest of her life. She had been begging her long-term lover in America to marry her. Though he wanted to, his family would not consent. Lya had already been married twice, and they were all too familiar with her vampish reputation. In a last-ditch effort to convince him, Lya went on a hunger strike.

When her lover turned up one afternoon, Lya was in bed eating a chicken leg. She had to hide the evidence. And quickly. She swallowed what she could. Her lover found her beneath the sheets, choking. She was taken to the Harbor Sanatorium on Madison Avenue, New York.

After her death, Lya's body was held in the morgue for several weeks while the Countess decided where her daughter should be buried. Believing it to be Lya's wish, the

Countess finally opted for St Patrick's Cathedral, New York, where the funeral service was conducted by Reverend Joseph Marczinko of New Jersey, a Hungarian, who, as fate would have it, had been a tutor of the de Putti children in pre-war years. Lya's ex-husband, Zoltan, sent a basketful of flowers, but not via a local florist. 'These flowers might wither and die before they get there,' he wrote, 'but at least they are Hungarian flowers.'

On Lya's grave, her date of birth is 1899, and not 1896 as it should be, or the 1904 claimed by Paramount publicity. Throughout her career her publicity team also added 11 centimetres to her height. Like all stars, she was an exaggerated being.

Which makes me wonder: since fleeing in pursuit of her spirit, her dream, had she ever really been herself?

I want to go to the theatre! There's a version of 'Hamlet' on here at the moment. The company is promising 'an experience of life-death intensity'. There is a rumour that they have forty actresses to play Ophelia across the forty-night run.

Back in '68 when your students in the West were demonstrating in favour of Marxism, our students were finding ways of eluding communist censorship. It was enough to see a czarist officer in a Mickiewicz play for everyone to think of the Russian troops in Poland. Mickiewicz's dream was that the word meant action.

I am sorry we have been talking less. You don't seem to ring much. Only late at night. I could picture your ankles sticking under the glass sides of the box. New socks, perhaps? Then you were gone. Between the tarmac and the trees. Pulling the damp night around you like the hood of a monk's habit. Along the paths of the city gardens, no doubt to join your friends, other poets of the crumbling stucco . . . sometimes I wish I could be there!

Strange variations of a continental climate. A couple of days ago we were on a trip to the south-west, not all that far from you. I thought of coming to see you. I wanted to ask my husband. He saw the question in my eyes. I saw the refusal in his. We were blown around the whole night and most of the day by mountain winds. The fir trees were covered in sticky snow. The air was sharp and fresh. The whir of the forest! A whirring silence punctuated by the crackle of twigs. Malena loved it. She is a robust child, and the air is so much better than in the city. They have bears here, roaming wild. We didn't see any, despite Malena calling to them. 'Misie!' Lynx, too, apparently. Many birds have come back for the spring. It might be up to 20°C next week.

You have seen for yourself what I mean about this country of contrasts. We live in our blocks of flats, match-boxes we call them, standing on their ends across the dark landscape. Then we escape all this concrete to snowy peaks where bears and wolves still roam, or we go to forests with depths unheard of in the West, or to lakes that promise the floating freedoms that this country, landlocked on three sides, can otherwise only dream of. On top of that we have very cold winters, very hot summers, and lots of ups and downs. What an effect this must have on a nation's psyche! Perhaps this is what makes us continental?

Letters

21 April

When we last spoke, why did you say I only have a fantasy of loving you? By doing so, you imply my lack of courage, and suggest that I'm not too good at life, not too good at love.

Joseph, there is no need to keep hurting me. So stop swinging an axe at your phantoms!

Later

I must confess I cried after our phone call – just hearing your voice. To say your name, to think of you so close. But when you sulk, you're so Polish! And when you're like this, your voice does not break your silence towards me, it emphasises it.

Don't turn an ode into a mazurka! Especially when you ask, with a little spicy sarcasm, if my world is made of books. As a child, books were a way of escaping the sadness that surrounded me. They were never the only way. A necessity, yes, but more like a beautiful accompaniment than a world apart.

I know one thing, Joseph, books are not sandbags.

Also, there are always strange men hanging around the phone box waiting for used phone cards. One guy, in particular, a giant with trousers that reveal his ankles as another set of eyes. If we were still under communism, I would say he was a spy. Yes, even at 2 metres tall! Besides, back then, the secret police were not so secret because they used to sit in little white Fiats. And everyone knew it was the secret police because of these two men trying to hide behind their moustaches while sitting in their dirty white clouds.

That reminds me of the writer Stanisław Jerzy Lec: 'He thought someone was following him, but it was only an agent of the State Security.'

Did I tell you about my grandfather, not the argumentative one, the other one? He survived the war, working on a farm in Germany. His two brothers were shot for being in the AK, the home army. After the war, because of his excellent record as a scholar, my grandfather was asked to attend an interview, with a view to becoming a secret agent under communism. Can you imagine? Asked to spy on his own community! My grandfather hated the idea!

During the war, working on a German farm in Zagan, he had seen the English POWs emptying their pockets of soil as they dug their tunnels (the 'Great Escape' camp). These prisoners would throw balls of tobacco over the camp walls in exchange for potatoes. He remembers their fondness for Chesterfield cigarettes. When he had a brief exchange with them, they gave him lots of these cigarettes which he sent to his delighted father. After the war he helped Germans who were running away from their country. He then walked home, all the way from Zagan to a village near K-wce. He kept notebooks of all the towns he passed through, the farmhouses, barns, shacks and forests he slept in. The soldiers and displaced persons of all nationalities he met on the way. Some returning from camps. No one knew who to trust. There were shots in the forest every night.

He is a good person. A kind soul.

Of course, he did not at all want to be a secret agent! He set about thinking up excuses. At the interviews, they were impressed despite his pleas that he suffered terribly from asthma (he tried to huff and puff), and that his eyes were bad (he kept squinting).

That night, he shared a room in the city with three other interviewees. The next morning one of them said to my grandfather, 'You talk in your sleep! How can you be an agent?'

Without finishing his coffee, my grandfather leapt down the stairs of the block – he was still a young man then, about 28 I think. He sprinted to the building where the interview had taken place. He asked to see one of the men who had interviewed him. Finally, he was called in. He tried to conceal his excitement. To talk in a solemn voice. In fact, an imitation of theirs, plus a trace of an apologetic tone. But this time his breathlessness was genuine. And the tears of joy in his eyes made him squint. Grandfather told the man that he talked in his sleep. That he had only just learned of this. That he was sorry that he could not have informed them yesterday. He said he was worried that this wouldn't make him a very good agent. Impressed by my grandfather's conscientiousness, the man said he'd have to think it over.

Three days later when he was back home in the countryside, my grandfather received a letter. The letter informed him that he had been unsuccessful in his application to become an agent.

Joseph, I never lost this love for you. But I cannot live pining for you. It is really only positive. I do love the two people in my family. Your image will not dissolve because of them. I am indignant only when it feels like you want to leave some lasting wound. Or word.

3 May

It's your birthday. I don't know where you are. You are always in between. So, zwischen-Europa is ideal for you. Especially as – fetch the trumpets and the vodka! – this country is now in the EU. At the weekend there were fireworks in the square. The event wasn't particularly well attended. I saw a busker with a tiny EU flag sticking out of his accordion, and a food-stall selling 'Eurozupa'. Lots of red and white flags, too – just to make sure we don't forget who we are. Especially as today is a national holiday, Constitution Day. We have the oldest constitution in Europe, the second oldest in the world. There's still at least one generation here who think these changes have come too soon, i.e. only fifteen years after we regained our independence.

My husband knows of two schoolfriends going to London to work as bouncers. You should see these guys, they look as though they are carrying a television under each arm. Their girlfriends are going to Dublin for a while, to work in a chocolate factory.

But where are you? Are you the one now hiding behind a pine? Or are you, as we say, sawing off the branch on which you're sitting?

Watch out! As for birds, so for human beings, there is a big difference between a migrant and a vagrant.

Ps Conrad wrote that 'All exile, like love, is not just a condition of pain, it's a condition of deceit'.

Does the sky here still look different to you, even in this warm and watery spring light? A different texture, you said, and less of it. Do the trees still look menacing? Is the darkness thicker, despite the quickly lengthening days?

Joseph, have you left your face in thse shadows? Have you blamed this all on me? How badly you carry your hurt!'

Boze moj! Is it really true that everything that floats must eventually burst: clouds, balloons, soap, bubbles, love?

Our religion?

Is this what your silence implies?

Or has something happened to you. Perhaps you have met a princess? Or fallen down a hole? Or vaccinated yourself with vodka? The perfect antidote to me! You once said that a drink every now and then makes you feel warm. 'Like putting my heart in a honey-pot' you said. I say, more like your liver in a leech pit!

Maybe the answer is more simple. And less crude. Maybe you have long since left my country.

Let me know where you are. Let me know you're ok. At least a sign.

Happy Birthday, Joseph.

6 June

I know one thing, the despair that was overbearing when we parted eventually gave way to brightness. Maybe I have increased my faith in other people, in my immediate world. These things that distance can bring. I have learned that the opposite of intensity is not, or does not have to be, indifference. My decisions did involve loyalty, but not a 'return to safety' as you once put it. Nor does my head rule over my heart, as you also implied. I am merely a seeker of those moments when, after all the fret and terror and uncertainty, the world starts moving again.

27 June

Still nothing from you. Perhaps you think your unconventional life is superior to my academic and domestic one? Are you drinking until dawn in a bid to remain undetermined? That's about as conventional as it gets for the rootless, unregistered ones, sorry, for noble travellers, sorry again, for bohemians like yourself! Tell me, are the small hours always the ones filled with revelations? All that beer glistening like amber from Gdynia. Perhaps you can only study yourself through a glass? Perhaps you'd be better off with a magnifying glass!

You once said that I keep you human. So tell me, Joseph, who or what is keeping you human now?

9 July

Last night I dreamed we were talking like we used to. How warm this dream made me feel.

Joseph, we must never forget how much we have given each other.

Forgive me another quotation. A Lithuanian writer: 'What matters is not where you come from, but what you bring with you, and where you take it, and with what care'.

Whatever happens, I believe I won't lose the Joseph who once kissed me gently on the lips and placed two small pebbles in my palm.

Besides, I am sure I can hear you listening, on the other side of your pride.

I'll be finishing,

32

How Quickly A City Suffers!

Everything gives in to gravity, except prices. And in this city, the prices are going up rapidly. The last of the day's light bounces off newly erected street signs. There are fresh notices in five languages. Joseph can hear his own language everywhere around him. All those vowels!

How quickly a city suffers!

The talk is of bargains, of property, of booze, of how best to market this beauty. Joseph is stricken with comprehension, assailed by words he understands, words that sound ugly in his ears. Some of the locals have picked up phrases from this language, too, like 'fuck!' and 'Oh my God!' and 'biznesmen' which drop like coins of an odd currency among those with eagles on the back. In an instant, it all comes back to him: the constant white noise of a life back there.

How quickly a city suffers!

There is drilling in every quarter of the old town. In every block. And from 7a.m. The church bells don't have a chance. The hourly trumpet may as well be muted. The horses don't have a hoof to stand on – that's to say, you can no longer hear their clippety-clop above the din of drills and dialects.

A few pretzel-sellers have started a new line: bags of popcorn! And there are 'Kantor' signs at every turning, exchange booths where men in leather jackets and black woollen hats – that give them the appearance of malicious sprites – grin to show the gold in their teeth. And there are tour guides in golf carts, and idiots in tandem, and a weekend couple astonished by the lack of fresh milk.

How quickly a city suffers!

But beauty has a knack of resisting. The sun squats on the copper dome at the end of Szewska Street, making faces as vulnerable as freshly-baked biscuits. Sick of lenses and disinterested eyes, buildings melt their dimensions and flow down the drains, only to re-emerge, as robust as history, a few doors further along. Balcony railings refuse to hum in the heat. Floating seed-pods, those ghosts of snowflakes, decide to land elsewhere. And the horizon itself is packing its bags in search of less congested skies.

How quickly a city suffers!

And the stucco looks stuck on! Where Joseph once collected curious pamphlets, they now hand out adverts for language schools and bank loans and *kredyt konsolidacyjny*. A church in the centre has closed; its board for death-notices is now covered in posters for 'Praca w [work in] USA'. And there's a sudden arrival of upmarket beggar-boys, men in suits selling from a briefcase: insurance policies, credit cards, plastic massage gadgets. Joseph spent one morning walking from one pair of polished shoes to the next, shaking his head, leading away preyed-upon old ladies, while saying to the young men who reeked of all-over body lotions, '*Nie kapitalizm!*'. He received, in return, a series of middle fingers.

And the spiders are three to a web! There is talk of

converting the city's cellars into an underground shopping mall, the art nouveau cinema, the oldest kino in town, into a supermarket! In Café Galka, there's a sad-faced male at nearly every table, masters of mid-afternoon yearnings, who bury their memories in notepads, their long-held gazes dreaming of all this beauty, the yellow walls, the eyes, the women, as if it might be here they can finally deposit their pain, whether real or invented.

How quickly a city suffers!

Joseph can no longer anticipate this city, he has seen it from every side. From a sudden dusk without an hour to follow daylight home, to a dawn of pigeon skin and coffee fumes. From dark afternoons that put ice in your endeavours to bright mornings when you inhale flakes of warm plaster, and the dogs lick the dust from the drains.

But now there are other tongues. And these tongues have found the milk bar on the corner, beneath the plastic Jesus, where they lick the froth from closely-shaven upper lips or order a breakfast in a 'Can I get?' way, a breakfast that now arrives on porcelain plates with thin slices of bacon, segregated eggs and a toss of lettuce!

When chestnut leaves and tired voices get together to form a dusk, Joseph leaves his retreat among the drunkards who have already laid down their beards. Like most people rising from a bench, he takes a look back as if to say, 'Where shall I find such peace again? And when?' He walks across the main square, its history banished by the chatter of tourists, and by people who view the architecture, at arm's length, via the screen on the back of their cameras.

'And the women!' says a bald middle-aged man in the middle of a group of bald middle-aged men in football shirts, each of their heads fitted on top of a glass of beer.

Gypsy musicians abound, licking their lips at the prospect of silver coins instead of the usual copper. Including a strolling band from a province of Bucharest whose double-bass player, only just held in by his cummerbund, can't keep up with the two accordionists and the trumpet player as they serenade the drinkers beneath the parasols. Yes, the bass player snatches his instrument by the neck as if uprooting a bunch of sunflowers, then he carries his belly and bass to the next café – a slightly different wicker set, and tin tables instead of plastic – and no sooner has he replanted the spike and plucked a few strings with his yellow-tipped fingers – dripping a few beads of sweat, like extra notes, from his forehead to the wooden neck – than it's time for him to twirl his instrument round, uproot more tenacious stalks, and dash to the next café – smart waiting staff, clientele with heavier jewellery and jowls – and here the band lingers a little longer (in anticipation of gold and not silver coins), and so the sweating bass-player can catch his breath, catch up with the melody, even dab his forehead with a red serviette. That is, until he remembers it's his turn to go round with the tin.

Led by his disenchantment, and perhaps also by a vague religious feeling that has grown within him all these months, even if he does still feel closer to his grievances than to God, Joseph attaches himself to three pairs of monks. Down Grodzka Street, he walks, among the procession to the cathedral at Wawel castle, falling in with sandalled feet and a devotional silence, until he comes to an open ground-floor window. Through this window he sees a builder in dungarees covered in white brick dust. The man's skin is also covered in plaster, so that he looks like an albino. His blue eyes stare without blinking.

How quickly a city suffers!

So Joseph goes to the market, the one only the locals know, that's squeezed between a disused tram stop and a row of tin shacks, and smells of goat's cheese and cheap tobacco, and where old women hold aloft the chickens they're plucking, beside buckets of dewdrops and marigolds, tomatoes like polished billiard balls, fat strawberries, enormous apples with yellow streaks where they have rolled in the sun, mini-cauliflowers in an old man's palm, sheets of feathery lettuce like a deep-sea sponge, bulbs of horseradish shaped like the tongues of the city's church bells, trays of walnuts, bitter berries, sweet fruit, sour milk, everything rising and rinsed!

I will walk and walk until . . .

History at heel, and lifted by everything that is crumbling or flowing, fading in or fading out, shimmering or scuttling, yes, by the familiarity of all faint things, Joseph then makes his way to the Jewish district. Along its short and twisting streets he goes, alongside dark buildings and rotten wooden fences, past blocks licked with leaves and light, where every street is a Yiddish lament intoned with a whistle or a wail, but no, it is silent, even bleak, an absence that has for a long time held the buildings in its thrall.

Joseph goes to his favourite café in this part of town. Even in the summer, it is lit only by patches of nicotine wallpaper divided by chocolate seams. He orders a coffee and a chunk of *szarlotka* apple-pie with a thick roof of pastry. He sits opposite the three-panelled mirror in case he needs to study himself in triptych. In any case, in all three, his features reconciled to a future without her.

So much for a self-portrait. But he is not unhappy. He has thrown out most of his work; it served its purpose.

He has kept only the smaller sketches, the drawings made on the move, down side streets, in trams, in milk-bars and stand-up drinking dens, once even pressing on the cold green tiles of a urinal.

In the café, he surveys the darkness of the other room: the charcoal sketches on the walls, the sepia photographs, a bright green scarf hanging on the coatstand by the door. He is visited by a sudden memory of Izzy Singer's dad. He wonders if he would like it here. On the far side, the bar rises like a wooden boat in the darkness. The brass pumps look like important controls. There are glass shelves, a vase of yellow flowers – each one a mini-sun on a stick – stools with chocolate button-tops, and tables finished with a sprinkling of sugar, no, actually it's lace.

Yet everything seems draped in the dust of departure, the dead skin of those who have already gone on their way. There are station clocks, sewing-machines in wooden hubs, a wind-up gramophone with a huge orchid for an ear, and a stack of travelling trunks whose fading stickers cover their sucked-in cheeks: Warszawa, Sopot, Praha, Wien.

The last rays of the sun enter the café, illuminating dust motes and other dimensions. Joseph notices new faces, and obviously from elsewhere. They have bloodshot eyes, perhaps from their first local hangover or from a freshly distraught love. They are scribbling in pads. Joseph has heard that a group of artists sponsored by some institution or other has been sent to produce official representations of 'New Europe'.

New Europe!

How quickly a city suffers!

He finds a bench in Szeroka Square. He can hear typewriters through the open windows of the police station, punctuated by crows and the rattle of dishes from the Jewish restaurant opposite. The pastel facades of small buildings glow in the twilight. Like the eager faces of a family huddling round the hearth, waiting for the storytelling to begin.

Joseph sits in near-perfect solitude, as if, like pigeon-boy, his thoughts are concealed by a cloak of wings. All the shadows he has cast since he came here have now assembled. Yes, they have gathered about him like a horde of spirits released at last from the hum of the engine, the weight of a heel, the vicissitudes of love.

He heads for the Remu'h cemetery. The iron gates are locked by the city's last remaining Rabbi as soon as darkness falls. Joseph must hurry. The sky is a four-cornered prayer-shawl. Taking quick strides, he cuts through an alley of buildings leaning on one another like a row of suitcases. Once inside the gates, he stands by the wall of the synagogue and looks across the rows of thick headstones, each with its own tin roof. Night-lights in red pots throw out tiny shadows of wings.

As the breeze stiffens, Joseph recalls the words of the Rabbi on his first visit here, when he quoted the prophet Jeremiah: 'The heart is deceitful above all things, and desperately wicked: who can know it?'

Reaching for his inside pocket, Joseph teases out a small pebble with his fingertips. He steps across a clump of grass and stands beside one of the graves. Then he places his last binding-stone on top of the headstone, a promise of return.

Acknowledgements

Deborah Rogers, for her green slips and unerring support; Andrew and Sam and Ursula at Picador; Peter Straus for his faith from the start; PH & SH & CB x 2; Simon, Chris, Hannah W; Johannes Zeilinger and Matthias Unger in Berlin; Arts Council East for chipping in when the soup ran out; and for all the souls who see – thank you.